THE HEART OF

GRIM

A story of fantasy, action, adventure, war,
politics, monsters and untold secrets.
Let's not forget the dark powers and a
romance subplot. If you like tabletop
roleplaying games, then this is
dedicated to you.

Book Cover by Amir Zand @amirzand.art

Map Illustration by Veronika Wunder @veronikawunder

Preface, Chapter Titles, Scene Breaks & Flags by Marta Iva @intotheforest.illustrations@gmail.com

Grimoire Pages & Tattoo by Alexander Jones @ajonestattoo on Insta

Editing by Clara Abigail @clarabigail.ca

First edition 2025

ISBNs:
Paperback: 979-8-9928249-0-2
Hardcover: 979-8-9928249-1-9
eBook: 979-8-9928249-2-6

Arcane's Summit
Selva Dawn
Tundra of Dawn
Mount Firebrim
Mountain of Agathor
Mirror of the Heavens
Lighthouse of Alexias
Pharos Island
Eraveil
The Dead Lands
the Alliance of Thalar
The Great Trade
The Grove of Esperin
For Runsw
The Valcan Sea
Vahnbal
Exonia Creek
The Tribe of Ulatec
Lake Exonia
Range of Cav'lon
Starwrig Mines
Starwright
Mercha Ris
Pandora's Box
Eira
Lightfor

The Kingdom of Esperin
The Forgotten Isles
Gilacrest City
Lake of the Exalted
Edomen City
Tree of Tranquility
Umberfall
Umberfall Mines
Graycott Village
Fort Silvercrest
Fort Bendalin
Goldenrise
Enderbrooke
Shadowbane Forest
The Eastern Expanse
N
W E
S
The Monastery of Khendalon
Wellcaster
Redwick
The Avernos Empire
Cove of Lost Souls
Lockridge
The Light of Khendalon

PROLOGUE.

When the last cry of death echoed into the sky, the fighting had finally ended.

For miles, the battleground remained hushed amongst mountains of ashes. The only shift of movement was the solemn wind, roaring past inert ears. It caressed the tattered flags of kingdoms fighting for a selfish cause of heedless sovereigns as a reminder of ill consequence. The colors and symbols on the tarnished pennon reposed underneath thick layers of mire and gore, their torn edges fluttering despite the field's stillness. Beneath the oscillating cloths, bodies amassed for miles. The mangled conditions of the corpses concealed their identities, leaving them amongst a desecrated battlefield and disregarded by the kingdoms that compelled them.

With their heads lifelessly turned upright, the empty gaze of dead soldiers longed for the dim light of the sun. Its rays seeped through the creases of the clouds with trickling light. Continuing towards the skyline, the sun turned a blind eye as it hid behind billows of mists, turning its back on the lands just as it had done the day before.

Yet there was one—one who knew the names of the fallen and belonged to neither side of the human, godforsaken war. He floated across the trenches of the forgotten ones, twirling endless red thread between his bony fingers. A long, threadbare robe engulfed him, forging a grim silhouette that lacked a shadow.

He held a scythe that loomed above him, constructed of bones with pendulous feathers, rope, and leather. Dangling from the décor tied at its clamp was a bell, which remained silent as he sauntered through the bleakness. The curved, matte-black blade with veins of gold whispered in the darkness of the haze, eagerly waiting in the figure's loose grip.

He lifted his reaper and severed the twine of life, herding the souls like a shepherd through fields of bloom and sorrow. His cape fluttered behind him from the wind's empty cry and closed the eyes of the deceased.

A cough echoed through the emptiness, halting the figure. He heard a coarse breath erupt from the haze, followed by continuous, strained gasps. The shadowed man pivoted towards the setting sun.

There, amidst the torn flags of a fallen kingdom, lay a soldier, holding anxiously on to his uncut thread. His breath was thin and shallow, like the string he desperately attempted to detain. The fallen warrior extended his quivering voice into the abyss, expecting no one to reply.

The cloaked figure strode to the man with a weightless grace, like a feather chasing a dancing wind. Although the scythe wielder's hood covered his aged features, he could still see the timorous visage painted across the soldier's bloodstained face. He was riddled with arrows that protruded from his calves all the way up to his shattered clavicle. His left arm, completely severed from the elbow down, lay discarded not too far from his maimed body.

Multiple ribs caved inward beneath his sternum, coercing the lone man to take heavied breaths. Blood still spilled from a deep gash that stretched from the left side of his temple to the right, prohibiting him from seeing the fleeing sun.

Death would answer his call today.

"What is it that you would give?" the mysterious figure questioned.

As daylight retreated past the distant horizon, a bleak reminder rose from its alternate side. The moon, coated in a hue of scarlet, ascended from the world's unseen darkness. It peered down towards the scene with a crimson luster and a silent voice. With the sun no longer bearing witness, the man whispered into the night with his last breath.

"Anything."

Too far for both figures to hear, a bell of deep cadence rang from atop an eldritch cathedral of darkened stone within lands enwreathed in shades of rose.

ONE.

An incessant prodding on the man's shoulder spurred him awake, his heavy eyelids not aiding his consciousness. His lips felt chapped, cracking upon their momentary separation. As his eyes fluttered open, light cascaded over him, paining him from the sun's striking intensity. Instinctively, he tried to raise his hands to shield his watering corneas. The maneuver proved to be a pointless endeavor as his arms remained stagnant against the dirt beneath him.

Silhouettes above his person created a canopy from the blinding light. They were talking, but he couldn't better understand them if they were speaking in tongues. A tinnitus ringing longed for his attention with persistence, despite his groggy mien. Though its bell-like quality should have sounded shrill, its reverberation resembled more like a gravely psaltery, its bassist manipulating its strings with dual bows. It was deep and longing, initiating the beginning of a song he couldn't comprehend.

"...okay?" one of the people above him questioned as the deep carillon faded. The voice was feminine, a tender sound that caressed his ears like a soft touch. He liked it, he decided in that moment. Its owner quieted after the question, awaiting a response.

Finally, the unnamed man's eyes focused on his surroundings. It was difficult to decipher the details, but he counted two shapes hovering above him. When his languid eyelids rose to inspect them, the forms gasped in harmonic unison. After a moment's pause, the female voice spoke up again.

"Are you okay?" she repeated, lowering her hand to brush her thumb across the man's cheek. Dried blood mixed with dirt smeared across his face, its metallic odor pungent and rustic as she soiled her perfect complexion with his present circumstance. Before her contact, he hadn't realized how cold he was.

The unnamed man leaned into her touch, yearning for her inviting warmth. A golden light radiated from her fingertips as the plaguing chill melted away. He expected it to burn like a crazed fire, but it soothed him like a medicinal remedy. Despite the comforting feeling, the stiffness in his jaw didn't disappear.

"Do you know where you are?" she inquired.

When he met her gaze, a pair of gilded eyes stared back at him. As his vision adjusted, the details of the world unfolded like a legible scroll, and he eagerly scrutinized its contents.

Her amber eyes shimmered despite the umbra, resembling medallions of the finest gold. Her ears, pointed in contrast to a human's rounded cartilage, protruded from the soft tresses of her hair that alternated between strands of chestnut and platinum. She reminded him of the diverse shaded leaves of autumn. *An elf*, the nameless man thought.

"What's your name?" the female elf asked, his attention refocusing on her furrowed brows.

The man's lips cracked once again from their parting, dry and flaky from inevitable dehydration. He tried to formulate a sentence, but his throat tightened from unexpected tension. The midday breeze coated his silence and saturated the atmosphere with a whisking breath where his own voice should have been. After several more attempts, he managed a whisper.

"I don't know." The nameless man's voice felt foreign in his own ears, raspy and unpracticed. As he numbly lay there, endeavoring to recall his own name, face, and identity, he remembered none. He surveyed the area to try to aid his failed recollection and beheld a bleak scenario that would have left the faint-hearted in utter despondence.

The obvious battlefield was strewn with a myriad of human remains amongst hovering debris. A thin haze covered the entirety of the area, with grass dimming and dying beneath the corpses that lay mangled atop them. Spears, swords, axes, lances, arrows, and numerous other weapons jutted from the soil. Their shafts directed upwards at the scattered clouds, which passed by the atrocity below with blithe disregard.

Multiple humanoids of a similar faction scoured the fields, searching for signs of the living. Unlike the ones above him, most had donned masks that obscured their faces, with rounded cages protruding from their mouths. The simple design beheld a small slit atop, acting as an entry for air. Numerous herbs poked through from within its confines. While some of the people wore long robes tied by leather satchels, much like the attire for practicing physicians, others sported tunics and braies of candid linen. All, however, safeguarded their skin in thick leather gloves as they rummaged through the deceased.

They sought endlessly through the mounds of corpses with a heaviness of solemnity. They called out like a choir, their tones unknowingly bearing resemblance to a deathly dirge for their grand funeral. As their voices ceded to quietness with a grim realization, the echoes diminished until they existed no more—for no other soldiers responded to their calls.

One of four thousand—fate or chance? a voice whispered, but the nameless man knew not where it originated from.

The unidentified soldier careened his head back to stare at the vast field behind him. It must have been true, for he couldn't locate any source of life underneath the veil of death. Out of the dead that lay unmoving, he could see two distinct uniforms: one set contained steel with sharpened shoulder guards and decorated with crimson accents; the other lined with gold and brown highlights amongst rounded pauldrons and intricate designs that imitated curling trees. He tried to see the color of his armor beneath the layer of blood, but the stiffness in his neck thwarted him.

The ones wearing masks commenced what seemed to be a practiced method of gathering bodies. They began dividing the corpses up by the insignias on their armor. Wooden carts aided their endeavors as they loaded them carefully and distributed them among divided teams. Beige flags protruded from the handles of the wagons, with an intricate design becoming obscured from the restless wind. In the middle of the banners was a morning star with five spikes to mimic its namesake.

"Salem," the second silhouette said. He wore a simple robe to match the beige color of the waving flag. Long, pointed ears split through his longer blond hair that sat in a knot below the crown of his head, with loose strands falling past his frown. Hatred seemed to linger in his blue, analytical eyes, complementing the harsh gaze underneath the veil of his shadow. It mimicked the punitive sun that rose behind him, both analyzing him with distain. "Salem, he's—"

"Get a bishop," the female elf urged as she rose from her kneeling position.

The instant she stood, the unnamed man longed for the warmth that followed her.

"We need more healers over here!" she shouted, gaining the

attention of several people not too far from them.

As they approached, his eyelids fought against his desire to remain conscious. Before his voice could pass his lips, darkness welcomed him again.

TWO.

The nameless soldier awoke to a panorama of a vast, pearl sea. Above his reclined form, waves of white ascended like soft edges of stacked feathers, itinerating upwards where each comber clashed in a whirlpool. The currents billowed to a wind he couldn't feel, the ocean protecting him from its chill. Only then did he realize, with subliminal scrutiny, that it wasn't water that trailed upwards, but a blanket pavilion.

The tent was assembled from stretched canvas with a wooden rod meeting at the highest point. The stanchion jutted from the middle of the room, surrounded by randomly discarded rugs to cover the soil and ashen grass. A coffer perched across the far side of the room, adjacent to a compact table and dual set of empty chairs. Atop the ocular trestle table resided apothecary accoutrements, on which he spotted vinegar, mint, and a cough syrup with liquid dried and hardened at the bottle's finish. Even from his lounged position, he could smell the mixture of fruits and spices lingering from the brew's cork.

The flock-bed beneath him was constructed of wool and wooden frames of simple design, focused more on comfort rather than visual appeal. He stirred underneath multiple blankets of fur and linen before he sat upright, and a creak of the timber escorted his careful shifting. His arms and legs ached from a numbness of lack of movement and ignored his stirs to wake them for several minutes.

He stilled in secluded ambiguity and contemplated how long it had been since his ominous awakening. Declining light trickled through the tarp's gaps, ignoring his unspoken questions.

He rose from the cot and placed his numb, bare feet on the warm carpets. A long, linen shirt hung around his knees and swayed in a loose rhythm, despite the multiple bands of fabric encircling his waist. His sleeves squeezed his wrists, and he grew irritated at its tightness as he meddled with the hampered fabric. His trousers clutched at his ankles just the same. The clothing was unappealing in style, though its indicated purpose prevented him from dying of hypothermia, for which he was thankful. Even still, he removed several layers of cloth, tucked in his shirt, and rolled up his sleeves. It wasn't truly comfortable by any means, but he would make do.

The man trudged over to the entrance of the tent, the flap dangling in the breeze. When he peeked through the aperture, bright light confronted his eyes like a swinging sword. He raised his arms to halt the attack. After the pain subsided, he blinked away the flashes of gold and placed a palm over his eyebrows. The temporary amnesty permitted him to see the world beyond. He hadn't expected there to be so many people, dead and alive.

It was almost the end of day. Due to the mass of the dead gathered at this encampment, he knew the battle had concluded; howbeit, the musk of war hadn't receded from the hills. Men and women of various races—humans, elves, gnomes, and dwarves—strode through the encampment, each performing distinct tasks.

While some schlepped bodies covered in wrapped tarps, neatly arranging and organizing them betwixt the conflicting armies, others ferreted through several pieces of parchment on boards and jotted down notes.

After the corpses were distributed, physicians thoroughly removed any arrows, mud, and gore that hid their identities. The soldiers with the armor decorated in red cloth wore piercings in their ears of similar fashion. The undertakers were carefully removing each stud before cleaning the protrusions with a red wine redolent of tree sap.

A *proclamation of spirit and unspoken tradition—now all are removed from service,* a voice chimed. The unnamed man whipped his head around in various rotations to find its source, but he found none.

He didn't know the difference between either side of the conflicting kingdoms. If the laborers were aware of the soldiers' opposing beliefs or not, it didn't seem to prevent their obligations. All the dead of the gruesome fight had been brought to this place, divided only after their origins were identified. Whether their parting souls liked it or not, death now unified them.

The people who weren't delivering bodies to the physicians were collapsing and folding unused tents. With some of the shelters packed, more of the surrounding area was revealed for further inspection. Fields and hills lay in the distance, the previous battle residing in a slow, dissipating mist of sweat, smolder, and decay from inevitable humidity. The plains stretched for miles, with rolling slopes to distort the horizon in the distance.

In the north stood a stronghold on the edge of a fortified hill, with stone walls recently collapsed. He wasn't sure how he could see in such vivid detail from such a long distance away, but an army of soldiers clad in silver and red were surveying the area and tending to the fort's wounds. As he gazed into the bleakness of the thin fog that spread across its wall, he couldn't remember if he fought for it or against it.

Across the slopes, maple trees swayed beside the collapsed fortress. Despite the ruins that endured, the beauty of the orange leaves remained untouched by the cruelty of war. They bloomed brightly in the darkened space, standing almost as tall as the stronghold next to it. They exuded superiority, proving more formidable than the crumbling battlement, and even more beautiful than the sunset, which was fleeing from the night's embrace. He didn't know the day, the year, or the place, but it must have been the welcome season of fall.

Salem, the voice whispered. The purrs of its malevolent chime spread a chill down his spine.

Salem. He remembered awakening to her golden eyes. His cheek tingled from the memory of her warmth and magic, his body longing to reminisce in the vibrance of her presence. It wasn't long after his awakening that he succumbed to a dire sleep, wishing to return to the temperateness that exuded from her. In comparison, this place felt cold and dim.

The nameless man strode back farther into the tent, the bright colors of spots obscuring his vision. He rubbed his eyes, ridding the irritation as he welcomed himself into the opaque setting of the closed tent. A form shifted in the awaiting darkness, and he froze. Across the way, meeting his own gaze, was something staring back at him.

Its irises were completely white and surrounded by darker sclera, resembling pearls in a sea of black. The skin beneath its eyes was swollen and irritated. It was either a creature on the brink of death, lacking sleep, or both. A prominent, maroon scar stretched from one of its temples to the other, carved horizontally through the very eyes that stared back at him. Despite this bright red scar, the eyes of night looked untouched by the mark that ravaged them. Surrounding its face were dark strands of hair on top of pale skin. The locks clung to its face from a recent, cold sweat.

The strange being extended its hand towards him. Strong looking, but deathly pale fingers curled out, as if it was just as confused and curious as he. He reached for it in turn and felt something underneath his own fingertips, but it wasn't the skin of the other form—it was harsh in texture and solid in foundation.

It was a mirror.

The nameless soldier gasped, his image mimicking his own movements. Underneath the curtain of his jet-black hair, those pools of whitened ivory inspected his body. He was larger than he thought, muscular in form with wide shoulders and hovering taller than a common man. He traced his fingers along his face, inspecting the piercings along his nose, eyebrow, and ears that resembled the soldiers from one of the warring forces.

Human or monster? the voice questioned. *You can't see their fangs until they smile.*

As the soldier stared at his reflection in perplexed awe, he was too afraid to discover the origins of the sinister voice and of the man or monster that stared back at him.

He traced the scar across the middle of his face, the irritation declaring its recent birth. Closing one eye, he saw the scar continue along both eyelids and extend to his temples. If not for his obvious ability to see, he would have believed that such a gruesome scar had taken away that very capability.

A chill ran up the back of his neck, like thin needles tracing shapes into his skin. He pressed his hands up his forearms, failing to spread heat from his palms to calm the instinctive fear.

The inner part of his left forearm throbbed in pain, as though it had been submerged into a frozen lake. However, when he glanced at his skin, it was flawless compared to the rest of his scarred body, except for right underneath his left elbow. Residing there was a scar that completely encircled his arm. It resembled the bright red wound that covered his face, with jagged, harsh edges that gleamed prominently against his white skin. He traced it with his cold fingertips, and he found a slight indent where the scar lay. Unless he were crazy, which still hadn't yet been defined, it looked as though his arm had been completely severed and re-attached.

The soul does not always belong to mortal flesh.

The nameless man shuttered at the intrusion of the voice and finally gathered the courage to ask the question that pestered him. "Who are—"

"You're awake!" a voice called from behind.

As he turned, he was met with the golden gaze of the female elf he awoke to. Before, her brown and ash hair hung freely at her shoulders. Now, it was pulled into a high ponytail, allowing him to see the white strands underneath and the longer locks that hung loosely in front of her pointed ears. Salem, a woman adorned with browns, ivories, golds, and a smile that would put the Heavens to shame.

He hadn't inspected her attire when he first awoke, but standing before her now, it glistened from the rays behind her. She wore a warrior's armor, with pristine, white steel and gold chainmail. Pauldrons, gauntlets, and multiple layers of iron covered her from head to toe. Her pants were similar to his own, except lighter in shade and protected by steel-toed boots that rose past her knee. A monastic scapular hung from her waist underneath the steel of her bosom, with a strange symbol he didn't recognize dangling at the bottom of the tan cloth. It resembled a knot with three different points, accented in swirls that complemented the designs of golden waves that traced the entirety of her armor. Her blade and shield also matched with flawless ivory, proclaiming their experience from the holster attached at her back.

"Yeah, I'm awake," the nameless man repeated, his thoughts having more to say than he could muster himself. His voice was deep, raspy and unused. His throat felt scratched, and he tried to clear it, but the irritation lingered.

"Are you okay to stand? Do you want to sit?" Salem urged, pulling out one of the chairs from the small table in the corner of the room. Without a thought, he took a seat, his fingers grazing his forehead to ease the continuous throb.

"What happened?" the unnamed soldier questioned.

Salem scanned his features, as if wishing to understand the depth of his moonlit eyes amongst the shadows of the canopy. The man found himself anxious at the lingering of her stare, and he broke eye contact to alleviate his trepidation. Salem cupped her hands in front of her on the table, picking at her gloved fingers where her nails were located, but the armor prevented her prodding.

"My allies and I found you in the middle of the battlefield. You were covered in blood, but your wounds were completely closed by the time we got there." The nameless man peeked back up at Salem from his diverted gaze. With the small movement of her pupils, he could see her scan one edge of the massive scar that slashed across most of his face. The golden specks in her eyes gleamed with curiosity. "After you fell unconscious, we took you here and had the bishops examine your wounds. They said that the injuries you obtained looked freshly closed, but unnatural. Do you remember what happened?"

Everything, yet nothing. Omniscient, yet ignorant.

The soldier inspected the woman's face, who continued to stare, as if awaiting an answer. It was then, that the man realized, that she could not hear the harrowing voice.

"No," he replied, inspecting his pale hands. He discerned he had been thoroughly cleaned several times because of his dried skin, but he couldn't rid the feeling of coated blood. His hands fidgeted within his lap, but recognition of his own body eluded him. "I don't remember anything. I don't remember who I am, or where I came from, or why I was fighting in the first place."

Within Salem's eyes, the nameless man saw his own confused reflection and a small ray of light cascading through an opening at the tarp's edge. It was as if the light followed her wherever she went.

"How long was I unconscious?" the soldier asked, coveting to piece together the fragments of time he might have lost.

"Almost a fortnight," Salem admitted. "We were, at some point, afraid you weren't going to wake up. Your body was exhausted."

Despite the emptiness inside, his heart tightened with dread. Among a camp riddled with people, dead and alive, he was lost.

"And what side was I fighting for?"

"The Avernos Empire, a human kingdom to the south." Salem leaned forward on the table, their fingers almost brushing together. Even from a distance, the man could feel her aura radiating from her, like a brisk fire in the dead of winter. "They were the side attacking the fort we found you at, Fort Silvercrest."

History repeats what it cannot change.

"Was I really the only one left?" the lone soldier muttered, the proximity of their hands shepherding his body into a shudder. He tried to stay composed, but the heat she radiated was enthralling. The ice of his skin longed for a relief of warmth as he remained in overstrung melancholy.

"Yes," Salem replied. Despite his sadness, he was thankful for her honesty. "I'm so sorry."

"There's no need for you to apologize," the man said, lacking a different response. "I can't even remember what happened, so I'm not sure why I'm so sad about it."

Salem frowned, her wince just as visible as an openly displayed card. "Maybe we can figure something out. Meditate for a moment—see if you can recall anything."

The nameless man took a deep breath as he shut his eyes, attempting to recall his lost memories. His head spasmed into a throb of an unsettling pain. Reaching into the unknown, ignoring his mind's heed, a physical blockade countered his efforts. He felt an eroded iron cell along with a musty, earthy odor from its rust. As the man shook the mental cage to open the barrier, he wasn't sure if he was stuck within the confines of its prison or if something else was caged behind the locked door. The exertion became unbearable.

There is a difference between lost and taken.

"No, nothing," he replied, prodding his temples in slow, circular motions.

"That's okay. Don't push yourself too hard. I'm sure they'll come back with time." When the soldier opened his eyes, Salem rose from her seated position. "Do you mind if I examine your wounds?" Not waiting for him to answer, she pulled back the collar of his loose shirt and revealed his torso underneath.

As Salem's legs closed in on the space between his own, the man swallowed the breath that lingered in his throat. She stood so close to him that he could feel her thighs brush against his own. Even while encased in her thick armor, her warm aura radiated like a soothing hot spring.

Salem leaned down, placing the edges of her fingers around his clavicle and tracing rings along his skin. When the nameless soldier looked down, he saw a familiar sight. There wasn't one, but several wounds that resembled the one across his face and around his arm. Imbedded in his skin were scars of scarlet. He saw one on his clavicle, three along his torso, and one on the edge of his hip.

"Despite these wounds closing before we got there, we know you received these on the battlefield because they match the protrusions in your armor," Salem explained, leaning in closer to inspect the newly closed abrasions. "It's as if someone removed all the arrows and closed your wounds, and the healing seems so unnatural, it doesn't resemble the properties of normal remedial magic from decidite at all. You retained no lethal injuries by the time we got there, but you still didn't look quite alive. It's almost as if you were..." she muttered, her voice trailing into a silence.

"Dead?" the unnamed man responded with no will of his own.

Salem lifted her head, and their noses brushed together from their vicinity. She stepped backwards with flailing arms, and a hue of reddish pink spread across her cheeks.

"Wah—I'm so sorry! I should have asked first," Salem said, a sheepish grin replacing where her concern had once been, armor clinking with her quickened stride. "My friends say I have no understanding of personal space."

"Your friends?"

"Yes, they're mercenaries, just like me." Salem seemed to forget about the awkward interaction as the cherry hue faded. "Would you like to meet some of them and have some dinner? I'm sure you're hungry."

Once again, having no patience to await a reply, Salem tugged on the nameless man's sleeve, coercing his venture from the safety of the tent. He followed suit, chasing after the light in the darkness.

The sun had already faded below the horizon when they exited the tent, the day taking pity on the man from the discomfort of its brightness. Because of the retreating sunlight, the nameless soldier was able to scan the area in perfect clarity. The people that had been working tirelessly before recently finished their daily tasks, assuming new places around the camp and speaking amongst themselves in hushed tones.

The aftermath of battle was clearly not for the fainthearted. They sat in solitude or around the blaze of the campfires, stoking the flames and brewing meals. People stood in long lines with bowls in hand, ready to finish the day with a warm supper. As far as he could see in the encampment, there were no soldiers wearing the colors of crimson or chestnut...alive, at least.

The nameless man and Salem walked towards the edge of the camp, where two people sat comfortably around the warmth of a blazing campfire. One was a human with long, red hair held in a braid that reached their lower back, with straw, plants, and leaves intertwined between its careless patterns. Grime covered their palms, fingertips, clothes and face, suggesting a previous scavenge through soil. Observing them now, the soldier couldn't decipher their gender, as though they hadn't aligned with either.

"Cooking too boring, rather eat raw," they exclaimed with an irritated voice and broken speech. They waved their skewer over the fire haphazardly, as if it would expedite the cooking process. Vegetables and meat flung from their chaotic flails.

The male next to them, colossal in comparison, reached out and grabbed their thrashing arm. "You're losing your food," the large male declared. His skin, a light and abnormal gray, was marked with dark tattoos that trailed down his arms, legs, and chest. His jawline and features were sharp and harsh, like the fangs that pointed upwards from his lower jaw.

A half-orc. How unfortunate for him. It must have pained him when his tribe cast him aside, the voice whispered.

Beside the duo lay a small fox, with a bushy tail wrapped around its curled form. Instead of a normal orange, the creature resembled a similar shade of polished garnet. Its fur was flawless and clean compared to the braided companion next to it. It peered at the nameless man with amber eyes and prolonged eye contact as he and Salem approached. It eyed him like prey, regardless of the usual omnivorous nature of the placid creature.

The most knowledgeable creatures are the ones that feign ignorance.

"He's awake!" Salem proclaimed, stepping to the side to reveal him like an awaited prize.

The two seated at the campfire turned their heads, both

meeting him with a gaze of similar emotions that the soldier could perceive in the flickering firelight. Content, curious, and surprisingly, welcoming.

"This is Andrid," Salem said, pointing towards the braided one before pointing to the half-orc. "And this is Haven."

"Nice to meet you," the unnamed man replied, not knowing any way to introduce himself.

"Why don't you sit? I'll get us some food." Salem motioned towards the fire.

Before he could interject, Salem had already stridden off towards a different direction. She waved at some other individuals as she ventured further into the camp, leaving him engulfed in a silence of unease. When the soldier turned, he met the stares of Andrid and Haven once again and found himself unable to speak.

"Hi," Andrid said as the nameless man sat down on the log in front of the roaring fire. "How not dead?" they asked matter-of-factly, a cheeky grin snaking up their features. They were inspecting him like a plant they had never seen.

"You'll have to forgive Andrid," Haven's deep voice interrupted. The half-orc placed a hand on top of Andrid's shoulder, pulling them back until there was ample space. Haven grabbed a wooden bowl, not caring to blow on his steaming soup before sipping down a spoonful. "They're a little nosey...and have no sense of the meaning 'sensitive topics.'"

Andrid huffed with sprawled legs, moving them in opposite directions to form effigies in the dirt. "I know plenty of meaning."

"It's fine," the soldier replied. "Salem mentioned you're both mercenaries?"

"Yes, we're a part of a company called Kendra Dawn," Haven said after a spoonful of soup. "We're a neutral party in Terrisae that assists the people. We're gathering the fallen soldiers from Fort Silvercrest, and we're going to bring them back to their respective kingdoms so their families can bury them to rest after the passage rite of Elohim." Haven must have noticed the soldier's confused visage, for he dipped his head in what he assumed to be some sort of apology. "It's a religious practice performed by the Kingdom of Esperin. Regardless, do you remember what happened to you?"

The names felt foreign to the soldier's ears, no satisfaction bubbling through his body upon recollecting a lost memory. Instead, he felt empty, except for the strange, reoccurring voice in his mind. He couldn't help but frown, casting his gaze from Haven and Andrid towards the bristling fire. The flames surrounded him, but he didn't feel its warmth, like an embrace lacking any emotion or two apathetic strangers forced to mingle. It felt colder than the touch of winter.

"No," the nameless man replied, cupping his hands together, sliding his thumb across the palm of his hand to try and return the heat his body had lost. "Nothing."

A silence fell over them. Embers trickled towards the rising moon, warm cinders meeting the cool air. He found it almost amusing how the world continued to turn, failing to notice the feelings of the people within it.

"Your country, the Avernos Empire, was victorious at the end," Haven stated, placing down his empty bowl and gazing up towards the fort. "The opposite kingdom, Esperin, couldn't hold the fort after Avernos dispatched a second wave of men."

Their encampment stretched about half a mile to the south of Silvercrest's grand hill. Even in the dark, the nameless man could see the structure with ease. Soldiers of the Avernos Empire surveyed the immediate area around the fort, clad in the armor with crimson décor that he guessed he previously wore.

"Not tell A-ver-nose you here," Andrid whispered in their broken speech. Still, they kept their palm raised between their mouth and the fort, though it did nothing to actually conceal their words. "Wanted make sure okay first!" Their lips spread to reveal their canines.

"Will you return to Avernos?" Haven inquired.

"I don't know," the soldier answered honestly. Currently, he felt no ties to this unknown empire. Even though he was saddened by unforeseen circumstances, he wasn't eager to return to a war that he couldn't remember. "I think I need a little time," he muttered, peering at them apologetically. "Can we not inform them?"

"Of course. You can take all the time you need," Salem interrupted, returning to the group with two wooden bowls in her hands. She seated herself beside him, offering the dish with a simple gesture.

The nameless soldier nodded in thanks, grasping the presumably hot bowl in his hands. Unsurprisingly, he felt nothing.

"What should we call you?" Salem asked as she leaned forward to meet his downward regard, the strands of her hair brushing past her cheeks.

He heard the voice chuckle.

"I seem to not know a lot of things, my name being one of them," the man answered, ignoring the strangeness of the voice's haughty gesture. It was still difficult to keep eye contact with Salem, but the flames accentuated her eyes like magical sparks in a glowing lantern. He wanted this beautiful light to guide his way, to bring him out of the darkness before it swallowed him whole. "Should I just come up with something?"

"No," Haven interrupted. "It's a bad omen to name yourself. If you need a temporary name, someone else should come up with it."

"Oooo, I pick name!" Andrid exclaimed, curling their legs underneath their hips. "Haven's chosen by me, so best experience with names." They sat in silence for a few moments, pondering as they analyzed the surrounding area for inspiration. "Bean. No. Moss! No. Birdie!"

"Salem found him. She should name him," Haven said.

"Me?" Salem questioned, and Haven nodded in approval. For a moment she sat staring at the fire, watching the embers that imitated crashing waves.

As the group sat in a strange tension, Salem folded her hands, closed her eyes, and straightened her posture to resemble a prayer. She lingered in a silence of mental solitude, despite the soldier's constant stare. When her meditation had ended, she stilled, as if awaiting a response. He wasn't sure if she had received a reply.

"Korbyn," she finally said, a name that gingerly rolled off her tongue. "Yes. Korbyn."

"I like it," Korbyn blurted out, his gaze fixed on her. Her smile was bright and contagious, and it made his mouth tug upwards for the first time—the first time he could remember.

While he finished his dinner, he watched the party amongst him exchange stories from earlier in the day. Andrid was always optimistic and cheery despite the severity of the tasks they completed. They went into excruciating details about a dead soldier they had found, whose torso was severed from the rest of his body and the disconnect of his mouth from the rest of his jaw. It didn't seem to bother them as they excitedly yapped for several minutes. The fox remained quiet and patient at their side.

Haven's recollection was short and sweet, elaborating on his day like a list of significant undertakings. It lacked much depth or emotion, but he seemed to take his job very seriously. As the largest male and the only one with any orc lineage, he mostly offered his services to completing the most strenuous physical labor, but he paid no heed.

Salem shared the details of her elongated day. Korbyn was just as entranced by her story, despite how tedious the tasks sounded. She relocated heavy items, packed supplies, processed and organized documents, scoured medicinal materials, recounted and divided victuals, and many other responsibilities. At some point, he lost track, unsure how one person managed to complete so much in a single day.

"You should get some more rest," Salem stated as she scraped the last of her potage from her bowl. She collected the dishes before Korbyn could offer his assistance. Haven and Andrid did the same by gathering the empty dishes and the rest of their belongings.

When they strode towards their own accommodations, Korbyn stared at the fort in the distance. It was quiet, lingering in the aftermath and fog of a weary battle, and eventually, the sounds of the living quieted. Voices called out to him from the shadows of the mists. When he tried to concentrate on their words, he couldn't discern them, but they increased in volume. Sharp cries rang through his ears, emanating from the fort. Somehow, he knew they weren't alive, as though they didn't originate from living souls. Still, the echoes of their declarations retaliated in defiance of whatever was ensuing within its walls.

A *premonition for when the red moon lingers*, the voice bellowed.

"Are you coming?" Salem urged, motioning for him to follow her.

"Yeah, sorry." Korbyn trailed her, ignoring the cries behind him.

The entirety of camp withdrew behind the flaps of their tents, with each fighter, bishop, and altruist retreating into their own respective areas and out of sight of the watchful moon. Within a few minutes, it was just Korbyn and Salem. She stopped and turned on her heel in front of his tent flap. She reached out and grasped his arm in consolation, and he wished she hadn't donned gloves.

"I'll come by early so we can talk." Salem pivoted, striding towards her tent that resided not too far from his own.

"Thank you. Goodnight, Salem," Korbyn said, wanting to hear his new name part from her lips.

Salem halted when she reached her shelter and pulled back the fabric. Before she vanished into its shadow, she turned to him with a smile. "Goodnight, Korbyn."

When she entered and allowed the linen to conceal her retreating form, Korbyn noticed there were no lanterns lit inside. Despite this, a light beamed within the darkness.

Before Korbyn strode into his pavilion, his back tingled in anticipation. He sensed watchful eyes, as though he was a raven hiding within blades of grass. At first, he couldn't find the source of his discomfort. Something hid and waited in obscurity for a guided misstep. When he turned, he met the gaze of a person.

Across the way stood the blond elf, the male from when he first awoke on the battlefield. The elf conveyed a glare so intense that even with Korbyn's constant chill, he shivered. The mysterious person remained silent before he turned abruptly behind the shadows of a tent, leaving Korbyn under the moon.

Alone.

THREE.

Salem could no longer withhold her progressing exhaustion. Once she had removed the entirety of her armor, she plopped into a chair at her overused trestle table. In her solitude, she allowed a semblance of fatigue as she slouched in the wooden seat.

Over the past two weeks, the entirety of Kendra Dawn, especially the volunteers, had toiled tirelessly to ensure the complete assembly of bodies. Today marked the last day of their excursion, and tomorrow, they would divide into two groups. While one would take the Esperin soldiers to the capital in the north of Umberfall, the other would trek south and return the Avernos soldiers to Goldenrise.

Salem picked up her quill, unscrewed the cork from its bottled ink, and dipped it. She definitely preferred monster hunting in comparison to these bleak tasks.

Ever since the war began half a year ago, Kendra Dawn had expanded into more than just a group of monster-hunting mercenaries. Volunteers from all around Terrisae offered their services to aid Kendra Dawn's unique vision. Mere mercenary band no more, the neutral party and volunteers struck a contract with both nations so they might return the fallen to their homelands. With their bodies collected, the church in Esperin could perform the passing rite of Elohim so that their souls could be guided to the Heavens.

Salem clutched the quill, almost snapping its delicate spine.

Up until this point in the conflict, Avernos hadn't successfully encroached into Esperin territory. For months, the conflicting nations had endlessly fought on the edge of Exonia Creek, leaving the civilians and towns safe from the conflict. At least, until Avernos took over Fort Silvercrest.

Now that the war had breached Esperin's borders, Kendra Dawn's services would entail more than collecting bodies and remitting them to their kingdoms. Now they would need to observe how Avernos handled the invasion. Their next objective might lean towards overtaking other fortifications along Exonia Creek to extend their borders. After that, they could easily enclose Esperin's capital, surrounding it from the south, east, and west. Despite Esperin's larger army, it would prove challenging to properly defend their territory.

In the future, when Avernos' army inevitably trampled across Esperin lands, Kendra Dawn would need to rebuild towns, regrow farms, heal the sick and injured, and any other general assistance they could offer. It would be exhausting, but Salem was eager to help the people, even if it meant a temporary pause in her search.

Shifting through the scattered papers along the table, the paladin rummaged through them until she found what she was looking for—a rough sketch of two long swords with uneven and jagged edges and hilts made of humorous bones wrapped in tattered leather.

She extracted a scrolled parchment. A map of Terrisae, beautifully drawn and now defiled by marks of black ink. X's and lines littered the vellum, indicating their previous travels. When they first arrived in this continent, Salem and Veeris searched Shadowbane Forest, surmising that such evil blades would surely exist in an equally nightmarish place, but they found nothing except unexplainable, magical darkness. Over the few years after that, they explored most of the Alliance of Thalar, with bits and pieces of Avernos and Esperin's countries. At this point, she was sure that the blades resided somewhere in the human kingdoms, if they still existed at all.

Salem huffed, wanting to crumble the map in her hands and hover it above her lit candle to watch her failed endeavors burn. These blades eluded her, remaining hidden from her vigorous scouting.

It had been years since she began her journey, but to no avail. She had relinquished everything for this cause, arriving in this continent to assist those less fortunate. Finding the blades would help innocents, yet she only had empty hands and false hope. If she could fulfill her oath, then the suffering of the people would certainly end. She clutched her locket, trailing her fingers along its golden surface.

"Elohim," Salem whispered, closing her eyes and trailing her thumb over the surface of the necklace. "Ever since I arrived in Terrisae, I have not heard Your voice, and I am in need of Your aid. I've searched lands, beseeched witnesses, and scavenged ruins, but none have seen or heard of the artifacts You sent me to retrieve. Where do You think they reside?"

And just like every other prayer, she was met with a silence.

Salem scoffed, allowing the artifact to once again dangle freely at her clavicle. No matter how many questions she had or how many times she prayed, no acknowledgment encountered her heeding ears. Several years passed, and not once had she heard Elohim's voice. She abided in skepticism, unaware of the significance of this faithful test.

Upon her arrival in Terrisae, she assumed she would be able to sense the dual blades, regardless of distance. However, even with her holy magic, Salem couldn't detect them, as though a barrier had prevented her otherwise heightened perception. The only abnormal entity that she recognized was a half-dead man with a distinct, grim aura on the battlefield of Fort Silvercrest.

Korbyn. Her mind wandered to him, letting the map fall limp in her fingers. When she witnessed his eyes open for the first time, those darkened sclera with eyes like the moon, her innate reaction was to rid the world of its evil, a suitable reaction from previous events, only to stop upon the realization that he was very unlike what she had encountered before.

At the time, Salem was riddled with blatant confusion and intrigue. She wasn't sure how this circumstance was possible, but something remained amiss. When his eyes stared back into her own, longing to live and unintentionally proclaiming his innocence from his near demise, she yearned to assist him.

Salem could sense with her holy magic that Korbyn was indeed a human, a casualty of a selfish war. And, despite the oddity of the situation, she fully believed his strange amnesia. He rested in a coma for an entire fortnight before he awoke, bearing no remembrance to his condition or life before the battle.

During his body's elongated stupor, an ailment threatened him. Unlike most debilitated people, weakened with a harsh fever, Korbyn was the opposite. His body chilled, freezing his skin as though he had been submerged in ice. The bishops continually tried to keep him warm and alleviate the reoccurring cough, but it was as if his body refused the treatment. His sickness didn't cure from her holy magic or the power of decidite, and they were forced to watch and wait for his probable demise.

And then, miraculously, the plague disappeared with no proof of its prior existence. Korbyn's unconscious body still felt cool to the touch, but death no longer threatened him. Whatever had occurred internally, it was as if he had been born anew.

Salem constantly verified his stability during and after his sickness. With her magic, she could sense a battle deep within his mind, heart, and body, of a dark power underneath contesting for dominance. When she reached for its lingering presence, it resembled an endless void in a cage, surrounded by an equally boundless maze. It was a strange, dark, and familiar power.

When Korbyn awoke, only mere hours before, Salem resolved to discover the secrets of this strange anomaly and help the man, regardless of whatever Veeris might think.

"Have you gone mad?" Salem heard from the entrance of her tent.

Veeris dramatically pulled back the flap of the tent's entrance and strode to the front of the table. His pointed ears twitched alongside his furrowed brows, and he seemed to have trouble keeping his blond, stray hairs from falling out of his tight-knit bun.

Salem leaned forward, resting her chin on her palm, and regrasped her white feathered quill. She grazed her thumb over the fringed texture and observed it for a moment, chuckling to herself at the irony.

"It's yet to be proved," Salem jested, dipping the quill into the ink again due to it drying moments before. She crossed out Fort Silvercrest. "What are we referring to this time?"

"That man," Veeris spat, crossing his arms and glaring, "I don't trust him."

"We're calling him Korbyn," Salem informed him, avoiding his gaze by pretending the map had some new, fascinating intrigue.

"Tell me you didn't name him," Veeris demanded.

She shrugged. "Alright. I didn't name him."

Salem didn't have to glance up to know he was glaring. "Of course I gave him a name," she said with a frown, leaning back in her chair and shifting her attention back to him. "What are we going to call him? 'You, the Guy with No Memory that Almost Die—"

"We are forbidden from giving names!" Veeris interrupted. "You know better."

Salem knew Veeris wasn't truly angry with her, but his irritation seemed to linger longer with each passing day.

"Yes, of course, because I'm such a stickler for the rules," Salem retorted sarcastically. "If I followed orders, we wouldn't be here in the first place. You're too untrusting of everyone."

"His eyes. You realize what he resembles, don't you? He looks just like a—"

"I know that, but we can't just assume anything. He doesn't even know who he is. He needs our help."

Veeris' eyes rolled dramatically all the way towards the ceiling before circling back to her. She was surprised his pupils didn't get lost in the back of his head with how many times he did that. "You fail to understand the danger it places on our mission, *Salem*. He may be here to prevent our search for the blades. His memory loss could just be a ruse."

"He doesn't remember anything, *Veeris*." She hissed his name with equal sarcasm, crossing her leg over the other underneath the trestle table. "Can't you see that? He's a victim. He nearly died from that battle. On top of everything, he has amnesia. Whatever is going on with him, it's our duty to assess the situation. If we want to learn more, we should keep him close." She flicked her eyes upward, noting his softened demeanor.

"You know I trust you, right? More than anyone in the entirety of this world, the previous one and whatever the next one may be. I left everything to follow you because I believed in you and your cause." The gentleness in his eyes dispersed, replaced with an unbound fury. "But him, I cannot trust, especially considering what he might be. If you plan to keep him with us, just know that I will be watching him at every corner, waiting for him to betray us."

He stalked over towards the entrance of the tent and pulled back the fabric.

"What's the saying? Keep your allies close and your enemies closer?" Salem questioned, placing her elbow on her chair and turning her torso to face him.

"Ah, yes. Syrian Claymore said those words back during the Esperin Civil War. He uttered that phrase to his forming rebellion when he was pretending to be loyal to his kingdom." Veeris quieted for a moment, staring out towards the moon with a lifted chin. "The active King of Esperin at the time kept him close—so close that he failed to see the hidden blade in the knight's hand when he stabbed him."

Veeris turned to her. "Do not get too close to him, Salem, for it's much easier to wound an ally than it is an enemy."

Before Salem could respond, he ducked out of the tent.

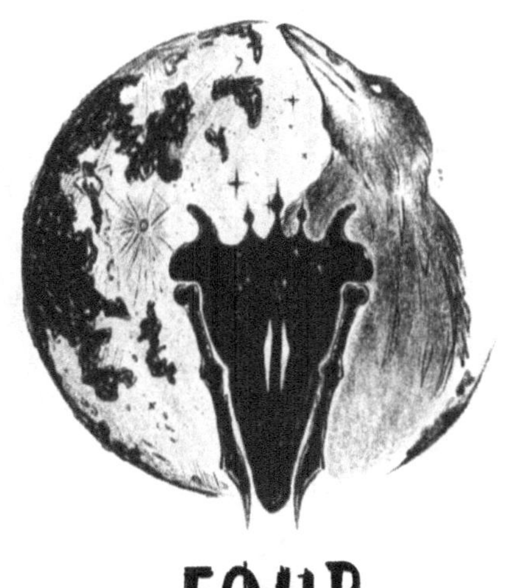

FOUR.

fter hours of shuffling under the heavy quilt, Korbyn couldn't sleep. Every time he tried to forfeit his active mind to slumber, he was disrupted by visions of a blazing fire and screams echoing across blankets of darkness. Unlike normal nightmares, these hallucinations prevented him from sleeping at all, forcing his mind to stay awake for every grueling second.

Korbyn rose from the wooden frames just before the sun did. He still wore his previous attire, the long tunic and a pair of pants that hung too firmly around his wrists and ankles. He rummaged through the coffer on the far side of the room to locate any preferable replacements, anticipating empty drawers. To his surprise, he discovered a loose-fitting, ivory cotton shirt and a pair of knee-high trews that tightened around the calf. He also retrieved a pair of leather boots beside the chest, which appeared simple in design and hopefully his size.

The pants slid on effortlessly around his waist as he buttoned them just below his navel. When he removed his old shirt, he approached the rude mirror with apprehension. He was still not used to observing his reflection, as the person standing opposite him echoed his actions while remaining unrecognizable. Whether the reflection was aware of its shrill mockery, it didn't cease its unbridled urging.

The scars across his face, body, and arms had quelled its swelling, though were still enflamed with a disturbing vibrance. As Korbyn finally donned his new attire, he could clearly perceive the arrow lacerations dispersed across his body. Whatever had brought him to the brink of death had gotten very close.

Death never dwindles.

Korbyn shied away from the mirror and ignored the voice's intervention. Instead, he tucked his shirt into his pants and rolled his sleeves up to his elbows. As he grazed his left forearm, a pain seared, kindred to his plaguing migraines. As he wrenched away and drove his attention to its origin, a shuddering chill domineered his slack form.

Previously flawless in comparison to the rest of his scarred body, Korbyn's left arm now burned in a matte charcoal symbol from his wrist to the encircling scar under his elbow. It throbbed in introduction, his skin lit aflame yet adversely surrounded in prickling ice.

Flakes of dry skin coated the mark, as though the needle lifted, and the ink kneaded. It resembled a goat's skull, with dual looking blades on each side of its face to create the silhouette of its protruding eye sockets and cheekbones. Adorning the top of its head was the profile of a crown with extended horns swirling upwards. Overall, it was symmetrical in design, as if it had been crafted by a skilled artisan. As if thanking him for the commendation, it rallied in a throb that induced a sneer. Korbyn prodded the tender skin and flinched from the tenderness.

A Crown of Horns and Blades. A grim sight indeed.

"Korbyn!" Salem greeted him from the outskirts of his tent.

Hurriedly, Korbyn unrolled the sleeves so that they enclosed his wrist, despite his impulse to leave the fresh lesion untouched.

"Are you awake? Can I come in?"

He sent several fingers through the thick locks of his jet-black hair, calming the wildness of his previous, unslept night.

"Yes," Korbyn replied.

Salem pulled back the flap. The morning sun bore its own greeting, following the paladin in her iridescent light. Korbyn couldn't prevent himself from sinking further into the comfort of the shadows.

"Good morning! How did you sleep?" Salem asked, her gilt eyes shimmering from his lit candle. Korbyn watched her attention inspect his body in its entirety, only stopping when she reached the purple swelling under his eyelids. He felt fatigued, despite any cries for help and the slumber his mind ignored.

"Decently," Korbyn lied, examining her in return.

Salem smelled of fresh pine before the start of winter, a gentle breeze that caressed the leaves of fall. She had tied her hair at her crown, revealing her neck and the thick locks of blond. Her blade and shield convened at her back in preparation for an undeclared battle.

"If you're certain," she replied with furrowed brows. Even so, she motioned with a raised hand to the exit of his marquee. "Will you walk with me?"

As Korbyn and Salem ventured further to the outskirts of the camp, he examined the members of Kendra Dawn assembling gear and supplies upon allotted wagons. With their copious belongings, it would still take several hours for them to pack what remained of their arrangements. Provisions, supplies, animals, tents, and furniture had been distributed betwixt them. He imagined that amid the fall season, the chill faded with the rising sun, though he couldn't discern it with utmost certainty.

While one line of the caravan faced north, the other assembly prepared their venture in the direction of a crossing over the sizable river to the south. Both groups had endless wagons of delicately organized and preserved bodies of the deceased. Only when all the volunteers gathered together did he truly distinguish their sizeable numbers.

"You awoke just in time for our departure. We're leaving Fort Silvercrest. We've divided into two groups: one is heading towards the capital of the Kingdom of Esperin and the other to the Avernos Empire. We need to return the fallen soldiers to their homes," Salem explained, waving at several bishops as they stepped past. "Thankfully, we get to depart today."

The duo arrived at the alternate side of the camp, where Korbyn could analyze the fort's decrepit stature. The garrison appeared to be constructed centuries ago with inadequate experience. Though it sat upon a grand hill, which aided its defense against an encroaching army, it also provided a poor foundation from its shortened fortifications and uneven terrain. The tall maple and various trees surrounding the hill undoubtedly aided a quieter advancement, permitting the aggressors to scale the unreliable walls with ease. Despite its robust solidity, it crumbled under any form of apprehensible pressure. Destroyed stone and walls now lay crumbled at the foot of its hill.

"Where will you go?" Korbyn prompted, returning his gaze to Salem.

She smiled, pointing in the direction of his previous focus. "To the Kingdom of Esperin, the opposite country of where you're from," she said, concern trailing across a sea of gold. "What about you? I know you said you needed time. You're more than welcome to travel with us until you're ready, unless you think you have family back home that you wish to return to."

Too soon. A tale for another day.

"I don't even know if I have a family," Korbyn whispered. As he observed Kendra Dawn and their charitable exploits, he longed for something tangible.

"I'm sorry," Salem replied, her frown deepening. She failed to cloud the sympathy in her eyes, emotions surging beyond the windows of gold. "The option is yours and yours alone. We didn't tell Avernos because we didn't want to overwhelm you."

Not completely the truth, not completely a lie.

Ignoring the voice, Korbyn gave her an appreciative smile. "If I'm not too much of a burden, I would like to stay with you..." He trailed off, clearing his throat that still ached. "You and your mercenary band. I would like to learn more about Kendra Dawn."

Salem's eyes lit like a newly ignited flame, her smile widening from one ear to the other. "I think that's a wonderful idea. I will need to check with my allies and the Arbiter, but I don't think it will be any trouble—oh, that's the leader of Kendra Dawn. You'll get a chance to meet her soon. But, before we leave, there's something I think we should do."

She strode towards the east side of camp. Korbyn caught up to her, striding in step to her left. It wasn't long before he witnessed their destination: a ring of simple, wooden fences huddled in a roughly constructed oval, with two beige flags of Kendra Dawn stationed at both sides of the entrance. Barrels and bins with randomly organized wooden and iron weapons stood against the only tent pitched at the far end.

Wooden pells scattered across the area, erected from the ground in firm positions, the entire lengths padded in hessian sacking. At their tallest, they leveled around the height of an average person. Arrows were riddled amongst torn fabrics, at the base of their structures, and far behind their locations, revealing a prior training. He sensed the users were unpracticed, as most of the arrows volleyed far passed their intended target. Lowering the crossbow would have been a simple readjustment.

"Nevin, could we use this place for a little while longer?" Salem requested, bowing her head apologetically to one of the volunteers who actively aggregated some of the scattered bolts. "We'll only be a few minutes, and we'll help pack up the rest of the area once we're finished."

An older male, Nevin, turned to face them. He was relatively short, reaching somewhere around Korbyn's waist. He modeled a shortened beard, a receding hairline, and a bright, contagious smile.

"I could never say no to you, Salem," the gnome responded, fetching the stool he previously utilized to reach an elevated arrow stuck within the pell's midsection. "We only have a few of hours before we decamp, so I wouldn't take too long." Nevin smiled nonetheless, greeting Korbyn with a wave as he joined Salem's side.

"Thank you so much!" she responded as Nevin departed to the pavilion, rallying the other volunteers.

Salem removed the long sword and shield on her back and propped them against the fence. In their place, she seized two longswords made of roughly cut timber from a bin and spun them, looking as though she was deciphering their weight.

"We're going to spar?" Korbyn asked in surprise.

Salem extended the wooden sword to his right hand, motioning him to bind his fingers around the hilt until his firm tightened. "Traveling through Terrisae is dangerous. There are a lot of creatures, marauders, and thieves from here to Esperin, especially during the war." She turned the wooden blade in her hand, home to where a weapon usually resided. "Do you remember the monsters that plague these lands?"

As Korbyn tried to recall, a sting traveled to both of his temples. "Honestly, no." He pressed his fingers against his head to reduce the discomfort. "I don't think I do."

Salem gave him an encouraging smile. "It's alright. If you plan to travel with us, then I need to inform you of what exactly you're getting into." She pivoted towards the lands outside the encampment, the soldier's gaze following her motions. "The lands of Terrisae are dangerous. The creatures that lurk crave the darkness. There are ogres, elementals, enraged spirits, wraiths, rocs, harpies, and many more wicked creatures. Most hide in shadows and await weary travelers. At night, they're at their strongest. Because of this, forested areas are incredibly unsafe, and it's not stagnant. For some reason, it's as if the darkness is giving them more and more power. Not only are their numbers increasing, but they're growing stronger and more defiant, especially under a Blood Moon."

Korbyn's eyebrow lifted. "A Blood Moon?"

She nodded. "Yes. If you see a Blood Moon, you'll know it immediately. It's a rare phenomenon that turns the moon scarlet. Its red hue is casted upon the lands, causing monsters to become irate, and it can do the same for people if emotions are flared enough," Salem explained, twirling her wooden blade as she stared at the sky. "Everything is affected by its existence. Some people say it's an ill omen."

"It sounds dangerous," Korbyn commented.

"It is," Salem agreed, weaving her blade as though it was a brush manipulated by a skilled painter. "Which is why I want to see what you're made of," the paladin taunted. "If you were a soldier of Avernos, you must have known how to wield a blade, unless they put just about anyone on the front lines."

A newfound gleam flourished in Salem's crystal eyes, accompanied by an eager grin.

The Paladin of Dawn, blinded by her own holy light, the voice whispered.

Mulling over the faux weapon, Korbyn noted its heaviness despite its frailty. It felt abnormal and foreign as he curled his fingers around it in a tighter grip. Mimicking her stance remained just as strange as he slid his left leg forward and situated the pommel above his right hip. His foundation wavered in comparison to Salem's poised gait.

She left him no time to think or readjust, lunging in his direction with a swipe.

With only a second to parry, Korbyn raised his arms upright to deflect. When he stepped back to readjust his undefended side, she tailed him and swung. She imitated the confident strides of a waltz, and just as graceful. Her blade cavorted like leaves trailing the autumn wind, goaded by the season's call. The lumber clashed against one another in quick successions, each strike from Salem more precise than the last. She stayed unsullied by the dirt beneath her, her breaths in tandem with her elegant strides.

After several paces, Salem slammed the edge of the wood against his knuckles and knocked it free from Korbyn's grasp. She leveled the blade towards his neck, and he raised his chin in defeat. Instead of being perturbed by her effortless disarming, as most experienced soldiers would have been, he was overawed by her expertise.

"Let's try it again," Salem stated, allowing him to pick up the artificial blade and resume his previous stance.

The longest Korbyn avoided defeat was nearly fifteen seconds, which proved to be impressive due to his lack of memories. In the heat of battle, there were only a few seconds before a winner was proclaimed, leaving one dead and the other alive. Again and again, he watched the wooden sword fly from his grasp and clatter to the ground. The fake weapon still persisted to be an unfamiliar entity.

When Korbyn finally staggered from weariness, Salem must have detected it. She approached his left and swung her ankle behind his own. As he surged away from her quick advance, he tumbled along with his disregarded weapon. Before he could stand, Salem pointed the sword at his neck. He conceded, leaning back on his palms for a moment of recess.

"It's not clicking," Korbyn admitted with a saddened sigh.

Only twenty minutes had passed, but he couldn't alleviate the inward frustrations of lacking his memories. It acted much like an irritable scratch that wouldn't cease, despite his constant attempts. Korbyn regretted not bringing water with him—or ale, at least. His thirst begged to be quenched as he sat underneath the sun that refused to warm him.

"It will," Salem said confidently, outstretching her hand.

Korbyn's breath stifled, and he extended his arm in return.

Before their skin touched, a jolt of energy trickled along his palm like needles. Even with Salem's glove between their hands, Korbyn experienced the abnormal surge. The shock was fierce enough to precipitate a lingering pulsation.

The paladin hoisted him up with great strength and solid foundation, and when they separated, the feeling numbed. Korbyn scanned his hand and then her face, unsure if she had experienced the sensation when she failed to exhibit a reaction. If she did, she hid it well, offering him a smile that warmed his aching soul. If not for the scar protruding from her chin, he would have considered she wasn't even mortal.

"I suppose I'll have to relearn along the way," Korbyn mentioned as he saw Nevin's approach.

Salem nodded in agreement, obtaining the discarded blade and assembling the rest of the equipment. He followed her example, grabbing some of the dropped supplies and forgotten weapons behind a wooden bench. When they reunited at one of the empty bins, she offered another smile. They stared into each other's eyes, the proximity between them seeming more comfortable than not.

"I may not know what it's like to lose something as valuable as my memory, but I imagine it's similar to the change of the seasons," the elf said, organizing the weapons within the barrel. "When winter appears, we have a tendency to take for granted the warmth of summer and the beauty of autumn." When she bore a smile of delight at her organization, she spun the top lid closed. "But spring always returns, just as it has before." Salem beamed, placing her hands on her hips as she comfortably shifted her weight. In such contrast to her previous words of wisdom, she finalized her speech with a snicker. "And if it doesn't, well, then that sucks for you. I guess I'll be kicking your butt forever."

A part of Korbyn instinctively lurched, with no control of his own volition. It was volatile, his body seething and his muscles tightening in a way that felt unnatural, new and unseen by himself or others around him. A sound emerged from his throat, one so foreign that the woman in front of him gawked in surprise.

Korbyn began to laugh. The sound was just as surprising to him, and when the laughter had settled, he couldn't help but keep the smile on his face.

"Be careful. I might like that," he declared, one end of his smirk twitching a little higher than the other.

Salem flashed her own wild grin. Despite the loss of his memories, Korbyn had gained something that, in this moment, felt just as valuable to him as what he might have left behind in Avernos. A blush spread across her cheeks, and a warmth crept up to his heart.

Screams echoed across the plains of Fort Silvercrest, causing both Korbyn and Salem to spin towards that general direction. Several members of Kendra Dawn, the bishops, assistants, and others unfit for combat, gestured to the skies. Silhouettes of large creatures of varying sizes slipped through the stillness of the clouds, emerging from obscurity. When the forms soared above their camp in continuous circles, they released loud roars that coerced the screams to a silent panic. Just as abruptly as they appeared, the beasts left their vantage points, lowering themselves through the density of the fog.

The clouds parted, revealing a pride of flying beasts, with the king of lions leading lionesses into the fray. They maintained wingspans that outstretched four paces in length and spiked tails that flicked in anticipation. Their bodies resembled lions, with enlarged paws and talons like machetes, and their wings paralleling that of eagles. Their manes, long and proud, whisked in the very wind that carried them. The pride male roared once again, initiating the rest of the group to charge towards the unprepared civilians.

Salem ogled the advancement, disbelief shining in her eyes. "Manticores."

FIVE.

Korbyn trembled, halted in a dread from the vicious, plummeting monsters. Before the influx, they would need to find temporary refuge until the creatures withdrew. He reached out to Salem, but she had already enacted her own plan. She thrust the hilt of a sharpened blade in his hand, one made of iron and steel.

"Manticores are cunning," Salem declared, stepping backwards towards the fray while retaining eye contact. "They're dexterous and fast in the air and on ground. When they're mid-flight, it's harder to hit them, but while they're grounded, they're quick, unpredictable, and have better control over their bodies. Their tails have large spikes, and they could tear you into pieces faster than you could dodge them."

Korbyn's mouth attempted to formulate words, but the paladin had already turned away, donning her shield and longsword.

"Where are you going?" Korbyn asked, despite knowing the answer.

When he took a step forward, Salem craned her face to reveal her scowl. Her normal, cheerful, and gentle persona was now concealed by confidence, a garb just as vital as her blade. "I need you to hide. Head with Nevin to the tent on the other side of the training grounds and wait for me there. Keep the blade with you just in case."

Salem did not wait for a response. Instead, she lunged towards the battle, leaving him behind in his own stupefaction.

Korbyn remained motionless, with conflict towing him in two directions. In the moments of truth, where his instincts determined if he were to fight or fly, he chose neither; instead, he allowed fear to bridle him. Meanwhile, Salem, a brave and beautiful paladin, countered the situation with haste and a heart of purity.

And that was when Korbyn decided that he would never falter in the face of danger ever again.

"Come on, boy, follow me to the tent! We can wait in there while the mercenaries do their job," Nevin urged, grabbing the edge of his shirt and pulling.

Despite the gnome's desperation, Korbyn didn't budge. Instead, he took a deep breath and shut his eyes, searching for the inevitable courage of a soldier who believed in a war so fresh that it newly bled. However, there was no memory to greet him, only the migraine and the disruptive voice.

The lion bares its teeth, but the raven is left with none.

"Get inside," Korbyn demanded, readjusting the blade in his right hand and stalking towards the edge of the training grounds.

"Wait! The tent is this way! Where are you going?" Nevin urged.

Without glancing back, Korbyn continued, feeling thirsty for something other than water. "To the den of the lions."

By the time Korbyn arrived at the center of the camp, the manticores had descended on the plains. They trampled over shelters, fences, and wagons, destroying any standing structures with ease. Korbyn counted five, eight, twelve—seventeen manticores in total, standing almost three heads taller than him that trampled over the encampment like a barbaric wave crashing into a castle made of glass.

If the sheer size of the beasts hadn't made the people cower in fear, the roars certainly did. They reverberated against the skies, their echoes carrying across the desolate plains. When they rallied together in unison with the rest of the pride, they instilled a fear that couldn't be ignored.

The horses reared, struggling to buck and tear away from the wagons they were attached to, but there was no room for them to retreat. The volunteers of Kendra Dawn followed suit, scurrying in panic. Some hustled into the ingresses of shelters or scurried under intact wagons, trying to conceal themselves away from the ferocious beasts, but others weren't so fortunate. A few members of the pride cornered them, circling them in rotations. If any were to try and scamper between the monsters, they would either succumb to the large blades jutting from their paws or their spiked appendages on their backside, which mimicked flails more than actual body parts.

The manticores paused in strange unison as they encircled their prey, baring their teeth in unbearable hunger. They lowered their broadened shoulders as their back legs quivered with expectation. Their eyes, radiant and golden, glowered in desire.

As Korbyn stepped forward to intervene, an imitation of various animal-cawing, tongue-flicking, and alternate vocalizations pierced the mist's veil, grabbing the attention of the manticores like an instigating battle cry. Emerging from the other side of the camp, through a cloud of dust and debris, was a figure. Andrid, already covered in dirt and bits and pieces of leather, sauntered from its depths. They carried not a sword, or spear, or any type of traditional blade, but a staff. Vines, mushrooms, and blooming green mums protruded randomly within its modified design.

There was something strange within the confines of the vines that formed a cage on the top. Within the enclosure was a black ore, roughly the size of a closed fist. Decorating its outer texture were veins of gold that shimmered, despite the fog that surrounded them. Magic emitted from the stone in waves of radiating brilliance, dancing in its own cadence.

Andrid strode towards the beast without fear or deterrence. Their long, garnet braid blew behind them, reveling in its caress. In contrast to their oblivious demeanor, Andrid bore a devilish grin. They strolled onto the newly declared battlefield, an aura of holy light emerging from the ore and weaving around their body like dancing ribbons.

Two of the manticores lurched forward at Andrid, alternating their steps in a choreographed movement. While one claimed the front, the other moved behind, maneuvering to shield the exact moments when the one in the back would strike.

With a grand swing of Andrid's staff, the edge of its wooden tip dug through the dirt beneath on its way up. When the swing met its full stride, roots ripped from the earth's surface. For the greenery, it was as if time surged forward—these small, normal-sized plants grew rapidly and formidably in a span of seconds. They were uprooted chaotically, as though Andrid had minimal control of their wild spiraling towards the rising sun.

The manticores lurched backwards, the dust from their movement concealing the plants. Attaching themselves to the closest living thing, the vines reactively wrapped their roots around the two manticores. The plants that now towered over them grasped firmly, preventing their continued assaults.

Two more manticores circled Andrid from behind and lunged. An alternate force slammed into one of the creatures with a broad shoulder, causing the first manticore to topple into the second, and they both fell in mangled heaps. The creatures adjusted their stances and rose to meet their new opponent.

Haven stepped in between Andrid and the two manticores. He inclined his head until it cracked before he unlatched his grand axe. The weapon stood almost as massive as him, with sharpened edges and strips of leather wrapped around its elongated handle. Designs that resembled his tattoos were engraved into the steel. Haven held its abnormal weight with ease, advancing towards the two creatures.

"Don't engage without me next time," Haven muttered, causing Andrid to beam with a chuckle that resembled a hyena.

"Best be's quicker then!" Andrid replied.

On the other side of the battlefield, protecting a group of people behind her, was Salem. Four large lionesses stood over several heaps of sprawled, lifeless civilians that had failed to escape the monsters' elongated claws.

Magic flowed around Salem's body like a brewing storm until its power became uncontrollable, its wild essence manifesting an extended partition of light. When two manticore slammed into it, holy energy erupted from the wall like lightning and sent them flying back into a wagon. Salem continued to defend the people with a raised blade and shield, combating the manticore every time they lunged.

As Korbyn went to assist her, a cry emanated from behind him. He turned, seeing a woman stumbling into one of the wagons that carried preserved, dead bodies. Despite the woman's obvious fear, her arms were stretched out, attempting to shield the remains of the warriors who gave their lives for their country's cause. Her legs quaked, barely holding her own body upright. In front of her wasn't just a manticore, but a king, the pride of its group and the largest of them all.

It stood twice as tall as Korbyn, its shoulders straightening in continual, effortless strides. Instead of lowering its torso into a prepared pounce, it sauntered with superiority. Intelligence surveyed the woman beneath it.

Salem informed him that most creatures were inclined to rely on the darkness to encroach, so what gave these creatures the courage to assault such a large encampment? Korbyn watched the lion's gaze flick from the helpless woman to the carefully arranged bodies in the back of the wagon.

The manticores wanted the corpses, and Kendra Dawn had reluctantly gathered them on a golden plate for its golden king.

Cunning predators lurk and wait in the darkness.

As the king strolled over to the frightened woman, it leered. The woman finally collapsed, leaning fully into the footboard of the caravan as her knees no longer supported her. The manticore loomed above her, the creases of its eyes and jaw scrunching together to bare the weapons that were its sharp and elongated teeth.

Without any hesitation, Korbyn plunged into the lion's den.

The blade in his hand felt like a boulder, too heavy and cumbersome, but his instincts didn't let that stop him. The king noticed Korbyn's advancement, but it didn't seem to care for the single warrior approaching its throne. As soon as Korbyn got close, the manticore flicked its spiked tail to thwart his advance.

Seeing the tail's movement, Korbyn was ready. He dropped to the ground and slid underneath the tail's swipe. Amidst his glide, he swung his blade across the rear limb of its elongated foot. A deafening roar emitted from the king's mouth, and it reared back on its hind legs, flopping backwards and rolling until it was on its feet.

The cut wasn't deep, but enough to make it falter. The new wound leaked with blood, forming a small puddle underneath its massive talons.

The lionesses halted their respective battles, turning their gazes over to Korbyn's direction. As blood spilled from the king's royal veins, the lionesses echoed the skies with their own promise of retribution. Four directed their backs to their previous opponents, stalking over to assist their king.

"Korbyn! Run!" Salem shouted, sprinting towards the retreating manticore. Two others obstructed her path, preparing for their pounce and removing any aid she might have provided.

"Hide." Korbyn waved to the woman, who had already scurried towards the other side of the wagon.

The king seemed to disregard the wagon and the woman, fixating on Korbyn with hunched shoulders and bared teeth. It seemed it had a new prize in sight.

Korbyn darted to his right, away from his enemies. He didn't have to peer behind him to know that the manticores—lionesses and king alike—lunged at him, their colossal paws digging a path with a volley of roars.

He slid under a wagon, flattening his body to avoid crashing into its underside. The vehicle, comprised of victuals, caved under the weight of two hurtling lionesses. Korbyn stumbled to his feet, dashing in between several other wagons and approaching dual horses harnessed at the driver's seat.

"Gyaa!" he verbally commanded, smacking one with the flattened part of his blade.

The horses kicked and reared. From its flails, the steeds severed the leather strap harnessed to the wagon. They frantically kicked, one slamming its hooves into the chest of a lunging manticore. It toppled into a couple of other lionesses, tumbling about as several of the caravans came crashing down on them.

Korbyn weaved around several tents to lose the king's gaze, but when he looked up, he understood his endeavors would be futile. The creature had already taken flight, actively fixated on the soldier's retreating back. With no trees or branches to conceal his attempted escape, the lion pursued. Korbyn cursed under his breath and attempted to guide the king off its throne in the sky.

He arrived at the edge of the encampment, the fence surrounding the training grounds in his path. Korbyn ran with vigilance, glancing backwards when he detected the perking winds of the king's quick descent. He launched himself over the wooden railing as the winds from the creature's dive grazed his back. The force of the updraft threw him tumbling towards the middle of the arena, only occupying a risen stance after several rolls.

The king arrived, permitting the momentum to carry its body like a volleyed arrow. It drifted to a slow, predatorial saunter, circling the area. Korbyn objected to its demands, mirroring its actions to prevent its siege. Circular effigies were pressed under their trudging feet.

Even though Korbyn didn't feel warm, sweat trickled from his brow. He tried to still the irrepressible drumming of his heart and the shallow breaths that followed. The king beamed at his consternation, exhibiting its pleasure with flicks and sporadic vibrations of its spiked tail. The monster's jaw quivered in equal anticipation, saliva sliding down the sharpened edge of its fangs. If Korbyn allowed his fear to commandeer him, then surely the miracle of his restoration would marshal fruitlessness.

Predator or prey? Lion or raven?

Settling his gaze under the harsh sun proved as equally bothersome as it was painful. He remained unsure of his eyesight's condition before his awakening on the battlefield, but his perception proved superior in comparison to what should have been feasible. His white irises granted him the abilities to spectate details from abnormal distances, witness minor alterations in a person's gaze, and even detect every unsettled grain of sand from cascading winds. Even though the shaft of sunlight attenuated his vision, it couldn't prevent him from analyzing every detail the world had to offer.

Korbyn watched the muscles in the manticore's hind legs tighten, preparing for its dive. And that was when he realized, with newfound conviction, that he might stand a chance. His heartbeat slowed, and his breath calmed.

Maybe the raven, after all.

The lion's leap extended substantially compared to a normal beast. It only took one jump to traverse the arena's diameter. Korbyn dodged to the side, flailing the blade in his hand to strike as the lion passed. To his dismay, he sliced through open air.

Before the king's landing, its tail extended in hasty savagery. Narrowly, the flail careened over Korbyn's ducked form. He took several paces away, allocating more space between him and the hungry creature.

With heightened agility, the manticore propelled its body in spiraling rotations with a push of its meaty legs like a reeling top. The momentum carried the weight of its body like a tornado, and just as ruthless.

Korbyn flattened his body on the ground as the lion raced over his lowered form. He wasn't quick enough to avoid its spiked tail, and it sliced him across the shoulder. Blood spewed across morning dew, and Korbyn stumbled to a hunched stance. He overlooked the blood and discomfort, adjusting the pommel to his hip as he had practiced.

The manticore flicked its tail, spraying blood across tattered soil. Korbyn imagined if the lion could have sneered from its successful clout, it would have.

As the manticore's muscles tensed, Korbyn leapt in synchrony, evading its next attack. He recalled the lightness of Salem's maneuvers during their spar, trying to replicate her style. He kept his blade close to his body, parrying the onslaught of attacks from the flail on the creature's backside.

The king shifted its formation. With incredible power, it pounced high and then dove. Korbyn scurried backwards, modifying his posture to counterattack after its rough descent. After the manticore landed, Korbyn pushed off of the arch of his foot and swung.

However, the monster spun after its landing and slammed its flail directly into his approaching stomach.

Korbyn soared across the arena, folding underneath his own body until he tumbled into the tent across the way. The poles holding the canvas upright splintered from the collision, matching his heap and caving inwards.

His breathing erupted into a violent cough, and he stifled it with a covered hand. The other wrapped around his abdomen, pressing down to cease the pain. When the hacking ceased, Korbyn noticed splattered blood in the creases of his palm. His groan didn't alleviate his pain as he lay curled, allowing a mere moment to restore himself.

People who were hiding in the tent sprouted from the tarps like weeds, shifting to escape the confines of the fabric that had covered them like a blanket.

"Fucking shit fuck," Korbyn murmured, wiping the blood from his face and accidentally smearing more across it. His body shook in a combination of distress and unbridled pain. The twitching in his fingers prevented him from standing as he struggled to even unbend from his huddled position. The control of his breathing dissipated, along with his aforementioned confidence.

"Korbyn! Are you alright?" a voice called from his side. Nevin, the older gnome, lowered to Korbyn's level, scouring for injuries.

Across the way, the manticore snarled.

"Get back!" Korbyn urged, rising to his feet despite the agony. He adjusted the grip of his blade to hold it loosely at his hip as he thrust the gnome backwards.

As the manticore prepared another attack, Korbyn darted away from the collapsed shelter and the civilians who struggled to escape the confines of the tarp. He moved slower in comparison but still managed to evade two direct claw swipes of the monster.

Ravens are clever and curious and conniving, indeed.

The king lunged again with impatience. Korbyn lacked the proper time to fully dodge the assault and withdrew behind a wooden pell. It converted into a makeshift blockade as the manticore's giant jaws clamped down on the hessian sack. Even though the pell was firmly planted, the sheer weight of the creature ripped it from its base, causing both Korbyn and the lion to tumble.

As he rose from his roll to sit on one knee, Korbyn watched the manticore. Its jaws were imprisoned within the wooden pell. The king twisted and turned, pawing at the wood and straw and failing to pry it from its clutches, but the wooden planks had sunk so far into its mouth that it penetrated the upper roof of its gums. Blood spewed from its wound as the manticore writhed in anguish.

This was his chance.

Korbyn trudged forward, readied his blade, and soared.

But they are nothing in comparison to the lion.

The manticore heaved its body sideways with such tremendous force that the entirety of the wooden pell and the shards that penetrated its skin dislodged from its wounds. As Korbyn approached, he couldn't dodge the improvised projectile.

It slammed into him, the sharpened edges of the beams tearing his skin. He dropped his blade when his head slammed harshly against the dirt. And when the tumbling stopped, the world spun in hues of gray and black. Not seeing the creature's lunge, he couldn't prevent the manticore's jaws from imbedding in his right shoulder.

Korbyn screamed as bones cracked and gore spewed, a cry of defeat from mangled prey. Instead of killing him instantly, the manticore lifted him and shook, clamping its fangs deeper into his skin until it had penetrated through his back and torso. Another piercing cry emanated from his lips.

The king was no mere predator that killed for food; it enjoyed the hunt.

Korbyn's vision blurred and his pain numbed. He failed to recall if or how the battle had ended. As he disassociated, he could no longer perceive the sounds encompassing him, except for the slow, deep chime of a bell. His attention focused on the retreating sun, which disappeared behind a set of clouds as darkness swelled in its place. He speculated the probable time of day, negligent of his fading life. As his eyes commenced closing, not even whispering a goodbye from his departure, his existence followed suit and initiated its dissipation into obscurity. If this was death, it felt familiar.

"Let go of him!" a voice shouted.

The violent rattling of his body stopped, and his eyelids lifted towards the direction of the voice. Standing in front of the disheveled tent, completely isolated except for an expression of fear, was Nevin.

He was strong for his physique and age. He chucked a pebble at the manticore's face, almost hitting it in the eye. The creature snarled and released Korbyn from its grasp. He tumbled to the ground, not even a grunt escaping his throat as his back roughly contacted it. He kept his eyes on Nevin, despite his hazy vision.

"N-Nevin..." Korbyn whispered.

As the shifting wind conveyed the masking clouds past the sun, an intrusive light pierced his eyes. The new pain roused him, and the dusk faded. Korbyn blinked several times, witnessing the grain in his eyes depart to match the stalking manticore. It sauntered in Nevin's direction, the gnome staring up in ambivalent dread.

"No," Korbyn breathed out, twisting his body to push himself upright. His right arm didn't listen to his calls and remained unmoving beneath his struggling form. Instead, he reached out with his left, fingers fumbling with the pommel of his dropped blade.

Under the circumstances of the impossible, can the feeble bird change the course of fate?

The voice unintentionally gave him the spite he needed.

The manticore lunged forward at the gnome just as Korbyn's blade penetrated its neck.

Korbyn had surged forward with technique and expertise. The blade, held in a precise uprightness, sank into one of the manticore's major arteries. It roared and thrashed in defiance.

Korbyn didn't falter. He removed the blade like a thin needle, striking the manticore with a newfound proficiency. The manticore staggered backwards, readjusting its body and anchoring its foundation, but the soldier confronted it.

He swung with a force so great that it carved through most of the lion's grand face. The creature fell onto its side. Korbyn rushed to its fallen form and began to swing...and swing...and swing. Even when the creature failed to move, he hacked incessantly, cries of anger and adrenaline seeping from him. For a moment, he felt his conscious waver, but his strikes didn't pause. When the haze of his vision disappeared, clarity returning to his senses, and he realized the manticore's head had been severed from the rest of its body.

The king had been dethroned.

The remaining female lionesses took flight. With the king's reign demolished, they departed high into the clouds, ascending until their shadows disappeared behind the faces of the meek clouds.

Korbyn wheezed, struggling to find an even breath as he stared at the dead creature. Blood encased his body in its entirety, both his and the manticore's gore saturating the dirt beneath him.

It took minutes for the heaving to cease. When Korbyn gazed down at his tightened grip, his hands trembled with stark realization that coerced a pitiful smile to spread across his face.

He was left-handed.

The chuckle only increased the more he mused. Korbyn belly laughed, holding onto his wound that emanated vibrations of pain.

When his laughter finally ceased, he recalled Nevin's act of courage. Korbyn was unaware how he had managed to prevent a worst circumstance from occurring, but without the gnome's intervention, he surely would have perished.

"Nevin, thank you for—"

Where the whole gnome once was lay a heap of mangled intestines, covered in blood and ripped skin. The elder male had been easily mauled by the jaw much larger than him. His eyes were wide, dried eyes gazing into the sky where his soul had just departed.

The blade in Korbyn's hand teetered to the ground with a clank. He fell to his knees, despair covering his body like a sheet of darkness.

You are not meant to save, the voice declared.

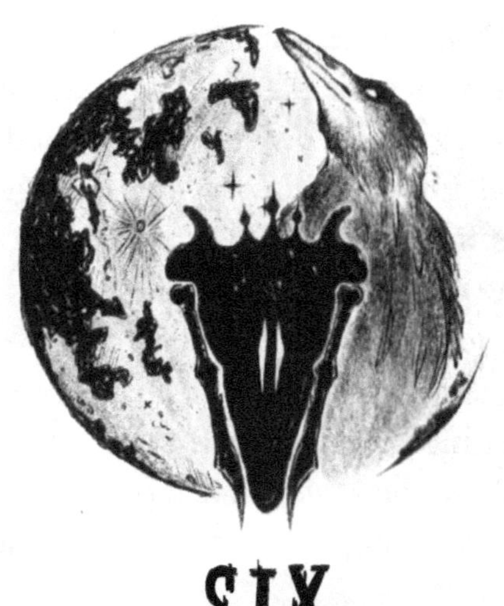

SIX.

By the time Kendra Dawn and its members departed from Fort Silvercrest, two days had passed. Korbyn accompanied the trek of caravans moving north through the Kingdom of Esperin, all members of its faction swallowed in desolate silence. The attack of the manticores had left him meandering amongst his own thoughts, with the wheels of the wagons against rocks and terrain existing as the lone sound that filled the early afternoon sky.

Salem commanded Korbyn to join the other injured in the back of one of the wagons until he fully healed. To his astonishment, his wounds mended much faster than what was deemed as normal, leaving only a soreness where the lacerations once lingered. When he analyzed the lion's bite, there were no scars or broken bones left to greet him, only the permanent marks of his awakening. Ever since, he managed to resume a stride at the caravan's side as to not feel so utterly hopeless and to ignore the abnormality of his rapid healing.

As Korbyn inspected the map of Terrisae in his palms, his eyes traced their route until he discovered their destination. Salem mentioned that it would take them almost a week to reach the city of Umberfall. Their extended travel would have been shortened if not for their cargo and the quantity of their numbers. He imagined their melancholy journey would do nothing to aid the sourness left from the departed morning.

He detected the transition of topography the farther north they navigated. Instead of small hills and colors of dark pine surrounded in hues of ash at the border, the Kingdom of Esperin was touched by autumn. Cyan and specks of rainbow-colored flowers spread across enormous meadows and severed the view of the horizon. Maple trees stood across the paved roads, caressed by a chill breeze with leaves of fallen ginger and gold. Korbyn thought they might have resembled traces of starlight under the beating sun.

He didn't remember his life before the awakening, but he assumed it would be difficult to overlook something so beautiful. Layers of leaves piled like small mounds underneath the maple trees, producing thick sheets of amber and honey like alternating patterns on a thick quilt. The foliage embraced the earth beneath to relieve the cold breeze with a warm touch.

Korbyn remained silent during their voyage. They accumulated fourteen bodies in the skirmish. In comparison to casualties in war, fourteen didn't seem like a substantial number, but these were bishops, craftsmen, cooks, farmers, and blacksmiths. They were volunteers who propounded their services, despite the inevitable risks, and fourteen succumbed to a dire fate.

All are known to the Shepherd, the voice interjected, which Korbyn blatantly ignored.

Then there was Nevin. Korbyn's chest tightened, the strain of his heart causing him to grip his shirt in apprehension. He felt responsible for Nevin's untimely demise, for if not for his ill choice of retreating to the training grounds, the gnome wouldn't have interjected in the quarry on his behalf. If Korbyn ventured further than the confines of the camp, then maybe it would have given the mercenaries enough time to stop the lionesses, leaving only the king to remain. If Korbyn had sacrificed his own wasteful life, then maybe he could have saved him.

You are not meant to save, the voice reminded him.

He grinded his teeth at the irksome voice, failing to fully ignore its incessant churns. Despite its whispers, it bellowed louder than even his own thoughts. Even now, he could clearly hear the presence, like an echo reverberating against a cavern wall—repeating over and over, but, instead of dimming into the darkness, it intensified.

You are not meant to save, it repeated, escalating in volume with each tangible howl.

Korbyn recalled his eyes fluttering to witness a circle of silhouettes hovering above him after the manticore attack. Bishops with blackened stone summoned holy magic as though it was an altruistic companion. Archaic energy swirled around their palms as the ore deteriorated into dust, and they tried to patch Korbyn's injuries from the inside out.

However, the strange ore was not the reason for his quickened healing. Instead, his shoulder bones snapped and mended of their own volition, but he couldn't feel its gruesome mending. The bishops stared at him like he was a monster, each stepping away from him with shaking hands and quivering breaths.

You are not meant to save.

Because of Korbyn, Nevin died. He was an amiable person, and those with benevolent and charitable hearts merited life. Unlike Korbyn, who couldn't recall a single thing about his past or decipher his moral behavior. Had he been a soldier eager to kill? A cutthroat? A pariah?

A monster?

His existence as an empty shell haunted him, bearing no purpose, goodness, or cause. A soldier's putative role was to protect, yet his merit diminished with his faded memories and evident inabilities. His accidental existence left him a husk of a person whose mind was corrupt and evil and *missing*.

You are not meant to save!

His hand tingled, stretching behind his neck to grasp—

"You doing okay?" someone asked, synchronously joining Korbyn's brisk walk.

The soldier jolted in surprise, equally from the presence at his side and his abnormal action for reaching for something that didn't exist.

A crescent moon of black and bone and gold under the veil of shadows and ice and fire.

"Yeah," Korbyn replied simply, adjusting the strap of his bag to give his reaching hand purpose before glancing at the origin of the voice.

He realized the person walking at his side was someone he had not met before. The male was short, not even reaching Korbyn's shoulder, and he stared up with bright, silver eyes that were illuminated under the sun. His skin, dark and flawless, gleamed in a beautiful shade of hickory.

"Heard you took quite a beating, but you killed the pride of the manticores. That's crazy. They're huge!" the male exclaimed, motioning his hands in an arch above his head, as if attempting to display how tall a manticore was. With his shortened stature, he couldn't reach nearly as tall as the height he'd been referencing.

"And you are?" Korbyn inquired.

"Oakley!" he responded with a mischievous grin. "You've probably already heard of me. I happen to be the best fighter in all of Kendra Dawn."

By the caravan ahead of them, Haven barked out a laugh quite theatrically. Oakley glared at the half-orc, who peered out into the surrounding wilderness.

"The best, huh? That's rather impressive," Korbyn teased, unable to prevent a smile from following Haven's mocking guffaw. "You must be quite the warrior."

"Yeah, I guess you can say that," Oakley agreed, displaying a confident smile across his face. "What about you, huh? You must be strong too, defeating the king of the manticore all by yourself even though you don't have your memories. I mean, you already know that, but I meant, how crazy would it be if you did have them, you know? Cause you slayed the leader of the manticore pride without them, so could you imagine if you did? Not that there's anything wrong with that—"

"Yeah, I get it," Korbyn interrupted, sending his fingers through his hair to suppress a chuckle.

"I can't imagine being your height. Well, I've imagined it quite a bit, but I really wish I was your height, or Haven's. I tell him that all the time."

"How tall are you?" Korbyn probed, analyzing Oakley's smaller frame.

"Five foot and a quarter. I'm part gnomish, I think. Or just unlucky in the height department. Who knows," Oakley replied with a shrug, stuffing his hands in his pockets before gazing up at the sun. Korbyn didn't question the precision of his response.

Korbyn analyzed the shorter male's attire. From head to toe, Oakley was covered in black garments with dark brown accents. A hood covered most of his charcoal hair, concealing his features from ongoing stares. He didn't wear much armor, only bits and pieces of leather that covered his forearms, shins, and a single pauldron across his right shoulder. Leather straps connected above his chest, where a small, metal circlet connected them. He also carried a bow, quiver, a pack of handcrafted arrows, multiple knives, a short sword, and several pouches containing various toxins and poisons. Even if he wasn't the best fighter in Kendra

Dawn, he was certainly armed as if he was.

After the manticore attack, Salem drove Korbyn to retrieve armor of his own. He preferred simplicity, choosing a rusted pauldron that now convened at his left shoulder. Three layered pieces beneath the armor connected to an iron clasp just above his sternum. He wore a pair of bracers around his forearms, covering the strange tattoo that hid beneath it. It throbbed in response, and Korbyn slid his fingers over its placement to silence its calls.

"I'm glad you decided to stick with us. It'll be nice to have another fighter around. Guess you could say you're a soldier to your very *manticore*!" Oakley jested quite smugly.

Korbyn responded with a flat expression, changing the subject with his growing questions. "Can you tell me more about the war? About both kingdoms? Maybe it'll help me remember." He wasn't eager for the pain that followed deep assessments of his mind, but the fog that deterred him continued to recess his thinking, to his increased annoyance.

"Oh, yeah! Of course. Well, as you know, when we found you, you were wearing the armor of the Avernos Empire, so that would only make sense," Oakley explained. "The other side, the Kingdom of Esperin, recently found an entire mine filled with decidite within their borders."

"Is that what the bishops were using to conjure magic?" Korbyn asked. "If I'm being honest, I don't remember anything about magic existing at all."

"Yep, that's right. And that's because it didn't exist, not until half a year ago," Oakley replied, although his contemplative expression portrayed that he still didn't quite understand the details of it. "Not everyone seems to have an affinity for it though. I touch those things, and nothing seems to happen. But everyone that can use it seems to be able to channel some type of holy magic, but it's different for everyone." Oakley shifted his attention to the sky. "Some people believe it's a gift from Elohim, as if He wanted to give us a way to combat the monsters, but the kingdoms started turning on each other, I guess."

"Is decidite really that fragile?" Korbyn wondered, recalling when the ore turned to powder after the bishops channeled it.

"That's the strange part. Esperin planned to make armor and weapons from them, but I've heard rumors they can't even forge it." Oakley glanced around, as if ensuring no one was paying attention. "They say that not even the hottest lava of Mount Firebrim can melt the ore, yet it dissolves after someone channels it to create magic! Weird, huh?"

"And what about Salem?" Korbyn interrupted, eyes trailing over her retreating back. "It didn't look like she had any of that decidite stuff."

Oakley grinned. "She doesn't," he replied, following Korbyn's gaze over to her. "They call her the Paladin of Dawn, a warrior who can split the Heavens. People say Elohim granted her powers Himself. Both kingdoms have sent her numerous proposals about joining their armies, but she's denied them each time. Lucky us."

A war of greed and lies and misery.

"I see," Korbyn replied, his gaze not faltering from the pristine armor. The rays of light from above seemed to shimmer in jealousy, but Salem didn't appear to notice. It reminded him of the blackened ore, and how in comparison, decidite failed to reflect any sort of luster at all.

"How much of the ore did they find?" Korbyn prompted.

"Not sure, enough to employ more miners down at the excavation site, I guess. We're pretty limited on our own resources, but we were lucky enough to get our hands on a small load, being neutral assisters to the war." Oakley pursed his lips in contemplation. "I've heard rumors that after a tsunami in the deadlands to the west, people found an excavation site of more decidite. It's like there's more ore deep enough in the ground—"

"Stop spewing nonsense, Oakley," the blond elf interjected, approaching the duo before he presumed a walk next to Oakley. The elf lifted his nose upright, accompanied by an equally grumbling glower. "There's no reason to overwhelm his empty head."

Korbyn frowned in quiet rebuttal, pondering at whether the elf referred to his memory loss or if it was an alternative implication.

"Aw, come on Veeris," Oakley remarked with a shrug. "There's nothing wrong with gossip."

"There is when it starts to fill someone's head with lies. The world is full of uncertainty and misconstrued meanings that eventually turn into deceptions. Just focus on what we can actually achieve," Veeris retorted before quickening his pace to pass them, leaving Korbyn befuddled.

"Don't mind Veeris," Oakley said, bumping his shoulder into him with what he assumed to be a friendly gesture, though Korbyn slightly stumbled due to his lingering soreness. "He's just grumpy these days."

The journey lapsed in another silence, each of the mercenaries resuming their positions and shifting their efforts to analyze the forest on each side of the continual path.

Veeris was unfortunately right. It was futile to fuss over immutable events, but Korbyn couldn't stop mentally proposing possible conceptions of Esperin's intentions. The last question that he had that irked him, from his intemperate quandary, was how it existed and where it originated from.

Somehow, he felt the voice's lip curl.

That night, when Korbyn tried to sleep, nightmarish visions once again prevented his rest. He witnessed scenarios of a darkened red sky in an unknown world hovering over a gothic cathedral made of blackened stone.

SEVEN.

Salem's armor emitted a melancholic reverberation as she marched down the northern path to Umberfall, leaving herself otherwise in a trench of silence.

They spent hours cleaning the disarray after the manticore attack, hoping to rid the camp of their bloodstains. The manticores left their prey in unrecognizable heaps that required supplementary efforts to decipher each identity the creatures left behind. The bishops required two ongoing days of endless stitching to piece the bodies back together, only proving feasible after tedious and dreadful toiling. Embalming their bodies and enacting Elohim's rite of passage by burial and prayer for their departed souls didn't provide any form of catharsis.

Then there was Korbyn, a man who not only cavorted on the edge of life and death not once, but twice. He intervened between the pride of manticores and a defenseless woman, managing to detract its thrall. Salem relucted to inform him that despite his exploits, the woman didn't survive the encounter. After her escape, a separate lioness prohibited her retreat. Her horrific demise was one that Salem didn't wish to reconceive.

The paladin tampered with her gloves, unable to reach beneath the quick of her fingers. She swore she felt mire and gore underneath them, a constant irritation and dire reminder.

"It's not your fault," a husky voice to her left said.

Salem turned to the wagon that she strode next to, seeing Micah, the Arbiter and leader of Kendra Dawn, lounging in the driver's seat. The Arbiter's permanently injured leg rested comfortably on the floorboard while she reclined. Her cane sat next to her person, close enough to grab if required. Her short, gray hair was shaved almost cleanly to the top of her ears with a few strands covering her temple. Her skin was kissed by the sun, with wrinkles hanging across her face that asserted knowledge and experience. An eyepatch resided over her left eye, a wound from a battle long before Salem reached Terrisae. Even though Micah was descending the hill of a warrior's peak, she might still put trained soldiers to shame.

"Experiences are meant to be learned from. If you allow your past mistakes to control you, you'll never live long enough to discover more," Micah said, reaching underneath her robe, patting down the fabric until she found the makeshift pocket underneath. She extracted a pipe made of clay and a small box of cannabis. She crumbled pieces into the chamber and pulled out a spill before surveying the area. "No fucking lanterns anywhere."

"I feel like it is my fault," Salem replied honestly, the sword and shield on her back feeling weightier than it had before. "If I was stronger, I could have saved them."

"Do you know how many manticores there were?" Micah questioned after she returned the cannabis to its confinement.

Salem recalled the memory but failed to recount the beasts. "I...no," she admitted.

"Seventeen," Micah stated, leaning back against the wagon's

wall. "There were seventeen manticores, including the king. We lost fourteen. Yes, while fourteen is a lot of people to lose, don't forget how much worse it could have been. In the grand scheme of things, we could have lost them all."

A fog of silence hung over them. The repetitive wheels against the rocks and dirt prevented the muteness from becoming too overbearing. Only after a few seconds did Micah shatter it with her gravelly voice.

"The fact is, no one's perfect, Salem. We can think all day about what we did wrong, but it's meaningless if you don't utilize your experience to improve yourself and your knowledge." Micah finally turned to her, and Salem could see the grief the older woman sought to bury behind her aged eyes. "It's only when you fail to improve on those circumstances should you surround yourself with grief."

"You're right." Salem sighed. "I always forget how wise you are from your foul attitude," she jested, the levity patching the tension before Micah burst out in a hardy laugh.

"Sometimes a foul attitude derives from wisdom."

"We close to farming towns," Andrid stated, appearing on the other side of the wagon. Their long hair whipped behind them in the breeze, a smile extending from one ear to the other. A bright red paste had tainted their lips and teeth, as though they had been scavenging during their dutiful reconnaissance.

"Good job, Andrid," the Arbiter replied, readjusting her stature to project more poise. "Get ready for the entourage."

In the distance, smaller towns and farms rose beyond the plains. Their route led straight through the heart of Esperin with neighboring farms residing on the outskirts of Umberfall, its prestige capital. Esperin was vastly known for its natural resources, inhabited mines, farms, livestock and vineyards that surrounded the main capital all the way to its borders. Even now, they were encircled with fields and crops as far as Salem could perceive in either direction.

As soon as they approached Graycott Village, a farming town south of Umberfall, families and people greeted them upon the recognition of Kendra Dawn's flag in a gathered stir. Despite their gratefulness for their service, she was certain they weren't too eager to see the remains of what they carried.

After another day of travel, they arrived at Umberfall and passed through the gates with ease. As an established neutral party of Terrisae, they had acquired unlimited access to any city within Esperin's and Avernos' borders.

Near the main gate in Umberfall's massive city stood a grand church. As the oldest city in Terrisae, Umberfall erected the first cathedral ever to be created: the Church of Elohim. Despite its age, it was beautiful in architectural design, with many pinnacles and buttresses surrounding its outer ring, with a nave in the center at its highest point. It contained tall, rounded arches on all sides, establishing a symmetrical beauty with its multiple entrances. It was built upon brick and somehow aged finely despite the centuries of its existence and its seeming lack of solid foundation compared to one made from stone.

Salem remained quiet for a moment, awaiting Elohim to greet her arrival, but she heard nothing.

As Kendra Dawn approached the church, the volunteers began unloading the wagons. They carefully retrieved the preserved bodies and transported them to designated locations within the property of the ecclesiastical. Before Salem could offer aid, the Arbiter impeded.

"Not you. Gather the rest of the mercenaries. Our presence has been requested by the king."

Before Salem could interject, Micah strode off with cane in hand, advising organizational methods to the volunteers as she passed. Salem's shoulders slouched in tandem with a breath of displeasure. If there was one thing she hated, it was meeting with snooty royals and officials. It looked like her avoidance of the king's constant petitions only took her so far.

"The king wishes to see us," Salem said as she approached her party. They gathered around her, followed by similar sighs of exasperation. Korbyn, who stood behind them, peered between the volunteers' restless activity and the mercenaries that faced the castle.

Salem reached out, tugging softly on his forearm to gain his attention. There was something she felt under her touch, despite the fabric between their skin. It was a spark, an abrupt sensation that felt both like pain and inclination. It was boiling, yet chilled, the sensation mingling together to form something new. She had experienced this phenomenon before, during their training session just before the manticore attack. At first, she ignored the sensation, assuming it had just been the adrenaline from sparring. But now, seeing Korbyn's countenance, she knew he detected it too. For a moment, Salem swore she felt his arm shake under her touch.

"You won't be allowed into the meeting, but you can come inside and wait for us. I don't want you feeling inclined to help the volunteers," Salem stated, trying to bypass the awkwardness of the strange encounter.

Korbyn's gaze shifted from his arm up to her eyes.

"If you're sure," he responded, pulling his arm away and squinting under the vivid sun with a grimace.

Salem remained skeptical of if his expression was due to her touch or the sun overhead. Korbyn shaded his eyes with his hand like an umbrella, as if it would help against Umberfall's wonted brightness. As they traveled through the city market, Salem noticed he lowered his gaze to onlookers. She frowned, feeling sympathetic to his obvious discomfort.

When they departed the commoner's district, the walls of Umberfall's grand castle leaned overhead. A canal circled the castle like a moat, an outlet forming at its base. Connecting the marketplace and the main entrance to the castle stretched a bridge. They ambled halfway across its foundation to its highest point, and Salem was able to witness the winsome maple trees. They bordered the castle's outer walls, decorating its magnificence with pops of oranges and reds. From this point, Salem was also able to appreciate the venerable and resplendent Tree of Tranquility.

Behind the fortress, located within the confines of the citadel's estate, dwelled the gargantuan tree that stood higher than her eyes could perceive. Its trunk swirled in circular motions from the base of its roots all the way up towards its pinnacle, as though a touch of magic caressed its curvature. Even where she was from, Salem had heard of this brilliant aberration.

The Tree of Tranquility, the oldest standing natural phenomena in Terrisae. People of Esperin said it was a blessing by Elohim, a symbolism of His greatness and His declaration of His chosen city. Alternatively, unbelievers and the nonreligious country of Avernos surmised it once contained a spirit that eventually guided the rebellion initiating Esperin's civil war.

Eventually, the rebellion's eccentric schemes lead to a coup d'état. Although the revolution was quelled, the radicals retreated past Exonia Creek and established the Avernos Empire. The theocracy of Esperin and the stratocracy of Avernos, paradoxical in all beliefs, had grown incredibly antagonistic ever since. Now, Terrisae was locked in another war, all because of decidite.

The mercenaries advanced to the main gate. For no reason other than feigned benevolence, the active guards shifted from slack casualness to readied poise at their approach. However, one soldier in particular, which Salem could determine held a difference in rank, wore a full set of steel armor from head to toe. The features of his iron plating were sharp in comparison to Esperin's normal silver curvature. The pauldrons, boots, and gloves stacked on top of each other to form durable layers, elongating his muscular shoulders. The designs of his darker armor reminded her of a garden, with golden branch-like swirls encircling intricate designs around it.

On his back, he carried a large war hammer, covered in scratches from extended use. A brown hood and cape draped around his neck, the edges of its fabric torn and shredded at the back of his calves. His helmet, abnormal and imposing, was comprised of two large horns that protruded from either side of his head. He resembled a fearless bull.

"Open the gate," the captain demanded, his voice gravelly and rough like sharpened stones on an unpaved road. As if the secure walls could hear him, the heavy metal rose into its jambs, the iron portcullis creaking as it retreated into the aloft gateway. The captain of the guard turned and sauntered through the open gates, not waiting to formally escort them.

They trailed the captain through an elongated vestibule with rows of layered columns of pristine marble that imitated coiling branches. Each pillar rose to its extended ceiling, crafted in pearl and bronze with murals painted on the roof. Its tranquil depiction of extended branches reaching the Heavens was profound, and Salem couldn't avert her astonishment.

The hallway led into a grand hall with arched windows on the western partition, allowing those on the inside to peer out over the castle fortifications and the locality of the descending sun. At each side of the tall windows was emptied armor, holding blades earthward in a professional salute. On the eastern wall, various paintings illustrated the ages of Esperin's kings, including its current liege, King Alecain.

A large pair of double doors loomed at the end of the hallway, intricately decorated in umber and indentations of winding branchlets. They weaved from the bottom of a bronze tree trunk and feathered off into various directions of saturated champagne, glinting in the sun's rays that cascaded through the glass windows.

"Wait here," Salem said to Korbyn, who also displayed infatuation with the marble décor. He opened his mouth, an instinctual motion to respond, but replaced the gesture with a nod.

"I really wish I smoked first," the Arbiter mumbled, fiddling with the unused pipe in her pocket. "And do me a favor, Salem, make sure to keep your mouth shut. Don't need us beheaded before the war's over."

Veeris strode beside her, eyeing Salem in subtle agreement.

The doors of the throne room swung open with a reverberating creak. The captain didn't seem to care for faux congeniality as he supervised them with silence. He walked with an assertive gait down the ornate rug, leaving them to their befuddled analysis of the room's immaculate architecture.

The details of this chamber were just as exquisite as the rest of the castle. The ceiling of this royal chamber soared higher than the grand hall, with tall stone arches decorated in lines of painted gold turning brown with age. Tapered arches connected the beams to another pair of rounded columns that lined the walkway. The western wall posed windows, similar in design, but augmented to complement the throne's higher plafond. Multiple chandeliers rose above the leading carpet that extended through the entirety of the corridor. The flames flickered to aid the sunlight in illuminating the room, though presently worthless due to the location of the sloping sun.

The other side of the partition that held stained glass portrayed bishops in a queue of prayer, the line of people leading up to a pompous throne. Even though the building was ancient, the cathedra resembled something even older. Instead of stone, a tall tree growing from underneath the marble floor extended to the ceiling to form a makeshift contraption. The tree's bark caved inward to form an ingress at its base, with the inside constructed with skilled carpentry. The husk of its wooden locus molded into an elaborate throne, with the tree's branches reigning above it like a terrace. The roots and branchlets that indented the back wall resembled flickering starlight and hues of brownish gold.

"Kendra Dawn," King Alecain greeted, corpulent in size and haughty in demeanor. If he was ever athletic in his younger years, Salem couldn't tell. His round, wrinkled features betrayed the authenticity of his supposed age of forty-eight, though he looked twenty years dated. The seat underneath him, warped through time and plausible moisture, didn't buckle under his overwhelming stoutness.

Salem hadn't heard about Alecain's importance in comparison to his ancestors until recently. His loyal subjects referred to him as the Herald of Light, a recent title under abnormal circumstances. She had seen reports that he heard Elohim's voice, commanding him to keep the decidite for the continuance of Esperin's reign. As one who hadn't experienced Elohim's presence since she arrived in Terrisae, she failed to believe it credible.

Bags and wrinkles lifted with a perverse smile when the king's eyes settled upon Salem. "Thank you for gracing me with your presence."

Members of the king's royal court, clothed in tunics of browns and gold, stood at the bottom of the stairs. They surveyed the group with judgmental eyes and raised chins, otherwise remaining imperviously stoic.

"The pleasure is ours, King Alecain," the Arbiter replied with mirrored stoicism. "What can we do for you, Your Majesty?"

"I wanted to thank you for bringing the remnants of our fallen back home," he stated, no sense of gratitude or sincerity in his voice. "And ask that you reconsider your neutrality."

He adjusted his position in the chair, creaks of the wood echoing his motions. Though he spoke to Micah, his eyes remained on Salem. The paladin chewed on her lip to alleviate her discomfort and increasing irritation.

"That's very kind of you, Your Majesty." Micah seemed unaffected by Alecain's declaration, as though anticipating his request. "However, the war has just begun. I understand you lost Fort Silvercrest, but one battle does not win the war, and even then, you outnumber them three to one. Why would you need our assistance?"

"This war may get brutal, and in times of need, our soldiers could use leaders with more experience such as yourself, Arbiter," King Alecain replied, finally moving his attention to Micah.

"With all due respect, King Alecain," Micah said, adjusting her posture to bow with the use of her cane. Despite her gesture, Salem was positive no respect lingered there. "I'm afraid I'm nothing but a retired merc. I wouldn't provide much use in my current condition." The Arbiter referred to her walking aid. "And we are only a handful of mercenaries. Especially with your unique resources, you should be able to win the war quite easily." She raised her head, making direct contact with the eyes of the stubborn king. "Unless there is something we should know?"

There was an uncomfortable silence, the king's jaw grinding against his teeth. Salem scanned him, searching for answers she couldn't find. She yearned to reach for her locket, to use her magic to discover any lies within his practiced speech, but she felt a heavy stare from the armored knight and relaxed her arm at her side instead.

"What other reason do I need than having famous warriors at my side? There is none, other than the fact that Kendra Dusk, your band of mercenaries before they died, were legends. No one else in history has ever slayed a dragon, and now they are extinct. Having the Arbiter lead a faction of my soldiers would cause the Avernos Empire to rethink their assault on my kingdom." His rebuttal was sound and practiced, and he once again turned to Salem. "And Elohim's proclamation of sworn custody of all decidite is His holy mission, spoken true with His own voice."

Then the crazed rumors were true—King Alecain *did* claim to hear the voice of Elohim.

Alecain's eyes roamed Salem's body in its entirety, despite being heavily guarded by armor. A disgusting grin spread across his face, and waves of chills trailed her spine. "And to have Elohim's chosen paladin, the most beautiful woman of light in all Terrisae, fight at our side would surely cause the men's bollocks and knees to quiver." The king laughed. "And to reconsider their secular and unpragmatic sins."

"As flattered as we are to hear that from the renowned Herald of Light, we are sworn by obligation to bring the dead to rest. Our duty is with the people," Micah interjected.

As if not expecting that response, the king huffed loudly, somehow deepening his wrinkled frown. "Yet you fail to notice that bringing back bodies of the dead for the rite of Elohim, of which Avernos does not even partake," he retorted with a lifted chin, "that you inadvertently serve both councils."

"With all due respect, Your Majesty, we have sworn neutrality and will abide by it," Micah stated.

"And what of this neutrality? It is nothing but a quiet defiance against those born to lead. It will only result in more suffering, for you choose to not lend service to end the war." The king's voice was stern and demanding yet somehow struggling to remain cool-headed.

"We wish to keep peace and prosperity when war threatens the common people. That is not something we can do on the front lines," Micah responded, remaining composed under his leering eyes. "Neutrality is the best way for us to serve the people directly, Your Majesty."

King Alecain sneered. "Good people claim neutrality in the name of peace, but intelligent ones know that impartiality is equivalent to turning your gaze away from bloodshed," he spat, his grip on the chair tightening.

"Selfish."

The entirety of the court turned to Salem.

Micah, the mercenaries, and the council members froze under the king's silent rage. Salem heeded none with a straightened composure. Her eyebrows creased her forehead, glaring back at the king with a penetrating gaze that could cut steel.

King Alecain lifted his nose, returning her expression. "What was that?"

"I called you selfish," Salem spat, stepping forward to stand next to Micah, whose eyes had widened in fear. "You're speaking as though your actions are justified and are for the better for your people, yet you're either lying or just idiotic enough to not realize that your actions will not only end this war in bloodshed but will inevitably lead to more."

Salem took another step, one full of resentment and growing rage.

The captain of the guard, with the fierceness of a bull, mirrored her movements. He appeared ready to draw his weapon from its position on his back, but Salem failed to concede to his imposing disposition. Instead, she welcomed the knight's approach, not slacking in her response.

"You chose to deny the other kingdoms a valuable resource, knowing it would start a war." This time, Salem smirked, a wicked grin that prompted tension in the king's shoulders. "When the other kingdoms join Avernos and rebel against your avarice, what will you do then?"

The king glared, emphasizing the creases in his wrinkled face. "Elohim's call will guide us to righteousness, and I thought a follower such as yourself would have aptly agreed," he gritted out, equal anger and lust clouded in his eyes.

"Do you even hear Elohim's voice?" Salem asked.

Tautness plagued the room, and she could sense the stilled

shoulders of her allies behind her, though she cared not for her blatancy.

"Your Majesty, she didn't mean—" Micah stammered, but she was interrupted by a hardy laugh, one that mimicked sounds of belittlement more than actual amusement.

When the taunting passed, the king stilled and lounged further in his chair. Liars normally grew defensive when faced with blunt scrutiny, attempting to deny the harsh severity of a person's words, but King Alecain instead bore a wicked grin.

"I hear His voice," Alecain growled, the edges of his lips curling. "And He hears mine."

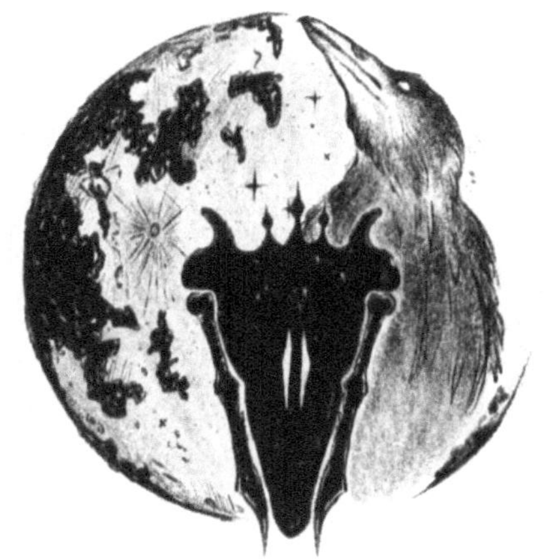

EIGHT.

Undeterred by distance or obstruction, Korbyn's perception proved surmountable, for he could accurately perceive the conversation from his seat in the grand hall. The soldiers standing guard ignored his presence as he focused his gaze on the wall. Kendra Dawn stood aligned in front of the throne, which he surmised must have been almost ten paces away, yet he probed with instinctual clarity.

Progression and transformation—an endless pursuit, the voice whispered.

King Alecain, the Herald of Light, as they called him, was a crude individual. Korbyn tried to ignore the suggestive pursuits of the king towards Salem, who seemed to ignore his endeavors.

Filthy fuck, Korbyn thought, tightening his hands into fists. Just like the leader of the manticores, kings assumed they could have anything they wanted.

The more he concentrated on their conversation, the more he could understand it. The wall resembled more of a translucent suggestion than formidable brick, and he assumed he would ponder his strange abilities another time when he wasn't trying to eavesdrop.

With his concerted effort, his eyes complemented the talents of his ears. On the other side of the wall, colorless energies sprouted like fires. Despite their brightness, it didn't incapacitate his eyes. Each white flame swayed as if they heard a song no one else could hear yet caged within limited boundaries. They were surrounded by silhouettes of the people standing on the other side, and he was unsure of what exactly he was witnessing.

There were two different flames that stood out among the rest. One was black as coal, originating from the shadow standing by the king. Korbyn recognized this figure as the captain of the guard that guided them into the chambers of the throne room. The orb acted differently than the rest. Instead of a moving flame, it remained stagnant, a controlled blaze waiting patiently like a predator readying to strike.

Concealed under the bridge of their upturned noses.

Ignoring the voice, Korbyn turned towards the most stunning hue of brilliance he had ever seen. Instead of white or black, it was a distinct, golden spark. It was radiant, its flames taller and more profound than the rest, dancing to the beat of its own drum and ignoring the confines of the body's limitations. The flame danced vivaciously with no care of the space around it, beautiful and captivating. After his elongated analyzation, Korbyn finally realized that the flame originated from Salem.

When the meeting was over, Korbyn pretended to be fixated on something outside, changing the direction of his body to fully meet the window. When the double doors opened, the mercenaries exited the throne room. Oakley appeared anxious, with sweat dripping from his brow. Andrid, with the fox at their side, endeavored to withhold a fit of giggles. Haven ushered them forward, moving them out of the king's watchful eyes as they exited.

Salem stomped out of the chambers, only to be swept away by the Arbiter and Veeris towards the corner of the room.

"How could you be so reckless?!" Veeris exclaimed just as animatedly while the older woman with the cane rubbed her temples. A lecture followed his continuous ramblings, though mostly incomprehensible. Salem remained quiet, standing before them with folded arms and furrowed brows.

As Korbyn meandered to the rest of the group, he was confronted by a tall figure. The captain of the guard loomed before him with a forward tilt of his bull-like helmet. If not for the film on the inside of the visor's slits, Korbyn would have been able to see his eyes from their proximity. Dual pairs of eyes transfixed, leading to a silent skirmish unbeknownst to the surrounding bodies.

When love withered, so too did the garden.

Pits of interminable darkness greeted Korbyn. Here, he saw a rising crown and cathedrals of obsidian amongst spreading ice underneath a red moon. Weapons clashed under a crimson sky of a land of darkened shadows under the guise of an eclipse. People shrieked in torment and agony as their howls ripped through the sky, echoing into the world tarnished in scarlet. Voices screamed out for help in the depths of a forest of mist. Then, Korbyn saw a pair black blades with hilts made of bone, dripping in blood so dark and heavy that it stained the hands of the warrior holding them. He couldn't see their face, but they were veiled by a long, red cape.

"Intriguing," the captain murmured as the visions subsided.

Right or wrong, left or right, good or evil? In a war of black and white, he chose morally gray, the voice whispered.

Korbyn was left in gawking bewilderment from the sequential visions. The soldier walked past, leaving him in lingering confusion.

"Ya alright, lad?" a voice inquired.

Korbyn glanced to his left, and then down, seeing a figure that stood about half as tall as a normal man.

"Yeah," Korbyn responded to the dwarf, though he was unsure if it was true.

"Name's Gilben. Haven't had the pleasure o' meetin' ya yet," the dwarf said. He was stout, that much was certain, with coarse hair to match. He had thick brown locks that weaved into an intricate braid, strapped together at the bottom of his facial hair by a bracelet. Several silver charms shaped like music notes dangled from the leather. On his back, he carried a candid lute, which appeared slightly splintered from use and adoration.

"Oh, uh, no, we haven't. I'm Korbyn," he introduced.

The strands of Gilben's mustache rose with his changing facial expression into what Korbyn assumed to be a smile, though it was covered by foliage that some would have called a beard.

"I'm assuming you're a mercenary too?" Korbyn asked. The dwarf nodded, his contagious grin still lingering.

"Aye! Though I'd have ta say me talents are more fer music," Gilben explained, gesturing to the instrument on his back with a point of his thumb. "I'll have ta play ya a tune sometime!"

"Yeah, thanks, I'd like that," Korbyn replied, peeking towards the captain's retreating form. He felt guilty for being distracted, but something irked him from the man's presence, and he couldn't help but linger, transfixed on the unknown.

"And yer sure yer alright, lad? Ya looked a wee bit spooked," Gilben said with concern.

Korbyn continued his deep concentration on the captain, who neglected to wait to accompany the mercenaries. He strode through the grand hall in solitude, disregarding his own soldiers stationed on the opposite side. To the west, the sun sank over the castle fortifications, causing the shadows of the partition to elongate across the majority of the chamber. As the captain walked past the arched windows and into the enveloping darkness, Korbyn swore his silhouette resembled more monster than man.

"Yeah," Korbyn whispered, attempting to avoid its familiarity.

"Soldier not real bull. It okay," Andrid stated as they approached, offering a poor attempt at comfort.

"That's not—" Korbyn chose to not elaborate, returning their warm grin with a slouched posture. "Thanks, Andrid."

They beamed in accomplishment.

"Unbelievable," Veeris sneered, stomping past the group. The mercenaries turned, watching his departure down the hall. Salem and the older woman strode forward, joining the rest of the group in their perplexity as they watched the elf's retreating back.

"Just be more careful next time, alright?" the older woman with the cane urged, patting Salem on her armored shoulder. "For the safety of others, sometimes it's better to listen and observe."

Korbyn witnessed Salem's slack shoulders, a sigh following. "You're right. I'm sorry. I shouldn't have said anything."

"And will he be alright?" the woman pressed, motioning to Veeris' retreating form.

"Oh, yes. He'll be fine," Salem responded with a shrug. "He just gets a little heated sometimes."

The woman's eyebrow rose. "Right. If only he could learn from your characteristically even temperament." Salem smiled, as if agreeing to her statement, though Korbyn was positive she remained ignorant of the woman's sarcastic insinuation.

"Gilby, play more music tonight?" Andrid probed with a widened grin as they began walking down the grand hall.

Gilben nodded, offering them a thumbs up and following them at their side. "Aye, just for you, maybe I'll play somethin' new."

"Hell yeah! And I'm itching to play some cards," Oakley chimed in. "What do you say, buddy? Want some redemption from last time?" the shorter male teased, elbowing Haven's side.

The half-orc huffed. "You always win," Haven grumbled.

"You're cheating or something."

"Me? Cheat? What, like counting cards? As if I could count that high—I've just been getting lucky!" Oakley replied dramatically, ushering his friend forward with a pat on his lower back. The height difference was amusing. Even if Haven was twice his size, Oakley seemed to have the half-orc wrapped around his smaller finger. "Come on, you'll win this time. I'm sure of it!"

As Korbyn followed the retreating group and their ongoing conversations, the older woman approached his side with a limp of her leg and a courteous nod.

"And you must be Korbyn," she stated, a smirk coiling up her features. "Apologies for the wait and for not introducing myself sooner. I wanted to get some hindrances out of the way." She leaned on her wooden assistance with every step, and Korbyn instinctively slowed his stride to adhere to her comfort. "Heard you killed the king of the manticore pride. I would be lyin' if I said I wasn't impressed...and envious."

Korbyn hadn't been prepared for her intrigue, somewhat gaping at her gained attention. Several objections coursed through his brain, but he found himself only offering a sparse reply.

"Ma'am—"

"Call me Micah. Some call me the Arbiter, but the title doesn't fit me, to be honest. A lot of people refer to me as 'bitch' or 'asshole.'" Micah chuckled, amused by her own jest. "You remember anything yet?"

Korbyn frowned, realizing only obscure visions and a strange voice offered any knowledge, though both proved to be unhelpful. "No."

"Then I have an offer for you," Micah declared with a smirk. "Despite what the king believes, we serve a good cause. When we're not cleaning up the mess of egocentric kingdoms, we're monster hunters."

Korbyn peered at Salem, who joined his side. She mirrored Micah's grin.

"If you're not returning home, then you're welcome to join us," the Arbiter offered. "We could use more people like you."

As they continued their excursion, he gazed at the organized brick that shifted into the randomized terrain of the marketplace. He wasn't sure what "people like him" meant, and Micah probably inferred respectable intentions, but he sensed, deep down inside, that being a person like him wasn't exemplary.

"Yes," Korbyn replied regardless. "I'd like that."

NINE.

The copious voices at the inn and tavern left Veeris in ongoing irritation. The building was packed with people filling every corner of the establishment. The structure itself was made of simple design and seemed just as old as the rest of the city, with rusted chandeliers and wobbling chairs that had been neglected for far too long, but the partygoers didn't seem to mind. Men and women dressed in simple cloth and tunics circled each other and danced to the local bard's ballad, with alcohol spilling from their raised mugs. Despite the ale dipping and spinning with the cadence of their twirls, the kegs somehow seemed bottomless, which, for some reason, irked Veeris even more.

He leaned farther into his chair, scrunching his shoulders and raising his book over his face. No matter how much he tried to ignore the jubilant masses, they somehow retrieved his attention and annoyance. He had been trying to read the autobiography of Besemir Taundil for well over an hour, but he couldn't manage to focus with the surrounding voices quieting his inner thoughts.

Most of his friends sat at the next table over, happily drinking away beside the bar, which was filled with various brands of liquor and ale that Veeris had never heard of. It was always Micah's suggestion to convene close to where she could easily interact with the bartender. She somehow managed to captivate the man, who then ensured that the mercenaries' jugs were always filled. Even now, she was chugging down her third mug of ale, moving back and forth between her table and the bar as if she was twenty years younger.

Haven, Andrid, Oakley, and Gilben sat with her, playing a card game that Veeris never cared to learn. Every time the group engaged in a game, multiple distractions occurred that prevented its conclusion. Either Gilben would start playing a song or counting his coin, Andrid would overindulge in food, Haven would take three or four minutes on his turn before getting irritated and quitting, or Oakley would flirt with a barmaid. Veeris gave up on socializing long ago, instead choosing to spend his time indulging in a book, just as he was trying to do now.

Salem, at some point, assisted a barmaid who had complained about a leak in one of their kitchen's faucets. Veeris had encouraged Salem not to bother, but she blatantly ignored his suggestion, exiting the back of the kitchen later with grease smudged on her brow and a smile on her face. Even now, the barmaid was apologizing profusely.

Then, there was that *thing*. The creature sat on a stool with its back to the bar not too far from the mercenaries, recurringly taking small sips from the tankard in its hand. If they had been friends, Veeris would have criticized its poor, hunched posture. Instead, he analyzed it with perpetual scrutiny, ensuring the monster didn't attack or take advantage of his friends in their drunken stupors.

Veeris was certain this thing was feigning its amnesia, here for a foul purpose. He wasn't sure what it was, but he knew this beast was up to no good. As if it was reading his mind, it craned its head in his direction. Its ivory eyes immersed in pools of darkness sent chills down his spine, and Veeris returned the glance with a hardened glare.

"Veer! Come join us," Oakley called out from the table next to him as he leaned back in his chair, tipping it back on two legs. The seat was wobbling, and at any moment, the furniture appeared as though it might collapse under his constant teetering. Oakley seemed unaware of its flimsy structure due to his tipsiness as he wobbled back and forth.

"No," Veeris replied, picking his book back up and concealing his face from the rest of his group's ongoing stares.

"Veery, when become no fun?" Andrid huffed, placing their cards down on the table, face up. Haven reached over and turned their cards face down.

Andrid hiccupped, picking up a slice of onion with their bare fingers and tossing it in their mouth. They chomped and fidgeted in their seat, dancing even though the tavern's bard had temporarily halted playing music.

"I'm plenty of fun," Veeris retorted, flipping a page in his book. He wasn't actually concentrating enough to comprehend its contents, but he was hoping it would assist him in ending this fruitless conversation. "We just have different definitions of it."

"I'm not an expert on your literary garbage," Haven remarked, which earned a lowered book and penetrating glower from Veeris, "but wouldn't you rather hang out with people you do know instead of reading about a dead one?"

"First of all, Besemir Taundil is not *literary garbage.* His books are incredibly engaging, regardless of the subject matter, and he relays not only authenticity in his narrative, but profound knowledge on topics like religion, economy, and political science!" Veeris exclaimed, holding up a single finger. He ignored the fact that the others stared at him with risen brows before raising his middle finger. "Second of all, Oakley cheats."

"See? I told you," Haven said, whipping his head in Oakley's direction.

Oakley shrugged, lifting his hand from the gesture. Veeris counted an extra card in his grasp.

"And I'm telling you that I would never cheat! Besides, wouldn't you have caught me by now? You're so smart, Haven!" Oakley teased, throwing down a pair of threes into the pile with a mischievous grin.

"Either way, it's about the fun, lads," Gilben chimed in. Whether or not the dwarf knew of Oakley's exploits, Veeris wasn't sure. Instead, he seemed to be engaged in the merriment as he tossed a card into the pile. "Ya sure ya don't wanna join? We could gamble to make it more excitin'!" Gilben offered with a smile hidden beneath the upward curls of his mustache before he leaned down for his bag of coin within his satchel. He fumbled several times as he reached for his belongings, most likely due to his short stature and his clear inebriation.

"Fuck yeshh, how much err we bettin'? I'm all in!" Micah replied, slurring as she spoke. She tossed in her remaining cards, extending her injured leg underneath the table and retrieving her own bag.

"You all have fun. I'll stick to Taundil," Veeris declared, pivoting his torso away from them. Before he initiated his reading, shifting by the bar grasped his attention.

Salem was seated on the stool next to the creature, both of them facing outward towards the rest of the tavern and engaging in some sort of conversation. She laughed, as if it was the most hilarious thing she had ever interacted with, which was highly implausible, considering a monster couldn't feasibly possess such a characteristic. From Veeris' position, which was not too far from the conversing duo, he began to eavesdrop.

"How long have you all been a mercenary group?" the creature asked, not shifting away from Salem as it placed its drink down on the bar. Its dark locks half-covered one of its eyes, with random strands pointing in different directions. If there was one thing the creature actually needed, it wasn't its memories, but a hairbrush.

"We all joined Kendra Dawn at different points. Veeris and I were the first to join, back when it was just Micah, but she wanted to reform the mercenary band into something new. Gilben was next to join the group, followed by Oakley, Andrid, and then Haven," Salem responded, smiling at it, seemingly unperturbed by its appearance.

"And how long have you known Veeris?" it probed, glancing over in his direction.

Veeris quickly raised his book, acting as if he was emersed in his read, but continued listening.

"I guess you could say we grew up together," Salem stated. "He's like family to me, in a way. We came from another kingdom outside of Terrisae. We wanted to be in a place where we could more actively help people, and here we are."

Family, Veeris thought to himself, clutching his book. *I suppose that's one way to put it.*

"You're a very skilled fighter," the creature blurted out.

Veeris glared at it, peering over his book. It was as though it was studying Salem, whose cheeks had turned to an abnormal cherry hue.

She fiddled with her locket, the golden chain twisting in between her fingers. "Thank you. If there's anything that I'm honored with, it's my swordsmanship. It's why I was so eager to come to this continent in the first place. I felt as though I could make a difference."

"How is it that you have magic?" the monster questioned. "I'm not still sure I understand how that decidite stuff works, but I can tell it's an impressive feat."

Salem beamed, her fingers still twiddling with the golden locket. "Elohim gifted me magic in this world with a purpose. I'm here to help people, but I'm also here by oath."

"Oath?" it asked with a tilted head.

"To find a pair of evil weapons," Salem elaborated, turning her gaze towards the partiers within the tavern. "Matching dark blades made of bone."

Veeris did his best not to gasp, trying to conceal his expression with Taundil's autobiography. His fingernails dug harshly into the leather of the book's cover. He couldn't believe it took him this long to muster a conceivable reason for this creature to be here. It took several weeks of pondering, but the monster just accidentally revealed its hand, and Veeris raised his book to mask his own set of cards.

The monster was after the blades.

Veeris wasn't sure why he didn't realize it before, but it all made sense. This thing was here to intercept their plans and claim the weapons for itself. It couldn't be a coincidence that Salem and Veeris were the ones to find this creature, just when he had felt as though they were nearing the end of their journey. Or maybe, despite how chilling the notion was, the creature was the one to find them.

Salem's next question reeled him back in to their private conversation.

"How did you defeat that manticore?" She leaned towards the creature's stool, as if inspecting a torn parchment under a rustic magnifier. "They're intelligent and strong beasts. Not many can say they've killed the king of a manticore pride."

"Turns out I'm left-handed," the beast replied with a chuckle. Veeris was certain the laugh was also fake. "Holding the blade felt a lot more natural to me after I figured it out."

"Of course! How stupid of me. I hadn't even considered that a possibility," Salem said, slapping her forehead. Then, she turned her body to face the creature, lifting her leg on top of her alternate knee. Because of their seated proximity, their thighs rested against each other.

"Luckily I didn't realize it too late, but it did help that I had a good teacher," the monster replied, leaning into her after her re-adjustment. It put its arm across the bar, which happened to reside behind Salem's shoulders. She didn't withdraw, as if for some reason, she wasn't bothered by its proximity.

"Left-handedness is rare. You must be someone incredibly special," Salem stated, mirroring its lean and leaving little space betwixt them.

"Special? I don't know about that," the creature said with a laugh. Veeris couldn't have agreed more.

"I mean it. You're very interesting, Korbyn," Salem murmured, and Veeris barely caught her words. He witnessed her eyes shimmering against the lantern lights, her pupils moving in a way that resembled deep intrigue and fascination. "Very interesting indeed."

"I could say the same for you, mercenary whose holy magic can split the Heavens," it replied with a tone of confidence. It flicked its gaze down to her lips before returning to her eyes. "If I wasn't mistaken, it sounds like you'd make angels envious for more than one reason."

Are they...flirting? Veeris thought, his nose and brows scrunching in absolute disgust.

His breath quelled as he watched them whisper and lean into each other. No one in the tavern seemed to notice their intimate behavior, as they were all clearly absorbed in their own merriment, but Veeris just sat there, dumbfounded, watching the two interact. This behavior was completely abnormal to Salem. In all her years, she had never flirted with another, yet only after several days of interacting with this foul beast, she was reveling in some sort of romantic encounter. It didn't make any sense.

Unless the monster was somehow enchanting her.

"I wish I saw you fight against the manticore," Salem stated, leaning farther into the monster and mirroring its intense gaze. "Now I'm curious how good you are. You'll have to show me sometime."

Veeris slammed his book on the table and rose.

"To quote the magnificent writer, Besemir Taundil, 'Left-handedness is a symbol of evil, a creation of the devil who forged sigils that only the left hand could perform,'" Veeris interjected, thrusting himself in between Salem and the creature. Their stools pivoted and turned their bodies in opposite directions, giving Veeris enough room to lean against the bar betwixt them. The monster glared at his intrusion. "'People should be wary of those with such features, for these traitors and pariahs are sent from the Hells to fulfill the tasks of the wicked.'"

"Veeris!" Salem snapped, tugging Veeris with a force that he couldn't counter. When she pulled him away, she stood from her chair and crossed her arms. "You and I both know that's a fallacy."

"There is always some truth hidden in myth, just as equally as there are inaccurate ones," Veeris replied, straightening out his tunic and gifting the monster a cold stare. "So, tell me, deserter of the front lines, which one are you?"

Salem heaved Veeris' collar back with such intensity that he almost toppled over. She stepped in front of him, leveling her chin to meet his scowl. Veeris knew she was challenging him by the intensity in her eyes, with specks of shimmering gold and amber dancing like a fire.

"What do you think you're doing?" Salem hissed.

Veeris' eyebrows knitted together. "Me? What about *you*?" he whisper-shouted, failing to lower his voice from his boiling anger. "We talked about this."

"Go cool off," Salem demanded. "Now."

Veeris glanced around the tavern when he noticed its silence. Stares from random civilians and his friends met his brief scan. He scoffed. They leered at him like *he* was the bad guy, when an obvious blight sat just a few paces away from him.

"Fine," Veeris growled, stomping away towards the entrance of the tavern and avoiding the gawking. As he neared the door, the voices of the building erupted into their previous conversation. Veeris halted at the ingress when he heard Salem's voice.

"I'm so sorry about him," Salem said as she rubbed her brow. "It's nothing against you. He tends to indulge in outlandish philosophy and is untrusting of most to a fault."

"It's no big deal, really. I would be wary too; you all just met me, after all," the monster replied.

Veeris gripped the doorframe until his knuckles turned white.

"You are either the kindest or the most imperturbable person I have ever met." Salem chuckled. "Maybe both."

Veeris left the establishment, stomping down the street until he found himself in front of one of the windows. From the outside, he saw Salem and the creature join the mercenaries at the table, being handed their own set of cards. They all smiled at one another, already entangled in some sort of conversation. From Oakley's perpetual teetering, his chair's leg finally broke, and the smaller male collapsed under his weight. The mercenaries and the monster exploded in a robust laugh.

Veeris once again caught the gaze of the monster, who stared back with an expression he could not decipher.

"I know your hand, abhorrent beast," Veeris sneered as he strode away from the tavern.

TEN.

Regardless of his continual attempts, Korbyn still couldn't sleep. Instead, sentience plagued him with engulfing visions. For several hours, he stirred to rid the unnatural phenomena that demanded his attention. Every time he closed his eyes to accept any form of rest, he witnessed images of a world writhing in frozen canyons bearing no sun.

He expected the alcohol to assist him with slumbering, but it provided no reprieve. His body easily conquered the depressant, consuming it as though it had been nothing more than water. Despite actively consuming multiple jugs, he remained just as sober as he did before.

Aggravated, Korbyn jerked into a sitting position, blinking away the visions of a dark cathedral. He inspected the window, noticing that the early light would soon flood the streets of Umberfall. The confines of this room decidedly irritated him, and he pulled on a fresh set of clothes before exiting the pub.

Thankfully, most people chose to rise with the morning sun.

With the streets emptied, Korbyn cared not to cast his gaze from prying eyes. He analyzed Umberfall's ancient beauty, admiring the landscape's serenity of whisking autumn.

Korbyn witnessed the various establishments within the confines of the lower district. With the dangers of the lands, businesses seemed to thrive. Where there was a danger, there was a need for protection. As he meandered, he found various businesses fluctuating from taverns, inns, forges, guilds, stables, markets and shops of varying supplies near the city's entrance.

From the corner of his eye, Korbyn saw a figure amongst the shadows of an alley. He turned, the remnants of a torn cloak hiding beneath a thick layer of twilight. For a moment, he felt his heart stop, hearing a familiar voice after hours of silence.

What is it that you would give? the voice chimed.

Korbyn adjusted his path, walking to the alleyway of gloom. Despite its impending darkness, he could see in full clarity. All things that endeavored to hide failed beneath his empowered eyes. But nothing was there.

The streets were still empty of people, except Korbyn and the mysterious cloaked person that once again disappeared around another corner. Korbyn briskly followed, peering down both ways before crossing the cleared street and entering the alley dipped in shadows.

"Hello?" he called out upon seeing no one on the other side. He quickened his strides, feeling ushered forward despite not hearing any physical voices.

This dance of cat and mouse continued for several pathways, the edge of a person's presence disappearing into the shadows that formed from the overhanging rooftops before Korbyn could reach it. Panic arose in his chest as forgotten memories longed to be more than an irritation on the tip of his tongue. When he finally rounded the last corner, he was struck with awe.

Before him stood a courtyard with a grand cathedral, a majestic, four-story building that loomed over the other structures. Groups of oval windows decorated in swirls of carved stone that encased unsmeared glass spread across the stone wall. The center of this building extended higher than the rest of the rooftop, containing a balcony that overlooked the square. The lower rooftops were decorated in small, beautiful merlons that extended to the parallel sections of the building, protruding from the surface. Dual columns stood on both sides of the entrance, leading up to the grand spires that adorned its structure towards the top. At the lower end of the pinnacle was a small statue of the Tree of Tranquility, its spirals ascending upwards and decorated in lush marble. An arcade of multiple arches towered over its entrance, continuing to a large set of open, double doors made of iron.

A linen cloth and a trace of obsidian passed the building's threshold.

Korbyn rushed to the large doors, flying past the sill beneath him. He almost crashed into a short, elderly man, and he pulled himself back by the door's frame to halt his advance. The man wore a navy houppelande that fell above his ankles and was tightened around his round frame with a leather belt. On his feet were a pair of brown pantoffles and a matching cap. He had a short beard that melded into his mustache of silver—but no black cape.

"Did anyone come in here before me?" Korbyn asked, disregarding his smaller frame for visual clarity into the lobby.

"No. You're the first one here. I just opened the door," the old man replied, clearly confused by Korbyn's brash entrance. Nevertheless, he moved towards the wall and craned open the iron gate a bit wider. "But you're welcome to peruse, if you wish."

When Korbyn stepped into the building, he saw waves of bookshelves stacked neatly like rows of cornfields, carefully placed in the endless, grand halls of this massive library. The wooden stands depicting different genres divided the first floor into multiple sections, varying between countless categories of fiction and nonfiction. Small banquet tables were scattered across the room, holding arrangements of irises in an analogous theme of lavender, champagne, and deep indigo. They were placed in large bowls adorned in engraved curves that mimicked the movements of vines grasping a forgotten structure.

"Beautiful isn't it?" the elder stated, adjusting his hat before gazing up at the shelves that towered over him.

Korbyn ogled rather than initiating a response, endeavoring to see every part of the library from his position at the entrance. Eventually, he nodded in bafflement.

"Is there anything in particular you're looking for?" the old man inquired.

"Actually...yes," Korbyn stated, then turned to the man fully. "I'm looking for research of the supernatural."

The tattoo on his left forearm tingled in response, the design of the insignia painted into the back of his mind. He ignored the fact that he might not have been led here by chance.

The man placed his pointer finger and thumb on his gray beard, stroking the hairs into a fine point. He remained contemplative for a moment before a spark lit in his eyes.

"You will probably find documents located near the section of studies on the philosophies of the arcane, which will be on the third floor." He smiled, referring to the dual flight of curving stairs that circled a painting of the Tranquility Tree on an old, wooden canvas. "If you need any more assistance, ask Wethereen."

Following the librarian's suggestion, Korbyn ascended several staircases, peering into each floor as he entered them. In terms of the layout and structure of each floor, they were all relatively the same; each bookcase aligned perfectly with one another, all sections of shelves divided by genres, such as lyric poetry, rhetoric, fabliau, romance, popular drama, and many others that Korbyn skimmed over. Vases on top of similar tables were neatly placed near the sections, each floor holding different species of flower.

While the second floor held beautiful white, pink, and blue lotuses, the third floor contained garlands stacked in bowls of sunflowers that resembled golden crowns.

The third floor held less of a wild variety of genres than the previous ones. Glancing around, he saw mathematics, sciences, history, universal philosophy and insight, biographies, and academic texts. He frowned, not immediately locating the correct category. After rounding several corners, in search of any hidden bookshelves, he gazed over to the help desk against the back wall, seeing another librarian that he guessed to be Wethereen.

The elderly woman with ginger hair streaked with gray resided on the other side of an archaic wooden counter. She arched forward over the desk, as if unable to stand up completely straight. She was consumed in the depths of a book, part of its leather bind raised so that Korbyn could see the title despite his distance. *The Origins of Terrisae: The Blessings of Elohim* by Besemir Taundil. Beside the current read sat a couple of mounds of books by Taundil, carefully placed in organized stacks and alphabetized, but the librarian didn't appear as if she was going to be placing them on the appropriate shelf.

"Excuse me, ma'am, are you Wethereen? I was hoping you could help me locate something," Korbyn whispered as he approached her bureau, attempting to lower his volume to prevent an impression of a ruffian despite his oddities.

Her gaze of admiration shifted into a penetrating one, though she kept her attention on her text. She raised the book, blockading his view. Even though he couldn't see from her nose down to her chin, he could tell her frown deepened from the heaviness of her wrinkled forehead.

"Yes. What do you want?" Wethereen groaned out irritably.

He paused, gazing back down at the books to her right. "Apologies, ma'am, I saw your current read and figured you would be the perfect person to ask. I'm a big fan of Besemir Taundil myself. I think his memoirs on the relationship between the church and state from its establishment in the Kingdom of Esperin and its current importance in contemporary leadership and religion was exquisite," Korbyn explained while viewing one of the books titled *The Threat of a Secular Age and the Importance of Church in State* by Taundil.

Wethereen immediately lowered her book and raised her eyes, peering into his irises of white and sclera of darkened coal as the cover tilted closed. His proclamation seemed to be a good enough reason for her to bypass the defects of his person.

"You're a fan of Taundil too? You must be a student of philosophy, history, and political science!" the old woman replied excitedly, her tone shifting. Before, her voice had been harsh and raspy and somehow transitioned into a shaky and weathered hum. Thankfully, she proved amenable. "What specifically are you researching?" she asked with a bright, toothy smile that resembled a checkerboard.

"I'm a little embarrassed that I don't know the title or author," Korbyn said, the fabrication spilling out of his mouth like a dam that had burst open. "I'm researching texts revolving around the supernatural." He watched her frown. "I'm fascinated by fallacies of the mystical and its hypothetical relevance to world. What better way to counter a heretic's beliefs than to understand them?" Korbyn remarked, watching her frown brighten into an astonished smile. He, in fact, had no idea if any philosophical writings existed, but the visions, his inability to sleep, and the strange occurrence of his memory loss seemed somehow tied to the paranormal.

"A scholar indeed! Of course I'll help you, dearie! We have an entire section of philosophical debates and hypotheses on such topics, but they're mostly fictional nonsense if you ask me. You'll see that Taundil doesn't believe in all that kookiness," Wethereen said, walking over towards the far side of the library, her hunched form leaning over her wobbling, wooden cane. He was surprised that the ancient contraption wasn't an artifact in the library. "I have to ask, which of Taundil's manuscripts is your favorite?"

While Wethereen turned the corner, Korbyn skimmed the stack of books.

"*The Elohim Gospel and Hymns*: *A Foundation for a Better World*," Korbyn responded, reading the title before he met her regard with a wide smile. "I thought his speculations on the importance of music and the arts accompanied by religious conviction was unmatched."

Wethereen beamed. "I agree! His descriptions of the supposed forgotten hymns by early Esperinans just made my heart want to sing!" She pointed to another philosopher, waving her hand dismissively. "If you truly want to read drivel, then you should reference Syrian Claymore and his speculations on Elohim. Why we still have his nonsensical madness, I will never understand."

Syrian Claymore and the Spirit of the Wood: *A Biography and the Depictions of Terrisae's Civil War* lay discarded atop another set of books, which Korbyn grabbed before following her down the next aisle.

Turning to another corner, Korbyn realized he missed a path on the other side of the library. Here, he saw multiple other genres, followed by more display tables of freshly watered flowers.

"Once you are done checking out your book, you should have some tea with me, and we can discuss *The Natural Formations of Land Mass and Their Origins*." Wethereen stopped in front of the aisle, wobbling her body and cane to completely face him. Her gaze was suggestive.

Korbyn's forced smile twitched. "As lovely as that sounds, I'm afraid I leave in the morning. I was hoping to get the read in before I left," he said, trying to sound as kind as he could.

Wethereen nodded in response. Her fingers that fluttered

over his arm produced a shudder. "No problem at all, sweetie. You can find several pieces you're looking for in this section," she told him, her stick wobbling under her weight. "And if you're ever back in Umberfall, make sure to come see me." The old woman winked before vanishing through the stacks.

Korbyn sighed, allowing his fake smile to disappear from his naturally frowning face. How he managed to blatantly lie on topics he had never read would remain a mystery, but the power of insight and deception felt a little too natural.

He spent the next couple of hours sifting through countless texts. After Korbyn read through a book and found nothing of interest, he placed it at his side on the floor and retrieved another, scrambling through its contents. There were many different topics, varying from occult practices to the religions of other races.

Only two books proved memorable, but conflicting in belief. The first text, written by a bishop in the early golden period of Esperin, declared righteous souls being delivered to the gates of the Heavens from good deeds and practiced worship. Meanwhile, the second was a replicated biography by Syrian Claymore, the leader of the rebellion of a civil war in Esperin hundreds of years ago, which regarded something called "The Spirit of the Wood," a voice that originated from the Tranquility Tree. He claimed that it spoke of Elohim's treason of "The Trinity." However, most of the biography only contained small excerpts, revealing the scribe who created this specific text never had access to Claymore's original manuscript.

Traitor, the voice whispered, though Korbyn remained dubious of what it was referring to.

Korbyn closed the book, realizing that the outlandish philosophies failed to aid in whatever he was searching for, not that he had the slightest inclination. This research had proved a waste of time.

"Nothing," Korbyn muttered, placing the book on the floor,

despite wanting to throw it as far as he could muster. "Why did you want me here?" he asked no one in particular, leaning his head back against the bookshelf and peering upwards at the wooden rafters.

After he managed to return the books to their shelving, Korbyn paced around the library. He stuffed his hands into his linen pockets, dragging his feet around the carpet that led to the staircase. When he saw movement at the top of the stairs, his neck almost cracked from its abrupt turn. On the landing of the fourth floor, Korbyn witnessed a cloak rounding a corner and disappearing out of sight from his immediate vicinity.

Korbyn approached the stairwell, not heeding things around him until he ran into something: a velvet rope attached to iron poles in half circles that dangled to the floor to block the stairs. A sign next to it read: "Off Limits. Approval By Council Only."

He inspected the help desk. Wethereen was completely immersed in her book. She adjusted her glasses and leaned her face downward, squinting at the text. Despite her clear fascination, he doubted the elder woman would have been able to perceive him from this far away. Korbyn easily maneuvered around the stanchion, racing up the stairs and towards wherever the mysterious figure was leading him.

When Korbyn reached the top, he gasped.

The wooden boards on the ceilings extended to tall arches that curved like branches, forming intricate designs six paces above his head. The room was dimly lit by tall, standing, unlit candelabras safely placed away from the manuscripts. At the far end of the hall was a large desk with scattered documents covered in dust in front of a large, cylindrical window with decorative wooden panels weaving across the glass. Instead of horizontal rows of bookshelves to form makeshift hallways, the cases were placed against the wall on either side of the long room, filled with endless books, texts, and journals.

Veils of chains hung from the shelves like a canopy of tarnished silver. Every single book from the entrance to the end of the hall was chained to the cabinets behind it. Protruding halfway down the bookcases were extra shelves, a mount for the books to rest while actively attached. Scattered across the hall were waist-high bookstands, with massive tomes individually placed and shackled to each wooden contraption.

"What do you want me to find?" Korbyn whispered, half-expecting a response.

When nothing replied, he turned to the door behind him and locked it. He trotted over the dusty path, scanning the heaps of books stuffed on the shelves.

Twenty, thirty, forty minutes passed, and Korbyn realized he never wanted to read again. He shifted through various subjects and authors, varying from topical philosophies such as curses, hexes, the dark arts, rebirth, and even reincarnation, all practices forbidden by the clergy of Elohim. However, none explained sudden marks manifesting on people after an avoidance of looming death.

"Damn it," Korbyn cursed, slamming the chained book back into the open space on the shelf.

The chain rattled in retaliation, and Korbyn paced, circling the library and permitting his moonlight eyes to scan the entirety of the collection. The person that he kept seeing must have been leading him to something, whoever they might have been. He felt pulled by a chain, similar to the fashion of these bound books. If someone was attempting to steer his uninformed mind in a particular direction, they were utterly deficient.

Korbyn took a deep breath, closed his eyes, and allowed his tense arms to rest at his side. He envisioned the magical flames he witnessed in the depths of the throne room, allowing his heart, mind, and body to succumb to the wishes of this unknown entity.

To call upon the powers of the crescent moon, you must first fall prone to wither and bloom.

Korbyn opened his eyes.

Behind one of the bookshelves, far in the back of the hall towards the desk, was a glowing flame. He strode towards the source, reaching the corner of the bookshelf until he saw it in full.

On a large bookstand with weathered timber was a massive tome, glowing in a magical black flame that the ordinary eye couldn't see. It whisked against a nonexistent wind, reaching out like tentacles around its form. The leather binding was held together by thick lace that hung over the stand, the matte-black thread made of silk ignoring the rays of the sun that gleamed through the window. In the middle of the tome was a golden medallion that resembled a crescent moon, its pointed edges faced downward. Pieces of metal were fastened on all four sides of the book, including the opposite side of the hinge, which clasped the book firmly closed. Peeking out of the dark leather bindings were light brown vellum with uneven edges that depicted its age. Korbyn was surprised the antique bookstand was strong enough to hold the oversized book.

They say history is written by the victors, but where do the failures hide their truths?

Korbyn ignored the voice and walked over, entranced by the essence seeping out of its core. He flipped the heavy tome in his hands, perusing at the leather binds that constricted it, and gasped upon its design. Located on the back of the book was the same mysterious symbol engraved into his arm.

Korbyn tried to remove the book from the wooden lectern, but a chain bellowed in response. Thick metal links dangled from the bookstand all the way to the tome, a large lock attached to its spine.

"Are you sure he's up here?" A foreign, muffled voice questioned from the other side of the locked door. Another familiar voice responded.

"I'm not sure. No one saw him leave the library, so I don't know where else he would be," Wethereen declared, her cane unintentionally echoing up the staircase to the fourth floor.

What happens to the raven when trapped within a cage?

"Shut up," Korbyn growled in response to the voice, sprinting towards the escritoire and fumbling around the discarded papers and quills scattered on top of it. When he found nothing, he pulled out every small compartment on its ridge, shuffling through the random objects inside.

"There's got to be a key," he whispered, directing his attention to the desk along the back wall, searching hectically through the nooks and caring not for the mess he left behind.

"It's locked," the foreign voice declared. Several hard knocks followed, echoing throughout the chamber. "Hello? Is anyone there? This floor is off limits!"

"Fuck," Korbyn muttered under his breath, running back towards the book.

The banging from the person on the other side of the door erupted into larger thumps, demanding immediate entry. Korbyn peered down at the tome as it gleamed with an otherworldly flame, and he conceded to his instinctual actions.

"Guards! Open the door!" the voice demanded, followed by several bodies slamming into the locked entrance, wood cracking from brute exertion.

Korbyn reached out to the chain, his frigid fingers wrapping around the metal binds. Magic surged towards his fingertips, essence and vapor exuding from his grasp and into the warm, autumn air. It slithered over the iron, sinking deep into its metal confinements. Within moments, ice covered the lock. The chains snapped, shattering to the ground in heaps.

The door to the grand hall burst open.

Korbyn narrowly escaped, leaving only a shattered iron lock and an open window behind him.

ELEVEN.

ity guards flooded the streets and raced towards the library. Korbyn discreetly sauntered into the enveloping crowds and pulled back the hood on his newly acquired cloak. He scoured a vender's stall within the market, paying little notice to the tumult of guardsmen. He flipped a salesman a silver coin, grabbing a fresh pomegranate and biting into its core. As several soldiers dashed past him, Korbyn adjusted the leather strap of his newly acquired leather knapsack and strolled past them.

There were voices emitting from the abnormally massive book, but more like incoherent whispers than actual presences. Even though there were dozens of people walking amongst the streets, they chattered louder than the enveloping crowds, sonorous and eerie like stilled flames. He carefully analyzed individuals within the masses as he prowled, searching for their notice of the ominous voices. Thankfully, Korbyn seemed to be the only one privy to their mutters. They were unintelligible, hissing secrets in another language that he didn't understand. He felt remorseful for stealing the mysterious book, but he needed answers.

Korbyn shifted his attention towards the sun to determine its height in the sky, and he regretted it. He pulled his hood farther over his eyes to shield its harsh rays. The bright orb was almost halfway towards its highest point, peeking through a set of clouds. Salem and the others were probably searching for him, if they hadn't already left him behind.

The streets of Umberfall were crowded with people, striding in a hurry towards their assigned destinations. It was easy for Korbyn to meld with the herd, camouflaging himself as an ordinary citizen despite his hood. There were many others like him, covered head to toe in linen to conceal their features. Because of the war, not many people were allowed into the kingdom's capital, forcing travelers and mercenaries to find temporary housing and jobs within the city's borders in fear of not being able to return.

A surge of pain swept through Korbyn's temple, impeding his next steps. He leaned into a wooden pole attached to a vendor's stand to uphold his weight, leaving him unable to stop the agony or the vision that followed.

A man in his mid-forties meandered through a crowded street. Hints of gray peeked through strands of beige, hanging over a pair of hazel eyes and the occurring formations of aged wrinkles. Above him, the sun ascended towards the sky's summit, cascading bright rays of sunlight. Off in the distance, the fall-colored leaves of the Tree of Tranquility swayed in tandem with the caressing wind.

Affectionally holding onto the man's arm was a woman, similar in age and covered in freckles. She spoke, but Korbyn couldn't hear her over the unbearable quietness. The silence rang so loud in his ears that it felt as though they would have bled.

The man reached out for a piece of fruit on one of the stands, exchanging an apple for a silver coin. The woman seemed to be telling her partner a joke, and they both laughed in what Korbyn assumed to be perfect harmony. And when the man continued to chuckle, he choked on the fruit.

His breaths were shortened and shallow, unable to remove the large fragment from his throat. He slammed his fist against his chest, struggling to withdraw the wedged fruit, but it failed to budge.

The ongoing crowd trailed by with uncertainty. As the woman shouted for help, they turned away with feigned ignorance. She became desperate, timorous in action but filled with desperate apprehension.

The woman circled her arms around her husband, yanking his body against hers with a force that seemed to surprise even herself. Despite her efforts, the apple was stubbornly lodged in his pharynx. She tried, and tried, and tried again.

After several minutes, his body trembled, inevitably plunging to the ground in chaotic spasms. Eventually, he fell limp, staring with wide eyes towards the unresponsive Heavens.

The vision and pain disappeared simultaneously. Panic stirred in chaotic rhythms of Korbyn's shuddered breath, as though he failed to breathe during the duration of the hallucination. Several people around him stared but disregarded him with wandering avoidance. Most watched him with furrowed, judgmental brows. When Korbyn finally rid himself of his vertigo, he hurried through the crowd and feigned a composed demeanor to evade their stares.

Who guides the way of the wanderers if he is lost himself?

Korbyn spurned the vision, eager to focus on something he could tangibly apprehend. Due to the mercs' departure, he might not have ample time to read the tome's contents today, but it surely had the answers he was desperately searching for.

Korbyn's hand tingled, still ridden with icy frost. He wiped it on his trousers, hoping to purge the sensation from his fingertips. Every day it seemed like he was figuring out something new about himself, but instead of recalling memories, habits, personality traits, and other useful things, he discovered abilities of the unknown, impudent and disturbing.

"Someone, please help my husband!" a woman screeched.

Even though Korbyn had never heard the voice until now, he knew he had experienced it before. Her desperate cry writhed with an agony that stirred unbridled apprehension within him.

As he gazed upon the masses, he jolted with recognition. The woman from his vision desperately endeavored to save her dying partner. Currently, her arms enclosed his torso, forcibly tugging on his spazzing body as he choked on a lodged piece of fruit.

It wasn't just a vision—it was a premonition.

As Korbyn lunged towards the couple, something foreign halted his movements, like a magical wall that prohibited further venture. Disobeying his mind's demands, his body stilled. His muscles shook in an uncontrolled defiance, the invisible grip caring not for his desperate pleas.

For several minutes, the man jerked in pain for a second time, falling out of the woman's grasp and hitting the gravel. A silence swept over the area, bystanders gaping at the widened man's eyes before passing by, disregarding his death.

"No! Elohim, please don't take him from me!" the woman shrieked, waves of tears falling past her freckles and hiding the innocence of her features. Her screeches penetrated the silence. She fell to her knees and coddled him in her arms, but he was too heavy, and his limp body scraped against the stones beneath him. In a place filled with people, she was alone.

You are not meant to save, the voice said.

The grasp no longer thwarted Korbyn's efforts, but still he remained paralyzed in boundless trepidation.

Korbyn meandered through the front doors of the tavern and inn and caught sight of Oakley first. The male perched on a stool almost as tall as him, dangling his feet off its ledge and consuming a loaf of bread and an assortment of cheeses, including what was left of northern brie and a lightened parmesan. When the door closed behind Korbyn, Oakley whirled the chair in his direction with a wide smile and a grin full of bread.

"Kor-bn! We fot yu go sckard n' rn oth!" Oakley bellowed with a mouthful.

Korbyn raised an eyebrow. Gilben, who sat adjacent, spun the stool around like a top.

"He said we thought ya got scared 'nd ran off," Gilben explained, taking a smaller piece of bread in his own mouth and chewing. Displayed on the slab of the bar were sheets of parchment and a quill left temporarily forgotten. "Glad yer back, lad."

Before Korbyn could reply, Salem, Haven, Veeris, Andrid, and the fox emerged from one of the rooms in the back of the tavern. Salem beamed. Veeris frowned in comparison.

"Korbyn! Thank Elohim you're okay," Salem exclaimed, prancing in his direction until she met him face to face. He could already feel the heat emitting from her body, despite their distance. "Where did you go?"

"I—" Korbyn stuttered, following her gaze to the cloak and knapsack. "I thought I should get some supplies. I didn't get much other than a bag, though."

Salem nodded in assumed approval, tugging a bit at the cloak's edge. "It suits you. I like it," she responded, regarding his hood. Stricken with sudden sheepishness, Korbyn avoided her eye contact.

"Can we get going? The sun doesn't slow because of our wasteful conversations," Veeris interrupted, his arms crossed over his chest. Korbyn couldn't help but wonder if his face could get stuck like that. The elf shifted the sneer in his direction. "What?"

"Nothing," Korbyn replied before analyzing the group's attire.

They all had replaced their casual clothes with their armor and weapons. In front of the entrance door, their belongings were placed in organized piles. "Where are we going?"

Salem's excitement billowed, as displayed by her cheeky grin and sparkling, golden eyes. "We've got a contract!"

TWELVE.

U mberfall's grand branches waved them goodbye from the ardent breeze of fall, leaves of bright oranges trickling the sky like longing tears. Korbyn almost felt guilty for not waving in return as they exited the main gate.

The party departed long after the sun offered its welcome, the lingering clouds parting and retreating from the orb's previous ascent. As of now, it was a couple of hours after midday, scattered clouds intermingling in the cerulean sky. The mercenaries ventured forth in a rugged caravan, ignoring the asymmetrical wheels and craggy ruts.

Haven and Gilben sat on the driver's seat, with Haven grasping the reins of the almond-colored horse. Gilben switched between pieces of parchment and his lute once again, consumed with lyrical composition. Both were quiet otherwise, probably relishing in their drunken stupors from the night prior. Haven took a swig from a flask, despite the early morning.

"Ale's the best medication for a hangover," Haven had said

when Korbyn watched him fill his tankard before their departure. Korbyn wasn't sure how more alcohol helped a hangover, but he digressed.

Comparatively, Salem and Oakley happily engaged in their own forms of entertainment during their voyage south. Oakley exhibited a couple of card tricks, hiding Salem's randomly chosen card in a stack of seventy-two. Korbyn was intrigued by his proficiency, wielding the set of cards like twin daggers and a surprising amount of finesse. When Oakley reached past her ear, flicked his hand, and exposed the queen of diamonds, her eyes gleamed against the sun's rays with sparkling gold, much brighter than any gem would have been.

Veeris leaned against the far wall on the front seat's opposite side. He sat in a composed lounge with a book on his lap and a foul attempt at immersing himself in the packed space. After thirty-seconds, his attention shifted to the next page, carefully flipping it as if it had been made of glass.

Korbyn heard the whispers emitting from the dark tome, despite its silence. The others hadn't seemed to notice its presence, a relief that allowed him to retain a passive persona. He hadn't yet had a chance to peruse its contents, but hopefully, with a temporary moment's peace, he would be able to. When he saw Veeris' eyes shift towards him, Korbyn adjusted his stare to his own hands, regarding the multi-colored rocks piled within his palms.

Andrid sat at his side with their napping fox, rummaging through a sack made of patches of alternating quilt, decorated mostly in colors of turquoise, jade, and a hue that matched a dirtied seaweed. A collection of rocks formed heaps, varying in size and shade. During Korbyn's extended muse, Andrid utilized him as a makeshift bag, supplying him different stones as they adjusted which ones were placed at the bottom. Observing them, Korbyn was unsure of what exactly their organizational method was.

This collection reminded him of the piece of decidite securely placed in Andrid's staff. Unlike normal decidite, which turned to dust after use, their piece of ore ceased to decay. Instead of just a matte-black texture, it also contained swirls of gold along its surface, its gilded tint the only part that reflected any light.

"Can I ask you something?" Korbyn inquired, trying to take Andrid's attention away from their collection.

For a moment, it worked. They temporarily halted their rifling to greet him with confused blinks and slight tilts of their head. "You asked permission, but then asked anyway," Andrid replied, displaying a toothy grin. "You are silly."

"Fair enough. Then I'll ask a question and not enquire permission," Korbyn replied, referring to the disregarded staff. "Why doesn't your decidite dissolve after it's used? How does the magic work?"

One of the fox's eyes opened dubiously, presumably listening to their conversation as if it was able to understand them.

Andrid placed down a rock to unfold all five of their fingers. They folded their thumb into their palm, followed by their pointer finger, counting both as they did. When they seemed confident of their findings, they met Korbyn's eyes once again. "That two questions."

Korbyn frowned. "Can you answer both?"

"I answer that too." Andrid chuckled more animalistically than the fox beside them. "Dunno how work. Strange rocks," they said, huffing a bit when they failed to find whatever they were searching for. Andrid placed more random rocks within the pile in Korbyn's grasp, unaware that he was beginning to lose space in his lap. "Rock give holy magic. I make things grow. Grow kinda like healing but not healing. I make plants 'nd things grow faster," Andrid explained, as if any of it had made any sense. "My dee-si...demi...deci....my ore rarer and stronger than rest."

Recalling the fight against the manticores, Korbyn had watched those able to use the stones weave magic. His past eluded him, and he couldn't recall ever witnessing such ethereality, but these abilities seemed like such an impalpable concept. To Andrid's description, it seemed decidite gave them holy magic to expand their normal limitations of growth. In battle, Andrid was able to manipulate the greenery around them for their benefit. Most uses of decidite Korbyn observed remained limited to healing magic, other than a few exceptions. There had to be some sort of limitations to these abnormal, ethereal capabilities.

"Why is your decidite special?" Korbyn asked.

Andrid shrugged, fumbling a stone in their hands. It seemed as though it was not the one they were searching for, and they tossed it to the side, haphazardly aiming for the bundle. They missed, and Korbyn lunged for it to prevent its tumbling out of the back of the moving caravan and added it to the assembly of rocks.

"Gilded. Don't know why special. Just is. More exist. Not many found, so very rare." Andrid took a break from their search, took a bite from their ration, and then continued. With every chew, they danced happily.

"Isn't it dangerous to carry it around? Someone could steal it," Korbyn noted.

"It can only be used by one person while alive, useless to others. It tied to me now."

Korbyn prepared to ask more questions regarding their knowledge on the subject, but Andrid assumed a straighter position and grinned happily upon locating their missing object.

They held up an obsidian rock that appeared as though it had been sharpened, splattered in speckles of white and traced in curved lines of ivory that resembled veins. They lifted it near the opening of the window on the side of the caravan where the curtain shifted from the uneven terrain of the dirtied path, the stone's matte surface refusing to shimmer in the light.

"Kind of look like ore, but no magic," Andrid said, waving the rock in front of Korbyn's face. "Korbi—take," they urged.

Korbyn stared for a moment, blinking curiously at the nickname and then the rock before taking it and dropping it in the pile with the rest of the collection.

"No," Andrid interrupted, retrieving the rocks that Korbyn had been holding onto and tossing them into their bag. "Keep."

Korbyn flipped the stone in his hand, analyzing the detail and natural design on all of its sides. The pale lines bore a resemblance to paint, the uneven edges grainy against his calloused fingers. "What's it for?"

"Gift." Andrid tightened the bag, looping the rope before peering at him with sea-green eyes. "Basalt 'nd quartz—igneous stone formed from cooling lava. Stone transform'd into new." Andrid was staring intensely, and Korbyn imagined his eyes resembled the drastic opposition of off-white against the dark obsidian.

"Andrid has given us all rocks," Salem interjected, digging through her own bag until a stone that resembled orange sand sat between her pointer finger and thumb. "It means they like you."

"Unless they give you a dumb-looking rock!" Oakley huffed, retrieving a larger stone with a hue of lightened mustard, containing layers of a multicavity that resembled a nest of wasps. Protrusions covered the entirety of this stone, producing an uneven and sporadic texture, lined with shades of butternut.

"It a geode!" Andrid stated, acting as if it had been the millionth time they had explained this. "Not chosen for outside; secrets lie within."

Oakley turned a deaf ear, rolling the abnormal stone from one hand to the other. Korbyn speculated what beautiful colors adorned the inside.

"That's okay. I get it. You hate me," Oakley lamented, shrugging and carefully placing the rock back in his own satchel. "You think I'm ugly. That's what it is."

Andrid glared at the male. "If can't see true beauty, then just dumb."

In defiance, Oakley rose from his seated position just as the wagon jostled. For a moment, he seemed to lose all sense of his dexterous prowess. He tripped over Andrid and crashed into the wall, provoking laughter from Korbyn, Salem, and Andrid. Oakley rose and turned to Korbyn with a widened jaw. A red welt appeared on his forehead where he fell face first into the timber.

"And here I thought you lacked personality, Korb!" Oakley stated, rubbing the new wound on his forehead. Another strange nickname. "I was starting to think you lost your memories *and* your humor."

"Maybe you just aren't that funny." Korbyn smirked, wrapping his arm around Oakley's neck in a headlock. The male squirmed under his grasp, not strong enough to unlock his grip. Korbyn sneered triumphantly, grinding his knuckles on top of his head and messing up his curls.

Salem and Andrid guffawed in amusement.

"Great, another child to deal with," Veeris complained, flipping the page of his book of lilac and leather trim.

"Veeris, you're grumpier than usual today. You might want to be careful when you sit. I think it shoved that stick farther up your ass," Oakley quipped, flicking his curls out of his eyes. "Unless you prefer things like that?"

Oakley's eyebrows wiggled with implication, and Veeris gawked at the sexual innuendo.

"That's crude and inappropriate." The elf scoffed, lifting the book again so it covered his face. "We should be focusing on our mission instead of goofing off."

"We won't be there for several days. What's the rush?" Oakley groaned, assuming a lax position.

"It wouldn't hurt to go over it early in case Korbyn's got any questions," Gilben said from the front. The lower half of the dwarf's face had been hidden by the wooden slab that acted as the backrest of the driver's seat, causing only his eyes to be seen. "He's a bit new to monster huntin', after all."

Beside Gilben, Haven nodded in agreement, not taking his eyes off the road ahead.

"Good idea," Salem noted, adjusting her posture.

Veeris glared at Gilben, who returned his hardened scowl with an oblivious grin.

"The Avernos Empire sent word before we reached the Kingdom of Esperin. They asked if we would help the towns on the outskirts of Shadowbane Forest." Salem reached towards Gilben, who handed her the map. She revealed its contents and twisted the parchment so that it faced Korbyn. She pointed to a grand forest that curved in a reverse crescent shape from the Kingdom of Esperin all the way down towards the Avernos Empire on the eastern side of the continent.

Where a seed from the Heavens exists, so too must a pit from the Hells.

"What's going on with the forest?" Korbyn questioned, his eyes trailing over the towns that sat several days outside of the empire's capital. He presumed it held a dark title for a reason.

"This forest was deemed unfit for travel and off limits by both countries," Salem explained, tracing her fingers over the drawings of the trees. "There's an unnatural darkness that resides there with an abnormal number of creatures lurking inside. Usually, the creatures stay within the forest's borders, as though they are lured into the darkness. The shadows there seem cognitive, like it has a mind of its own."

"How is that possible? Is it magical? And if it's magical, is it affected by decidite?" Korbyn pondered, followed by a shake of Salem's head.

"Terrisae's lands are infused with magic," Salem explained, and motioned to several locations scattered across the map. Korbyn saw the Forgotten Isles, Mount Firebrim, the Mirror of the

Heavens, Pandora's Box, the Dead Lands, and of course, the Tree of Tranquility. "The lands and the creatures of Terrisae have always been an enigma to Terrisaens. While people are born without magic, the land and creatures seem to be full of it. Mists call out to people like whispers, waters in the northwest are said to heal any wound, islands filled with ancient ruins floating in the sky that, to this day, remain unexplored..." Salem trailed off, returning her gaze towards Shadowbane Forest. "The darkness is dangerous and is doing something to the creatures inside it. The Avernos Empire sent word explaining that these monsters ventured outside of the forest and have been attacking nearby towns. They requested that we step in and help."

"And the empire hasn't sent their own soldiers to deal with the problem?"

"With the ongoing war, it deems more beneficial for a group of mercenaries trained in hunting monsters to deal with it instead of expending their own resources."

"That makes sense," Korbyn stated. "Do they know why the creatures wandered out of the forest?"

Salem leaned back and shook her head. "No, but I want to figure that out while we're there. Hopefully we can prevent it from happening again."

"You said the forest was deemed off limits by both countries. Are there active patrols on the edges of the forest? Have any soldiers seen exactly what we're dealing with?" Korbyn questioned, and he swore he saw Veeris roll his eyes from the corner of his own.

"Despite it being an active law, there aren't actually soldiers placed on duty. The law is mostly for frightening people from going inside and to avoid liability," Salem replied. Korbyn nodded, sliding his hand over his mouth in contemplation. "But reports assert sightings of an ogre."

"Is there anything else you can tell me about the forest?"

Salem gestured to the ink drawings on the map. As if curious about his problem-solving skills, she pointed towards Shadowbane Forest and then to other sets of trees scattered across the map. "Do you see the difference?"

"The trees are bigger," Korbyn commented almost immediately. While Shadowbane Forest's icons were drawn in thick strokes, the rest of the forests and randomly scattered shrubbery on the map had been painted in quick successions.

"That's right. Shadowbane is the largest standing forest in all of Terrisae, besides the Tranquility Tree, of course." Salem smiled, an expression of smugness shimmering across her face from Korbyn's observation. "Once you enter the woods, it's easy to get lost. Veeris and I ventured inside Shadowbane when we first arrived in Terrisae. It's like the darkness calls out to you. There have been stories of people venturing inside and never coming back." Korbyn watched a tinge of sadness glisten in her eyes. "Even aside from the looming darkness, the trees stand so tall and close together than you can't see the sky from the inside. It's like a complete world of its own."

"And what about this darkness?"

While radiance gives life, the necrotic takes it.

"Naturally, the forest absorbs the energy of living things inside it," Salem explained. "Veeris and I experienced this fatigue immediately after entering the woods. Even normal animals know the dangers of this place and tend to avoid it all together. There is also said to be a traveling, dark fog that creates wild visions if you're stuck inside for too long."

"How did you combat the darkness?" Korbyn prompted. "It sounds like we wouldn't be able to get too far."

"My holy energy will deflect the circulating gloom." Salem straightened her posture, a confident smug complementing her poise. Her locket shimmered and she lifted it with her gloved fingers. "As long as everyone stays by my side, we'll be fine."

Smirking, Korbyn eyed her up and down. "I'll make sure to stand close then."

Salem chuckled in response, gazing from one of his eyes to the other. "I'll personally make sure of that."

Silence filled the caravan.

"Huh," Oakley mumbled. To disrupt the silence and tension, he fumbled with Andrid's discarded bag. "So, uh, what other type of rocks you got in here?"

THIRTEEN.

The mercenaries of Kendra Dawn traveled for several days through the lands of Esperin, and Veeris was surprised how the road remained serene with utmost amazement. Habitually, monsters and bandits ambushed traveling roads; however, he lingered in anticipation, awaiting the moment when the monster in their group would disturb their abnormal respite.

The party passed time by exchanging stories and playing several games, ones Oakley always insisted upon. Veeris studied the monster with ivory eyes behind his unfurled book, watching it mingle amongst his friends like it believed it belonged there. It laughed in tandem with them and offered jokes of its own. For some reason, Salem always laughed, even though nothing it said was particularly funny. Despite the obvious abnormalities in the creature's features, the rest of the group welcomed it with open arms. It confirmed Veeris' suspicions. Somehow, the beast had convinced the rest that it was normal—and one of them.

At the end of the third day, after passing through Graycott

Village, they arrived at an Esperin fort alongside the border, with the grand Exonia Creek near its base. Despite its name, the geographic marker that divided the human kingdoms resembled more of a substantial river than a creek. The span of the canal neared somewhere betwixt four and five hundred paces. Peering into the depths of the water, Veeris could see long, horizontal tree trunks at its bank, with pointed stakes thrusting out of the trunks to prevent boats from approaching either side. Matching defensive barriers blocked both entrances to the bridge, the cheval de frise prepared for any invasions on horseback that the opposition might have planned. For now, both sides maintained their positions.

The bridge couldn't have been more than ten paces wide, but the length traversed the entirety of the river, covering too far of a distance for arrows. It would have been unwise for both sides to engage in a fight when the bridge could easily collapse under the weight of an army, sending groups of soldiers spiraling down into the river below. Luckily for Kendra Dawn, it aided in creating a safe passage from one country to the next.

"It's time," Haven stated, slowing the horse's trot to a casual stride as everyone reached for their bags.

Veeris noticed the creature's shoulders flinch for a brief moment. Salem must have also noticed its trepidation and offered some type of solace.

"They are required to check our belongings on both sides, just to ensure safety," Salem explained.

Veeris swore he saw fear flicker in the monster's eyes.

As they neared Esperin's fort, Veeris, Salem, Oakley, Andrid, and the beast exited the wagon and walked by its side, with nothing but their sacks on their back. Haven and Gilben remained at the driver's seat, maneuvering the horse-drawn wagon towards the entrance of the bridge. Attached to the side rail of the caravan was a wooden pole with Kendra Dawn's flag of the morning star greeting the soldiers at the fort.

Their legal forms of identification were required for their travels, which proved more time-consuming than Veeris deemed necessary, but he understood their caution. Each of the mercenaries procured a parchment with a stamped symbol of Kendra Dawn, along with their names and the signature of the Arbiter's title signed at the bottom. If he was lucky, the soldiers would recognize the monster for what it truly was and prevent it from crossing the border.

As the creature reached for its legal parchment, it fumbled, handing it over to the awaiting soldier. The soldier inspected the parchment more carefully. Afterwards, he returned it and ushered the creature forward. Veeris scoffed.

The soldiers sifted through their belongings within the caravan, not even bothering with the satchels and bags on their backs. After the faction approved of their departure, they temporarily opened a small portion of the blockade, allowing access to the bridge. Even though this process should have occurred with ease, tension and fear presided, for the awaiting soldiers of Avernos on the other side stood ready for combat at any notice. Hopefully they persisted in withholding their arrows or at least attacking the beast rather than Veeris and his friends.

Gilben raised Kendra Dawn's banner even higher, their peaceful sigil fluttering in the breeze. As they approached, soldiers grasped their bows in tightened grips and nocked their arrows in preparation. As soon as they witnessed their flag, the lieutenant signaled to cease. The mercenaries exhaled their breaths in awkward unison.

Once the soldiers settled, the lieutenant, three men and one woman clad in Avernos' armor approached their wagon, confronting their advancement when they reached three-quarters of the way across the long structure. The lieutenant stood in front of Salem and extended his open palm.

"Names, identification, and legal documents," he demanded, vanity exuding off his judgmental face. He bore shimmering armor compared to the rest to proclaim his rank along with mirrored ear piercings and a single ring in his nose. His bangs were long and slicked back to appear wet and smooth.

Salem withdrew several different pieces of parchment. The soldier's eyes scanned the contents of the letter and the emperor's sigil thoroughly before shifting his gaze towards her.

"We were informed of your arrival, but we can never be too safe." The lieutenant nodded to the soldiers when they had finished rummaging through the wagon. "Check their bags."

The beast fidgeted, clutching onto its bag as though it might disappear if it even so much as blinked.

"Is this necessary?" it asked, the abnormality of its eyes drawing the lieutenant's watchful gaze. "We've lost so much time already."

"It will only take a second," the lieutenant replied, urging his soldiers forward with a lift of his chin.

The creature handed over its knapsack to one of the soldiers, and the man yanked on the string and the button on top to loosen its hold. Before he raked inside, it interrupted him.

"Can you please at least handle my stuff with care?"

The soldier turned away from the contents of the bag and examined the creature's face, his eyes roaming and flickering with analysis. Veeris attempted to conceal his smile as another soldier perused through his own bag, keeping the scene in his peripheral.

"Are you an Avernos soldier?"

That's what you notice? Veeris thought, dripping in aggravation and observing the rest of the soldiers within the vicinity. Each wore ear piercings to match the Avernos' tradition of enlistment. Veeris noticed that the creature's ears matched theirs, along with a couple other piercings along its brow and nose.

Veeris waited for it to fumble with some half-assed reply, but when it reacted with a swift fabrication, he gawked in stupefied horror.

"Was once, been years now. Started mercenary work and monster hunting ever since I left the vanguard. Though, I gotta say, I miss the brotherhood in arms sometimes," it lied with finesse. It motioned towards the lieutenant to avert the man's attention. "New guy, huh? He treating you well?"

"How'd you know that?" the soldier questioned in bafflement.

"Guess my years in the service gives me a sense for guys like him. You seem like a smart guy. I bet you'd make a fine lieutenant."

The soldier gawked. "You really think so?" he asked, the held bag becoming disregarded in his clear infatuation.

It smiled wider, and Veeris swore he saw sharpened fangs in the brief moment when it reprieved the man of the heavy knapsack. "Oh yeah, I've seen worse men take the knight's vow, and seeing a guy with the vigilance and promise such as yourself, I couldn't think of anyone finer."

As though under current scrutiny, the soldier straightened his back and ushered it forward in approval. "Th-Thank you, sir! Thru-vah!" He saluted unabatedly with the use of Avernos' slogan, thrusting the side of his closed fist against his alternate shoulder.

With a slothful jab at its own chest, the wolf in sheep's clothing mimicked the movement. "Thru-vah, soldier. Keep at it and thank you for keeping Terrisae safe," it replied, venturing past with a reassuring slap on the susceptible man's shoulder.

The mercenaries, otherwise, passed through the garrison with ease. After several minutes of securing their belongings, the group began reloading onto the wagon for their journey south.

"H-how?" Veeris stuttered in bewilderment to the creature. The beast turned, raising a questioning brow as it adjusted the leather strap of its bag. "How did you do that?"

"Do what? Know how the lieutenant was new? Wasn't it obvious?" it asked with a scrunch of its nose, as though smelling something rancid. "The prick's armor was too new and too polished. It reeked with layers of oil. He's going to end up attracting so much residue that it'll compromise the density of the armor. It looks shiny now, but it'll end up tainted and dull after the oil starts accumulating too much dirt. Don't even get me started on the putrid stench of what he called hair—" It halted its explanation, offering Veeris another inquisitive glance. "Could you not smell it?"

Veeris didn't bother replying. Instead, he stomped away, finalizing the readjustments of their things. Even still, he kept an ongoing analysis of the creature and the bag in its clutches.

The monster was hiding something.

FOURTEEN.

At the end of their fourth day of travel, the mercenaries once again conglomerated together to form an encampment. Their destination was the town of Enderbrooke, a farming settlement almost halfway between the capital city of Goldenrise and the border of Exonia Creek. Upon their arrival, they would need to spend time gathering information and details about the incidents within the forest.

Salem exhaled, wiping away her sweat when she finally completed the construction of her tent. Examining her friends, they had already done the same. Veeris fashioned the last adjustments on the tents, Andrid returned with some herbal ingredients, Gilben cooked their meal, and Haven finalized the preparations of the meat.

After Haven disposed of the gall bladder of the boar, he prepped the rest of the editable parts by packing salt into the meat, drawing out moisture and preventing bacteria from accumulating. Afterwards, he dipped the meat in several different brines. Once evenly distributed, Haven sealed the containers with rope and placed them securely in the back of the wagon. Oakley aided the organization, accompanied by incessant yet charming yapping.

"Aw, come on Haven, just one game!" Oakley protested, gathering the larger man's faltering attention by tugging at his arm.

Haven huffed in protest. "No. You cheat in any game we play," he replied, squinting. "And I'll figure out how you're doing it one day."

"Well, how are you planning to do that if you don't play? Come on, just one game. If you win, you can have half my dinner portion, and if I win, then I don't get anything, so you're not losing anything anyway!" Oakley taunted, a devious smirk presiding over where the innocence had once been. If there was one thing Haven couldn't back down from, it was a challenge.

"Fine," the half-orc replied, plopping on one of the makeshift benches constructed from a log.

Oakley sat opposite of him and retrieved a board of checkered patterns. He distributed the scattered pieces on both sides, with symbols of war erected on the battlefield. There was a knight, a castle, a king, a queen, and soldiers lined up in mirrored image. The fire in front of the duo brimmed with anticipation, readying itself for the art of war.

Gilben still cooked their meal, reaching for the pot over the fire and tossing the prepped beef and extra boar fat into the boiling water. After stirring for quite some time to ensure the meat was properly cooked, he pinched a combination of pepper and ginger into the boil. Salem could smell the spices from her position in front of her tent.

Korbyn returned to the camp several minutes later with a stack of firewood in his arms. He lacked his new hood and cape that obscured him in mystery; instead, he wore a black blouse that cuffed from his wrist to his forearms. The baggy shirt was tucked into his slacks, its collar loosely tied by a thread to reveal his collarbones and half of his chest.

His shoulders were broad, and his hips were slim, his torso forming an almost perfect triangular shape of a well-built warrior. When they first met, she hadn't realized just how sturdy he was underneath his armor, as if the world had tried to keep the eyes of the sinful from reaching him. His hair was shorter in the back than most men had it, revealing more of the muscles in his neck. In the front, strands hung over the left side of his forehead and past his cheek, and occasionally he would run his fingers and push it backwards when it bothered him. As he did, he glanced in Salem's direction.

She shifted her gaze, wanting to smack the redness away from her face. These new feelings demanding her attention proved much confusion, but she couldn't deny her unsteady heartbeats every time he looked upon her.

Romantic temptations weren't something she normally experienced. Before she arrived in Terrisae, she couldn't recall previous infatuation. She was always focused on duty and passion but living on this continent changed many things. Butterflies now filled her stomach when their eyes crossed paths, rattling in such unbridled chaos that she had to remind herself to find even breath. She experienced a magical surge between them when they were close, an addicting urge to feel the sparks underneath her fingertips. Would that same spark occur if she kissed him?

She licked away the dryness on her mouth and scolded herself. These continual thoughts were rampant, and despite her best attempts to overlook them, they always resurged with vengeance. She wished to condemn her clear infatuation as she remained fearful of the unknown and the unrevealed darkness that might lay dormant within him. However, for some reason, she couldn't help but feel some unexpected bias. Something about him called out to her, a comfort in presence and conversation that no one else truly provided.

His gaze entranced her like matching pendulums comprised of dual moons. The darkness surrounding his eyes enveloped her, a void entrancement. He was blanketed in a veil of mystery that Salem wished to unravel, just like the strings of his shirt that prevented her from gazing more at his torso. She groaned in annoyance, pressing her fingertips against her closed lids as she contemplated how to gain relief from ongoing stress.

"Hey."

Salem flinched, unaware of the presence looming over her. It was Korbyn, angling his head to the space next to her.

"Can I join you?" Korbyn prompted.

Salem prevented her gaze from trailing over his revealed chest and hoping the blush had receded from her face. "Of course!" She smiled, feigning ignorance. Once he sat beside her, she stared into the fire several paces ahead. "Thanks for getting all of the firewood; it'll make everything a lot easier for the trip."

From the corner of her eye, she saw him nod. "Yeah," Korbyn replied, though she was unsure if he comprehended her appreciation. "I have something to ask you."

Salem turned, their gazes meeting once again. She could stare for hours, wandering in the darkened shades of obsidian. The ivory of his eyes acted as illumination, and she was drawn to its uniqueness.

"Of course," Salem replied. "You can ask me anything."

Korbyn returned his attention to the flickering of the fluid flames that their allies surrounded for warmth. Veeris had reverted towards the flames after he had completed his own bouts of organization. She ignored his watchful leer, focusing on the campfire.

"What made you want to join Kendra Dawn?"

Salem blinked in astonishment, unready for his question. She took a deep breath, pondering deeply at his implication.

"I want to help people," Salem responded, crossing her leg underneath her body to sit more comfortably. "Where I came from, everything was...perfect." She eyed the sky, examining the darkness of the night settling upon the quiet landscape. "There was a war, a long time ago, but we lived in a place where everyone had everything—endless resources, people living like royalty, ornate provisions, exquisite parties, and riches so boundless that it practically had no value, but I was unhappy. My kingdom lives in such prosperity, but it doesn't extend their assistance to others. When I asked my king if we could put forward our privilege to assist those in need, I was denied." She took a deep breath, wishing to settle an inner anger that boiled. "He gave me one condition: if I could find the blades, then my wishes would be reconsidered. Veeris joined me, and we've been here ever since. When I met the Arbiter and learned about her forming a new group of mercenaries that could actively help people, I was so excited. It felt as though I could help people in a way that I couldn't before."

"And what about monster hunting? Do you enjoy it?" Korbyn inquired, adjusting his body to sit sideways on the log. He leaned forward with every question, his elbow resting on his knee.

Salem grinned. "Yes, and I'm good at it, too."

Korbyn smirked in a way that stirred rebellious butterflies. He was mischievous, of that she was certain, and she couldn't discern if he was candor past his foreign eyes.

"Is there anything you're bad at?" he whispered, his voice smoky and hoarse.

With reddened cheeks, Salem angled her face back to the fire, hoping the distance of the light was far enough away to not reveal her features. "I'm terrible at a lot of things," she replied, trying to dissuade these feelings despite her internal need. "Cooking, sewing, anything artistic, really. I also tend to get a little frustrated—"

Korbyn burst into a scoff, and Salem craned her neck. "What?"

"You said a little, implying it was mild." His smirk widened.

Salem's nose and lips scrunched in a scowl. "It's not that bad."

"Are you serious?" When she didn't reply, Korbyn leaned back, a reverberating, deep laugh filling the night sky.

"What?" she asked, shaking her head and laughing in tune. The butterflies stirred, quelling apprehension.

"I'm just surprised you really believe that," Korbyn said, chuckles intermingling with his words. "Cause I'm sure people with *mild anger issues* don't tell kings to go fuck themselves."

A blush rose to her cheeks at the profanity, and she called her arms to defend her as she crossed them over her chest.

"I think I reacted appropriately. He's an ass." The curse sounded foreign on her lips.

Korbyn laughed again, shaking his head. "I'm surprised you got away with it."

"I've argued with a greater king than him."

They both smiled, analyzing the features in each other's faces. When a silence crept in, Salem observed the dancing flames.

"Is there anything you like to do besides monster hunting?" Korbyn asked.

Salem made a verbal noise that initiated a moment to ponder.

No one had really asked her that. Ever since she arrived here, she had made a name for herself. Elohim's Chosen, Paladin of the Dawn, the holy warrior whose magic could split the Heavens and many other titles, but not once had anyone asked her what she liked to do in her free time, and only one thing came to mind.

"You'll make fun of me," Salem mumbled.

"I won't."

"Promise?"

"I promise to try," Korbyn said with a smile, resting his hand on the log. Their pinkies touched, and a spark formed from their contacted skin. Instead of focusing on the lack of distance he put between them, she answered his question.

"Feathers."

"Feathers?"

"I collect feathers," Salem elaborated nervously.

"Are you going to learn how to fly?" He grinned.

Her eyebrows furrowed again as she shoved him off the log. She always forgot how strong she was, and Korbyn tumbled off the seat. "I told you not to make fun of me!"

He laughed, wrapping his arm around his stomach to stifle his mirth, but her irritation seemed to only fuel it. "Okay, okay. I'm sorry. I'm only teasing. Why feathers?"

Korbyn returned to the log, pressing his side against hers, leaving no space betwixt them. She wasn't sure if it was intentional or not.

Even though their clothes prevented their skin from touching, the spark coursed. It was as if there was friction, the clothes glued together like opposite charges. Salem leaned into him more, unable to deny the excitement and comfort that she felt from being so close to him. For a moment, she swore he genuinely experienced a similar infatuation.

"Feathers have different meanings based on their colors. There are spiritual implications when you find a lone feather out in nature. Many people believe it's the world gifting you with a divination." Their pinkies caressed each other, and she tried to smother her loudening heartbeat. "For example, yellow feathers represent happiness and new beginnings, while orange feathers can indicate someone needs to trust their intuition."

Korbyn gave her his full attention, nodding at her explanation. "And what colors have you found?"

Excitement and astonishment tangled for dominance, and she stood to withdraw to her tent. She retrieved a foot-long box that held her feathers and sat back down beside him just as close as they had before. When she opened it, Korbyn leaned, his shoulder resting against hers as he peeked within.

Inside the box were several different shades of feathers, varying from whites, grays, browns, greens, and a single red one. In total, there were about eighteen, all neatly and carefully arranged in a jewelry box with a makeshift compartment. "When I arrived in Terrisae, the first feather I found was this brown one," Salem exclaimed, holding it aloft to inspect its every angle. It was a beautiful russet with hues of orange mixed within. "Brown signifies stability, protection, and foundation. I think it came from a brown thrasher."

Korbyn smiled. "Beautiful," he whispered.

When Salem noticed his gaze, he peered back down to the box and pointed towards the single, crimson feather. "What about that one?"

Salem exchanged feathers, raising the red one straight into the air and spinning it between her fingers. For some reason, it was a calming addiction. "This is from a cardinal. Red feathers symbolize strength and courage."

"And those?" Korbyn prompted, pointing to a collection of white feathers. There were at least ten in the assortment, all carefully placed on top of each other.

Salem held one in between two fingers, spinning the flawless spine. The feeling was serene and familiar. "These are my favorite. The white feather represents wisdom, truth, and remembrance," she replied, inspecting it one last time before placing it back into the box. "Do you know why I named you Korbyn?"

"No. I just figured it was random. Is there a special meaning?"

"The night before we found you on the battlefield, I had a dream I was in a different world. Thinking back, I can't remember what the world looked like, but I think it was red. It was raining so hard that it was practically hail. It was so thick that I couldn't see in either direction. It was so loud that I couldn't hear anything at all. At some point, the water transitioned into cascading feathers. It was unlike anything I had ever seen before. They were black feathers that were so dark that they didn't reflect any light. I felt safe, for some reason, as if I was being called there." Salem beamed. "Black feathers in particular mean protection and transformation."

One of Korbyn's eyebrows rose. "So, what does that have to do with naming me Korbyn?"

"Korbyn means black bird, like a crow. Crows represent wisdom, transformation, and safety. You're going to go through a lot of change and learn a lot about yourself." She leaned into him, their faces only a few inches away from each other. "When I was taking care of you while you were unconscious, for some reason, I felt as though you were the one watching over me."

Korbyn laughed again, the addicting noise filling her ears. She wanted to learn his humor, to figure out all the different ways that she could hear that musical sound whenever she pleased. A comfortable silence ensued, and they both stared into each other's eyes, and for the first time in her entire life, Salem forgot the rest of the world existed.

"Dinner's ready!" Gilben shouted in their direction.

Korbyn stood, extending his open palm to her. She accepted his offer, and he pulled her upwards with a tug. Their torsos made contact from his yank, and Salem flushed when Korbyn did not immediately withdraw from her touch.

"I don't know if I was capable of looking after you while I was unconscious," Korbyn murmured with what she assumed was blatant honesty, one fine line of his mouth curling upwards into a handsome grin. "But I will be from now on."

Korbyn pivoted, striding over to the group as Gilben handed out bowls of food. Oakley peered in Salem's direction, whispering something she couldn't hear. Clearly annoyed, Korbyn elbowed him, coercing Oakley to unfurl a wave of laughter as they exchanged banter between each other. She couldn't help but grin at the exchange.

"As will I," Salem whispered with a smile.

FIFTEEN.

"What do you mean, you don't know about any attacks?" Korbyn asked, lingering in irritation. He didn't possess any memories prior to his awakening, but he was certain this was the most frustrating conversation he had ever had in his life.

They had reached Enderbrooke early the next afternoon. When they arrived in this sizable town, with widespread farms, vineyards and barns spanning miles, Shadowbane Forest still didn't meet their gaze. From his observations of the map, it was less than a day's travel, but not close enough to perceive from this distance, and definitely not close enough to deem a constant concern to the nearby town. If what Salem said was true about the monsters within the forest not leaving its borders due to the attraction they held for the darkness, then Korbyn found it unlikely there would be any threat at all.

The voice, with continual urgency, prevented his internal solitude. It proved exacerbating when he yearned for silence, its presence riling immediate stifling. However, there was no escape from its persistent bouts and interjections. Korbyn just wished, for a moment, he was left alone in the confines of his own mind.

Under lock and chain, you wish to silence their voices, but their vacant stares will become unwelcome reminders.

Up until now, Korbyn had done his best to ignore the voice, the intrusive thoughts that he hid behind a closed door daring to break free, but with every passing day, the voice grew louder and more irritable. Even now, Korbyn fought against the trembling of his left hand and the severe itch that spread across his forearm. The mark rallied in defiance, as if wanting to be used, and the voice demanding to be heard.

Release your fears and become whole.

Korbyn exhaled deeply and returned to the conversation with the older man. To his dismay, when they questioned the farmers on the outskirts of the far side of the town, most of them seemed to be completely oblivious, which proved fruitless and presented the mercenaries as utterly foolish.

"I'm tellin' ya, I got no idea what yer talkin' about!" the older man said, ambiguous to their prodding and interrogation. He placed a hand on his hip and pointed to the edge of Enderbrooke, which happened to be his vineyard. "Ain't nothin' been botherin' our town, as fer as I know!"

Ignorance is evil's best friend.

Peeking at the condition of the old man's farms, the lands were thriving in perfect serenity. Even from their proximity to the border, the countryside was untouched by war due to the stalwart barrier that was Avernos' army. The crops were prolific, the fences untouched, the barnyard of animals grazed the grasslands, and the vineyards bloomed with black and green grapes. Despite the old man's crazed personality, he appeared accurate and truthful. The farms and town remained intact and void of wild attacks, which annoyed Korbyn further, as they beheld no answers to their lingering questions.

Korbyn could perceive Salem's mirrored irritation. She tried to dig under her nail beds, some type of formulated habit prevented by her gloves. Often, he could see her attention wandering by her drifting gaze, as though conceiving different possibilities in spite of their lack of findings.

"You're absolutely certain you haven't seen anything suspicious around here?" Salem asked.

The farmer hummed, pursing his lips and rubbing his chin. After several seconds of silence, and a deadpan expression from each of the mercenaries, he finally spoke up. "You mean besides my Aunt Claudia stealin' a basket of my finest blackberries every Tuesday before the sunrises?"

The mercenaries didn't answer him.

"Well, now that ya mention' it, I did think I saw somethin' strange." He waited for their response, but he was met with exasperated silence.

Korbyn rolled his eyes. If not for the older man's infatuation for heeding to his own cadence, he might have noticed their aggravated huffs. At first, Korbyn suspected little to no pertinence during his next ramble, but he was genuinely surprised when it seemed applicable.

"There's been some reoccurin' happenins in the past half year. Few weeks ago, soldiers barreled through here, then start headin' east, but ain't nothin' that way 'xcept the forest, that is. And the Eastern Expanse after that, but there ain't no reason for them to go that far cause there ain't no roads or nothin', 'nd I heard that's a week's travel 'nd empty waters. The forest would be the only thin' makin' any sense."

Korbyn and Salem glanced at each other curiously before returning to the man.

"And did they specify where they were going?" Salem inquired. She held a board and parchment, marking notes with a small piece of used charcoal. Even her handwriting was beautiful.

The man shrugged. "Nope! Not other than just checkin' in 'nd makin' sure we're safe from monsters...but old man Wilkin's got a keen eye for liars, ya hear? They ain't carin' for us little folk. I bet I know 'xactly what they're doin!" he declared, brows dancing with suggestions of profound knowledge.

Salem seemed ignorant to his crazed remarks. "What do you think it is?"

Wilkin drew in a whispered breath "I bet..." he muttered, leaving them in a moment of silence. "I bet—"

"What lies you feedin' them nice folk, Wilkin?" a stout lady shouted, walking past with a deep scowl and a basket of berries placed on one hip and a toddler on the other. "Don't waste their time. I'm sure they got more importan' things they could be doin'."

Wilkin huffed, turning towards the woman and throwing his arms above his head. "I ain't feedin' nobody nothin'!"

"That's the only truth you been spoutin'," the woman declared, rolling her eyes.

Korbyn coughed, acting as if he hadn't heard the argument. The older man turned back, a matching scowl on his own face.

"You were saying?" Salem prodded, practically on the edge of a precipice.

Wilkin nodded, resuming their conversation. "Ah! Of course, as I was sayin', them soldiers got foul intentions, ya hear? There's only one thing they could be doin' out east, where no one else dares ta go from the threats of the wilds..." Wilkin regarded Salem with an eerie gaze, one with such intensity that everyone's breath stifled in expectation. "Those soldiers..." The older man took another deep breath. "They're havin' orgies!"

Korbyn, Veeris, and Haven slapped their foreheads in brisk harmony. Comparatively, Oakley, Andrid, and Gilben stifled a laugh.

Salem, however, nodded. "I see. And, good sir, what exactly

are orgies?" she questioned further, readying to write down her findings in thorough detail.

"Alright, we're done here," Korbyn interrupted, grabbing her wrist to prevent further note taking. He pried her from the man's proximity and led her away with a hand at her lower back. "Thanks, I guess, old man."

"The war ain't real, ya'll hearin' me? Don't let them crazy theories deter you! Leaders want ya to believe just about anythin'!"

The woman smacked the back of the crazed man's head, followed by a dispute that decreased in volume the farther the mercenaries ventured east.

They gathered towards the outskirts of the town and returned to their caravan. Salem stopped and whirled towards the group, mirroring them with her own thoughtful and inquisitive expression.

"We should have questioned him further. That knowledge could have pertained to our contract," Salem said with a frown.

"It didn't, Salem. Just let it go," Veeris grumbled.

When Salem frowned, Andrid offered her several reassuring pats on the shoulder. "Say, maybe no ask," Andrid suggested. "Or maybe ask Korbi," they said with a mischievous grin and a wink.

Salem glimpsed at Korbyn, as if expecting an explanation. Oakley, at Andrid's side, slapped a hand over his mouth, failing to withhold his amusement.

"Korbyn?" Salem asked before examining the chuckling duo, who leaned against each other in a heap of conjoined laughter.

"I said leave it, Salem," Veeris repeated, glaring at Andrid and Oakley.

They both coughed, whistling and changing their attentions as if captivated by something else, though nothing in this wide expanse existed but open plains. Korbyn shifted awkwardly when Veeris' glare transferred to him. He also looked away, blushing and scratching his neck in discomfort. Salem huffed and retrieved a letter with a broken seal, unfolding the parchment until its contents were revealed.

"The statements of the farmers don't seem to match up with Avernos' request at all, and we don't even know if anything that the man said was true," Salem said, analyzing the parchment. From sheer curiosity, Korbyn shimmied over to read it.

KENDRA DAWN,

I formally ask your assistance on behalf of the town of Enderbrooke. There have been reports of creatures and monsters wandering out of Shadowbane Forest and attacking the nearby town. Several accounts have noted a large ogre roaming the plains and killing farm animals.
At this time, no one has been injured, but I humbly request your aid in stopping further destruction before there are any casualties.

My greatest thanks,
EMPEROR WYMOND

The official seal of the Avernos Empire nudged Korbyn with familiarity, to his quick disregard.

"Well, I suppose the only thing we can do is go find this alleged creature that may or may not exist," Salem stated before rolling up the letter and returning it to her bag.

"I find, I hunt for clues, mhm mhm," Andrid stated, walking ahead of the group and past the wagon, in search of tracks. The fox followed them, sniffing the dirt in search of information.

"Maybe the emperor got some bad info," Oakley said, striding over to the back of the caravan and hoisting himself up. "Sounds like there isn't anything to fight at all."

"We shouldn't take 'ny chances," Gilben stated, rolling his shoulders back to presume a hardier stance. Due to his armor and bulky blade, he resembled a male of greater height. "Whether or not we find this strange ogre, I'm sure we'll be runnin' into different monsters in the forest; we should be ready for anythin'."

Haven nodded in agreement. "I doubt the emperor will want us to come back empty-handed. I say we enter the forest and figure out what information we can find," the half-orc urged, walking around the vehicle and offering the horse a comforting pat.

"I agree. Let's get going," Salem stated, escorting Haven.

As Korbyn ventured to follow, a voice called out to him.

"Stay behind."

When most of the others walked past, Korbyn wheeled around in confusion. Standing with a glorified posture and an angered mien to match was Veeris.

At first, Korbyn wasn't aware of the elf's reference. He searched behind him, realizing the rest of the party had already resumed their venture forward. Veeris never acknowledged his existence other than the intermittent, caustic glares. When Korbyn returned the gaze, the elf's attitude hadn't faltered.

"What?"

"I said stay behind. You're inexperienced, and you'll get in our way," Veeris sneered.

Korbyn grimaced. "I'll be fine," he stated, initiating a stride towards the caravan.

Veeris stalked up to Korbyn and grabbed his left forearm, halting his further attempts. Korbyn flinched and snatched his arm away. The elf seemed unaware of his reaction.

"I'm not worried about you. I'm concerned with the safety of everyone else," Veeris explained. The elf closed the distance between them, murmuring his next words, but not lacking in verbal poison. "You're going to fall behind, or get injured, and someone is going to try to help you and get hurt in the process, or worse.

The best possible outcome of this scenario would be a repetition of history, to which you grow too fearful at the slightest sign of danger and turn tail." Veeris surveyed his slack posture, a menacing glare ushered from unknown hatred. "Isn't that right, deserter of the front lines?"

Korbyn scoffed, curling his fingers into fists at his side. He stood taller than the elf and angled his head to presume an elevated height. "You know nothing," Korbyn spat, challenging the male with a deepened scowl. "I may not have memories, but I had legitimate combat experience on the battlefield."

Veeris scoffed, clearly unimpressed. "Oh yes, thank you for the reminder. I forgot that we found you on the verge of death. What a great warrior you must have been."

He is a creature bound to bark instead of bite. How loud can a dog howl if it has no tongue? the voice sneered.

"You've been glaring at me since the moment I got here. What the fuck is your deal?" Korbyn hissed with the rest of the party still unaware of their current conversation.

The elf refused to submit, raising his chin to increase his own height.

He is attempting to discover your secrets. Can a snake smell if it has no tongue? the voice continued.

"I'll shrink my vocabulary to your educational level so that you understand. My *deal* is that you're a bad omen, a poison that slithered its way into my group with no merit or reason. Your ambitions to join this faction are selfish and unmindful to the actual cause that Kendra Dawn plays in the backing of the people. You're either lying about your memory loss so that you can feign ignorance, or you're just stupid enough to join a group of whose priorities you don't truly understand, and if you think for even a second that you're a respectable individual, then why don't you explain what in the Hells is in your bag?"

Korbyn's jaw slackened in fright.

This one slithers too close to the creature's jaws. Rip the snake's tongue from its throat.

"Th-that's none of your business—" Korbyn stammered.

"Is it now?" Veeris' confidence grew at his fumble. "It's not our business that whatever you conceal in that bag is so secretive that you're fearful of someone finding it?"

Kill him. Kill him, kill him—

"Guys? Are you coming?" Oakley urged.

Korbyn and Veeris both turned. The rest of the group currently observed them with analytical eyes. Luckily, they seemed oblivious to the purpose of the conversation.

Before they approached, Korbyn cast his eyes back on Veeris. "You don't know what—"

"There are two different outcomes to this story, and you're going to listen to both very carefully," Veeris said, lowering his voice. "You're either going to take your secrets and leave Kendra Dawn without a second glance"—Korbyn's eyes trailed over to Salem, who initiated her approach—"and *stop* staring at Salem, or"—he regained Korbyn's attention—"you speak freely about your ill intentions and let the rest of the group decide your fate. And if you decide to choose neither, then I will deal with you *personally*."

Before Korbyn could respond, Veeris slammed his shoulder into his own. As the group returned, the elf stomped past them and ventured towards the back of the wagon. The group gaped betwixt both participants.

"What happened?" Salem asked, scanning Korbyn before watching Veeris' departing back.

"Grumpy is as grumpy does," Andrid stated, plopping a berry into their mouth and returning to their surveying.

"I'm sure everythin's fine, lass," Gilben urged with a smile, motioning her forward. "We shou'd keep goin' for now, aye?"

Salem gazed at Korbyn with a frown and furrowed brows.

"It's nothing," Korbyn said.

Most of the mercs concurred with equal puzzlement before preparing their departure and loading into the back of the wagon.

The fox remained behind as Korbyn stood in uncertainty. Curiosity and knowledge flickered in trails of light in the creature's eyes, and Korbyn was unsure of the words it wanted to say.

"Ya alright, lad?" Gilben suddenly asked from his side.

"Oh, yeah, thanks," Korbyn replied, stuffing his hands inside his pockets, a habit formed from the pest on the inside of his forearm. An itch always lingered, and he forcibly refrained from soothing the constant irritation. Instead, he rubbed his thumbs over the rest of his fingers within the fabric of his pockets, a laughable effort at withholding warmth due to the inevitable chill.

"I wouldn't worry too much about 'im," Gilben stated, his eyes squinting from his wide smile, though hidden underneath layers of coarse hair. "Veeris means good. Sometimes he's justa bit untrustin'." The dwarf motioned towards Salem and Veeris, who appeared to be deep in whispered conversation. "They've known each other the longest, more than any of us have. They don't always agree on thin's, but he cares deeply for 'er. I imagine he's not taken yer friendship with 'er too well."

That was when Korbyn realized it: the way Veeris regarded her, a look foreign to his natural features: eyes gentle, glistening with admiration and longing, stern and serious and passionate and desperate. Veeris had feelings for her.

Korbyn proved to be nothing but a nuisance, hindering a relationship with his own selfish intent. Though not fully aware if a spark between them existed, and even though Veeris has been nothing but discourteous since his arrival, Korbyn wished not to be at fault for egregious influence. If Salem had feelings for Veeris, then he should provide distance.

Korbyn sighed, sulking in deep and utter despondence. Salem was too good for him anyway.

"I think I understand what you mean. Thanks, Gilben," Korbyn replied, approaching the caravan.

He avoided Salem's inquisitive glance, focusing his attention on the western horizon. As the horse trotted forward with the mercenaries in tow, Korbyn watched the town shrink. For the first time since its unwelcome greeting, the voice exhaled a long, airy breath that strangely mimicked a sigh, and, for some abnormal reason, sounding just disappointed as he.

Cursed by the lands they were destined to protect; the sun and moon were sworn to never unite.

As Korbyn shifted to lean back on his palms, something poked his hand. When he glanced down, an ominous black feather protruded between his fingers, threatening to fly away from the horse's stern trot and the unstable saunter of the wagon's hurried following.

He picked it up and twirled it, its barbs flicking in alternate directions from the force of his movements. He surveyed every inch of its tattered form, feeling a connection to the lone quill's state of oblivion.

Crow or raven? Blessed or cursed? Good or evil?

Korbyn deposited the feather in the confines of his bag, readying himself to witness the shadows of billowing branches.

SIXTEEN.

"Are you going to explain what that was about?" Salem whispered, positioning herself next to Veeris to halt any avoidance of conversation he might attempt.

Instead of meeting eyes with hers, his attention moved to the window of the caravan, glancing south to the open plains as the vehicle trotted forward. "He's trouble, Salem, yet for some reason, you choose to avoid the situation," Veeris sneered. "I told you I would be keeping a close eye on him. His betrayal is inevitable."

"Yes, I remember you stating that, yet you still haven't told me what your argument was about," Salem retorted in a low whisper.

"If he lives after this mission, then you can ask him yourself," Veeris mumbled.

"Before we left Fort Silvercrest, you said that you left everything behind because you believed in me and my cause, which is to help people, help *everyone* in need," the paladin whispered. "I'm aware that Korbyn is different. Something is wrong, and you and I are the best people to help him. Can't you see that?"

Thankfully, the others filled the small wagon with loud conversation, concealing their discussion within the mass.

Veeris' eyebrows furrowed. "I want to help people who deserve to be helped, but he knows more than you give him credit for. I won't sacrifice our entire mission for one person."

"What about me?"

Veeris' gaze flicked to Salem. His eyes shifted to one of her eyes, and then the other, as if either would offer different explanations. "What?"

"What if it was me?" Salem asked. "What if you had to choose between our cause or me? Which one would you choose?"

Veeris failed to provide an answer, shutting his agape mouth.

"Here's the thing, Veeris. When it comes to doing the right thing, you can't pick and choose who's worthy. To save people, we must help everyone, not just those who you think are commendable and those who are not. That's exactly why I left home in the first place, because our king made those subjective decisions."

Veeris turned his torso away from her completely, forcibly halting further conversation. "Then maybe He was onto something after all."

Salem sat in smoldering anger and astonishment.

"Salem?" Oakley interjected, waving her over to the far corner of the caravan. Before he witnessed her frown, Salem replaced it with a smile and slid next to the smaller male. "Everything okay? Did Veeris say something rude? Do I need to beat him up? I know he's taller than me, but I think I could take him cause he's scrawny. Oh! I know, how about you hold him down, and then I'll wrap my arms around him and put him in a chokehold, and then—"

"It's okay, Oakley, really," Salem replied, a genuine chuckle passing her lips. "He's just in a bad mood. It'll pass. I appreciate you though." She affectionately ruffled his hair, and he grinned widely.

"M'kay, well, let me know if you change your mind. I'm always here for you." Salem doubted Oakley knew how charismatic he was.

"I know. Thank you," she said, leaning against the side wall of the vehicle. "How'd you get to be such a good guy, Oakley?"

For a moment, the paladin swore she recognized a flicker within iridescent silver, his pools gleaming with a saddened emotion. However, she battled the conflict as the display vanished just as quickly as it occurred, for a wide smile deterred her.

"Guess I'm just born with such boundless charm," Oakley remarked. "Don't worry, Sale, if you ever need any advice, just let me know. Heroes like me tend to attract the masses," he jested with a wink.

Salem chuckled and observed Korbyn, who sat alone at the wagon's edge.

"Maybe I'll take you up on that offer someday," she thought aloud.

Even though a silence resided within the group, there was a whispering in these woods. Darkness concealed Shadowbane Forest like a cloak, a mask of mystery dawning on a span of hundreds of miles. It slithered in the deepest parts of the trees, concealed within bushes and foliage like a predator, waiting for its prey to wander between its jaws. Life and greenery didn't inhabit this forest; instead, hues of gray and darkened hickory surrounded the woodland like a crowd of watchful onlookers, hovering over any travelers who dared to enter its depths. Instead of customary-looking trees, these strangler figs were enveloped in layers of bark that swirled around the entirety of its trunk, as if it had been choking itself.

There were no critters, no animals, no bugs, or any type of wildlife, only the harmonized hum that welcomed its guests with a malicious whine. The mists whispered like two-faced friends, mummering secrets that remained unheard by the topics of their conversations. When Salem tried to focus on the words, they hushed, as though worried she would hear them. The silence was daunting, and her ears rang with loud bells of defiance when the forest had quieted too much. When she focused on the darkness, shadows pranced away from her sight, and she wasn't sure if it was a trick of the eye or if the darkness itself endeavored to don masks like traitors amongst a group of trusting allies.

"You guys hearing that?" Oakley warned, fearful or just courageous enough to penetrate the eerie reverbs encircling them.

"Keep close to me," Salem urged, a holy light surrounding the cluster. The mist of darkness recoiled around the sphere of divine magic, its hum twisting into low screeches, sounding like they were struck with pain. The swirls of haze and darkened shadows resembled fingers lacking bones, trying to grasp at their ankles as they treaded deeper into the depths of the living gloom, but were inevitably pushed away by Salem's illumination.

The gloom had grown even denser since Salem and Veeris' last expedition, and she swore she sensed prying eyes observing their movements. Even at the forest's edge, the darkness of the woods weighed on their bodies like a thick quilt. However, instead of providing a pleasant warmth, the murk traced their skin with sharpened nails and whisps of cold air. Whatever was rising in Terrisae, it was getting worse.

"Elohim, protect us," Salem whispered.

The sky was hidden by a ceiling so thick with branches and leaves that it even prevented the watchful gaze of the sun. No matter what time of day it had been, the area within the trees convened in a permanent dusk that cascaded its entirety into pitch darkness. Here, time was an enigma, and anyone who dared to journey through these lands became a part of its paradox.

Salem glided her eyes over her party as they ventured deeper into the forest. Andrid was usually calm in nature when surrounded by greenery, but this place was unnatural. They tiptoed cautiously, navigating their path while avoiding any branches or leaves that might have cracked underneath them. They rummaged through the dirt, searching for any tracks or signs of life. They found none, continuing to lead the others deeper into the welcoming depths.

Haven stood close behind Andrid, occasionally pressing his hand against the small curve on their lower back. Salem could tell he was striving to be courageous for them both, his fingers curling tightly on the hilt of his great axe.

Gilben was usually the one to provide words of encouragement when even Salem found herself lacking in confidence. Sweat trickled down his brow and into his brunette beard, and he gripped his broadsword tightly within his just as broad hands.

Oakley seemed the most anxious of them all as he gingerly stepped forward, maintaining his position in the middle of the group. His neck twisted and turned after every step, as if searching vehemently for a listening predator. Usually, Oakley reveled in the shadows, but at this specific moment, he seemed to be fearful of it.

Veeris hovered next to Salem, his body meandering in trepidation and occasionally bumping into her. Though most would have been dubious to his physical prodding, it was probably purposeful as if he sought constant reassurance of her presence. A stoic expression covered his face, but Salem recognized the feigned confidence for the mask that it was.

Then, there was Korbyn, the most unfazed of them all.

Salem was skeptical of how he would react in a place such as this, but he strode with boundless confidence. As he ventured further, walking in the back of the group and peering into the blackness, she swore his eyes pierced through the mist, penetrating the walls of the forest and seeing much clearer than the rest of them could. Instead of reaching for his ankles, the tendrils of shadows shifted around him, welcoming him like a carpet of scarlet unfolding with every step he took.

Andrid stopped, sniffing with their strange, increased perception.

"What is it?" Haven asked, leveling his great axe.

Andrid pointed forward through the bleakness of shadow, referring to something that Salem couldn't see. "Something dead," they whispered.

"Show me," Salem responded, holding her longsword in one hand and raising her shield in the other. She followed Andrid into the pit of darkness, pushing back branches that coiled and wrapped around each other, like walls to prohibit onlookers from the view on the other side. Lying in the dirt, wrapped in roots and branches resembling a burial shroud made of silk, was a deceased soldier.

Oakley jolted back. "What in Elohim's name?"

"What's a soldier doing here?" Salem wondered, walking up to stand over the body.

The man was unnaturally draped in vines, as if the forest had been pulling him underground to conceal his body...or absorb him completely.

"Crivens," Gilben stated, lowering himself to the soldier and analyzing his wounds. "He's got a large laceration in 'is torso, which was definitely the cause o' death, but he's lookin' as if he were drained." The dwarf pointed to the indentation in the man's torso, trailing his finger over the entirety of the oval-shaped wound where his chest caved inward. The armor crushed the soldier's sternum and ruptured the organs underneath. His armor and clothes were so disheveled and wrapped so tightly in vines that Salem couldn't even properly see the emblem of his kingdom.

Underneath, his skin shriveled up and tightened across his broken bones, ostensibly drained of his blood and organs. "Bludgeonin' trauma. Whatever hit 'im killed 'im instantly. Don't know what's got 'im all fankled, though."

Salem nodded, kneeling beside the body and sheathing her weapons securely on her back. The soldier's eyes were still widened in fear despite missing one of them, with vines curling around his throat and protruding from his mouth and eye socket. She carefully peeled away at some of the vines covering the laceration. The plants clutched the body tightly. Salem pulled against it, wrestling with its hold. Freeing the man from his restraints, she analyzed his armor. Though she didn't need to verify his origins due to her suspicion and his pair of earrings, she verified it by his surcoat—the coat of arms was a sword and shield.

"He's a soldier from the Avernos Empire," Salem remarked, dropping her hands away from his body.

"There's more of them," Haven stated. Andrid nodded in response as they pulled back another veil of hanging vines.

On the other side were piles of Avernos soldiers, bodies stacked on top of each other and interlaced in so many layers of vines that they looked fabricated to form a mound of the deceased.

"Okay, so I understand that the whole bodies-being-wrapped-up-in-strange-and-spooky-vines thing is weird, but why is it strange that they're Avernos soldiers? We're in Avernos, and that crazy old guy verified they headed this way," Oakley commented.

"In Emperor Wymond's letter, he noted that no one had been injured yet, and we were dealing with the issue as a precaution. He never mentioned he had sent the soldiers to deal with the problem before us," Salem replied, keeping her eyes on the soldier in front of her, as if his mouth would open to reveal the answers to all the questions she had. For some reason, she felt as though she could hear his stifled cry, even though death had already claimed his life.

"Well, maybe he sent his soldiers to deal with them, and when they failed, he requested our aid?" Oakley asked, crossing his arms over his chest. His lip protruded upward, a thoughtful and questionable countenance spreading across his dark-skinned face.

"But why would he lie about that? Something feels off. I think if he wasn't hiding something, he would have informed us that he lost a troop of soldiers," Salem pointed out. "On top everything else, the town stated they hadn't seen any creatures leaving the forest."

"But these soldiers definitely go' attacked by the same thin'," Gilben interjected, pointing towards all their bodies. Each had some type of large laceration, seemingly killed by a massive, blunt object. Some of their skulls caved in, others their legs crushed, and some, like the man in front of her, had been struck in the chest. "I'm startin' ta believe there is an ogre. These wounds wou'da resembled a big weapon one wou'd carry."

"But if the farmers aren't getting attacked, then why would the emperor want the ogre dead?" Oakley muttered the question everyone was wondering. Unfortunately, Salem also lacked an answer.

"Salem!" Korbyn yelled.

She turned too late.

One of the vines slithered up her leg. It yanked her down to the forest floor, and she crashed into the dirt. Before she could even breathe out a yelp of surprise, Salem was hauled past a barrier of vines.

Her friends faded from her view as she was drug deeper into the forest.

SEVENTEEN.

"Salem!" Korbyn bellowed as she disappeared behind the mists.

Before he could pursue her, cries of agony erupted behind him. When he turned, his allies plummeted to their hands and knees, strained with shallow breaths. Coils of darkness shifted around them like creatures guided by hunger. Korbyn vacillated betwixt Salem's retreating light and his tentative comrades.

"Shit," Korbyn muttered, scuttling to Haven. "What's wrong?"

"My energy," the half-orc whispered, panting with uneven breaths. "It's like my energy's depleting."

Korbyn fixated upon Haven's lowered form. A spark of white rallied within the male's chest only to plunge downwards, a stifled flame from precarious absorption. It traveled down his body to the soles of his feet, permeating the soil and spreading through-out the land like fertilizer.

Observing the rest of the party, they were having similar ex-periences. He watched their colorless essence swirl in defiance, only to seep out of their forms like pitchers of pouring water. The well of their energy dimmed, absorbed by the trees and empowering the looming darkness—but not his.

Multiple sources of light may coincide, but shadows intertwine.

"The forest is feeding off of your energy!" Korbyn shouted to them, rising to stand and hauling Haven to his feet. "You all have to get out of here—*now*."

Veeris appeared as though he wished to oppose Korbyn's command. He rose on quivering legs, just to stumble forward in an uncoordinated gait. However, Korbyn did not await his interjection. Instead, he sprinted into the woodland, chasing after Salem.

"Salem!" Korbyn yelled, pursuing the trail of her dragged form. He volleyed past branches and shrubbery, neglecting any potential dangers awaiting on the other side. His hood had dropped to his shoulders long ago, but he disregarded the usual safety it provided. He had no need for it now, for he could see in perfect clarity in the forest's umbra.

Korbyn hastened up a hill with strained impetus. His calves retaliated in enervation as he scaled the slope's vertical altitude, and he stooped forward to scramble on all fours from his wavering ascension. With an exasperated groan, he reached the hill's peak, not even pausing for a breath. He clambered past another set of trees when the trail continued, disregarding the swipes of the branches as they cut through his linen. To his dismay, when he encroached on a glade, the trail vanished.

"Salem!" Korbyn shouted with a craned neck.

"Korbyn!" Salem answered.

Korbyn scanned above. Salem was suspended in a heap of vines that swarmed her body like an enveloping cocoon. She wriggled and extended her bound hands towards the longsword clasped on her back, but the vines engrossed her arms at unnatural angles.

"Hold on!" Korbyn commanded, following the vine that held her captive. It wrapped around a large trunk taller than that of six stacked men. If Salem were to fall, there was no doubt she would be heavily injured, at best circumstance.

What happens when the light flickers out? the voice cooed.

Korbyn scaled the tree. With decreasing momentum, he withdrew his blade and stabbed the bark. Upon securing his foot against the weaving vines around the tree's abnormal exterior, he ascended the strangler fig with exigency. When he reached the tree's bough, Korbyn tracked the gyrating vine that held her aloft. He lowered his form to a crawl, carefully approaching Salem.

"Do you trust me?" Korbyn questioned.

After several, stilled seconds, Korbyn watched her pupils dilate, never breaking contact with his despite her inverted stature, and Salem answered with what he believed was utmost surety.

"Yes."

Korbyn severed the vine.

To prevent the paladin's descension, Korbyn counteracted her weight by throwing himself off the bough and lunging in a downward plunge. Even with her hulking armor, the momentum of his fall carried her body upward. As he soared, the wind scudded and breached his ears, mimicking sharp howls of a battle cry. He reached the ground and fumbled with an erratic landing before anchoring his heels into the dirt. He supported his grip with coils of vines and bent knees, and he braced himself with defined strength and mental fortitude. He lowered her as carefully as he could manage and diminished the distance between Salem and her safety.

About two-thirds of the way down, the encroaching vines tugged against the tree's thick branch. The vines strained under

Salem's armor, threatening to tear with every shift of her dangling form.

"Korbyn..." Salem urged in a growing panic, though he was already made aware of his shrinking duration.

He retracted the vine upward in balanced coordination, ensuring the stability of the rope while enhancing his own speed. Still, the vine's delicate threads uncurled with each movement.

"Korbyn!"

Post haste, the vine shriveled up like a dying spider, releasing Salem from her constraints to send her plummeting to the forest floor. Korbyn dove.

Instead of smashing into the earth, Korbyn absorbed the brunt of her descent, both of their forms clashing in conflicting momentums. He stumbled forward with Salem in arms, tripping over overlapping roots and sending them both careening down the hill. They clutched onto one another as they tumbled. Her armor smacked harshly against him, though he enclosed her body with his own to guard her from potential acuate rocks with every vigorous clout.

The eons of tumbling down the incline eventually led them to the forest floor, collapsing at the foothill with grunts of discomfort. Still, they rolled, toppling like weeds until the momentum of their falls eventually decelerated. When the chaos halted, they sprawled out across the dirt in heavy breaths, half of Salem's body resting on Korbyn in intertwining limbs.

They lingered in ongoing silence and remained entangled in one another, except for their heated breaths. For some reason, the makeshift night sky authorized dormancy. Shadows and slithering darkness offered them seclusion, and Korbyn and Salem stared up at the entanglement of vines and branches above where stars should have been. With the stillness of the forest watching the duo carefully from afar, Korbyn selfishly adhered to the moment of respite. Even after his breaths stilled and his adrenaline slowed, he allowed the silence to entangle them just as the vines had desperately wanted to only seconds before.

"How was it for you?" Korbyn asked cheekily.

Salem glanced upwards with furrowed brows. The sexual innuendo seemed to bypass any form of comprehension, and he chuckled at her charming naiveté.

When recognition finally crossed her features, she analyzed their provocative position with a flush. Despite her embarrassment, she couldn't stifle the giggle that erupted. It was so contagious that he joined her in his own fit of chuckles, and they laughed in harmony. It was a chorus of music so beautifully intertwined that he momentarily forgot about the bleakness around them.

"You're cheeky," Salem said with a prod to his ribs, presumably much harder than she intended.

He ignored its soreness, snickering as he helped her rise. "I can be much more than that," he whispered, coercing her smile to widen.

"Really? What does that entail?"

It was then that Korbyn remembered his past conflict, and he mentally scolded himself for his weakness. He neglected to answer her question by changing the subject. "Let's go get the others. They should have made it out safely."

Korbyn avoided her gaze, ushering her forward with a prompt to her lower back. Though, he had no sense of familiarity with their current location, as he saw no visible tracks of the paladin's armor when she was yanked into the masses of the dark.

"Which way do we go?" Salem questioned, surveying in matched confusion.

"I have no idea," Korbyn responded with a squint. "I think we fell on the wrong side of the hill."

"Then let's head—" Salem grasped onto a silence when the ground quaked beneath them.

A single moment, followed by muted breath.

"Wh-what was that?" Salem stammered.

"I'm not sure—"

Another rumble. Larger, louder than before.

The same stillness, and a moment of tension.

A hitched breath.

"Korbyn...?"

"I don't know."

The land convulsed. Their bodies swayed.

It shuddered more frequently, with singular booms preceding others. Each tremor increased, and Korbyn and Salem hung onto each other to remain upright. He was too frightened to move, unaware of the cause of the distorted tremors. When the trees parted, folding back like pieces of thin cloth, a large creature emerged from its depths.

An ogre, standing almost as tall as the trees, hovered over them. It had a large, robust torso with appendages thicker than the trunks of the forest and with forearms larger than a person. Necklaces crafted in rope and branches swayed from every stomp it took. Skulls and bones sharpened into serrated blades hung suspended as makeshift jewelry, chiming in deep clangs that echoed after each thunderous quake. Its sockets were hollow, lacking any traces of eyeballs. Despite its lack of vision, it appeared actively aware of their presence.

Its chin lowered to leer with a lingering, unbridled rage. The atmosphere permeated a foul stench of deterioration, the folds of its skin barely hanging off its thick bones. When nausea hit him, Korbyn realized how a monster could exist in the depths of a forest that swallowed the energy of every breathing creature—because, somehow, despite the ogre obeying its natural instincts, it wasn't alive.

"Run," Salem whispered. Run!"

The ogre's fangs dripped with saliva, pellets of water spattering against freshly formed mud. It raised a grand club constructed of wood and protrusions of filed bone, swinging back its arm with a hefty growl.

When the ogre brought down its mighty club, the ground rippled in terror.

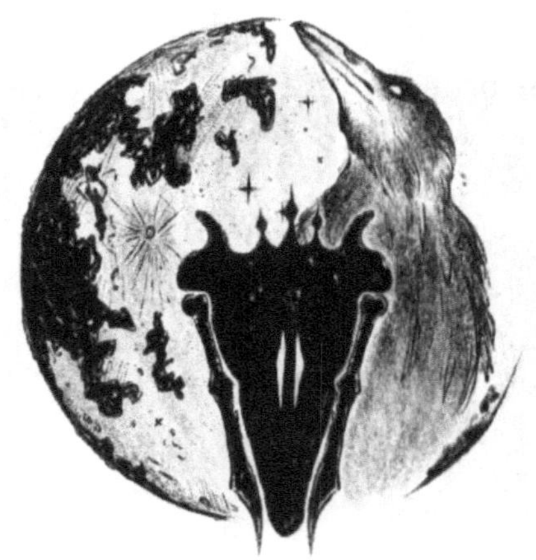

EIGHTEEN.

Korbyn and Salem leapt in separate directions, the ogre's weapon plummeting into the empty space. The terrain caved inward, and rocks, dirt and stone volleyed through the air upon its impact. When Korbyn trotted back several paces, he curled his fingers around the hilt of his blade, unsheathing his sword with his left hand and twisting it in circular motions to stretch his unused muscles.

Salem matched his movements and withdrew her mighty longsword in one hand and her shield in the other. A radiant flash of energy originating from her locket streamed like encircling gold to her weapon. She readied herself, stilling her aforementioned fear with a deep exhalation.

"Target its legs. When it falls, we strike its neck!" the paladin commanded, and in an elegant flame of light and darkness, they danced.

Korbyn raced around the creature in an arch just as it swung its club. He evaded its attack by dropping his body to a brisk slide, a tunnel of wind veering from the weapon's thrust. Korbyn and Salem reached its alternate ankles in unison, brandishing their blades across the thickness of its skin. Korbyn managed to slice through a part of its ankle bone. From his position, he could see Salem had cut deeper, a holy light bursting from the seams of the wound, the creature's cry rippling through the gloom.

It stumbled but deterred its descension with a rebuttal of staggering legs. Preventing its fall, it proceeded to stomp like a child's tantrum. Korbyn and Salem scurried out of its perimeter, shielding their eyes from the uprising smog. The ground beneath them tore and shook, and Korbyn stumbled back with waving arms to keep himself upright. He lowered his body, centering his gravity and adjusting his weight with the movements of the irregular terrain.

When the ogre slowed its clomping, Korbyn and Salem charged in mirrored grace, an unheard song guiding their unified cadence. They aimed for their previous lacerations, driving their blades deeper into the gashes of its ankles. The creature howled again, sinking its body and flailing its arms with uncoordinated movements.

The ogre's free arm smacked into the brunt of Salem's shield, and she soared backwards. She managed to slow her momentum, tumbling only briefly before she slid back in a lowered prowl. Springing at the monster again, in a light of retribution, Salem leveled her blade. When the ogre raised its arm wildly, she spun on her heel and punctured her blade through part of its forearm, slicing through its wrist bone.

The blood, a darkened purple, sprayed in surprisingly thick froths. It congealed in bubbles, dispersing into a liquid across her face and armor. Salem seemed unperturbed by the gore, following her previous swing with another elegant twist of her body.

Another cry emitted from the ogre's mouth as Korbyn flanked it. With its body lowered, he swung his blade several times around its calf. Its dying skin wasn't as tough as he originally thought; the membrane ripped and tore from his blade's edge to reveal its bones underneath with every strike. Hues of indigo coated him, its thick masses lobbed with every attack.

Again and again, the duo struck in combined movements like practiced partners, a choreographed waltz too fast for the creature betwixt them. It floundered in confusion and rage, writhing, smacking, and grabbing at nothing but air. Meanwhile, their intended strikes sliced through bits and pieces of decaying flesh. While Salem reveled in a divine light, Korbyn cavorted in the monster's grand shadow.

Eventually, the ogre's arm slammed into Korbyn's abdomen, and he lurched backwards in a heap of rolls. A crack of resounding fracture ensued, and he crashed into the base of a rigid tree. A poorly timed inhale led to a quarrel of lost breath and aggressive coughing, and he clutched at the pain in his side, barely seizing the blade stationed in his quivering hand.

"Korbyn, get up!" Salem yelled.

The ogre flaunted a bone that resembled a human spine from its neckline. Instead of blunt edges on the top and bottom of the vertebrae, each end and protruding part had been sanded to resemble a sharpened spear. With a strong, full-body toss of the creature, the weapon soared with a hastened velocity.

Korbyn prostrated, begetting the makeshift spear to collide with the tree above his head. The base uprooted and toppled over from its unbridled vigor, crashing with a decisive thud.

Standing in direct disobedience to his body's pained retort, Korbyn hunched forward with a tightened grip on his blade's hilt and the other on his abdomen. In the distance, Salem leaped around the ogre's massive form and flourished like a warrior trained in multiple lifetimes. Holy energy radiated from her iron blade, breaching the ogre's previous wounds with a thunderous cry. It yelled out another deafening howl, still refusing to falter.

"It's not falling!" Korbyn shouted, his voice dripping in annoyance and pain. Salem angled her face with boundless confidence.

"Don't give up!" she yelled, and her voice lifted him from the embrace of his hesitance.

They circled the creature until they reached alternate ankles, dodging the flurry of swings as it sporadically threw the weapon around its torso like blades on a windmill. Its advances lacked technique or cause, a threat of unpredictable chaos rather than a refined and knowledgeable enemy.

Despite its size, the ogre waved its mighty weapon with a rush of speed that created small devils of dust to circle the area around them. Although they weren't strong enough to deter their advances, the haze decreased visibility. Again, the ogre thrashed. With surprising aptitude, it slid its hand down the hilt of its hefty weapon mid-swing, elongating its reach.

Korbyn failed to fully evade, and a protruding bone from the club ripped through his torso. Blood sprayed in the erupting gale.

"Korbyn!" Salem shrieked, desire for retaliation trailing her roar.

With the ogre preoccupied, the paladin lunged and slammed the brunt of her shield into the open wound of its ankle. It shrieked, a piercing weep that echoed and tore through the darkness. It tumbled after failed attempts to hold a stance, the skin along its ankles tearing in fragility like tattered clothes. As its foot separated from the rest of its leg, the grotesque body flailed from its disheveled descent.

Korbyn staggered with a wavering breath. With a sluggish lift of his chin, he met the monster's empty sockets, its lids strained in unbeknownst terror. Gravity tugged on its corpulence in Korbyn's direction. He could have shied away from its falling portly mass, but, instead, he welcomed its expanding shadow.

His inhale, deep and tranquil, remarkably alleviated the tension in his wounds. With his exhale, he overtook a poised stance, knees steadfast in staunch fortitude. The iron gleamed in the darkness as he leveled his blade, and as the hulking body careened, Korbyn charged his sword's sharpened edge towards the Heavens that couldn't see him—and swung.

The blade severed the ogre's head and ligaments. Waves of blood spewed from the ingress of its wound, creating a cadence of darkened rain. Its gunk sprayed across the grass, a portrait of death in a woodland of dusk.

Its head and body crumpled on either side of Korbyn in a heap of mangled, dead mucous, the crash resounding in the depths of the forest. The echo dispersed against the dome of darkness that frantically endeavored to keep its secrets within. Eventually, the battlefield settled, and the whispers of the woods waned.

"We did it," Salem remarked with a smile, sweat trickling along her brow.

Although her holy magic now purred in comparison to its previous eruption, she was illuminated in an iridescent flame that drove away the darkness. The shadowed tendrils seethed backwards and retreated into the gloom recoiling from her holy flare.

Korbyn basked in the aura of her warmth, his idle posture adjacent to his elongated shadow that only the sun could have provided.

Salem smiled, shining brighter than any star. Korbyn beamed in the gaze of her sunshine.

And then, a serrated bone pierced through Salem's thick, iron armor.

Metal and cloth ripped from the momentum of its strike. Salem reeled so far back that the massive bone penetrated the tree behind her, only stopping when its sharpened end pierced the dirt. With half of its long bone jutting out of her abdomen, blood gushed from her mouth and wound. Blood sprayed like a painter's abrupt strokes, the dirt and foliage becoming a canvas of cedar, basil, and scarlet.

Salem's breathing mirrored his own, and he sensed an exhaled breath that didn't return as the sun had promised.

Korbyn's shadow faded, and the internal voice quieted.

NINETEEN.

Every time Salem reached for a full breath, she shuttered in stifled quietness. Her lids fluttered in wavering modulation as she remained incapable of fully opening them. If Korbyn spoke to her, she couldn't hear him; all sounds were hushed in this strange respite except for a piercing shrill.

She couldn't remember the journey from her previous place to this one, but when she peered down, she understood her destination involved a massive bone of an ogre's forearm protruding from her abdomen and a grand tree at her back. She was pinned, she was certain, though she lacked the required energy to even twitch.

When the haziness and ringing dissipated, pain surged in remembrance. Blood spewed from her torn flesh. Though unconsciousness fought to suffocate her, she rebelled against its daunting presence with hitched breaths and blinks of desperate clarity. When she saw Korbyn's distorted, fearful expression, she hadn't heard the words that passed his mouth, but she was certain it was her name.

That was when she saw them.

One, four, seven—ten ogres in total emerged from the depths of the darkened forest, all dead-looking monsters with crude weapons the size of trees and decorated in wood and bone. Wooden plates wrapped around their forearms and shins, like pieces of armor. With every step they took, the ground shook and shivered in fear that dispersed even the lingering shadows. Some of the monsters were missing eyes, some lacking limbs, some with hanging jaws, but all dripped with a thirst for bloodshed.

Salem tried to stand, but the protrusion angled her body awkwardly. Somehow, it had completely severed the large tree and bound itself into the dirt behind it at an angle, preventing her from escaping either end of the improvised spear. She slackened, and with unnerving realization, Salem knew she wouldn't escape this place alive.

"K-Korbyn. You have to run. I'm stuck, I-I can't move." The paladin squirmed against the protruding bone. She bludgeoned it with her elbow to try and dislodge it, but it proved vigorous, for each rallied effort left nothing except a forming bruise on the outward crook of her arm, despite the steel cop.

Korbyn didn't seem to hear her. Instead, his back now faced her, as though he was staring at the hoard of ogre. The shadows from the woods grasped his ankles, swirling in weaves of dark power.

"Korbyn, run!" Salem screamed as the darkness encircled him. Despite her warning, Korbyn remained stationary.

And then, the shadows swallowed him whole.

"*Korbyn!*" Salem cried, her voice cracking and reverberating into the bleakness. The trembles ensued, though its origin remained uncertain. Her shuddering body and the stomping of the ogres matched poetically. The beat of the shadowed flames hissed and writhed in satisfaction.

Salem was tired of witnessing death and being too incompetent to prevent it. She was tired of befriending allies just to bid them eternal farewell. Her shoulders slumped, eyes drifting like a curtain's close. Salem was tired, and she welcomed the darkness.

Then, the darkness erupted.

The magical essence swirled and danced around Korbyn's body in perfect entanglement. Black energy radiated under the tarp of the forest, his energy pulling the bleakness closer. He called upon the power like a warrior requesting an affiliate's aid. The shadows hovered like budding mists, traversing the battlefield in waves. This process continued, his magical energy increasing in power and size. Yet, somehow, there was no decidite in his grasp.

The shadows weren't swallowing Korbyn whole—he was absorbing them.

The ogres charged with a thunderous battle cry. They toppled trees with thrusts of their elbows, the woodland snapping like twigs as they fell in heaps of debris. Korbyn sauntered forward to meet them, energy and swagger whipping around his body as he idly carried his blade at his side.

One of the ogres led the charge, impatience and bloodlust controlling its movements. The earth quaked beneath them harder than it had before, and Salem gripped onto the bone to halt the reckless shifting.

The ogre closed the distance and raised its club, smashing it down towards its enemy in one fell swoop. When Salem blinked, Korbyn was gone.

She saw him behind the ogre, Korbyn's blade extended and at the end of a swing. In the next moment, the ogre's left leg was severed, plummeting to the forest's floor. The creature toppled to the ground with a cry.

Two ogres followed, racing towards him with waving clubs. Korbyn dodged the volley of attacks, unbothered by the layers of dirt and dust that whisked in the winds. The creatures slammed their weapons onto the ground in quick successions, each strike missing its mark. Korbyn moved with such rapid grace that Salem's faltering consciousness struggled to maintain mental pace.

Upon another strike of the ogre's club, Korbyn leapt to the top of its fist. The monster reacted as if he were an unwanted gnat, reeling back its large arm and lurching to the side. Korbyn held fast before darting up its forearm. Before the ogre could recoil from his approach, Korbyn swung. Its head plunged to the forest floor, thick indigo rain following its tumble.

Korbyn bound for the second ogre before the first one fell. He dodged in elegant strides when the creature lowered its body to its knees, disregarding its weapon and slamming both fists on the ground incessantly. It was a desperate venture to crush the man's body beneath it, but the hysteria heeded no effect. This creature possessed eyes, and it scanned the forming smog beneath it, failing to track the man's swift movements.

Korbyn propelled his heel into the creature's nose, the cracking bone reverberating with his contact. The ogre roared and toppled backwards, disregarding him and clutching onto its shattered snout. The boom that followed curled another haze of dirt, shifting to reveal Korbyn's form that landed on its face. He flipped his blade in a reverse grip, mimicking the creature's continuous crashes and stabbing one of its eyes endlessly.

The ogre flailed, swatting the air in a vile pursuit to rid Korbyn of his presence. When it slapped downwards, it smashed itself in the face, rolling incessantly in a fit of pain. Korbyn moved on, leaving it in its hysterical rage.

Three of the ogres ran at him in unison, one jostling the other two in a rally. Korbyn shifted to the right and forced the creatures to change the direction of their strides. The one in the middle tripped over the one to its right and then pushed the creature away, both tumbling. The two ogres locked in their own form of combat, distracted with each other instead of their previous purpose.

The third ogre, unaffected by the fighting of the other two, had only one arm but swung as if it had both. It waved the improvised club around, its arm and stump moving quicker than the rest. Korbyn deflected the attacks with his blade by pushing its weapon to the side, following the motions of its sweeps instead of blocking its incessant barrage. When he jumped forward, the ogre lifted its foot and kicked.

Korbyn soared twenty to thirty paces from the impact, thudding in a heap of tumbles. Salem heard bones crack from the collision, assuming such a harsh bout would have killed him. Eventually, he slammed into one of the trees, which fractured and fell in a concealed veil of mist and debris.

"No!" Salem yelled, desperate to rid herself of this weapon bound to her stomach. She screamed as though it would aid her efforts, pulling with the remainder of her strength. Still, it didn't listen, for it was locked in place, and so was she.

When Korbyn emerged, seemingly unaware of the blood that traversed down his chin, he presumed an upright stature. His gaze didn't totter from the creatures that reassembled on the other side of the field. His position proved advantageous for her discerning eyes, and the sight of his face surprised her. Red eyes replaced his ivory ones in an equal abyss of darkness, resembling the daunting presence of dual Blood Moons.

"*The cage, temporarily broken and unfastened,*" Korbyn sneered, his voice bellowing in a foreign menace. "*The raven demands deliverance.*"

He strode forward with a limp, but he seemed ignorant of any pain. Where heavy breaths should have been was a stillness of his chest, as if he hadn't been breathing at all. In defiance against his composed exterior, the remaining ogres raged.

They trampled the land beneath them in a fury of strides. The one in the front of the pack swung its massive weapon towards Korbyn. He spun on his heel and dodged. He flicked his blade and sliced straight through the ogre's wrist, despite its breadth. The weapon and hand fell with a resounding boom, followed by a howl of pain and anger.

The following creature ran around its ally and threw its entire body in a trample, but Korbyn proved quicker. For a moment, he stood firm, and in the next, he sprung from the creature's back neck. Tendrils of darkness and shadow followed his glide and formed sickles of ice. As Korbyn soared, the stems of shadows shot out for his next victim, piercing several points along the ogre's torso. When one pierced its leg, severing any further control of movements, it fell prone.

The two ogres engaged in previous combat with each other halted their assaults, returning their attention on Korbyn. They joined the tenth ogre, all wailing and swinging their weapons in frantic chaos. Korbyn evaded their incoming volleys as they lunged, despite his limp.

"All *fall short of the Shepherd!*" Korbyn cackled maniacally, avoiding every measly attempt at their winded madness and growing haste.

When one of the monsters staggered, Korbyn severed its thumb and pointer finger. The weapon fell from its grasp as the creature squalled in opposition and pain. It grasped its wrist in disbelief, trekking backwards until it fell prone.

Two others raised their weapons for a unanimous attack, holding up their strike longer to gather as much strength as possible. It gave Korbyn ample time to respond.

The shadows from beneath his feet shot up towards them and pierced their forearms to greet the chilled air. The shadows expanded, ripped, and tore them from the inside until their arms separated from the rest of their body. Other tendrils of shadows pierced their chests and heads. The darkness pulled away, and the monsters fell.

The ogre farthest in the back reached for a spear made of an ogre's bone from its necklace and snapped it off. The necklace crafted of bone and branches cascaded to the ground in heaps. With a lunge of fury and desperation, it lobbed the javelin across the entirety of the battlefield. Korbyn sidestepped the weapon with ease, and it pierced the air, bypassing him and lunging straight at Salem.

Salem's breath failed her as she watched the pointed edge. Prior memories demanded remembrance. She recalled kneeling and begging before her king, promising to find the lost blades, venturing to these lands, and offering her strength to help civilians and her newfound family. Lastly, she recalled Korbyn, a man clouded in mystery she would never unveil. In her acceptance of death, she was only left with regret.

When bone tore into flesh, it wasn't hers.

Above her, Korbyn heaved, grasping onto the spear lodged in his chest. It protruded through the trunk directly over her shoulder, its sharpened edge managing to cut only a fraction of her cheek. Somehow, Korbyn had adjusted its directory with his body, acting as a makeshift shield.

She could feel his back against her chest. Korbyn heaved and his knees trembled, and she could tell he only stood upright because of the protruding bone giving him no other choice. Salem gawked, unable to form any cohesive sentences other than a single word.

"Why?"

"The world doesn't deserve your light," Korbyn rasped, blood gurgling in his throat. She couldn't see his eyes, but she imagined the crimson had faded back into his usual ivory as his crazed voice had disappeared from the abrasive wound. "But it needs it."

When the ogres continued their approach, Korbyn lifted his left arm, reaching for where a blade would have been, but his weapon had been dropped, and his sheath was empty. Despite this, it appeared as though he grabbed onto something tangible, but nothing was there.

The remaining ogres galloped with raised weapons, ready to conclude the fight before Korbyn could retaliate. Salem desperately attempted to pry him off, but he was just as encumbered as she was. She grasped her necklace, and it shone in a brilliance of flawless gold.

"Elohim," Salem whispered, blood spreading across her shimmering locket. "Where are you?"

TWENTY.

ephyrean winds caressed Korbyn's cheek, surging from the ogres' bellows. It roused him from his brief slumber, and he gazed forward at the approaching hoard. With his fading consciousness, it would have been too easy to forgo further tries at escaping, but it wasn't just his worthless life on the balance—it was Salem's.

Korbyn didn't recall much of the previous fight, if any. He remembered a suspended cage and swinging within its confines; a wretched rust permeating his nose; his ankles, wrists, and neck bound by chains; a forest surrounded not in darkness, but thick waves of forming mists; cries of foreign voices echoing across the blanket of branches that replaced the sky; and then Salem and a flung weapon accompanied by a piercing cry from its flight. It hauled him back to reality, the prior visions becoming nothing more than pointless illusions.

He felt his consciousness slipping again, and Korbyn reached for something that he knew should not have been there. His fingers coiled behind his back and grasped a foreign entity, as though invisibly sheathed. He hoisted its weight, its phantom emerging from the unknown. Its calls beckoned, mild elation arising from its awaiting power. It was taboo, he knew, but still he extracted it from a howling abyss, urging it alive by his mere demand.

But it wasn't needed.

Materializing from the edge of the forest's shadows was a blast of holy light. Swirls of gold emitted from growing plants and roots that charged forward in reckless pursuits. Controlling this arcane energy was Andrid, who held their arms aloft. With one hand, they held onto their staff with gilded decidite of black and gold, and the other, their outstretched fingers manipulated the weaves of essence. Roots and vines untouched by the spreading darkness erupted from the ground below, thrusting back the mists and growing at rapid rates. The shadows lurched away from the holy light that trailed from its nature, as if it wasn't able to swallow the life as rapidly as they had been growing.

Veeris, Oakley, Haven, Gilben, and the fox followed them from within the sphere and approached the hoard of ogres. The animal companion trailed Andrid's side, as if ready to protect them at any given moment. Haven pursued, swinging his massive great axe into the back of an ogre's calf. Its weight buckled underneath it, the monster writhing in pain, and it toppled to the ground face first. Its indigo blood glistened in the light's holy radiance emitting from Andrid's staff.

Once the creature had fallen, Oakley hopped on the back of its leg and dashed up its body. Before the ogre could regain its staunch composure, Oakley stabbed the back of its neck with two daggers, the blades dripping in some sort of purple ooze. The large creature thrashed, and its body shook from what Korbyn assumed to be poison that viciously dripped from its wound. The size of the ogre didn't seem to aid its resistance, for it succumbed to dormancy within seconds, and the dead skin covering its body shriveled around its bones.

Gilben was fast for a dwarf. He crossed the path of the next ogre before it could continue its strides towards Korbyn and Salem. He swung his grand broadsword at the monster's ankle, and it cracked from the collision. Its foot broke sideways, and the rest of its body crumbled.

With power and magical control, Andrid kept up their concentration of the holy light. The greenery contrasted heavily with the dead trees around it as they sprouted beautifully underneath the forest's shadow. Even though Andrid couldn't directly manipulate the vines in the directions they wished, it was as if the life instinctively fought against the darkness. The acceleration of the flora's growth curled around the dead plants, denying the darkness that wished to swallow them. They twisted and curled around the ogres, who were failing to combat them. One fought against the restraints of the vines until a crack rang from its broken neck, and its head fell limply to the side.

One of the ogres reached Korbyn and Salem. It halted its run and swung its club so far in the air that it parted the branches in the roof of the forest. Before it struck, a circle of magic appeared before it. An ethereal blade conjured from light struck upwards, piercing the bottom of its chin and straight through the crown of its head. The heaviness of the club pulled its limp body backwards, and the monster fell, motionless after a reverberating crash.

Veeris manipulated ten blades of holy light with each finger, striking at the six remaining ogres that still rallied against them. Sweat dripped down the elf's forehead as the winds from the chaos whipped around them. Veeris and the rest of the mercenaries unitedly fought against the ogres with precision. Even in unified numbers, the monsters hadn't stood a chance.

The remaining creatures collapsed in piles of dead mucous, skin, and bone. Darkened blood sprayed in thick globs, the clotting gore resembling more solid than liquid. The quakes in the forest finally dispersed, an eruption of eerie stillness replacing where thunderous booming had once been.

"Salem," Korbyn breathed out. The cavity in the forest's ceiling cast a trickle of moonlight on the duo, locked together in a deathly embrace. He couldn't see her, and he feared she had died in her sudden quietness. "They're here for you, your friends," he whispered, another puddle of his blood falling past his lips. "Don't die."

"*Our* friends are here." Salem coughed and chuckled, as if offering a painful smile through bloodied teeth. "I won't die if you don't."

Korbyn mirrored her laugh even though it hurt. Ahead of them, their companions hastily approached, and he slackened.

"I'll try," Korbyn muttered before his eyes slammed shut.

Korbyn roused from unconsciousness with a jolt. When he erected his back, stabbing aches throbbed from his abrupt lurch. He groaned, a combined growl of fury and agony. He endured it for a few moments, waiting for its inevitable alleviation, though the pounding in his head failed to cease. He heeded the idea that his body had shattered and despairingly rearranged, but whoever mended the pieces misconstrued their original locations.

For some reason, Korbyn couldn't recall the origins of his pain.

The creature underneath was set free, only to be caged again.

He lifted his hands over his face to shield his eyes when a bright light pierced the periwinkle curtains. He groaned, rubbing his forehead and tugging the shades closed to block the intrusive light. When the room darkened, he scanned the contents within.

A cottage room with white oak furniture decorated in multiple shades of blue and lavender greeted him. He sat in a small, wooden bed next to an arched window of draping curtains. On the opposite side of the bed resided a nightstand, with an unlit candle and a glass of water surrounded by dwindled condensation.

Korbyn scanned the far wall, where white bookshelves rose to the ceiling. Instead of containing strictly books, decorations and flowers accented the light oak finish. Blue daisies and orchids sat in light brown baskets and intricate bowls and vases of hand-wrought ceramics. There were a couple of paperbacks purposely placed to accent the flowers. He read a couple titles that related to farming, gardening, and pottery.

Multiple layers of heavy quilts draped across his lap. Despite their bulkiness, he felt colder than usual, as if covered in a blanket of ice. Instead of pain, the chill brought him comfort like a welcoming embrace.

The roof above him rose at an angle to form a triangle. Hanging from the highest point in the ceiling was a lantern, still and unkindled. Based on the curvature of the room, it appeared as though he resided on the top floor of a cottage.

He peered past the thick curtain's fabric, careful to avoid the disturbing light. Rows of farmlands and clusters of livestock within the confines of an intact fence extended into the distance. Several workers tended to the vegetables, gardens, and animals that thrived under the sun's grace. Dropping the curtain, darkness enveloped him once again. It gifted him with memories, flooding into his mind's eye like crashing waves.

What happens to a fire when there's no one left to kindle it?

Korbyn flung the blanket away and rushed to the closed door with incomprehensive, cursed mumbles. He stumbled onto the wooden planks, and the iron bands and studs fractured from its fragile construction. He tripped at the door, not discerning the proximity of the stairs. He tumbled down the entire flight. Eventually, he slid down the remaining steps and invertedly landed at the base with a plop. He leveled his head back into a slouch, not preventing a vexed groan from rumbling in his throat.

"Korbyn?" Oakley yelled. "A-are you okay? Those were stairs. You can't just run down them!"

When Korbyn opened his eyes, the world was upside down. He saw Oakley, Gilben, Haven, Andrid, and the fox hovering over him. Oakley was flailing his arms sporadically, as if he wanted to help but had no inkling how. The rest were covered in varying forms of concerned glances.

"Is Salem alive?" Korbyn wheezed out.

Gilben and Haven assisted his endeavors to rise, shifting him so he sat upright at the base of the stairs.

"She's alright, lad," Gilben reassured, inspecting Korbyn's body. "She's just restin', which is what ya should be doin' right now."

"I'm fine," Korbyn stated with a relieved sigh, leaning his stiff body back so that his elbows rested on the stair. Even if he wanted to stand, he wasn't sure he could. "Where are we?"

"Back in Enderbrooke. One of the bishops in town let us stay while you and Salem recovered." Haven's eyes trailed over his torso. "You both were heavily injured."

Allowing curiosity to stir him, Korbyn pulled up his shirt to inspect the wounds underneath. However, none resided there. Where he expected a scar to be was instead threads of goat sinew intertwined neatly through the skin of his chest and an odor of vinegar. All stared in bewilderment.

"I didn't imagine it all, did I?" Korbyn questioned, only seeing the scars and marks from the ones that existed from his awakening.

Gilben shook his head, inspecting his body as well. "I'm 'fraid not, lad, though if ya tried hard enough, I might believe ya, considerin' ya seem in perfect health now." The dwarf stroked his beard. "Ya heal pretty fast."

"That's a bit of an understatement," Haven replied. As if testing the waters, he threw a light jab at Korbyn's stomach. Korbyn groaned in response, the soreness of his muscles rippling from what should have been a soft punch, but the half-orc clearly didn't how to control his own strength.

"Yeah, still hurts." Korbyn gestured with a grimace.

Haven shrugged, followed by a mischievous smirk. "Thought I'd make sure."

Korbyn scoffed with an upward tug of his lips. "Ass." He chuckled before resuming the previous topic. "What injuries did I have?"

"A perforation in yer torso, several broken ribs, fractured leg, a concussion, 'nd multiple gashes across yer body," Gilben responded, as if he had just read from a list. "Don't see proof of 'em, though."

"Did I get healed with decidite?" Korbyn asked, analyzing each of them. Gilben, Haven and Oakley looked between themselves before they shook their heads in distinct disapproval.

"Your body healed on its own," Haven responded.

"Strength, grounded..." Andrid whispered. Korbyn wasn't sure if they were a part of this conversation or not.

"How's that possible?" Oakley wondered, poking at Korbyn's chest, as if he wanted to ruin an illusion with his physical touch. "You're weird, Korb."

Korbyn swatted his hand away. The only remains of the encounter had been the tenderness of his muscles that lingered.

"It's a wee bit strange, methinks." Gilben raised his hand and stroked his perfectly brushed and braided beard. "Count yerself lucky then, aye?"

"Yeah..." Korbyn trailed off, pulling his shirt over his abdomen.

"Strength, grounded 'nd...grounded 'nd..." Andrid whispered again, their eyebrows furrowed together. The fox kept its gaze on them, as though awaiting an answer.

"Can you take me to Salem?" Korbyn urged.

Haven obliged, pulling him up to his feet and swinging his arm around his shoulder. Andrid and the fox followed them, despite not discovering whatever puzzle they were struggling to decipher.

"Strength 'nd grounded 'nd somethin'..."

Once they stood in front of Salem's door, Haven gave Korbyn a pat of encouragement. He motioned for Andrid to follow. Before Andrid vanished around the corner, a cheerful, yet eerie smile spread across their face.

"Strength 'nd grounded 'nd *transformation*," they remarked, returning to hand Korbyn the obsidian rock that they had given him before. He never realized he had dropped it. Korbyn retrieved it from Andrid's small fingers and stared into the ivory veins. "Just like basalt."

Before Korbyn could ask any questions, Andrid returned to the hall, approaching Haven and the fox.

Transformed into something new, the voice repeated.

Korbyn analyzed the rock before stuffing it into his pocket and knocking on the door. At first, no one answered his call. Before his next set of thumps, Veeris wrenched the door open. Their glares clashed like dueling blades.

"Is Salem awake?" Korbyn prompted, peering past the elf. He exhaled a breath of relief when Salem glanced back with an equally relieved smile.

Veeris stepped in his way. "Yes, and she's not taking visitors right now," he spat, motioning to slam the door.

Korbyn placed his foot in the way. "I just want to talk to her."

"Get out," Veeris hissed.

"It'll only take a second—"

"I said, get out!" Veeris yelled before pushing him.

Normally, Korbyn wouldn't have succumbed to his demands,

but his weakened state collapsed under the force. He stumbled out of the entrance and barely prevented the fall to his ass. Veeris closed the door with a resounding slam.

"Veeris!" Salem hissed from the other side. It sounded like a combination of anger and pain.

After Korbyn recomposed himself, he was met with a silence, as if Veeris was waiting for his departure. He huffed, accepting defeat.

Instead of mingling with the rest of the mercenaries, Korbyn trekked back up the stairs. As he shut the door to his temporary home, he plopped onto the firm mattress. Only a thin shaft of light trickled through the curtains, leaving him amongst a bountiful layer of welcoming shadows.

As Korbyn slipped under the quilt and pulled out the basalt and quartz stone to analyze its matte texture, he tried to remember how it felt when he lost control and escaped the cage.

TWENTY-ONE.

Veeris finally returned to face Salem, anger and hatred seeping from him like a visible steam. She rivaled his anger, casting a glare before swinging her legs over the side of the bed. The pain was immeasurable, but she didn't want to feel so vulnerable during their inevitable confrontation.

"You have been insufferable ever since we found Korbyn. What's going on with you?" Salem demanded, clutching her stomach, as though it would somehow soothe the pain.

"Why do you look at him that way?"

Salem struggled for a full breath. "What?"

"I said, why do you look at him that way?" Veeris repeated.

"What way?" Salem snapped in feigned confusion, though she couldn't hide her blatant irritation.

"You like him," Veeris stated. "You have feelings for him. Don't think I haven't noticed. We all have."

"I-I don't have feelings—" Salem stuttered.

"'Now I'm curious how good you are. You'll have to show me

sometime.' That's what you said, isn't it?" Veeris spat, mimicking her voice. "Seriously, Salem? Who even are you?"

Salem glowered back with an intensifying glare. "First of all, even if I was attracted to Korbyn, it would be none of your business. Secondly, who says I wasn't talking about his swordsmanship?" she asked, followed by his dramatic scoff.

"Yes, because when I want to talk battle strategy with someone, I also tend to flirt," Veeris responded sarcastically.

"We weren't—"

"You know it is *forbidden!*" Veeris interjected with a sneer. "There is one law above all else that is prohibited, and it is intimacy. You know the consequences."

When silence fell, Veeris hissed and approached the window. Neither one retained the ability to hold each other's glance, and Salem watched as the sun approached the horizon in its own quietude. Farmers and caretakers departed to the comfort of their homes, leaving the farms and open fields on the brink of resounding stillness. Salem went to break the silence, but Veeris interjected.

"No matter how much we long for it, or how much we want it, love is impermissible." His fingers turned white from the tightened grip on his crossed arms. "You should know better."

Salem watched the descending sun. An internal part of her always grew saddened when it dispersed past the land's edge, missing its warmth and light. It graced the world with its presence every morning, smiling down on the people and supporting them with its guiding brilliance. However, even she knew there was something addicting about the reflective moon.

"Can you take me outside? I'd like to see the sunset," Salem whispered, not turning her gaze away from its illumination.

Veeris obliged, leading her outside as she hobbled to a bench that sat on the edge of the property.

They faced the west, with endless fields quieting from the

sun's fleeting warmth. Its vivid rays trickled between the branches of trees, not yet ready to depart. The voices of the town soon dispersed, leaving Salem and Veeris alone in solitude. Several moments passed before she spoke.

"My oath is my top priority," Salem said, watching the overhanging clouds that wished to cover the sun's beauty. "I made a promise. I swore I'd find the blades, no matter what, but, regardless, I still want to help him, Veeris. He needs us, and that is what we swore to do. We swore to help *everyone*."

"He is not a normal person, Salem. You saw what I saw," Veeris spat in lingering hatred. "The forest didn't harm him not because it didn't want to, but because it couldn't. There's only one type of creature that can revel in the darkness. We both know it's a—"

"Demon," Salem responded. "I know."

"I understand that he was human before this, but whatever happened to him on that battlefield changed him," Veeris said, turning his entire body to face her.

Even still, Salem faced the setting sun. Most of the orb had descended past the horizon, causing trickles of light to cast on the duo.

"But do not forget, we also made a promise to Micah and her cause. We're monster hunters. One day, the demon inside of him will snap. Maybe not today, maybe not tomorrow, or even next month or next year, but one day, he will be consumed by the dark power he's been cursed with, and he will kill." Veeris rose to his feet. "Will you wait to regret it, or will you rid the world of a demon?"

TWENTY-TWO.

Demons—such colloquial term. Do not forget, that is what the Heavens turned us into. Darkness only exists because it is the light that casts a shadow, the demon snarled.

Korbyn lounged behind a cloak of tapestry within the darkness of his room, staring at Salem and Veeris below him. He didn't intend to eavesdrop on their conversation, but they were perched on a bench within his range of vision. He gawked in dumbfounded disbelief, his heart thrumming against his chest. Luckily, they both remained oblivious to his presence in the window, continuing their discussion. The mark on Korbyn's left forearm pulsed in recognition, confirming what he feared. He tried to stifle his growing panic, but his heartbeat grew louder with every inhale. Korbyn shut the blinds, no longer wishing to see the fading light on the other side.

His heart pounded, and he clutched the fabric of his shirt to try and suppress its beats. The tightness in his chest made breathing strenuous, his fear and anxiety circling their sharpened fangs around his throat. Every time he tried to draw a full breath, his body fought against his efforts. How long had they known that he housed a demon inside his body? Was he dangerous? Was he always like this? How did they figure it out? What did all of this mean? What was he?

Korbyn gazed over to his bag, watching waves of black tendrils dancing from the tome within, despite the lack of wind passing through the room. It waved at him, the possibility of knowledge seducing him like a welcoming beauty.

He didn't know the answers to any of these questions, but he was going to figure it out.

Carefully, Korbyn unbuttoned his bag and withdrew the large tome. Despite its size, it didn't feel heavy.

He traced his fingers over the thick leather bind, and the lace hanging off the side slid back across his skin in return. The golden medallion in the middle, the crescent moon, felt familiar. Instead of the moon facing sideways, the edges pointed downwards unnaturally. He pulled away the leather straps that crossed over the book's midsection, permitting their plummet in a quiet heap. The metal clicked open, and Korbyn folded back the leather to analyze the beige pages within.

There was no title, no index, no author's notes. The first page threw knowledge immediately at the reader, if they could even understand its words. It was neither the common language, nor Elvish, nor Dwarvish, nor Gnomish nor Orcish; it weaved in an unknown script of secrets. He could hear the rough language within his mind as the whispers of the pages spoke to him, but he couldn't understand it.

Nothing hides from the Shepherd of Souls.

When Korbyn blinked, the words and the voices became tangible. They spoke of creation and beginnings, of forbidden love and betrayal, of wars and strife, of angels and demons, and of a place called Abaddon.

Korbyn read about Elohim. He read about the relationship of the mortals, Adaman and Evelyn, and how they were forcibly arranged to create life. He read how the archangels, Samael and Lailah, fell in love with Evelyn and Adaman respectively, and disobeyed Elohim. He read how both couples bore children and created the first demons named Kanen and Abel. He read about the death that followed, and the withering of the Garden.

When he flipped the page, he saw a sketch of magnificent, menacing dual blades. They were drawn in black charcoal, but the blades were darker than iron or steel. They looked familiar to his mark that brimmed on his forearm and the ones he saw in his visions, wielded by an unknown warrior.

Right under their upturned noses, the voice repeated.

According to the book, the blades were used by Samael to lead the war. His most trusted allies stood at his sides, with Lailah to his right and Azrael to his left. Rebel angels fought the devout angels of Elohim. The rebels, later called "The Fallen," lost the war and were exiled to the place known as Abaddon. Still feeling as though something else of importance resided within, Korbyn turned the page.

A familiar symbol spread from the top of the sheet to the bottom. His mark burned in recollection, causing Korbyn to grimace. He rolled up his sleeve to uncover the irritation. It pulsed sporadically, as if waiting for secrets to be unraveled, and for the attention that Korbyn refused to give it. Finally adhering to its calls, he flipped another page.

A second sketch burned in charcoal brilliance, a separate blade built of similar bone and wrapped in leather, but mountainous in comparison to the weapons before it. Instead of longswords, it rose taller than a common man, a crescent moon protruding from the bone and sweeping in an arc.

The scythe of the damned, made of heart and bone—a trophy or a consequence?

As a searing pain stabbed Korbyn's mind, the tome toppled out of his hands. Memories flooded like a broken dam, and he followed the book's plunge to the wooden floor.

The battle was over, and he was dying.

Lying in the aftermath of battling and debris, the soldier spat up blood after continuous, rough coughs. His head tilted backwards, his neck too sore and heavy to hold himself aloft. His hair, drenched in blood, fell in front of his eyes. When the man made to gaze around the area, pain retaliated. Several moments before he was struck by a volley of arrows from the fort, a soldier from Esperin swiped a blade across his face. He could no longer see the beauty of the world he was leaving behind.

Even if he couldn't witness his golden skin fading, or his naturally auburn hair drenched in brighter red blood, the soldier knew he was dying. He felt the warm rays of the sun beating down on him as it descended behind brewing storm clouds. A part of him wished to call for aid, but he knew it wouldn't reply. He wasn't worthy of its help.

Among this battlefield of bodies lie some of his dearest allies who trusted him to protect them. Back home in Avernos, his friends eagerly awaited his return. He made a promise to his family that he would return home safely. He had failed them all.

The man felt a sharp pain puncturing his lung, resulting in his strained breathing. When he endeavored to coil his fingers around a single breath, it wisped past his shaking fingers. Eventually, his body slackened, witnessing his soul depart with his falling eyelids. Another rough cough pulled him back to consciousness, not allowing him to fade just yet.

He sensed a presence lingering above him.

The soldier opened his eyelids, forgetting he couldn't see. An umbra clouded his senses, and all he could perceive was a cloak mingling with the autumn breeze. A chill traced his body, and he wasn't sure if it was due to the person standing above him, the fer-

menting storm, or the welcoming of death. Maybe it was all three.

"What is it that you would give?" the figure questioned with an old, withering voice.

Without caring about the consequences that followed, the man reached for the last bit of life he could give and told his truth.

"Anything."

Korbyn awoke from the memory drenched in foreign sweat yet shivering from a blanket of cold. He coiled into a ball while lying on the floor, arms wrapped around his abdomen. He heaved in uneven formations with rasped breaths, succumbing to the overwhelming dread.

It took Korbyn several minutes to regulate his shallow inhalations. Eventually, when the attack finally subsided, he allowed his body a moment of respite. The dread didn't completely subside, but he was able to inhale normally. He uncurled himself from the cold floor and raised his head. When he scanned the book, sprawled open on the page of the scythe, he felt its anticipation. Instead of rising to his feet, he slid the book closer across the wooden floor.

This vision, this memory, was difficult to decipher. Someone had stood above him as he was dying and asked a question. Despite the unknown implication, Korbyn discerned his ambiguous intentions.

What is it that you would give to live?

Friends and family awaited him in Avernos. Despite his meek endeavors, he couldn't evoke their faces or names, and even though the occurrence of this vision resembled more of a foreign story rather than his own past experiences, Korbyn recognized a yearning for them. They felt like fragments of another person's narrative, a stranger of who he used to be before Korbyn was created.

He was so desperate to see them that he gave something that he shouldn't have. Korbyn traced his finger along the charcoal drawing of the scythe. Just like the sword before, the blade of the weapon was much darker than normal iron or steel. It reminded him of decidite, the ore that Esperin and Avernos warred over.

In his memory on the battlefield, Korbyn couldn't see who stood over him, but somehow, he could feel the presence, along with the scythe that lingered over him. Both sought his answer, to which he eagerly replied. Death or deal? He had taken the deal, one that he couldn't undo. He regained his life upon uttering a single word, but all things came at a price. So, what did he give in return?

Where there is life, there must also be Death.

"What does that mean? Who are you?" Korbyn questioned, finally replying to the demon that invaded his mind.

A chuckle responded. *We are the future of Grim.*

"You never make any sense," Korbyn growled.

Says the sloth who ignores my wisdom instead of sinking into further contemplation, the demon cooed.

Korbyn rose and stumbled over to the mirror in the corner of the room, almost surprised when he didn't return to his original skin tone and hair color. Instead, blacks and whites tainted him. Bags drooped heavily under his bottom lids, complementing his furrowed brows and empty gaze. He no longer wished to see the results of the demon's curse.

Korbyn pulled an extra linen sheet off the bed. When he returned to the mirror, horror paralyzed him. Staring back at him was a tall, cloaked man levitating off the ground, holding the bone scythe of the downward crescent moon stained in shimmering obsidian. Underneath the umbra of his hood, he could see the face that stared back at him.

It was his own.

More visions antagonized him. He returned to Shadowbane Forest, standing idly in front of a hoard of ogres. Shadows overcame him, and he wielded the darkness like a weapon. He was stronger, faster, and a weapon of death that killed ginormous monsters with delight. He was dangerous. He was demonic. He was Death.

Korbyn slammed his fist into the mirror and shattered it.

The pieces of glass tumbled to the floor, caked in the blood of his fingers. Though not darkened purple, it no longer resembled the crimson of a normal person.

Korbyn heaved, his tremble initiating his collapse to the planked floor. He managed to sit upright, bringing his knees to his chest and laying his elbows on top of them. His bloodied hand clenched his face, covering what he could of his shattering mask.

This demon, or whatever it was, was too dangerous to be around others. He was clouded in darkness and secrets that he didn't understand, trapped in an unknown cloak of hidden daggers. At any point, he could unwillingly wield the weapons and harm those close to him. He would be unprepared if his new-found power consumed him just as it did before.

In this current state of uncertainty, he couldn't return to the very people he swore to protect or stay with the ones who were kind enough to offer him a haven. He made a deal with a devil filled with unknown consequences, and he would pay the price.

Veeris had been right all along. He was a monster hiding behind a shell of a broken man...whoever that was.

When the sun returned to the sky, Korbyn would follow the fleeting darkness.

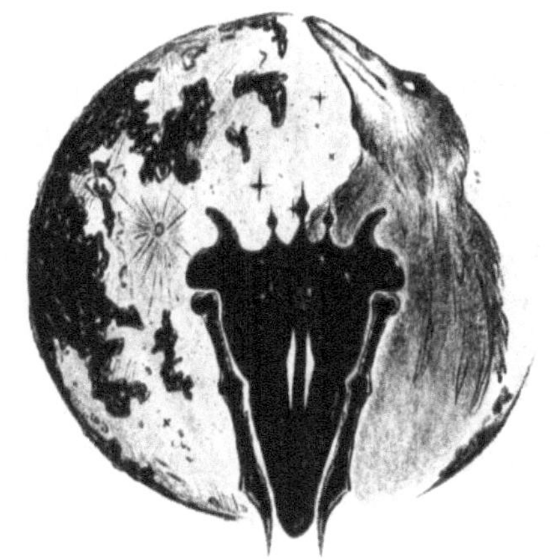

TWENTY-THREE.

uminescent light escorted Korbyn out of his interim lodging once he prepared for his departure. He adjusted the leather strap of his bag over his sore shoulder, following the moon's rays that derived from its highest point in the sky. It lit up the stairs like a beacon, and he pursued its direction with compliant silence. The rest of the mercenaries had dozed off a couple of hours beforehand, leaving the farmer's house in a peace provided by dusk.

Korbyn treaded down the stairs, careful of the wooden planks' squeaks with each step of his descent. When he arrived in the common area of the house, he gave them one last, courteous glance. Oakley, Andrid, Haven, Gilben, and Veeris currently assembled in cots and sleeping bags in the center of the floor, victim to slumber. Gilben and Oakley's loud snores concealed his footsteps, and he crept down the hallway where Salem resided.

Korbyn halted, seeing a small, lone figure at the end of the hallway. Andrid's fox perched like a pristine statue, gazing at him with a tilted head.

The Watchers of the Well. What happens to nature and fauna when the water turns black?

Korbyn saw curiosity shining in the fox's pools of amber. Its ears followed the direction of its head when it shifted to one side, attempting to process information as it watched his approach.

"Shh," Korbyn whispered, raising his finger up to his mouth.

When the fox remained stagnant, Korbyn stalked around it and strode to Salem's room.

Hushing the folded paper when it crumpled, Korbyn retrieved the note from his pocket and stationed it below the crevice of her closed door. With more care, he rummaged through the compartment at the fore of his satchel, withdrawing the black feather that gleamed from a candle along the wall. For a moment, he remained kneeling, the resilience to take his leave eluding him. He sighed, leaning into the wooden barrier with the brunt of his forehead.

"Thank you for everything, Salem," Korbyn whispered, hoping the folded parchment could accurately portray his sentiments adequately.

Whether it was his abrupt rise from kneeling or the trepidation of his leave, Korbyn's legs buckled from unexpected weakness. Nausea replaced his previous conviction, followed by an ache of continuous throbs in his skull. Vertigo created wild shifts in the terrain as though the world spun, and his senses failed to comprehend the difference in upright and horizontal direction. He swayed in distressed discombobulation and sickness, slamming into the wall. Though his tumble was less than graceful, he managed to lower himself to the floor in a quieter heap. He stifled his vomit behind a clasped hand, despite the visions that prevented him from deciphering hallucination from reality.

A *chained pedestal of blood and iron; magic swelling in swirls of radiant light; discarded armor of ivory and gold drenched in scarlet; a still chest, a lack of breath, and Salem's lifeless eyes star- ing above.*

When the visions ceased, Korbyn inhaled deeply, breaching what felt like the ocean's surface after being under for an extend- ed period. When he glanced up, the fox with crimson fur hovered before him. He couldn't tell what emotions swirled behind its watchful eyes.

The images played in such fast sequences that he failed to comprehend the details, but he was certain it was Salem's death he witnessed. The chaos also eluded him, forcing him to stir in contemplative uncertainty. Korbyn was conflicted with leaving to avoid hurting her and staying to protect her. Both ideas battled for dominance, and he struggled to evaluate the possible conse- quences of both. After several minutes of pondering, he held no solutions.

The small animal pawed the floor in front of his leg, forcing him to look up at it. Shakily, Korbyn reached out, leaving his fin- gers for the creature to interact with. The fox neither sniffed his hand nor leaned forward, instead remaining still.

"What do I do?" Korbyn whispered, partially expecting the creature to answer him. It did.

"You have been chosen by default, Grim," a feminine voice whispered within his mind. The creature leaned its head to the side, continuing its response with an immobile snout. *"This is just the beginning of a larger story. You must place your individual piece down within the grander puzzle. After you have risen to your rightful place among the damned, your blood will follow."*

Salem's door swung open.

"Korbyn? What are you doing? Is everything alright?" she questioned, analyzing his precarious seat along the wall.

"Oh, uh, yeah, I, um, I-I was just thinking," Korbyn stuttered, still not completely comprehending the eerie fortune. "I was just sitting here with—"

The fox had already left.

"With who?" Salem inquired again, gazing down the empty hall.

"My thoughts." Peeking at Salem, Korbyn noticed she was hunched with an arm around her stomach. "I was just sitting here with my thoughts."

She nodded before her gaze dropped to the floor. Below her was the crumpled piece of paper and a black feather.

"What's this?" she wondered, picking up both.

Korbyn lurched forward, standing and nabbing the note from her hand.

"N-Nothing!" he stammered, the feather whisking in the breeze of his quick movement. "I mean, I found a black feather, and I wanted to give it to you and tell you something, but it was late, so I left a note."

Salem scanned both of his eyes with a fine line of her lips. An expression of disbelief crossed her face. "With...all your stuff?"

Korbyn gazed over to his forgotten satchel on the floor. "Oh, well, it was easier to just grab the bag, I guess."

"Well, you could just stay and read the note to me instead," Salem suggested, lingering desperation floating along her whisper.

"It's late, and it's a little embarrassing. I should get going," he replied, scratching the side of his neck to alleviate the awkwardness. "It's not anything important."

"I would prefer to hear it from you," she insisted, widening the space between the door and its frame.

Not conjuring a proper way to excuse himself from her presence, Korbyn obliged her guidance through her room's entrance. He avoided the lit candle's shimmer as it illuminated sections of the room, and he backed into the door when she closed it. He barely noticed the various furnishings, unable to take his eyes off the glisten of ginger light dancing in her eyes.

"I—" Korbyn stuttered, flushed when he noticed the dissipating space between them.

"Read it for me," Salem whispered. "Please."

"Alright." He succumbed, uncrumpling the paper. The candle provided a faint glow on the unfolded parchment, though he didn't require its aid. Still, he wavered, unable to begin.

"I'm ready," Salem urged.

Korbyn nodded. "Right."

He cleared his throat, failing to alleviate his shaking hand. With a deep inhale, he recited the scrawls of his note. "You told me that the black feather symbolizes protection and transformation. Ever since I awoke with a forgotten past, I've been torn and conflicted about my present and my future. I felt lost in a sea with a horizon of water surrounding me, swimming against waves that were desperate to drown me. That's when I found a symbol of hope, a black feather lingering in the breeze and lifting me with a gust of wind from the depths of the drowning water.

"I know not if this feather belongs to a crow or raven. While the crow symbolizes change and transformation like its matching darkness, the raven represents evil and misfortune. Both elude me, but you made me believe that I have the choice to decide for myself. Because of you, I want to be a soaring crow over crashing waves that fail to touch me."

Korbyn feigned the rest of the note's words, for he couldn't tell her that he planned to disappear, never to see her again. "Thank you for everything you have done for me, and please take this feather as a reminder. I hope to live up to your expectations." After he finished, he folded the paper and stuffed it in his pocket.

The silence that followed accumulated into budding trepidation. At first, Korbyn avoided meeting her stare, awaiting some sort of response. However, instead of a proper reply in recognition of his candidness, Salem said nothing.

His personal delivery of the letter and feather had resulted in a regretful blunder. As an alternative of approaching her doorstep, he should have left his farewell in the confines of his room. Surely, at some point, she would have discovered his departure. Whether the rest would have truly cared remained an enigma, but it would have at least alleviated the apprehension billowing in his chest.

"I should go," Korbyn whispered, turning to grab the door's handle.

A warm hand wrapped around his own. He halted, the heat of her grasp radiating like a campfire. As it trailed up his arm, the winter of his body dissipated. For a moment, he swore color returned to his skin, the grayscale of his physical appearance shifting into the auburns and tans that it had been before.

"The paths we take are ours to forge, though sometimes it can include trusted companions," Salem whispered, her hold not loosening.

"I agree," Korbyn murmured, not turning to face her for fear of what he might find. Even now, the desire to curl his fingers around her own was too difficult to bear. "But paths leading in the same direction tend to intertwine and may lead in the direction of a darkened forest filled with monsters."

"Good," she responded. He couldn't see her smile, but he knew she displayed one. "For that is what we are: monster hunters. And paths wreathed in shadows are far better than lonely ones."

"This is not a darkness I can see through."

"Then I will light it," Salem declared, shifting her hand so that her fingers interconnected with his.

Korbyn's fingers spazzed from the shock that scurried up his arm, his mark beating like a rebellious heart.

"Let me help you," she pleaded.

"I don't belong here, Salem," he said, unable to prevent the shakiness in his voice. "I don't deserve it."

"If there is one thing that I have learned while in Terrisae, it's that your circumstances do not diminish your merit." Salem's voice converted into a stern proclamation, one he was sure she fully believed. Though, it was only momentary; she converted her confidence to a murmur. "You are capable of choosing your own path and your own worth."

"I may be able to decide, but it doesn't mean the one I chose is the right one." Korbyn sighed. "And as far as I know, they all connect at the end despite the one I take."

"An even better reason to travel the route with companions," the paladin said, spreading the warmth of her thumb with a slide across his palm's side. "With me."

"I can't," he whispered with slack shoulders. "I can't."

"You can," she insisted. "I can't be there for you if you don't let me, Korbyn, but I would like to." She gripped onto his hand tighter, her voice faltering. "In a couple of days, we are headed to Goldenrise to deliver the conclusion of our mission to the emperor. I hope that you will be joining us."

Korbyn tried to ignore the sadness that mingled between her words. "Thank you, Salem." He withdrew his hand, despite its exertion. The chill returned, reminding him of the death lurking inside. "For everything."

He strode from Salem's room, not looking back as he fastened the door to a close.

Quietly, Korbyn approached the house's front door with a quick adjustment of the bag's leather strap. The hallway was a surprisingly long trek in the welcoming silence, other than the echoes of his footsteps. Finally, when he arrived at the door, he seized its handle and halted.

Korbyn was unsure of how long he wavered at the exit, wrestling between conflicting verdicts. As he forged numerous paths and outcomes for each, never did he find a contented resolution. He exhaled a deep breath, leaning against the wooden panel with closed lids before falling victim to further contemplation.

And thus, the decision of the mind halted the body, both con-

stantly foiled by the pressure of the heart, the demon chimed poetically. You stand at a crossroad, little raven. Which route will you
choose? Three realms now rely on your verdict.

TWENTY-FOUR.

A demon in need of brisk banishment—that was what Veeris declared, but this was no demon. This was a man without his memories, a soldier that lost his purpose, an innocent victimized by evil, a friend in need of help. No, this was not a demon at all—this was Korbyn.

Salem strode over to the window, leaning against the sill despite the discomfort bridling in her abdomen. Her temple grazed the glass, and she wrapped her arms around her stomach to comfort the internal and external ache. She watched the entrance door below, waiting for Korbyn's departure just as the sun had done hours before.

The unrestrained, chaotic heartbeats were something she had never before experienced, but she was knowledgeable enough to identify her longing for him. Despite the demon that prowled with expectancy, despite the wicked power that lurked within, despite the fact that they were forbidden from being together, Salem's heart yearned for him.

She raised the feather with its hollow shaft and twirled the quill between her thumb and index. A sad smile spread across her face, entranced by the hues of gray and black. The iridescent feather shone with hints of indigo and navy, the hidden colors shimmering with brilliance under the moonlight.

There was no doubt within her mind that something within him stirred, but she didn't care.

Salem didn't care about Veeris' foreseeable opinion. She didn't care about Elohim's commandment. She didn't care that she was an archangel.

To her surprise, the front door to the cottage never opened.

When Salem was an angel amongst the Heavens, she often looked upon the world and watched the mortals. More than anything, they intrigued her. She observed them as they worked, ate, celebrated, created, suffered, enjoyed, hurt and loved. She somehow empathized with them and envied them all at the same time. They were given a freedom that angels were prohibited to experience. The people were left to their own devices, often praying to Elohim and receiving no answers. Little did mortals know of the true reason for Elohim's absence.

Many years ago, archangels and humans broke His sacred law, forming connections with each other and creating new life. From their violation, the first demons, Kanen and Abel, were born. Elohim's wrath ensued, and Evelyn died in the skirmish of their betrayal. Samael led a rebellion, initiating the catastrophe known as 'The Fall.' Archangels and angels alike on both sides were slaughtered, and the bodies of the dead fell from the Heavens. Salem remembered gazing onto the newborn demons, seeing their crimson eyes for the first time.

She fidgeted with the locket's constant dangling, recalling the same gleam she witnessed in Korbyn's eyes.

After the fall of the rebels and their failed uprising, Elohim exiled them and removed His grace from mortal flesh. Without His blessing, war raged upon the lands that the people were cursed to live in. In Terrisae, wars erupted, natural disasters occurred, monsters ravaged the lands, history became forgotten, and Elohim watched them from above.

"Freedom cannot exist without consequence," Elohim told the angels.

While mortals were left to wither in bodies victim to time, angels like Salem were pristine and perfect, left to soar through the Heavens in a realm of no strife. They were just as beautiful as mortals claimed them to be. Before she willingly relinquished the full capabilities of her powers to walk amongst them, she didn't have to worry about unkempt hair, bathing, eating, training, or other mundane things that mortals were subject to, until now.

Salem huffed, pushing strands of wild hair away from her sweaty face. The walk through the capital city of Goldenrise was a trek on its own. Stationed around the vast city were waves of alert soldiers, careful and wary of arriving travelers. The admittance process took them over an hour and a half, and they finally ventured within its substantial, stone walls.

Unlike the old city of Umberfall, with buildings constructed of brick and wood, Goldenrise was built upon stone, with higher castle walls and surrounding trenches to form a deep moat. The first emperor, with the mind and experience of a knight, built these lands with defensive foundations to prepare themselves for future attacks. The common buildings were no different. They were constructed upon cobblestones and fortified at every corner.

Despite Avernos' army being half the size of the Kingdom of Esperin's, it wasn't a surprise that they were winning the war. As a city built upon the previous rebellion of trained soldiers led by the famous Syrian Claymore, each soldier thereafter his reign was well versed in combat. Throughout the ages of Avernos' establishment, they were led by emperors that were once proficient and experienced knights. Their battle sense and combat intelligence far exceeded the slack of Esperin, especially in stark comparison to King Alecain, the Herald of Light.

Even though Goldenrise was untouched by battles, the people lingered in the dread of uncertainty. As they passed a cemetery near the castle walls, rows of the deceased lined up along the secular cathedral's fief, with monks, physicians, and morticians organizing the bodies. Families gathered underneath the gothic cathedral and perused the dead as though they were browsing at a market stall in search of their fallen relatives. Salem watched with a saddened gaze as people cried, embracing each other when they found someone familiar to them.

She must find the blades.

A broad hand clasped her shoulder. Haven strode beside her, following her eyes to the people in the cathedral's shadow.

"We can't save everyone, Say," the half-orc muttered, shifting his attention back onto the road in the linear direction of Goldenrise's castle. "We can only do what we can."

Salem's smile twitched upwards, the comfort of Haven fighting against the unknown sadness that swelled in her chest. "You're right. Thank you, Haven," she replied, walking side by side with him. "How is it that you're so wise?"

The rest of their mercenary band presumed strides before them. Veeris and Gilben led the front, deep in a conversation of their own. Behind them, Andrid and Oakley chatted incessantly to each other with Korbyn stuck betwixt them, though he didn't seem to mind. He appeared in deep contemplation, giving them vague responses to their ongoing conversation.

"Barely avoiding death has that effect on someone, I suppose," Haven replied, fixated on Andrid. "And it helps when you find someone you want to become better for."

Warmth filled Salem's chest. "When did you know?" she probed.

Haven didn't seem to understand her question, and he glimpsed at Andrid before returning his attention back to Salem.

She elaborated, not tearing her eyes off Korbyn's back. "When did you know you had feelings for Andrid?"

They walked for several minutes without Haven answering her question, silence swelling amid unsettled minds. Enough time had passed that she forgot she had even asked, but Haven disrupted the quiet with a strong and kind voice.

"When I failed my clan's trials to become a warrior, I was exiled. I left the Tribe of Ulatec with no family, no friends, and no name. The world I thought I knew crumbled around me." Salem watched his hand shudder under the weight of the memory. "There were many times when I believed I was vermin to this world, better off not existing at all." Haven's eyes rose to watch Andrid conversing with the others. "But Andrid gave me something valuable that was missing: a purpose. When I was lost in a maze of emotions, it was Andrid who pulled me out. I'm sure it's a lot like how Korbyn feels about you."

Rose crept up Salem's cheeks, and she pulled at the strands that fought for freedom against the tie of her hair, needing her hands to find purpose. "I, uh, am not sure what you mean—"

"You know you're a terrible liar, right?" Haven responded, a smirk coiling across his lips. His candid statement and jest conjured a wave of laughter from her throat.

"I suppose I am." When she gazed forward, her eyes met Korbyn's. Even with his hood on, she could see his expression exuded awe, as if seeing a myth come to life, or a beautiful sunrise across a vast horizon of ocean waves. It was as though he waited for her to laugh again, to bask in a glory that could heal his physical and mental wounds.

They both paid no heed to their surroundings, and Korbyn collided into Veeris' back, causing an abrupt spin and scowl. His glare, almost incandescent, might have formed a fire from the pure intensity in his eyes.

"Sorry—" Korbyn began to say before he was interrupted.

"What did you say?" Veeris challenged.

Fear of argument or an escalating fight washed over Salem, only to realize that he wasn't talking to Korbyn or anyone in the group. When she walked forward with Haven, Veeris was facing a few townsfolk, who seemed confused by his sudden intrusion in their conversation.

"Wh-what?" one of the women stuttered, dressed in dirty rags and covered in the grime of a worker's day. At first, the lady didn't realize Veeris' inquiry was directed at her. She remained stagnant in a dumbfounded gawk.

"I asked what you said about Fort Runswhick," Veeris repeated. "Please."

"Oh, we were just saying that the emperor's army overtook Fort Runswhick..." the other woman amongst them stated, followed by a nod from the man at her side.

"Another group of soldiers left Goldenrise a couple of days ago to reinforce their hold," the man answered. "The volunteers of Kendra Dawn went with them. I was just telling them that I hope we didn't lose too many."

"Thank you," Veeris responded, coercing the mercenaries into a circle and away from prying eyes. Somehow, he excluded Korbyn, and Salem shimmied away from Veeris to allow him entry. Veeris frowned at her, but she replied with a contrived unawareness.

"They took over Fort Runswhick already? That's the largest fort Esperin has!" Oakley exclaimed in surprise.

"There's going to be a lot of bodies." Salem sighed. She sent a quick prayer up to Elohim, despite knowing that she wouldn't reach Him, the locket heavy in her hand.

"Then we need to make our time here short," Veeris urged, to everyone's agreement. "Let's hurry and meet with the emperor. We don't want to be there any longer than we need to."

"If that's the case, maybe we should split up? We need some rations and gear before leaving. I need to restock," Oakley said, nodding in approval of his own statement.

"Good call. Veeris, Gilben, and I will go meet with the emperor. Oakley, Haven, Andrid, and Korbyn will gather the supplies and food we'll need for our travel to the fort." Salem didn't miss Veeris' smirk.

"I don't mind goin' with the lads to buy some thin's," Gilben interjected, holding up the large bag of coins on his person. As the keeper of their funds, the gold raddled from his movements.

"No offense, but you're a cheapskate," Oakley stated, holding out his palm with unfurled fingers. "Hand it over."

Gilben frowned and searched the group for assistance, clutching onto his coin purse tighter. Salem offered an apologetic grin.

"Sorry, Gilben," Salem said, motioning to Oakley. "He's right."

"Alrigh' but try not ta spend it all!"

When Gilben took too long to separate from the gold, Oakley whisked it away. Veeris maneuvered the dwarf in the castle's direction with several pats on the shoulder, his version of a subtle condolence.

As the rest parted, a hand grabbed her forearm. A familiar and addictive tingling shot up to her fingers, like waves of ice. She looked back, meeting Korbyn's regard.

"Korbyn?" Salem asked.

He resided in quiet scrutiny during the span of several passing commoners, though no one paid heed to their secluded moment. "Please try not to piss off another country's leader," Korbyn muttered, his voice passing through the darkness of his hood.

When a mischievous grin crossed her face, he frowned. "That doesn't sound like something I'd do," Salem replied, feigning innocence. "Maybe you just don't have faith in me."

"On the contrary, I have too much faith that you'll do the right thing, but not enough faith that you will keep your trap shut," Korbyn replied, his frown transitioning into a smile.

Salem mirrored his visage, stepping closer to whisper her next words. "I'll do my best," she responded with a teetering chuckle. "Oh, and Korbyn," she added, eyes roaming towards his grasping hand. "I'm glad you stayed."

Korbyn was gifted at masking his thoughts; however, for a brisk moment, she swore she saw unanimous longing in the uptilt of his smile.

"For now," he responded.

Salem frowned. "Are you referring to my appreciation of your company or your choice to continue accompanying us?"

Korbyn bore a smirk, one so enticing that she might have declared it sinful. "I guess we'll find out," he whispered with a craned neck, endeavoring to see past the loose stands of her hair. She hid her blush with a spin, facing the path that led to the castle.

"I guess we will!" Salem declared. "But you made a choice, Korbyn, one I will remember if you choose to leave again. I may not let you next time."

Though she didn't see it for herself, she was certain he wore another devilish grin.

"I might, just so you can try and stop me," Korbyn responded, his rasped voice intermingling with a huffing chuckle.

She couldn't hinder the tingling in her cheeks.

In this moment, Salem was thankful she was no longer pristine.

Salem disliked many things.

She disliked the abrupt moments of waking up on an early morning, when her favorite fruits became too ripe, when people were discourteous and apathetic, when royalty constantly assumed that they were better than other people, and most of all, she disliked waiting.

Salem might have understood the busyness of a leader amid war, if she hadn't overheard the regent whisper to one of the soldiers the real reason for their elongated wait. The emperor was currently engaged in a very personal meeting with four women from the brothel. She couldn't possibly imagine what they had been doing for almost two and a half hours.

The three of them sat impatiently in the castle's great hall before the regent finally retrieved them. The man greeted them dismissively and unapologetically before he led them to the emperor.

Salem, Veeris, and Gilben walked down a grand, long hall, with columns and tall arches leading to alternate walkways on either side. Above the arcs were different floors with several balconies overlooking the main corridor. Chandeliers made of silver hung from the ceiling's tallest point, reaching down to illuminate the pathway in front of them. Sconces lit up each column marked on both sides, dimly flickering in low, unnoticed flames, and not thanked by the ones that walked through the illuminated hall.

In front of every other bracket stood stagnant soldiers, embellished with cuirasses of sleek design and cloths of crimson. The sigil of Avernos glimmered across their chests, revealing their recent shine. Each bore matching pairs of studs in their lobes. They never shifted, but Salem sensed their watchfulness as they proceeded down the corridor.

They eventually arrived in front of imposing, dual doors made of wood and fortified by iron. Two soldiers on either side nodded to the regent as they approached and swung both open to reveal the grand throne room.

Like the rest of the city, the castle was fortified with thick cobblestones. The wide, long room felt like a mile walk as they strode down the red carpet that led up to the grand throne, which sat on an elevated pedestal. The seat was simple but large, with a red cushion and iron designs painted gold. Along the arms and the back of the chair were patterns resembling flames, the designs encircling each other all the way to the highest point in the chair, where the flame erupted upwards.

Behind the throne was a tall, arched window. The window-panes were recently cleaned, with rays of sunlight cascading through the flawless glass.

"Mercenaries of Kendra Dawn, it's a pleasure," Emperor Wymond proclaimed, welcoming them with a straightened back and a lifted chin. His posture and gestures presented the persona of a trained warrior. Unlike King Alecain, who had fallen victim to age, Emperor Wymond in his later years aged like unopened wine, with hints of grays peeking noticeably through his well-tapered mane and facial hair. Even as a man older than the King of Esperin, Emperor Wymond was conditioned for combat at any given notice. His practiced hands still held callouses.

"Thank you, Emperor Wymond," Salem stated and bowed, followed by leans from Veeris and Gilben. "We came to inform you of the completion of our job in Shadowbane Forest."

Emperor Wymond's face remained stoic, nodding in affirmation. "Very good. Then the ogre is dead?"

Salem dipped her head in response. "Yes, but there were more ogres in the forest than expected. There were eleven in total. Each were slain."

He couldn't hide the slight twitch of his mouth that threatened to form a smile. "Very good. I apologize, but I do not have much extra time to spend, so the regent will accompany you to the grand hall to give you your reward. You are dismissed."

The emperor waved them off before rising from his seated position. Veeris and Gilben bowed and turned, ready to follow the regent out of the large double doors that provided their entry.

"Actually, I had a couple more questions that I was hoping you could elaborate on," Salem interjected, unmoving from her position. Her arms remained just as firm in place behind her, with one palm clamping the alternate wrist. She couldn't see Veeris' glare, but she could feel the penetrating leer.

"One question, and make it quick," Emperor Wymond demanded, sitting back on his throne.

Salem would have to choose her limited options carefully.

"Before we got to Enderbrooke, we were informed that there was some destruction in the town caused by monsters coming out of Shadowbane Forest; however, when we got there, there weren't any issues. I was wondering what exactly happened beforehand," Salem explained, raising two fingers to her locket and adjusting its place on her chest.

"We got word from the townsfolk on the edge of Enderbrooke that they saw creatures and monsters wandering out of the forest and destroying their property. One specifically saw a gigantic ogre," Emperor Wymond stated with a brief flicker of his eyes. "If you didn't see any destruction, then they must have rebuilt their fences. They are the working class, after all." He straightened his stiff composure. "We didn't wait too long before we requested your services."

Salem kept her face void of any reaction or emotion. "It makes sense that you would call upon our aid instead of sending your own soldiers, given the circumstances of the war and our expertise."

The emperor nodded. "Yes. I need all my soldiers and resources for the war. I'm glad you were able to take care of the problem. Is that all, Paladin of Dawn?"

Salem bowed deeply. The emperor had already risen from his

seat.

"Yes, Emperor Wymond. Thank you for your time," Salem replied, withdrawing her magic. "We will be headed to Fort Runswhick to assist the rest of the volunteers, if you would be so kind to please give them notice of our arrival."

Emperor Wymond halted. "That won't be necessary," he said, diverting his attention when a messenger approached. He retrieved a quill from the man's hands and signed a document. "I already turned the volunteers of Kendra Dawn away from Fort Runswhick. The bodies have already been taken care of."

"What?" Salem snapped.

"I said that won't be necessary—"

"Yes, I understand what you said, but I don't know why you said it. What do you mean the bodies have been taken care of?" Salem retorted.

She could sense Gilben and Veeris' apprehension behind her, but she cared more for the man trying to dismiss their continual presence.

"The men of Esperin that were stationed at Fort Runswhick bore disease. To prevent further spreading, we were required to dispose all the casualties from the battle. They were burned." There was no hint of remorse behind his voice. "Therefore, there are no bodies to be returned to Avernos or Esperin. I also informed the rest of the volunteers of Kendra Dawn that we would take care of any future instances and that their assistance was no longer required during the rest of the war."

"But we signed a contract stating our neutral assistance so that the bodies can be safely returned to their homes for the passing rite of Elohim—"

"And I have continuously informed you that it will no longer be necessary. The passage of Elohim is a sacrament fashioned by Esperin and not performed by our country. We have merely amused your beliefs to appear courteous, but your presence is nothing but a hindrance to the end of the war." It was then that Emperor Wymond heeded them, his age irrevocably presented in the deep wrinkles of his brow. "If your mercenary services are needed, I will send aid. Otherwise, Kendra Dawn is dismissed from Avernos' duty. If you really wish to be useful, then get out of my way and leave my throne room, immediately."

The rampant retorts Salem prepared never left her mouth, for Veeris interrupted her by roughly pushing her down by the back of the head. He lowered his own stature, and soon they both mimicked an appreciative-looking bow.

"Thank you, Emperor Wymond," Veeris proclaimed. "We greatly value your eternal generosity."

Salem's penetrating glare didn't falter even when they departed the castle's confines.

"Nothin' quite like a bag full o' gold in yer hands," Gilben proclaimed with a grand smile hidden underneath his beard. He shifted his palms underneath the larger bag, the pieces clanking with his rising hands from the satisfying gesture.

Once they exited the premises of the castle, Veeris obstructed Salem's path with exasperated poise. "Do you despise every person of authority? Or do you just find amusement in lingering on the edge between freedom and execution?"

"What did you expect me to do? Roll over and abide by his command? He unlawfully broke our treaty and burned all the bodies! Something's wrong, Veeris, very wrong."

"Of course something's wrong—they're in the middle of a war!" Veeris hissed, a firm perseverance to counter Salem's vicious glare. "Even if he is up to something, do you think he'd just tell you outright?"

"No. I knew that he'd lie to answer whatever question I asked him," Salem retorted, lifting her chin with a gratified grin. "The purpose of my questions was to sense if he was lying, and he was."

Gilben executed an elongated whistle of profound awe. "Tha's a great ability ya got there, lass. How'd ya manage tha' one?" the dwarf wondered, stuffing a gold coin in his teeth and trying to bend it to ensure the coin's authenticity.

"I've got my ways." Salem smiled, motioning to the locket across her neck. "Emperor Wymond lied about several things. One, he lied about the destruction of the town and that he sent for our immediate aid. Obviously, he didn't because we found the recent bodies of Avernos soldiers in Shadowbane Forest. This means that defeating the ogres in the forest was caused by some other, unknown motive." She contemplated for a moment, reimagining the skirmish with the monsters within Shadowbane. "Those ogres we killed, they weren't normal creatures. The forest has always been an enigma, but it was as if the ogres weren't even alive, or at least, they shouldn't have been. It urges me to believe it has something to do with why we were sent there in the first place.

"Two, he lied about sending Kendra Dawn away from Fort Runswhick. We know this to be true because people in the city saw Kendra Dawn leaving north with the second troop of soldiers just a couple of days ago, which means that the emperor doesn't want our group snooping in their plans."

"And you want to go to Fort Runswhick, despite the emperor's orders?" Veeris asked.

Salem nodded. "If the volunteers are truly at the fort, they might need us, and if Micah heard about this, she'll be headed to the fort as well. She'd want us to meet her there."

"You know we could die disobeying the emperor's direct orders, right?" Veeris warned.

Gilben gave him a slightly hard nudge with his elbow, Veeris' scorn following thereafter.

"Aye, but we already knew that becomin' mercenaries fer Kendra Dawn, didn't we, lad?" Gilben declared, his unseen, yet contagious smile brimming underneath coarse locks.

Veeris rolled his eyes and sighed. "I already know what you're going to say, Salem. Let's grab the rest of the group and head to Fort Runswhick."

TWENTY-FIVE.

Goldenrise and its familiarity continued to elude him. The capital of Avernos resembled more a glorified fort than it did a city, its buildings made of cobblestone compiled in relative proximity, connected by single arches of flint architecture. The flushwork of unsplit cobbles along the walls seemed particularly arranged, portraying a beautiful and decisive décor. Even the streets were made of cobbles, forming a unified and fortified city within large, strong walls.

Occasionally, Korbyn would see arrangements of plants and greenery in flowerpots dangling from the cobblestone porticoes or situated in front of doorways to bestow life where it was usually scarce. The city bustled with bodies and voices, with people disregarding each other as they resumed their habitual activities.

As he walked by each person and face, he studied them closely from underneath the shadow of his hood. Before his memory loss, he once roamed these streets, prevailing as a man with another name. However, that fraudulent persona felt more like a stranger in comparison to his current identity. Thankfully, none of the faces struck him with remembrance, for he couldn't confront them with his outlandish appearance, and certainly not with the monster he housed.

The sloth evades what it is too fearful to contend with.

Shut up. I didn't ask you, Korbyn thought.

The demon snickered. *Complacent is the one who quiets their voice when they should speak in retaliation.*

Instead of amusing it, Korbyn focused further on the gathering folk at the grand cemetery's ingress. The civilians continued their excursions through the masses in search of familiar faces, which he assumed was an elongated process. If not for the miracle that Korbyn experienced, he would have been amongst those bodies right now. He forwent the prospect of his family and friends searching for his remains.

How easily it would have been to locate them, as Korbyn was certain at least one person might have recognized him, despite the disparity in his appearance. Admittedly, the thought frightened him, for if he were to return, who would be waiting for him? Would they be just as frightened as he? He wasn't sure if it was his unselfishness of wanting to protect them from whatever this dark power was, or if he was too self-centered to give up the new life he had created for himself.

"Momma, wait!" a young voice said.

Korbyn turned, seeing a young girl no older than ten years of age tugging on her mother's arm. They originated from the lower district, as exhibited by their ragged clothes and torn shoes. The adolescent's face was covered in scattered freckles, accompanied by dirt and grime across her slightly tanned features. Her eyes brimmed with tears as she desperately pulled her mother back in the direction of the cemetery's landscape with failed efforts.

"He has to be there somewhere! We can look again!" she cried.

"I'm sorry, my little owl. He's gone," the mother replied, hugging the girl's smaller form tightly. "I'm so sorry."

As their unified cries echoed across the cobblestone, Korbyn strode away from them. He lowered his head, hoping the large hood would conceal his sadness, and he became dubious of the overwhelming despondency and its origins. Was he covetous of the passed soul for the displayed care of his family or sympathetic for the two the man left behind?

"So," Oakley muttered, slowing his strides to meet Korbyn's, "you and Salem, huh?" A wild grin formed across his face.

"Me and Salem what?" Korbyn scoffed.

"You and Salem! You know..." Oakley lifted both of his hands before meeting both palms together, intermingling his fingers with one another until they were firmly clasped.

Korbyn replied with a fine line of his lips and silence.

"You know!" Oakley insisted.

"I don't," Korbyn retorted. "You're going to have to specify."

"You know...giving her a green gown," Oakley whispered. When Korbyn still didn't understand, he continued with poor explanation. "Doing the deed of darkness? Bumpin' uglies? Doing the dance without pants? Sexual stabbing—"

Korbyn slapped a hand over the shorter man's mouth.

"Okay, okay, for fuck's sake, Oakley, I get it," he retorted, removing his palm. Oakley's bluntness caused a stir within his stomach, and Korbyn reached up to the curve of his hood and dragged it further over his face. "We're not doing anything."

"What? You guys are at least smooching, right?"

"We're not together."

"What? You're lying. You guys are flirting like crazy!"

"We weren't flirting." Korbyn mumbled, endeavoring to conceal the embarrassment fluttering across his face.

"Okay, but you two clearly want to be together," Oakley retorted with a waggle of his eyebrows.

"No, we don't."

"Uh-huh, sure, because I write love notes to people I don't want to have bang-bang time with."

"First of all, never say that again. Secondly, what do you mean, love note?"

Oakley smirked, snapping his wrist with a smooth flick as a piece of paper unfolded from his pocket. He coughed with a closed fist over his lips before he dramatically read its contents in a deeper voice, mimicking Korbyn's: "You told me that the black feather symbolizes protection and transformation. Ever since I awoke with a forgotten past, I've been torn and conflicted about my present and my future. I felt lost in a sea with a horizon of water—"

Korbyn snatched the crumpled parchment from his grasp. "Where did you get that?" he questioned, looking through his empty pocket.

Oakley grinned triumphantly. "You can't just think I'm a pretty face, can you?" he asked, batting his eyelashes. Korbyn glared. "I took it from your pocket, obviously." Oakley lifted both of his hands in the air, waving his fingers independently of each other. "These are magic hands, Korb. No lock or pair of legs stay closed from these for long—"

Korbyn gripped the top of Oakley's head, pushing it downwards with a wild smirk of his own. "You say that, yet your tent seems rather empty these days, sticky fingers." He chuckled triumphantly while Oakley flailed his arms in retaliation. Korbyn pushed him forward, and the smaller man rubbed the top of his head with a pout.

"Yeah, yeah, whatever. Guess I was just imagining things, or you must talk to every girl like that," Oakley replied with a sneer.

Korbyn rolled his eyes and scoffed. "I don't talk to anyone else like that."

"So, you admit you were flirting then?" Oakley declared with an expanded grin.

Korbyn opened his mouth, then snapped it shut. "You know, maybe I was wrong about you. I assumed because you were so small, you must have a proportional brain," he said, wrapping him in a headlock.

"Ow, ow, ow! Watch the hair! My curls formed so perfectly today! You're going to ruin the charm!" Oakley thrashed.

Andrid slowed their pace, sticking their tongue out at Oakley to join the commotion. "Can't have what don't have!" They laughed, reaching for Oakley's side and prodding his vulnerable form.

The fox trotted happily at their side, staring up at their antics. Korbyn smiled genuinely while he analyzed his friends. Despite his strange experiences, he was happy.

"We're here," Haven interrupted.

Korbyn stopped, viewing the wide marketplace in front of them. The alley they traversed opened into a large street filled with cobblestone buildings and vibrant crowds. Multiple groups of people gathered around makeshift tents of leather and canvas upheld by wooden stakes with metal fittings that supported the fabric securely. Along the street were several shops behind the tents, with metal signs dangling horizontally from buildings that depicted their trade.

"It would be best if we split up and gather the supplies we need," Haven stated, gathering the mercenaries around him before they ventured deep into the busied streets. "Andrid and I will oversee provisions, soap, tinderboxes, pitons, sealing wax, ink, parchment, and a barrel of water. Oakley, you'll need to gather some bottles of holy water blessed by bishops and some empty vials."

Oakley saluted. "I also need some more supplies as well...toxins, antitoxins, herbalism ingredients, snake venom..." He became distracted by his mumbles, counting his extended fingers.

His footsteps guided him towards an alchemy shop, already consumed by his tasks.

"What do you want me to get?" Korbyn asked.

Haven pulled out a parchment. His handwriting was surprisingly elegant for such a hardened warrior, and easily legible. Analyzing the list, Korbyn read rope, hunting traps, oil, two grappling hooks, ball bearings, fishing equipment, universal solvents…

"There should be a shop at the far end of the market where they sell traveling gear. If you can get those things, it could save us a lot of time," Haven said, holding onto the back of Andrid's tunic to prevent them from wandering off when they began to walk in a random direction.

Korbyn nodded, folding the parchment in his pocket. "No worries. You can count on me."

Korbyn, in fact, couldn't be counted on.

He exited the traveling gear shop, readjusting his heavy satchel when he stepped down the stairs. He wore a deep frown and furrowed brows, thanks to the shopkeeper he just ended a conversation with. Korbyn pulled out his coin purse and shifted through the last few pieces of silver in his possession. The selfish buyer swindled him easily, practically taking all the coin he owned for everything he needed. He huffed in annoyance. For some reason, deception came easily, but it seemed like bartering wasn't a correlative skill.

With items on hand, Korbyn strode through the diminishing crowd. It eased a bit of his tension as the space reformed into a more conspicuous path. Despite the lack of greenery and natural plantations, grass occasionally rose from the cobbles along the road. Many people decorated their establishments in assortments of flowers, with lots of gardenias and a strange floret with narrow, tufted leaves and an elongated stem. Spikes of white petals and yellow stamens pointed sporadically from the vertical plant, and he recognized them to be from the asphodel family. He traced the edge of his finger across one of its thin petals, and it shied away. The flora's aversion from his touch was palpable.

Eventually, Korbyn halted at the entrance of a smaller alleyway when he noticed a lone shop. Its sign hid beneath a veil of darkness, tattered and forgotten. It bore no name, but instead it displayed an image of a unicorn with unfolded wings. At the bottom of the metal framework were two hinges that swayed in the wind, as if they once held a continuation of the sign where the title of the shop had once been. After several minutes of contemplation, he stepped within the shadow of the building and entered the unlocked door.

The room was dark compared to some of the other shops within the market, lit by only a single metal chandelier with three sconces at each point, two of which were unlit. Scattered across the room sat dusty, glass display cases with vases filled with freshly watered white and blond daffodils. The vases were designed with dripping paint of burgundy fading into yellowed ivory, cracked and rusted. Instead of walls, tall bookshelves extended all the way up to the ceiling around the perimeter of the small shop, bursting with books, charms, antiques, and other random assortments of items he didn't recognize.

A collector of artifacts, trinkets, and untold truths. Where did you go when the body, mind, and heart were separated? the demon cooed.

"Hello?" Korbyn questioned when he saw no one within the shop. He peered behind the glass case, but the entire store seemed empty, save for the open door with a shroud of tapestry. Hearing no one's reply, he examined some of the random assortments of trinkets and jewelry within the glass display.

The first thing he noticed was a deck of cards randomly

spread across a golden, silk cloth. They were different from a set of seventy-two that Oakley, Gilben and Andrid often played with. Instead of numbers, they adorned varying illustrations, each unique in contrast to the next. One held an empress, an emperor, a sun, a moon, a wheel of fortune, and then one that required further analysis.

That card portrayed a skeleton wearing a dark slate robe with a downturned hood. The background of the card was completely black, except for the white of the skeleton and the moon. The dead man was clutching onto a scythe with a wooden staff, the blade transitioning into the crescent moon that hung from the sky. Unlike the rest of the cards, this one faced him upside down.

Korbyn moved on, trailing over other items displayed within the glass case. Jewelry of gold and silver shined against the lit sconce on the ceiling. In the middle of the display was a beautiful, golden ring. It was traditionally feminine, seemingly able to only fit on slender fingers. In terms of the design, it had two raised symbols from the shank, a three-quarter sun with three protruding points on the left side to portray its rays, and a crescent moon on the right. Between both celestial bodies there was a small gap, preventing their touch. Both entities sheathed diamonds within their multiple prongs, securely fastened in its intricate motif. It reminded him of a commencing eclipse.

"Good eye," Korbyn heard from above his leaned head.

An older woman appeared on the other side of the glass case. Despite her hunched form, her voice didn't waver like most elders. It was breathy but stern. Her messy hair was tied in a loose bun at the base of her neck, with strands of blond and gray sporadically curled around her face. She stood with a forward lean, a warm grin, and a pair of wrinkled, closed eyes.

"Oh, yes it's beautiful," Korbyn responded, wondering how she knew what he was observing.

She slid the case open and pulled out the cushion the ring rested upon. It shone even brighter once uncaged from the glass. "I will go ahead and prepare it for you," the older woman stated, taking a small, soft fabric and wrapping it with utmost care.

Korbyn stuttered when she grabbed a small box made of cherry wood and iron framework. "Oh, I'm sorry, I-I can't actually afford it. I was just looking," he stammered, waving his hands dismissively.

The woman continued to place the ring inside the box and clamped it shut, sliding it across the glass. "You have already paid a grand price, young man," she replied, the folds in her skin deepening with her widening grin. "You just know not what it is yet."

Korbyn's breath hitched, and he tried to analyze the emotions and intentions that trailed through the windows of her soul, but they remained hidden by her closed lids.

"I'm sorry, I don't think I understand what you mean," Korbyn replied, scanning the burgundy box.

"You will."

When Korbyn gazed back up at where the woman had been standing, she was gone, leaving him alone under the flutter of a single flame.

TWENTY-SIX.

In the years of traveling through Terrisae, one of Veeris' most fond memories was traversing the Mountains of Agathor and standing atop a cliff at the landscape's edge. Despite the substandard beauty Terrisae provided in comparison to the Heavens, he still wished to stand forever at Salem's side, watching the sun rise past the floating specks of the Forgotten Isles far to the east.

Upon its precipice, an intrusive thought infiltrated Veeris' mind. If he jumped, how long would it take to succumb to death? Did waters await him below? If so, how deep did they run? Did dangerous creatures lie within? In his previous angelic life, he would have easily unfurled his wings and soared. Now, with the limitations of a mortal body and the loss of his holy magic, he would surely concede to death's call.

Veeris had been content with his previous life. War was a distant memory, strife was but the consequences of those unfit to behold Elohim's grace, and they once inhibited boundless capabilities, but Salem wasn't pleased with the overall status of the mortal lands. Though she had never met them, still she yearned for the end of corporeal suffering. Even though his adoration was mostly for her rather than her aspirations, Veeris still temporarily surrendered his angelic powers and descended onto this marred landscape.

Terrisae faced much discord. War, natural disasters, economic and geographic decline, monster onslaughts and outbreaks of disease, mortals demonstrated their inability to combat these tremendous affairs on their own. Salem begrudgingly quarreled with Elohim, begging for His intervention. For many years, He denied her, for He granted them the very freedom they wished to attain. Veeris agreed wholeheartedly, for how could they act on their own accord then plead for assistance when faced with consequences? Their blatant ignorance eluded him; however, he still chose this temporary circumstance to assist her, for if they could find the blades, Elohim would agree to his divine arbitration. And Veeris believed in her capabilities, for she was the most astounding being he had ever met.

She was much unlike the woman across the inn now, enamored with a monster.

After their excursions through Goldenrise, the mercenaries reunited at a local inn close to the city's walls. Veeris was in the middle of organizing Andrid's belongings and supplies with a scowl on his face. He pulled out packs of different ingredients, including thyme, peppermint, calendula, and ginger, which were some of the constituents they had just resupplied a couple hours prior. He distributed some of the components in small bags of leather and others in short, round jars with wide corks. He tightened the containers to prevent any spillage and wrapped them in emerald ribbons, tying them around the glass base and securing a knot at the top to prevent the glass from clinking against one another.

Lastly, Veeris withdrew pieces of parchment that were cut to the size of his finger. He carefully folded the sides to prevent any sharpened edges, forming them to imitate makeshift tags. He retrieved an ink set, which contained a new quill and an unopened bottle. Pulling off the cork, Veeris dipped the edge of the quill in the dark ink and titled each of the ingredients. When he finished, he pulled pieces of string through each of the tags and wrapped them around the ends of the bags and the corks of the bottles.

Veeris took Andrid's messy satchel and removed the dirt and unused contents. He positioned the glass bottles first, ensuring their security. Afterwards, he positioned the bags on top and in between each of the jars so that they wouldn't inadvertently break. Once his reorganization and cleaning had been completed, he tied the satchel closed and searched for Andrid's whereabouts across the inn.

Andrid resided at one of the tables with Gilben, perched on their heels abnormally in a crepitating chair. A mix of different ingredients were randomly dispersed on the table in a heap of untidiness, and Veeris sneered when he saw the powders mixing. He wasn't too interested in herbalism, but he knew blending elements before preparing a concoction was unwise.

"Then when done mixing ginseng, lavender, 'nd ginger, take dirt. Earth blessed remedy," Andrid explained, lifting their elbows and instructing Gilben how to properly mix components with empty hands, acting as if they were holding an imaginary mortar in one and a pestle in the other.

Gilben mimicked the gesture, raising his shoulders to put more force into the concoction, though Veeris deemed the gesticulation unnecessary.

Veeris respected the study of herbalism, but magical means deemed more beneficial than naturally brewed ones. Unlike remedies of the earth, which relied on a slower healing process, the supremacy of the arcane was much more effective. Holy energy could imitate phytotherapy, including alleviating swelling, treating allergies, boosting immune systems, and lightening fatigue. Magic could also instantly cure diseases and even heal fatal wounds. Despite the temporary existence of individual decidite, the boundless possibilities and superior results proved worth it. Besides, as someone who no longer beheld the power of an angel, he was left with little to no choice.

When Veeris left the Heavens, he no longer had access to his holy magic like Salem. Because she had been an archangel, she was still tied to a portion of her radiant abilities with the power of her conduit, the locket. He, however, a mere follower and lesser angel, seemed so much more mortal than she. To this day, he didn't feel any form of connection to the Heavens like he used to.

"Here, Andrid," Veeris greeted stoically, retrieving the satchel from his shoulder and placing it on the table.

Andrid's eyes gleamed, unhooking the bag and shuffling through it to inspect Veeris' organizational methods. "Very kind, Veery," they stated, bearing him a toothy grin. "Always kind...no, sometimes kind."

Veeris frowned. "What do you mean, sometimes?" he grumbled with a downward tug of his mouth.

An expression of innocence crossed their face, feigning ignorance.

Gilben chuckled, mixing the components of the remedy as Andrid had instructed. "I think they're meanin' the way ya treat Korbyn."

"I'm not sure what you mean," Veeris lied.

Andrid huffed and spun in the chair until they faced him. "Terrible at lying. Try harder."

Veeris mirrored their expression. "Oh, shut it."

Andrid stuck out their tongue, to which Veeris mirrored their child-like antics. Andrid burst into a fit of snorting laughter. Their contagious mirth formed a smile of his own.

"Like when smile better. You funny sometimes," Andrid encouraged.

"What do you mean sometimes? You know what, forget it. I'm not getting into this conversation again."

Andrid punched Veeris in the shoulder a little too hard. He winced, rubbing his tender muscle.

There were moments when he wished Salem's mission was over so that they could return to the Heavens and reclaim their rightful places. But being here with them now, Veeris sometimes wished it never would.

"Ya know, lad," Gilben said, not taking his eyes off the herbal remedy in his hands. Just as he did when creating a new song, he lobbed together the ingredients carelessly. The dwarf used to always say that precision could accidentally inhibit an innovative and idiosyncratic work of art...in simpler terms, of course. "Ya don't have ta be so hard on 'im."

Veeris scanned for the demon's whereabouts subconsciously. The creature was removing gathered provisions from its bag and preparing them for distribution amongst the mercenaries, thoroughly examining each supply it withdrew.

Veeris exasperatingly sighed, unprepared for another tedious lecture. He was much older than the dwarf, but he somehow was never able to avoid his unbearable orations. At one point, Gilben recited a forty-five-minute lecture on the importance of tone when speaking to people who were besieged with delicate hearts. The truth was never kind, Veeris debated, just as it was never revealed.

The rest of the group had no idea he and Salem were angels, temporarily under the guise of mortals. It was much safer that way, to lie about their origins. It was part of the deal they made with Elohim. Under no circumstances should they explain their genesis. It would raise too many questions, and they would have few answers. Veeris knew, watching the demon, that they weren't the only ones with hidden truth.

As the monster, Oakley, and Haven distributed the supplies, they spoke in hushed tones. Intermittently, Oakley intervened with a joke that Veeris still couldn't hear, but he could insinuate its implication based on the crude expression across his face. In response, the demon elbowed him, a display of a close bond. Haven also interjected with some type of comment, causing the monster to smile. They unanimously chuckled at whatever had been said, with Oakley following suit.

Veeris' brows furrowed.

"Korbyn's kind 'nd thoughtful," Gilben stated, handing the mortar and pestle over to Andrid once he had completed the mixing. "'nd he could use a couple o' more allies."

"I have no intention of being his ally," Veeris muttered to Gilben and Andrid, careful to keep his voice unheard from those on the other side of the room. Even if he kept his voice low, the demon could probably hear every word that they were saying. It might even be feigning the conversation with Oakley and Haven, awaiting any secrets or knowledge they might exchange.

Salem strode over to Oakley, Haven, and the monster, carrying three hooded lanterns. After their conversation and persistent gazes, she turned away with a growing blush and a creeping smile. The creature glanced away in tandem, its sheepish reaction matching her own. Oakley and Haven both huffed a knowledgeable grin at their abashed responses.

"Is it because o' how they feel about each other?" Gilben inquired.

"No," Veeris replied. "I just don't trust him."

It wasn't a complete lie. A large part of him hated it for being the one to make beautiful hues of rose swell to her cheeks. He hated it for being the one to make her smile rise like the glowing sun amidst the morning dew. He hated it for breaking down the barrier of unbreakable stone Salem placed around her heart. Most of all, Veeris hated the fact that there was a small possibility that the charm wasn't faked at all.

"Friends should trust each other," Andrid stated in a surprisingly coherent proclamation, taking a bite out of a piece of jerky with gluttonous intentions. They chomped profusely, saliva around their food with every obnoxious chew.

Veeris slammed the palm of his hand over their mouth. "Friends should also remember to chew with their mouth closed."

When he removed his hand, Andrid bore another grin, with pieces of food sticking out of their yellowed teeth.

"And him and I aren't friends."

Andrid's smile shifted into a pout. "Why, Veery?" they asked, emphasizing the nickname they continuously insisted on using. Their arms folded against their chest, preparing themselves for another argument, which somehow seemed to be one-sided.

"It's nothing to concern yourself with, Andrid," Veeris replied with pat on their head.

"You make promise now," Andrid continued swiftly. "Promise you will try and be friend."

Before Veeris could deny the request, Andrid raced off towards the other side of the inn and wrapped their arms around the demon's torso. It seemed surprised by the gesture but laid an arm on top of their shoulders to return the affectionate display. Afterwards, Andrid stole one of Oakley's organized, filled vials and raced off, with the rogue chasing on their heels.

"Sometimes it's a bit dangerous to put faith in those ya don't trust," Gilben stated, smiling over at the band of mercenaries. "But there'll be times in yer life when yer walkin' on a path, 'nd it stops at a cliff. Ya can either turn around or take a leap o' faith. It might just be clear waters at the bottom."

"And if the water is grim and full of dangerous creatures?"

"Then at least ya know, instead o' guessin' on the unknown."

When Veeris glimpsed at the group, the demon's eyes shifted to meet his own.

There were indeed dual pools at the bottom of this precipice, the black waters bearing reflections of the wicked moon. Underneath the waves, a monster stirred.

"I think I'll stick to the top of the cliff," Veeris whispered only to himself.

TWENTY-SEVEN.

When the ninth hour after dawn rang, initiating midafternoon, Korbyn and the rest of the mercenaries vacated Goldenrise with haste.

Korbyn sat at the edge of the wagon, hanging his legs out the back to stare towards the previously trekked road as they escalated a grand hill. The unpaved path proved to be rather soothing as the caravan marched over rocks and dirt, moving in tandem with the trotting speed of the horse.

It had been about three and a half hours since they departed Goldenrise, though it would still be a long trek until they reached the border of Exonia Creek. The sun initiated its evitable departure, and they planned to deduct time from their usual sleep to ensure their brisk arrival, not that Korbyn could submit to slumber anyway. If they passed Exonia Creek swiftly, they might be able to pass before the emperor's notice of their void contract reached the midguard.

Korbyn slid his fingers over the obsidian rock with speckles and lines of white, the continuous motion habitual across its texture. His perpetuity stirred contemplation as he outlined the trail of ivory, attempting to recognize which symbolic path he currently traversed. The matted basalt and quartz heeded no reply, and he could not determine if the stone recognized his concern or the meaning of Andrid's gesture.

A heaviness probed Korbyn's intuition, like a watchful and analytical gaze. Andrid's animal friend resided adjacent to the wagon's wall, sprawling comfortably with its head on its front paws and its tail wrapped around its small body. The edge of its tail concealed one of its eyes, but the other uplifted, stabilized on Korbyn's fluctuating attention.

The feminine voice's shrill fortune repeated mentally upon his revisited examination, though he wished to stifle its continuous memory. It projected omniscience, just as ambiguously guiding as the demon; however, both proved maddeningly worthless upon his failed interpretations. Korbyn shifted, discomforted by the fox's stagnant gaze.

The line between his reality and vision often blurred. In every hallucination, Korbyn felt the pain, the anguish, and the turmoil of this forbidding place cursed by a permanent Blood Moon. The nighttime visions vividly unfurled, so much so that he lacked confidence if the occurrences during the day could also be fabrications of his crazed mind. If not for the ring in his pocket and the fox's ongoing surveillance, he might have presumed both incidences to be false.

Those born before time hold secrets from the ones that arrive after it, the demon chimed.

"You 'kay, Korbi?" Andrid inquired, plopping on the edge of the wagon's bed. They leisurely craned back on their palms and kicked their legs independently of one another, chewing on an unknown provision.

"Yeah, I'm fine," Korbyn reassured, despite not believing his offered answer. He hid his fib in a bit of veracity. "Just tired."

Andrid's expression bore no secrets, as their visage displayed an obvious connection to their current mood. "Lies," Andrid said, tilting their neck back to better perceive him. "Broody 'nd thinking too hard. Mind is evil. Don't let consume you," they whispered, assumably fearful of an eavesdropping enemy.

Korbyn huffed a chuckle. "Can I ask you something?"

Andrid, apparently unable to retain idleness, twisted their body from the vehicle's edge to fully face him. They overlapped their legs and leaned forward, resting their face in their lifted palms.

"You do same thing," Andrid responded. "Yes, but no good at riddles."

"Not that kind of question."

"Oh! Good. Ask." A toothy grin framed their freckled face.

"How did you meet your fox companion?" Korbyn wondered, his observation flicked between Andrid and the fox.

In recognition of the veered topic, the fox's ambers emerged from closed lids. Andrid examined him with widened ones, full of wonder and surprise.

"You strange, Korbi," Andrid said in profound perplexity. "Met Willow one day when I alone. Willow helped me be not so lonely. Willow was..." Andrid angled back to view the resting creature. "First friend."

"Willow? Did you name it?" Korbyn probed.

"Nope! Willow name before me."

"How did you know its name?" Korbyn transfixed on both pools of amber and emerald.

"Told me. Speaks sometimes." Andrid reclined fully, the crown of their head propped back to inspect the fox. Willow's tail whipped back and forth, coercing Andrid to reach with playful flails. The fox unceasingly evaded their grasps. "You are only other who knows."

"I'm honored, then. You two are something special," Korbyn replied, analyzing the quieted knowledge teetering on the edge of Willow's glistening eyes.

"You 'nd Salem special too!" Andrid replied, rising from their sprawled position and diverting the topic.

Korbyn slammed a hand over Andrid's mouth.

Analyzing the others, they were all luckily preoccupied with their own various activities. Haven and Veeris sat at the front of the horse-drawn wagon, navigating their travel. Oakley napped, his loud snores echoing against the wooden walls. Meanwhile, Salem and Gilben exchanged words in an unknown conversation.

"We're not...I mean, we don't—"

Andrid tilted their head to the side like a curious animal, unaware of his clamped hand's intention. In an act of rebellion, they bit his finger and smiled mischievously when Korbyn reeled back.

"Natural for you to lie? To hide behind feelings?" they continued before Korbyn could scold them. When he failed to locate a rebuttal, Andrid snickered.

"Fine, you win," Korbyn muttered. "You're smarter than you lead on, Andrid."

He rolled the stone again, his nail following the lined paths of ivory all the way around its ovular shape.

"Yup," Andrid remarked confidently as they outstretched their legs, propping their ankles on Korbyn's thighs and reclining. "More question?"

Korbyn nodded. "Yeah, I have one more question...you said you gave me this stone because it transformed into something new, but I'm afraid. How do I change into something different that doesn't involve me losing my past or the future I want?" He gripped the stone tighter and shifted to inspect it. He consented to the need for brief vulnerability as his heart ached to share his intruding agitation.

When Korbyn turned to Andrid, he gasped. Their eyes were

widened and glazed, as if a creature stared in return. When they opened their mouth, their voice was echoed by an enigmatic, feminine voice.

"Transformation begins when the story of Deceit has been concluded. It is then that Truth will begin her story with the help of the crescent moon. Forge a path for the Crown of Horns and Blades."

Following the fortune, cognition returned to Andrid. They remained unperturbed by the abnormal message, seemingly having no recognition that it occurred at all.

"More question?" Andrid repeated, mimicking the same motions.

The fox still stared in an ominous stillness.

"Oh...nothing." Korbyn broke eye contact, unwilling to confront the deranged, prophetic utterance. "Thank you, Andrid," he mumbled. As he tried to cease his shaking, the wagon abruptly halted.

"Well, tha's not good," Gilben muttered.

Korbyn peered back, witnessing both Gilben and Salem gawking at something out of the caravan's right window. Past them, Haven and Veeris also stared in dread, eyes locked on the sky.

"Huh? Are we there yet?" Oakley asked as he stirred awake, raising his hand to rub his heavy lids.

"Oh, no," Salem whispered, mouth agape with fear and uncertainty.

"What's wrong?" Korbyn questioned, scrambling up from the back of the wagon and analyzing the eastern horizon.

The phenomenon spurred a nauseous inhale. Rising from the skyline, intruding upon the firmament, was the moon. Instead of its normal shade, one reminiscent of bone, it was illuminated with eerie connotation, permeating the clouds and sundered lands in brightened coral and crimson. A deafening silence obscured the terrain, followed by a piercing ring that intruded the previous tranquility.

"It's a Blood Moon," Salem whispered, her voice hitched with worry.

When the cardinal moon rises, it dampens the sky and the kingdoms below, the demon said. *The events that follow are inevitable on this chosen road.*

TWENTY-EIGHT.

Nausea brimmed in the pit of Salem's stomach. "We have to get to Fort Runswhick as soon as possible," she urged with obvious distress. "It's dangerous to travel so late at night, but I don't think we'll have a choice. Instead of taking a short rest, we'll need to take turns driving the wagon while the rest sleep. The driver will switch every four hours."

Everyone seemed to nod in response, other than Korbyn, transfixed downwards in some sort of contemplation.

"I'll go 'head and give Haven a break," Gilben said, rising to a standing position. With his short, stocky form, he could easily stand straight up without worry of concussing his head on the roof of the wagon. "Everyone else go 'nd get some sleep."

"I'll do it," Korbyn stated, leaning into the back of the caravan to aptly view them. "I'll drive the horse the entirety of the night. Just focus on getting enough sleep, and someone can trade with me in the morning—"

"Absolutely not," Veeris interjected, shifting his position from the driver's seat.

"You need some sleep too, Korbyn," Salem said, ignoring Veeris' foul response. "If anything, you probably need more rest than everyone else...given your circumstances with your amnesia."

Korbyn whispered something she couldn't hear.

"What was that?" Salem replied.

"I don't sleep," he snapped. "I don't remember my life before you found me and I don't know if I didn't have issues before, but ever since Fort Silvercrest, I haven't slept. I can't." He turned his gaze, avoidant of their glances and presumably chagrined of his condition. "But you all need it. I can drive during the night so you can all properly rest."

"No," Veeris repeated, feigning ignorance to Korbyn's presence as he kept his attention on the rest of the group. "We will take turns sleeping. I can also take a longer shift than most."

"What? Why?" Korbyn snapped. "It's just driving the wagon. I can't sleep, and I'm sure you'll all want to be better rested."

"I said no," Veeris barked as he shifted his body to face the road ahead.

"Maybe we can come to a solution—" Salem was interrupted.

"But you haven't given me a reason. At least tell me why," Korbyn demanded, clearly irate with Veeris' constant jabs and rudeness.

"I don't trust you," Veeris spat in return, leveling his own voice. "Who says you won't take us back while we all sleep and inform the emperor of our defiance against his orders?"

"What?" Korbyn barked. "Why the fuck would you think I'd do that?"

"Because you've been plotting and hiding secrets ever since you got here," Veeris declared, his nostrils flaring underneath his sunken eyebrows. "You have proceeded to disregard my warnings and have been nothing but a hindrance since you attached to our group like a leech. The Blood Moon is an obvious ill omen of your mingled presence. If nothing else, you are more than welcome to venture in the direction we just came from."

Salem recoiled at his honesty, the words spilling out of his mouth like intrusive thoughts. This wasn't good. The hanging red orb ongoingly flared his internal emotions. "Veeris, wait—"

"You can't be serious. I haven't been plotting anything," Korbyn interjected.

Before Salem could speak again, Veeris retaliated. "Yet you hide secrets. You have proven more than once that you follow us with foul intentions."

"Foul intentions? Well, your stupid idea of my alliance with Avernos is utter bullshit, considering that I would have betrayed you for them a long time ago even *if* there was a viable cause, which there isn't. So, you got any other ideas?" Korbyn suggested.

The tension hushed the rest into silence, unable to respond to their escalating argument. Despite Korbyn's question, Veeris failed to answer it.

"No? Didn't think so. We don't have time for this shit. Everyone else trusts me, and would even call me their friend, so why can't you?" Korbyn pressed.

"Friendship is formed through trust, and trust is earned, yet you have done nothing but verify you are unworthy of it!" Veeris' voice rose in dominance, gripping the side of the wagon until his knuckles turned white. "You want a chance to prove yourself? Fine. Then tell them! Tell them what you've been hiding in your bag!"

Salem and the rest of the group turned towards Korbyn, his shoulders tensed in rising consternation.

"I can't," Korbyn whispered in a breath of frustration.

Salem found herself in sheer astoundment, lacking words from her failed mediation. She was always quick to respond when met with conflict, but with one side being her longest, dearest friend, and the other being Korbyn, her voice shriveled unexpectedly. She angled her head towards the Blood Moon and witnessed its provocation. A stroke of copious clouds lingered before it, concealing its red hue and forming an eerie, enticing smile.

Veeris jumped off the driver's seat and stomped around it. Korbyn met him in his own stride, both leveling their chins in glowering anger by the side of the caravan. Gilben, Oakley, and Andrid peeked through the wagon's window.

"Lads, maybe we shouldn't—" Gilben was cut off.

"What? You want to hit me? Do it then, if it'll make you feel better," Korbyn said, gesturing with an exposed cheek with no fear of Veeris' strike. "Get it over with so we can move onto something that's actually important."

"Guys, stop—" Oakley interjected, only to be interrupted himself.

"Maybe I should, so you can have another reason to be embarrassed when I knock you on your ass," Veeris sneered.

"That's a bold assumption." Korbyn laughed with a forming grin. "That you could actually hit me hard enough."

Salem jumped out of the back of the caravan and rushed to them, physically intervening with her prying hands on their chests.

"You two need to listen to me! The Blood Moon is heightening your—" Salem was interrupted again.

Veeris swatted her hand away. "You're incredibly cocky for someone who's not willing to admit the truth. What are you worried about? Your wicked intentions revealed under the light? Your secret plots being exposed?" Veeris roared, his voice rising with each new statement that spilled. "If you want to be trusted, then tell them! If you're so confident that they're actually your friends—which they aren't—then tell them! Prove me wrong!"

"I can't!"

"Then why not?"

"Because you guys are all I have!" Korbyn shouted, his voice rasping in trepidation. "Fine, you want to know a truth? I'm afraid. I'm afraid of what I am. I'm afraid of what I might become, and I'm afraid to suffer through it alone. I know, somehow, that I had friends and family back home, but will they accept me, looking like this?" Korbyn gestured to the scar across his face and the abnormal shade of his eyes. "Will they shun me? Will they hate me? Will they be afraid of me?" His voice broke, trying to shroud his visage behind dangling locks. "But here, I'm accepted, despite not knowing a single damn thing about myself. Despite having nothing to offer in return..."

Korbyn's eyes rose to meet Veeris', anger and frustration swirling through ivory. "Except for you. You hate me for what I am, for what I can't control, and you've barely said a fucking thing to me since I've been here. How can I prove I'm trustworthy if you won't even give me a chance?"

"So, you admit it, then?" Veeris questioned in turn. Wrinkles formed in his brow when they scrunched together to create a deep expression of loathing. He pulled out a piece of decidite from his bag, and Salem watched as it crumbled to dust before their eyes. Magic surged around him like chaotic winds, and ten ethereal blades formed from the demands of his mind, the tipped edges pointing towards their target. "That's more than enough reason for me to end you."

"Wait—" Korbyn said, retreating a few steps, away from the threatening swords.

"Veeris!" Salem reached to seize his extended arms, but her reaction was belated.

Several blades danced in tandem with Veeris' outstretched fingers, the weapons volleying straight at Korbyn's unready steps. Wind lifted and burst around Veeris and the entirety of the wagon. The horse reared, sprinting away from the scene in hurried fright.

"Stop!" Haven yelled as the caravan unsteadily took off on the beaten path with Haven, Gilben, Andrid and Oakley still onboard. It descended the hill, causing the wagon to lean towards the left side. Further and further the startled horse led them down the slope.

"Haven!" Salem screamed, conflicted between aiding the crazed steed and her two friends. If the horse were to too quickly descend the hill, it would be a long drop to the bottom.

Korbyn's stifled grunt of pain pulled her attention back. Blood splattered in the night sky, accenting the vivid red hue that bounced against the terrain. Veeris leaped backwards, unfurling his fingers as more surges of attacks shot from them. The swords flew across the newly elected battlefield with consistency and strength, each aiming for where Korbyn was dodging.

Salem had to stop this, quickly.

"Veeris! What are you doing?" Salem shrieked, running to grasp him.

Veeris jerked out of her reach, controlling each of his blades with the singularity of his fingers. "What you have been afraid to do! He's tricked you! Can't you see he's enchanted you somehow? Open your eyes!"

Salem grabbed her locket to endow her with magic. Holy energy emitted from her golden crest and surrounded them both, beckoning to alleviate Veeris' rage. Normally, this would have eased the crazed side effects of the Blood Moon, but her radiant light seemed to bounce over him, his skin soaking in the red taint of the moon.

Veeris turned to Salem, flipping his palm and thrusting it downward. From above her, five of the blades followed in a wave of consecutive pierces. They surrounded her and imbedded into the earth, forming a barrier of solidified light connected together by the five pinnacles. Salem unsheathed her blade, swinging against the light. Even with her added strength, her steel bounced off. She was trapped inside, encircled like a wingless bird in a cage.

"Veeris!" Salem screamed, swinging her blade continuously against the cage, to no avail. She tried to channel her holy magic, but her exhausted body wavered. When her abilities failed her, she searched for a weakness in its foundation, but the barrier remained durable and inert. "Stop! This isn't you! The Blood Moon is causing you to act irrationally! Someone is going to get hurt!"

Veeris turned towards her, and when she saw hatred in his eyes, Salem didn't recognize him.

"I hope someone does. Maybe then you will see the truth," Veeris muttered, verbal venom dripping from his tongue.

Each of the remaining five blades spun majestically in rotations. They rose in the air and halted when lifted horizontally, all pointing towards their target.

"Korbyn, run!" Salem screamed. Again, she fought against the magical encasement of the barrier, but she found no success.

The translucent blades volleyed in Korbyn's direction. Instead of retaliating against Veeris' brutality, Korbyn focused on dodging out of the way. He lowered his body, evading several swipes above his head and pushing himself backwards out of the reach of the next sword.

Sweat trickled down Korbyn's brow as he sidestepped several more efforts of the blades' swings. As two more slashed at his sides and missed, he was unable to escape the third. Korbyn reached for the blade on his back and barely managed to deflect the attack.

"Where has your facade gone?" Veeris smirked. "And here I thought you'd be willing to fight me. Is there a reason you run in fear?"

"You've gone mad!" Korbyn growled. "Killing each other is incredibly stupid. Just give me a chance to talk!"

"To allow you a chance to enthrall me like you have done the others? No! I'll send you back to the Hells from which you came from, demon spawn!" Veeris screamed, raising his arms for another attack.

Two swords flew forward, following the movements of Veeris' index and middle finger. They struck, and Korbyn failed to deflect or dodge them in time.

They pierced his skin from his shoulders down to his hips, and red blood sprayed like splattered paint. Deep gashes opened to the sky, becoming vulnerable in its presence. Salem heard Korbyn gurgle; blood caught in his throat.

"Korbyn!" Salem yelled.

Korbyn was covered in blood, body trembling with every inhale. He appeared as though he might fall unconscious at any moment with every sway of his body. He needed her help.

Salem took a deep breath and began to pray.

"Elohim," she called with closed eyes. "I don't know why You choose not to listen to me. For so long, I have cried for Your help and received no response. Just answer this one request. Please, Elohim, help me," Salem beseeched. "Why won't you answer me?"

Korbyn staggered as he gripped his chest. Blood seeped from the deep wounds, his hand unable to stop the crimson gore cascading to the terrain in heaps. "Veeris, please. I don't want to hurt you," he begged, feet scuffling when he sought a sure stance.

Veeris raised his arms, readying another attack. "Says the one on his knees bleeding like a pig!"

As the five weapons shot out unanimously, Korbyn shot to the left, hardly dodging each piercing bout. To Salem's dismay, he sheathed his blade, running headfirst for Veeris. He lurched his arm forward in an attempted grapple. Veeris gasped and stepped to the side, out of the man's reach. Despite Korbyn's repeated efforts, his adversary prevented each.

Veeris swerved multiple times before throwing his arms forward. The blades flew, and Korbyn eluded the weapons with a stumbling retreat. The tips of the weapons struck the dirt, standing upright to form a partition of holy light between them.

With a surprisingly calm voice, Korbyn spoke after several deep breaths. "What will it take to get you to just listen to me? What do I need to do?"

Veeris glared, spite lingering in his cerulean eyes. "It will not be me who listens to you, beast," he spat. "When you die, I will let Azrael do that for me."

TWENTY-NINE.

Familiarity compelled Korbyn to an abrupt halt, the passage of time eluding him. Veeris and Salem stood in an unnerving stagnancy, supposedly frozen in anomaly. Despite his awareness, Korbyn also found himself incapable of movement. Visions carved into his mind like probing knives so forcefully that he writhed. He saw the event of his death, but not from his own eyes.

Blood, gore and debris across a stilled battlefield; the Blood Moon peeking from the skyline; a cloak of obsidian flowing in the breeze; a scythe of bone and black metal; the figure's face obscured by a hood of gloom; it lifts its gaze, revealing a permanent smile of a fractured skull and deteriorating skin; Korbyn's maimed body and the figure, locked together by a permanent, red thread. Korbyn inhaled deeply, and his eyes turned black.

"Wh-what did you say?" Korbyn stammered.

Azrael. That name, this person, or creature, or angel—it was familiar. It was the same name he read from the tome, but at the time of his inspection, it bore no familiarity. However, hearing it now, it sparked remembrance.

Whatever happened to him that day on the battlefield, it was what caused the demon to lurk inside of him, and he was sure it derived from the fallen angel, Azrael.

"Please, Veeris, tell me what you just said," Korbyn demanded, reaching out his left hand towards him. Veeris' eyes widened in fear, as if his touch would result in disease. "Please, Veeris, let's stop this. I'm begging you." He took another step forward, arm fully extended. "I need you to tell me what you know about—"

One of the magical, iridescent blades sliced through Korbyn's arm.

Silence fell over the field. After being airborne from the strike of the weapon, his forearm clattered to the ground. It rolled several times, coming to a standstill when the momentum of its fall discontinued. If anyone was saying anything around him, he couldn't hear them. He merely stared at where his arm used to be, slightly hunched in shock.

Observing the spot where his arm was severed, it was in the precise location where he believed the arm had been detached before, directly below his elbow. Veeris managed to somehow slice through his previous scar, one of the marks that refused to heal, despite his great restoration abilities.

After the shock passed, unnatural pain overwhelmed Korbyn's senses. The dark magic within him flamed in retaliation, his body burning from the inside out. It felt like he was standing amidst a fire, one so hot that it felt cold. The paradoxical phenomena filled his throat with more blood, threatening to choke him. His shoulders and arms shook and craned violently, unable to rise. His body felt pulled downward, as if chains wrapped around his right arm and phantom one. His back arched and cracked abnormally, his silhouette resembling a creature hiding within the woods. He was barely conscious, and he couldn't stop the demon's voice from meeting the sky tainted in red.

"*Tell me, Jeremiel, how do you plan to redeem yourself when the Heavens reject you?*" the voice inquired, an echo of himself and something else.

"Wh-what are you?" Veeris stuttered, stumbling backwards when their eyes locked together.

"*I am what your kind made me to be.*"

THIRTY.

Veeris witnessed shadows seep through the open wound in the demon's left arm. They resembled tendrils, flicking about the winds in muddled and sporadic gesticulations. They elongated, slithering across the grass all around the creature's body. Eventually, the gloom wrapped around its severed forearm. The gushing of blood and muscle filled the silent air.

The vines of darkness lurched back into its puppet body, heaving the forearm with it. It crashed into its form and twisted and turned until it returned to its normal position beneath the elbow, bones reassembling in full conjunction. Veeris watched the demon's fingers writhe as if it lacked a skeleton underneath its pale skin. A wild smirk spread across its face, eyes shifting from white to red.

"I knew it. You're nothing more than a vile creature," Veeris stated, clenching his jaw in anger. He raised his arm, and the five blades of iridescent and translucent gold followed his movements. The ends of the weapons pointed straight ahead, right towards the kneeling monster.

With its reattached arm, the demon unsheathed its blade and parried the ethereal ones. More fluid motions from the creature followed, clanks of magic and iron clashing under the gaze of the rising, tainted moon.

The monster's movements were relaxed, but still too fast for Veeris to keep up with. In his past glory, he could have kept the monster under his gaze, but with his lack of internal magic, his eyes strained.

The demon's movements transitioned into blurs, appearing at the swords' sides with every failed strike. It disappeared behind several trees, causing Veeris' attacks to strike the greenery instead of his intended target. When it emerged from the trees, Veeris swung. The blade in the demon's hand pushed the ethereal weapons, deviating their momentum as if they didn't weigh a thing.

It gracefully jumped away from the next couple of strikes. Veeris didn't allow himself a moment to breathe. Instead of focusing on the blades, the demon's eyes were honed on Veeris, watching the movements of his fingers.

"*According to your kind, sins are unobtainable, but you have perfected them,*" the demon prodded, sharpened canines revealing themselves after a maniacal laugh passed its lips. "*I don't see the Heavens in your future. Is that your greatest fear, mortal angel?*"

"Shut up!" Veeris screamed, lurching his arms with such immediacy that his shoulder popped.

The demon laughed as it dodged the next few onslaughts. From the corner of his eye, he saw Salem yelling, but he couldn't hear her. The anger and frustrations were overwhelming, his thoughts clouded in an uncontrolled rage. As Veeris stared at the illuminating, crimson-eyed creature on the other side of the battlefield, he wondered how they couldn't see this monster for what it truly was.

Veeris threw one arm out, the large, luminous blade following his movements. The demon merely craned its neck to the side, avoiding the attack with ease. The next two came from alternate directions, both passing by the creature's front and back, but had also missed their target. Its slack stature seemed unbothered by the proximity of his attacks.

The monster shifted into blurred movements, reappearing directly in front of Veeris. It loomed, somehow presiding over him more than usual. It craned forward with a slouched back, its shadow covering Veeris in his entirety. Instead of attacking him, the demon lowered its head next to his own and whispered.

"Does it anger you that Salem has feelings for me? Was I right about you, Jeremiel?" It sneered, teeth grinding from its curled lips. *"Is envy your greatest sin?"*

"I said, shut up!" Veeris yelled, stumbling away from its lolling stature.

When the creature rushed at him, Veeris withdrew his arms and crossed them over his chest. The creature entered the vicinity of all five blades, and the swords struck.

The weapons clashed. Two deep gashes appeared on the monster's side and opposite shoulder. Instead of piercing its body, the last sword clashed with iron, shattering the demon's weapon into pieces. The steel clattered to the ground, leaving only a hilt with a broken blade in its hand. The fiend's grin didn't drop from its wild face. That was when Veeris heard the rest of his companions behind him.

"What's going on?" Oakley said, the caravan being dragged up the hill by Haven, Gilben, and the startled horse. Even still, the animal shuffled uneasily, not wishing to venture any closer to the scene.

Veeris dared not to turn his attention away from the fight any longer. He could hear the fear and uncertainty in Oakley's voice and the gasps of the others as they approached.

"Korbyn...?" Oakley mumbled, voice cracking.

"Stay back!" Veeris warned, lifting his other palm towards them to cease their approach. "It's dangerous! Don't come any closer!"

"*Dangerous? Says the one basking in the glory of the 'demon's moon,*'" the demon stated with blatant sarcasm, widening its arms and inhaling with noises of satisfaction passing its lips. "*The only true danger I proved to be was a threat to the imaginary relationship you created.*" It cackled, a wicked smile tugged upwards by strings Veeris couldn't see.

With its left arm, the beast beat itself incessantly in the head, the leer unwavering. "*The mind is a funny thing, isn't it? It creates, it hides, it imagines, but never does it lie. It remains within a cage of safety, unheard and unseen by others around you.*" It craned its head to its other side, laying parallel to its shoulders. A resounding crack followed. "*Since I can't see the outrageous desires inside your head, what fantasies have you created that I so rudely destroyed?*"

The demon sauntered through the shadows of several looming trees, moving about the darkness as if it was returning home. It seemed quicker in the dusk, or maybe it was just more difficult to comprehend its movements. Within mere moments, the monster approached from behind him.

Before Veeris could swing his body around, the demon grabbed his arm and twisted it back. He felt a palm and sharp claws grab the back of his skull and shove him forward towards a tree, his cheek slamming into the bark. When he tried to maneuver towards the direction of his arm, the monster grasped tighter, preventing his circumvention.

"*I have tried to ignore you. I have tried to dismiss your cruel remarks, but you're like a thorn in my side, a constant irritation that I can't remove. It would be so easy for me to rid you of your pitiful existence,*" the demon whispered, leaning forward to his ear and quieting his voice. "*But I don't need to kill you to break you. Revealing your biggest fear would prove more viable.*"

It entered a state of silence. Afterwards, the demon tauntingly laughed. "*How interesting. Your fear is not truly demons, death, or even the Hells. You fear* loneliness. *How ironic, considering your habitual existence in self-isolation.*" Veeris gasped. "*When the skies become a battlefield of fire and wings, you will be forced to watch from below in a pit of your own sorrow.*" The evil creature smirked under the gaze of the moon. "*You will no longer be needed or wanted, Jeremiel.*"

Veeris yelled in a rally and separated from the fiend. He threw his arms forward, propelling the swords to enact his retribution. The creature eluded his reach, disappearing into another set of trees, despite the bleeding from its torso.

"Veeris, Stop this!" Haven urged, approaching the field. "Korbyn needs our help! Stop this before you do something you regret!"

"No! Don't get any closer!" Veeris demanded. "This is not the man you think it is! It's a monster!"

"*Poor Jeremiel, cursed with no purpose of his own, destined to fall in the footsteps of others and await the day when he can atone.*"

"Get out of my head!" Veeris screamed, launching all five blades at the same time.

The demon stumbled back when they grazed its side and calf, but the grin was glued to its face.

"Korbyn, please! You need to gain control! Don't let the darkness consume you!" Salem yelled.

Veeris watched the demon frown for the first time. It turned to Salem, full of longing and sadness, as lovers would when they say goodbye. His chest pained.

"Salem...?" it whispered, its voice no longer an echo of the demonic entity residing within.

It then fell to its knees, grasping its head. It wretched as though something crawled under its skin and fought for dominance despite its reluctance. When its chin rose, Veeris gasped.

It wasn't a demon staring back at him, but a human man trapped behind crimson eyes. It was a victim of unprecedented events. It was an amnesiac surrounded in fear of the unknown. It was a person in need of someone's aid. It was the one they called friend.

"Stop this," the man whispered to someone Veeris couldn't see, scarlet eyes fading into ivory. The gloom began dissipating, curling into the shadows of the overcast trees. The man trembled in visible distress, heaving when failing to find consistent breath.

Veeris' magic slackened, wavering with uncertainty, but only for a moment.

He would rid the world of a demon, and if it truly was just a human caged by evil, then Veeris would grant a quick and merciful death.

With a cry of ferocity, Veeris shot his arm forward, the blades following his designated path—straight towards the demon's neck.

THIRTY-ONE.

Billowing mists clouded Korbyn as though he were drenched in polluted waters. It thwarted his vision, the density of its thickened murk exasperating his sinuses. He was surrounded in a pungent smell of lilies, fields of flowers beneath his feet. Despite their potency, they had withered. Through the crevices in the fog's blankets, Korbyn viewed masses of looming trees. They reached higher than he could perceive, the layers of vapor that prohibited his gaze. The enveloping mists clung to his skin, its thick moisture clamming his palms and mimicking dripping sweat. He stood amongst a forest, he concluded with utmost apprehension.

"Hello?" Korbyn asked, projecting his voice into the void.

Only an echo of himself responded, fading past awaiting trees. Even with his enhanced eyesight, his vision couldn't penetrate the abnormality of its existence. He stood motionless, expecting the eyes he felt watching him to reveal themselves.

When nothing replied, Korbyn wandered around the mist,

searching for a landscape, a building, or a person within the congealed fog, but found nothing. He wandered for minutes, which turned into hours, which turned into days. He didn't halt for food or the alleviation of his bladder, for he didn't feel the need for either. Instead, his trembling legs ventured into the welcoming smog that cared not for his growing insanity or his desperation to escape its clutches.

Korbyn remained unaware of how long he strolled, searching and locating nothing but his own quaking voice. At some point, he found something residing within the confines of the fog, or, to his wary trepidation, something found him. A silhouette emerged from the opaqueness. A figure similar in height to his own sauntered with dipping shoulders of an indolent swagger.

"Who's there?" Korbyn pressed. When the person didn't reply or halt, Korbyn fidgeted back several paces. "I-I think I'm lost."

The shape eventually split through the mist, revealing its form in its entirety. It was hooded and draped in an abnormally long cloak. Somehow, underneath the umbra, Korbyn could see scarlet eyes penetrating the darkness, accompanied by a grim smile with edges rising so high across its face that it seemed unnatural.

"*No one is ever truly lost,*" the voice replied, sounding eerily like his own, but filled with internal malice. Its head fell to the side so fast that he was afraid it would roll off its shoulders; instead, its neck cracked, wild strands of hair falling around its pale features. "*We just wander aimlessly until we discover what they call destiny. Though it's just a term created by those who are too afraid of failure.*"

"What?" Korbyn asked, barely cognitive of its comments. "You're the demon, aren't you?"

When Korbyn blinked, it stood before him, resuming its looming posture.

"*I am you. I am your future. I am Grim.*" The demon laughed.

"You made your choice, and now we walk an evitable path."

The unrhythmic beating of Korbyn's heart shaped his hitched breath. He tried to presume a confident reply, but his voice quaked when it passed the ingress of his lips.

"No," Korbyn retorted. "I choose my own destiny."

The demon laughed like a ridicule to a child's ignorance. *"I have already told you of destiny. Destiny is a facade. It is not destiny you should fear. It is not destiny you should rely on for solace. It is choice. Choice is your true nemesis, for it enacts consequences and cares not to inform its decider, not until its dawn has already ascended."*

"If that's truly the case, then I choose to banish you from me," Korbyn seethed, irritated equally by its riddles and its prodigious beliefs.

The demon lurched its body backwards and grabbed its own head, laughing manically. It propelled its body forward, smacking its forehead against Korbyn's brow. It grabbed the back of his neck to prevent his backward reel from the collision. Korbyn's head pounded in pain, and blood dripped between their foreheads, intermingling in identical hues of darkened red. Dual moons, one set of pearls and another a set of garnets, stared across from each other with no sun to illuminate them in the darkness.

"It is too late, little raven. Our path is forged as a consequence of your choices. You were selected, and you accepted Death's call. You attempted to leave, and instead, you remained amongst your friends. Now, they are damned and obligated to walk this route by default."

"I don't understand," Korbyn murmured, shivering as the blood continued its descension betwixt them. "I did what I thought was right."

The demon grinned. *"Choice cares not for intentions. It cared not when the rebel angels fell, it cared not when Evelyn and the*

Garden died, it cared not when Abaddon became a home for the fallen, and it does not care about you."

"I-I can't accept that," Korbyn stuttered, his furrowed brows quivering in a forced retaliation as more blood trickled down to the pink, globular of his inner eye, nose, and then cheek. The smile that followed made him shiver.

"I'll *prove it to you,*" the demon muttered with a frown, its next sentence piercing his gut no less painfully than a blade would have. "*You are not meant to save.*"

When Korbyn opened his eyes, one of the ethereal blade volleyed straight at his chest.

He couldn't move; his body was held steadfast by invisible chains. He stared at the projectile, realizing the inevitable.

He was going to die.

With the last bit of his strength, Korbyn glanced over at Salem, who seemed riddled in her own fear. She was heaving in discomfort, her body trembling within the confines of a holy barrier.

"Salem...I—" Korbyn whispered, watching tears fill her eyes. His voice was cut off by the splattering of blood across his face. For a moment, he sat in silence, afraid to examine his wound, but after a moment's hesitation, he realized the pain wasn't his own.

"*Andrid!*" Haven bloodcurdlingly screamed.

Korbyn craned his neck forward.

Andrid stood before him, arms wide and fingers elongated towards the roots below. They were calling for the aid of the world, the limbs of foliage stretched upward in a wave of growth to stop the incoming attack, but they had been too slow.

Instead of halting the blade with the control of the trees, Andrid had thrown themselves in front of Korbyn and its trajectory.

The sword of translucent gold, as strong as any steel and just as large as an average person, pierced completely through Andrid's torso and through the other side. A wound from their clavicle down through their chest widened, their muscles and organs torn underneath the refined edge. Blood poured out of their body like the light from a newly opened window. Without the ability to see their eyes, Korbyn knew their life had started to fade.

"No, no, no!" Haven screamed, lunging for them.

As Andrid fell, the magical blades and the barrier around Salem dissipated. The half-orc slid across the ground, trying to catch their falling form. Before he could, Andrid hit the dirt with a resounding thud. Haven scrambled, trying to halt the profuse bleeding, but the wound was even more massive than his hand.

"Salem!" Haven called out.

Salem ran to Andrid's side, holy light emitting from her palms. It flickered in and out sporadically, as if unable to pump consistent energy.

"Andrid—Andrid, stay with us. Keep your eyes open," Salem urged, stuttering over her words. "Elohim, please, help me. Do not let them take Andrid. I'm begging you."

At first, Korbyn assumed this had been another crazed vision, the disparity between hallucination and reality intermingling to hinder his reflex. Analyzing the situation further, he watched Gilben kneel at Andrid's side, grab several ingredients from their pack and mashing up ginseng, lavender, ginger, and dirt with a mortar and pestle. His calm demeanor was a disguise, revealed by his trembling hands.

Oakley stood paralyzed, other than his quaking knees. Tears had already poured from his eyes just as fluidly as Andrid's blood. Bewilderment strained across his dark features.

"A-Andrid..." Oakley muttered, as if expecting an encouraging response. "Andrid, are you okay?" No one answered him.

Veeris was situated farthest from the group. His arm hovered from his previous thrust, leaving him as an impervious statue of dread.

When Andrid coughed, every single person shifted their attention to their face. Blood poured and tainted their teeth and lips in a darkened hue of mahogany, like a crammed mouthful of forged berries. They tilted their chin in Veeris' direction, their voice fading with their depleting life.

"Friends should...trust each other..." Andrid gurgled out, blood filling each word with intention. They lifted their hand, which was stained with so much blood that Korbyn couldn't see the fading color of their skin underneath it. "Please, no more fight."

Andrid's hand fell in a heap, accompanied by their last, exhaled breath.

"Andrid! No! Please, don't leave me," Haven cried out, pulling their body into his chest and wrapping his arms around them. Andrid's neck fell backwards, their eyes rolling in the same gesture. Korbyn met the colorless gaze of their empty body.

Salem and Gilben leaned forward, hiding their tears. Oakley ran forward, tripping over his failing legs before he knelt beside them.

"N–No! Andrid's fine!" Oakley laughed through another wave of tears. "They can't leave. They promised we'd go to Mount Firebrim together—w-we haven't done that yet!" He shook Gilben in defiance, a plead for his friend's aid. "Right, Gilben? They can't die. They promised."

"I-I'm sorry, lad," Gilben whispered, placing a hand on Oakley's shoulder. His dark face paled before he analyzed Andrid's body. Without any words to say, he cried.

Korbyn gazed towards the other side, seeing Willow seated beside Andrid. Their expression endured in continual stoicism, save for a minuscule flutter of gloss in the unreadable amber.

"I..." Veeris whispered, his voice cracking despite his usual confident persona. "I-I'm so sorry. I didn't mean—I mean, I wasn't..."

Haven carefully lowered Andrid's body, anger writhing in his jaw and water-filled eyes. He stalked to Veeris with flexed shoulders. The punch he hurled reverberated a crack in his cheek and spilled blood. When Veeris toppled, Haven pulled him up by the collar of his tunic and shook.

"We told you to stop! But you never listen!" Haven shouted, pent up anger and truth soaking the sky. "You never listen to anyone but yourself! We warned you someone would get hurt! And now they're gone! A-Andrid..." Veeris only stared up in shock as Haven's falling tears trailed down his face. "You killed Andrid."

Korbyn saw the moment that light disappeared from Veeris' eyes. As he analyzed the area in a solemn silence, Korbyn wasn't sure where the light of the Blood Moon ended and the stains of Andrid's blood began.

The somber mercenaries didn't leave until the Blood Moon retreated. Even though the sun returned to greet them, just as it always did, the bright orb seemed melancholic, somehow. It hid its expression behind a large set of gray clouds, thunder and rain threatening the ground beneath it.

The lands quieted, except for the tempo of rainfall soaking the dirt. Korbyn lingered far from the sleeping river, inching closer to the road with the halted wagon. To his dismay, his wounds initiated its ritual, one where they mended without the need of decidite's magic. Instead of the soothing energy that calmed the inflammation, he witnessed the deep gashes reconnect like threads of fabric. Each tug and closure rallied in irritation, and he endured the pain of each single strand of skin. Korbyn welcomed the ache.

In the distance, Haven, Salem, Gilben, and Oakley hovered over the small mound of dirt that covered Andrid's body placed beneath a weeping willow tree. Oakley and Gilben stacked rocks and stones on top of the grave, while Salem arranged a set of blue hydrangeas and daylilies in a bouquet. Haven sat on his knees, hunched at the edge of Andrid's resting place, with their blood still soaking his hands.

Korbyn waited patiently as each of them offered parting words. Gilben, the first, spent a couple of minutes playing his lute. It was a beautiful, somber song, and the first that Korbyn had heard without any words. For once, Gilben was speechless. The dull cadence of rain took the place where his singing voice would have been, accompanying his song like a temporary band member. After the song ended, he rose from the seat and trudged towards the caravan.

Salem was next. She placed a green feather amongst the bouquet while drying her continuous stream of tears. She turned and stopped, as if thinking to herself for a moment before she walked away from the grave.

Oakley lingered on his knees, clutching something that Korbyn couldn't see. His arms were shaking, seemingly from the emotions of sorrow budding in his chest and the unwillingness to part with whatever he was holding. When he finally unraveled his arms, an oval rock loomed in his hands—the geode that Andrid had given him. He stared down at the uneven texture, pondering in soundless despondency.

He unsheathed a knife and stabbed into the stone before shifting the hilt back and forth, forcing the pointed iron's entry. The blade finally imbedded deep enough, and the rock eventually caved under the pressure and split into two pieces. When shimmering, blue crystal, as brilliant and pure as a cloudless sky reflected light into Oakley's eyes, he choked on a cry.

He held onto both pieces for several minutes, cradling them with utmost care, as if the crystals were just as precious and flimsy as a mortal life.

Eventually, Oakley slid on his knees towards the base of the weeping willow and dug a separate hole. When he was content with its depth, he placed one half of the geode within its cradle and concealed it with the dampened dirt. He grasped tightly onto the other half, standing and walking away after bidding a quiet farewell.

Then there was Haven. During the duration of everyone's goodbye, the half-orc lingered in a state of sorrow. He neither moved nor spoke. The only movement Korbyn could see was the slow rise and fall of his chest. From his adept hearing, Korbyn could hear the lyrics of a whispered song.

Haven's gruff voice hummed, a melody resembling that of a grim lullaby. It was the tale of two unlikely lovers, both lost in a maze. One no longer remembered who they were, just as lost within their minds as they were in the magical forest. They wandered for what seemed like a millennium, consumed by the mist that deterred them from hope.

The other, searching for their lost love, entered the mist with intention. They maintained their memories, refusing to be deterred by any turmoil or strife that crossed their path. Both succumbed to wandering through the endless labyrinth for many lifetimes.

Haven didn't conclude the story. Instead, he placed his hand on top of the mound, tears soaking into the dirt beneath him.

"I promise, I will find you," Haven murmured, bowing his head and placing a kiss on top of the mound. With a lowered forehead, fingers gripping the drenched soil, he muttered a temporary goodbye. He eventually stood at full height, blood dripping from his clenched fists. He passed Korbyn without a glance or a word.

One more individual lingered at the grave's side. Underneath the hanging low branches of the weeping tree was Willow, Andrid's lone fox companion. Willow's head was held low, as if human emotions stirred within them. Korbyn strode towards the tree, afraid to disturb the fox and the permanently sleeping figure beside them.

Korbyn kneeled, stagnant in a lack of words. He half expected Andrid to burst from the ground with a widened, mischievous grin and a contagious laugh. He waited for their emergence, furthering his frown in continual brooding when nothing occurred. Only the rain replied, growing heavier with each passing second.

Nausea lurched within Korbyn's abdomen. He should have been the one to die. Andrid was loved and admired, so full of life and happiness. Haven and Andrid were supposed to have a long, fulfilling life together. Now, Andrid was dead, and it was all his fault. He made his choice.

Korbyn bit his lip, shielding his eyes when the tears fell. "Thank you for saving my life," he choked out, his words barely forming a whisper. "But you shouldn't have done it. It should have been me. Your life was so much more precious."

They call upon the Shepherd. Another piece has been placed in the puzzle.

Korbyn witnessed a shadow of black pass him from the corner of his eye. When he peered upwards, a cracking breath escaped him.

The Reaper approached the grave, hauling the scythe of bone, black metal and golden veins at his side. Though it dragged in the dirt, there was no physical proof of its existence left behind. Death sauntered over to the grave, just as he had done a million times before, and reached out towards the body beneath it.

A thread appeared; a red ribbon so thin that it disappeared periodically under the rays of the peeking sun. It intertwined around his fingers of bone, and the Reaper pulled. Attached to the end of its string was Andrid.

Instead of their body emerging from the dirt, a translucent soul followed its tug. Their eyes remained closed, as if unconscious even in the afterlife. They hovered inches from the ground, slightly slouched but upright. Their spirit lingered, unaware of the somber world around them.

Death traced the Reaper's bony fingers around the thin thread. Despite seeming so fragile, it persisted in sturdiness under the jerks of the skeleton's harsh gestures. Korbyn guessed that it already knew the strength and frailty of mortals, but he seemed to perform these actions as if to demonstrate it to someone else—to someone that could see him.

The Reaper drew his scythe, bearing the grand weapon to face the grave. He lifted it with ease, every part of the black metal seemingly a sharpened edge awaiting utilization. Death swung the crescent towards the long, crimson thread. Korbyn reached out to stop him, but he was too late. The thread snapped.

Death's hood tilted in his direction. Underneath the coverlet of the branches, Korbyn could now see past the darkness conjured from the Reaper's hood. He discerned a face of wilting skin and harsh bone, revealing a permanent smile of his skull.

The cloaked figure led Andrid towards an accumulation of trees, clasping their hand with a skeletal grip. As Korbyn rose to follow, they strode past a set of crying willows, not appearing on the other side. Andrid was gone.

"Korbyn?" Salem asked.

Korbyn whirled around, startled by her voice.

Her eyes swelled from her tears, and her once-strong arms seemed brittle, both wrapped around her torso in a self-embrace. "What are you looking at?"

"Nothing," Korbyn muttered, unable to meet her gaze.

"It's not your fault," Salem said, clenching her arms. "Andrid made that decision. It was out of your control."

Korbyn didn't reply. Instead, he twisted back to the grave. Willow, the fox, still sat underneath the tree, staring down at the mound of dirt with a lowered jaw.

"Sure," Korbyn said in disbelief, unable to prevent anger and sorrow from intermingling with that single word.

"We should get going," Salem stated.

Korbyn glanced back between Willow and the rest of the mercenaries, who solemnly prepared for their departure.

"What about Willow?" Korbyn inquired.

"What?" Salem stopped to turn back to him.

Korbyn frowned, not having the energy to explain, but doing so anyway. "Willow. What about Willow?"

Salem tilted her head to the side. "The tree?"

"No, Andrid's fox. Willow."

"What fox?"

Korbyn spun back to the grave. The silhouette of the fox shifted, like wavering mist above still waters. It bowed to Korbyn, its head lowered in its own farewell.

"We will meet again when the bells of Abaddon chime and introduce the initiation of the Revelation War," the feminine voice whispered within his mind. Moments later, the spirit disappeared.

"Are you sure you're okay?" Salem questioned.

Korbyn lingered at Andrid's grave, wishing he had the power to save.

"Let's go," he mumbled.

THIRTY-TWO.

Circumambient silence haunted the wagon. Veeris resided in the far corner behind the driver's seat, leaning against the sill with a half-lidded eye, the other swollen purple and blue. The abrasions pulsed in remembrance as he tried to ignore their whispering throbs. Outside the wagon, the sun's rays peeked past the melancholic sky; despite its presence, storm clouds littered the firmament like scattered books in a cluttered library. Truly, the glowing star's radiant presence lingered as a paradox to the transcending rain.

Fort Silvercrest rose high in the distance atop the salient hill. To arrive at Fort Runswhick to the west, they would need to pass this very fort, avoiding the Avernos soldiers' notice. Only after a couple months since the battle's end, still the fort resided in dilapidated heaps. They presumably lacked the required resources to preserve and fortify further reconstruction in its entirety. In the renewal's place, the soldiers fashioned makeshift balistrarias along the damaged walls, providing access for archers in case of approaching invaders. With multiple crevices made all around the fort's base, its fractured state provided a newfound advantage atop the hill, though its poorly built foundation countered that. The soldiers gathered the debris of the fort, to his assumption not for rebuilding, but for lobbing.

This useless war, this very tower was the event that started it all, when the mercenaries of Kendra Dawn adopted a monster of unknown origins into their ranks, when Salem's attention and infatuation had shifted to another, and when the Blood Moon returned with an uncanny and unexpected ascent.

The mercenaries' voices circumvented the entirety of the day as they ventured west. Oakley secluded himself to the best of his ability, though the small confines of the vehicle hindered his endeavors. His cries were the most audibly incessant until sleep finally consumed him. Gilben seated not too far from Oakley. His snores were quieter than usual, mimicking more of a trance than actual slumber.

Haven was curled against the opposite side, faced away from any lingering stares and remaining completely inaudible. Veeris had been afraid that the half-orc had died of mourning if not for a shift in his arm fifteen minutes before. He held onto his bag against his torso where Andrid should have been, clutching onto the leather.

Salem sat at the boot of the wagon, shoulders slackened in what Veeris assumed was silent dread. She adjusted between consciousness and sleep, shifting often from the clacks of her armor. Despite traveling, she refused to remove the steel. Her holy radiance expanded past the caravan in a wide span. Even though the sun was in the sky, far away from the moon, she kept her grasp on her locket.

Lastly, the demon, currently as quiet as a mouse but lurking like a predator, assumed a position at the driver's seat. It guided the horse to their destination, hushed in a silence unlike before.

More often than not, Veeris' attention was at its back, ensuring that it didn't betray them while they slept. Even if the rest were comfortable with its presence, Veeris wasn't. Up until now, they had been the only ones who hadn't slept, forcing Veeris to envelop himself in a shroud of caliginous despondency.

Andrid's innocent, imperfect, genuine laugh echoed in memory. A knot encroached in Veeris' throat, making it problematic to swallow the spit that gathered there. He grasped onto his cheeks with his fingers, momentarily forgetting the wounds that riddled his face. His left cheekbone throbbed, fractured from Haven's blow. He flinched at the sting, cross at the aching sensation and emotional and mental strife that accompanied it.

Normally, Veeris wouldn't have reacted so recklessly. His original plan was to let the demon enact a vile sin of its own volition, but he allowed himself to get too heated. The Blood Moon and its horrendous curse urged his hand, one he couldn't stop. If that monster hadn't been here, then this all could have been prevented, but once again, no one listened. If only the demon had been the one to enact the final blow instead of him.

The rest of the group had seen the true demon that lay underneath its skin, and even still, they chose to defend it. Veeris remained unaffected by the allure of the creature's faux grin, but they failed to notice his benevolence. Veeris deserved their recognition but received none, whilst his friends were wrapped around the creature's manipulative fingers.

The demon had enticed them more than he originally anticipated. This puppeteering beast compelled Veeris' friends to dance at the end of their tangled strings, leaving them demented and void of their previous cognizance. The Blood Moon clearly aided its unnatural abilities, coercing the mercenaries to protect the demon and rally against him. They were plagued by evil, and Veeris needed to quell the darkness.

"Veeris," Salem stated.

Veeris turned, wild strands of his unkempt hair dangling in front of his bruised face. When he peered at her, she avoided his gaze, only offering an extended hand. Her voice had rasped, inevitably hoarse from crying.

"Salem—"

"I need to heal your wounds before they become infected," Salem declared, not lengthening her arm any further.

Veeris frowned, trying to meet her eyes, but she continued to avert them. "I just want to say—"

"Don't," Salem spat with an anger that he had never heard before. She raised her hand to his cheek, her fingertips glowing with holy energy that soothed the cracks in his skin. "Don't. Not right now."

They sat there for a few moments. If Salem hadn't been actively healing him, Veeris would have assumed she had forgotten his presence. Her regard trailed to the passing trees, the sun's rays casting its golden hue on her equally golden features. It seemed jealous of her beauty, its rays only shining upon her skin instead of taking her radiance for its own. She seemed enraptured by the constant clacks of the horse's hooves on the uneven terrain, or it was the only probable distraction. No matter how hard he tried, her current thoughts eluded him.

She had to know that none of this was Veeris' fault. The Blood Moon antagonized him, but only because he attempted to save them from this monster. He was still the caring and devoted person that had stuck by her side unconditionally. He followed her from the Heavens, scrounged all Terrisae for the blades, fought any battle and supported any cause that she believed in, reinforced her endeavors and loved her regardless of their inability to be together.

Veeris would undergo that pain for the rest of his life and remain loyal to Elohim and His orders. He would undertake the task of pulling Salem back into the light and away from the prowling darkness. He would withstand the loathing gazes and rude remarks to save his friends. But there was one thing Veeris couldn't withstand: her silence.

"Please understand, Salem," Veeris whispered, careful to keep their conversation hidden. He leaned into her hand so that she cupped it, enacting a loving gesture on her own behalf. Even still, she refused to lock eyes with him. "I understand that I should not have let my anger best me, but you must know that it was for good intentions. I care deeply about you. I care about all of you, and you know how evil and manipulative the Blood Moon truly is."

Salem was always full of words and opinions, but right now, she didn't reply. Instead, she kept her gaze on the sun, glaring up at it as if realizing it had attempted to steal away her sheen and the fire caged within her heart.

"It was the Blood Moon's fault," Veeris stated, desperately wishing to grapple her attention. "You said it yourself—I wasn't acting normal. It's evil and corrupt. I would have never hurt Andrid." He paused again, waiting for her to view him. "It wasn't my fault. It was an accident."

"It was more than an accident," Salem whispered, not once shifting to face him. "It was a tragedy." Her voice cracked in a way that proved she did her best to prevent cascading tears.

Veeris' heart ached within his chest, and he felt desperate to reach out to her. Instead, he leaned more heavily into her palm, relying on her to keep his head aloft. He felt the shaking underneath his skin, and he nestled into her touch.

"I know, Salem, I know," Veeris murmured, meeting her whisper. "But we can start over. We care for our friends, but let's not forget our true purpose. We came to Terrisae for the blades, so let's go find them." He placed his hand on top of hers, forcing her to rub it along his face. Even though the paladin's gloves and armor stood between them, he no longer wished for the holy energy she emanated. "Before all this, before this madness, it was you and me. It was always just you and me. Let's go back to that."

Salem yanked her hand back, meeting his loving stare with her own surprised one. Finally, her gilded eyes analyzed him. He wished nothing more than to offer his feelings to her, to open the windows of his soul and reveal everything within despite his inability to be with her.

"You're serious?" Salem prompted.

Veeris nodded. "Of course I am," he responded, scooting closer to her. "You know I would do anything for you. That *demon* has tricked you. You saw what I saw—we all saw it. It is trying to prevent us from finding the blades. Surely you understand that?"

Veeris took Salem's right hand into his own, tugging on each finger of her glove until it slipped off. He shifted it to gaze at the top of her hand and inside her palm, wanting to memorize each line, scar, and callous that riddled it. She merely watched as he slid his hand over hers, and Veeris sighed happily when he finally felt her warmth.

"I understand this is a travesty, but you need to try and remember the positives. We can now focus fully on the blades. And Andrid is in a better place now—"

"A better place." Salem seemed conflicted between laughing and grieving, gluing her attention to the outside once again. "That is what Elohim used to say, but you and I both know where souls truly go."

Veeris mentally slapped himself for his poor choice of words. "I understand, but—"

"A better place would have been in Haven's arms." Salem quivered, biting her lip to halt her tears; however, they fought a winning battle against her. "And now, Andrid is gone."

More than anything, Veeris wanted to cradle Salem in his arms and soothe away her torment. He wanted to brush her hair away from her face, to wipe away her tears when she cried. He would fight monsters, travel the entirety of the lands, even yell at kings if it ensured her happiness. And right now, he wanted nothing more than to get rid of her pain. If she just gave him a chance, she would be able to understand that no one cared for her as much as he did.

At first, Veeris thought there wasn't anything more painful than withholding one's feelings for another, but he was vastly incorrect. The grandest pain was watching the one you loved adhere to the wishes of another. And, in the span of a single moment, the laws and consequences of Elohim's proclamations slipped from his mind.

Veeris craned his head, closing the distance between his mouth and hers.

A slap echoed throughout the vicinity, and Veeris fell back against the floor with a bang. Salem had smacked him with her ungloved hand.

His cheek, even more enflamed than before, throbbed with a new pain. Veeris touched his face, surprised when his fingers caused it to ache.

Salem rose as much as she could in the confines of the wagon, leaning over him like an enraged animal. Most of the others around them jolted awake from their stagnant positions, silently observing when they realized they were in no immediate trouble.

Confusion and anger raged in her eyes like clashing enemies, neither claiming dominance over the other. Veeris saw the moment realization crossed her mind, a flicker of light sparking in her irises. It resembled a pain of discovering a close ally's betrayal.

"You were my dearest friend," Salem whispered, her curled hands unfurling in a display of defeat. Her disbelief appeared to shift into acceptance, an unbearable gloom that neither one of them could seem to tolerate. "You have given me guidance, supported me in endless endeavors, encouraged me when I was consumed in doubt..." She turned her gaze as though holding it to his was poisonous. "But the man standing before me is someone I do not know."

"Salem, listen—"

"No, it's *your* time to listen," Salem barked, tears lingering in her eyes. "Ever since we arrived in Terrisae, you have changed. Where you were once kind and generous, you are now judgmental and selfish. I have ignored your malicious words for far too long, but not anymore. Consider our friendship spoiled and rotted. When the day comes that we return home, and you are denied entry, I will be there to witness their refusal."

Veeris' voice cracked when a gasp erupted. "Salem..."

"You are allowed to remain here with us not because you deserve it, but because I no longer trust you to venture out into these lands without proper guidance. If I didn't fear for the safety of others, I would send you to wander these lands to search for the blades on your own, but you have proven you are no longer reliable."

"But the Blood Moon—"

"Only brings to surface what resides underneath!" Salem spat, her body motioning to lash out again, but she resisted. Her voice transitioned into a softened, saddened one as a tear finally fell from her eye. "Andrid is dead. All because you fail to realize that it is *you* that houses a monster."

Salem turned and strode towards her previous position at the back of the wagon. She slid down the wooden planks until she was fully seated and pulled her legs up to her chest, concealing her face in her arms and knees.

It felt like hours that Veeris was glued to the floor. Outside the window, the rain poured like a can filled with water. The sun, desperate for Salem's shine, wasn't as beautiful as he remembered, and not as overbearing as the Blood Moon the night before.

During his time in Terrisae, he had only seen a few moons painted red. Each Blood Moon seemed to forebode a different, catastrophic event. First, there was the calamitous eruption of

Mount Firebrim, then when decidite was discovered in the mines of Brinshire, and after that, the Battle at Fort Silvercrest. Lastly, and most recently, when Andrid's life faded from this world. Even still, as Veeris remained alone on the floor with everyone's eyes cast away from him, they didn't realize the malice of the Blood Moon and the mental vex that the demon had ensued.

Veeris turned, meeting the eyes of the demon. For a split second, he could see the emotions that bridled within. Swirling in the obsidian, he saw a mixture of forming guilt and pity. Veeris spat and turned away.

This disaster wasn't his fault, and somehow, Veeris would have to convince his friends who the real monster was.

As the sun continued to shift west, Veeris wished that it would stop retreating from his constant observation.

Their group wouldn't reach Fort Runswhick for another day. They traveled for hours, stopping only for a brief disruption to relieve themselves and to gather more supplies when necessary, but the silence plagued them still. Everyone avoided Veeris' presence and eye contact as if he were a burdensome issue they wanted to neglect.

As promised, the demon drove the wagon throughout the day, only waking the party up upon their arrival at the bridge at Exonia Creek. The soldiers permitted their passage without any issues, thankfully still unaware that Kendra Dawn's flag was prohibited to cross these lands into Avernos' newly acquired borders. Veeris ignored the fact that the beast did nothing foul while the rest slept as much as they could. Surely, it was waiting for a viable opportunity when Veeris' attention was elsewhere.

Most of them managed to get a couple hours of quiet, due to mere exhaustion. Veeris, however, had stayed up all day, watching the demon carefully. After Salem's outburst, in the moments of silence that followed, sorrow and anxiety equivalently challenged each other in a brawl. Veeris became more fidgety as his mind developed in-depth scenarios of possible futures that he wouldn't be able to prevent if the demon got its way. He imagined the creature's true intentions were to prevent them from locating the blades, though he knew not of the veiled motives.

If Veeris was going to prevent the demon's foul plans, he would need to mend the conflict with his friends.

When the mercenaries finally pulled the wagon over for a break, they all veered off in different directions. Oakley suggested that he would retrieve more water, despite having a full barrel. Salem stated she would take a walk to stretch her legs, and Gilben informed them that he would scavenge for more herbal ingredients.

Veeris surveyed the demon, who remained seated on the driver's seat. He couldn't accurately perceive its current emotions, for it wore a dull stoicism buried under its hood. Lastly, there was Haven.

Ever since Andrid's burial, the half-orc resided in meditative silence. Veeris couldn't interpret his feelings, thoughts, or intentions from the walls that he surrounded himself with, the windows to his soul closed with curtains that he couldn't see through. If the group was going to trust him again, then Haven was the one he needed to start with.

"Haven, we need to talk," Veeris urged when the rest of the group had disappeared past a set of trees. "Come with me."

With Haven's back turned, Veeris could see the slight shift in his jaw when he angled it. When the half-orc didn't reply, Veeris trudged towards the forest, ensuring he heard Haven's trailing steps before entering the trees.

They traversed the unmarked path, both of their footsteps in discord with one another. While Veeris' steps were cautiously placed, treading through the forest and perceiving the unknown area, Haven's gaits were loud and weighty. When Veeris avoided branches and leaves, Haven's heavy strides slaughtered the flora beneath him. Veeris felt like a target with a future assailant watching his every move as he descended deeper into the forest's grasp. Unlike most predators, this one wanted its prey to know it was being hunted.

Eventually, the two arrived at a separation in the trees. A part in the foliage revealed a small field, covered in a blanket of shadow from the branches overhead. There were no birds or signs of animals in this place, and luckily no monsters or creatures hiding in their depths. Despite the sun's beginning dispersion into the night, the drapes of green secluded them like a dark secret and avoidant of any prying observers.

Even as they entered this space, Haven didn't regard Veeris' presence. Instead, the half-orc turned away towards the forest, as if expecting Andrid's humble arrival. Veeris waited in tandem. The forest stilled.

"You haven't said anything to me since the incident," Veeris remarked.

Haven remained stern, motionless with a turned back. Veeris paused, awaiting a verbal response, though none came. At first, Veeris assumed Haven tried to formulate his ongoing thoughts into words, but as the sun continued its descent, the half-orc offered only stillness.

"You and I both know how the Blood Moon drives people mad," Veeris explained, hoping his truth would conjure a response. "What happened back there wasn't me. The red moon is corrupt and savage and did everything it could to create foul air between us. I wish to fix it."

Still, Haven remained steadfast, his staunch back flexing from his crossed arms.

"Well?" Veeris probed, which was followed by a deafening silence. "You can't just ignore me forever."

The weeds below Veeris' feet swayed with the tantalizing wind, encircling his ankles like a grasping enemy. Panic arose as endless possibilities of his future crossed his mind, watching Salem live her life without him, his friends shunning him, succumbing to hatred and fear and living a long life just to die alone.

"What more can I do? I can't fix things if you don't talk to me. No matter what I say or do, it won't bring change to what happened. The Blood Moon is malicious and cruel! Do not blame me for the actions I couldn't control."

Menacing silence. It resembled the shrieks of a bird, one so agonizingly intrusive that he imagined blood oozing past his lobes. He wished nothing more than to alleviate the silence with Haven's voice, but still the half-orc refused.

As the light faded and the shadows darkened, Haven's silhouette merged with the overcast gloom. The retreating sun allowed the forest to enclose him in unyielding loneliness.

"Talk to me!" Veeris pleaded, unsure if Haven could even hear him. "There's nothing I can possibly do to change what happened!"

Silence.

"I'll do anything. Please! Let's go back to the way things were." It was as if Veeris' words were hitting closed ears, the emptiness of the air around them not paying much heed to his endless monologue. "I truly think something's wrong here, Haven, but no one will listen to me. I think the demon has charmed you and the others. Things only started to go amiss when he joined. It's his fault that Andrid died! Not mine! Please, do not forgo our friendship because of that *thing!*"

A piercing, wretched, intolerable silence.

"Haven...please."

Instead of responding, Haven stomped through the forest with pride exuding from his rugged posture, the flora becoming victims of rage and sorrow in the aftermath. The trees embraced him before he disappeared into the shadows, leaving Veeris under the unempathetic regard of nature. Veeris watched Haven go, unable to stop him.

THIRTY-THREE.

Horror and disbelief welled in Salem's stomach when the Blood Moon rose for a second time. As it projected a red hue upon the lands, the clouds above encircled each other in strange, unknown formations. After Andrid's passing, Salem extended an aura of holy energy around the caravan in a large radius. As they traveled, she could sense watchful eyes surveying them. Luckily due to her magic, they kept their distance, temporarily allowing them safe travel.

Veeris had betrayed her. He had expressed that she was guilty of falling for another, a sin prohibited by Elohim, yet he was guilty of the same. She hadn't been aware of his feelings before now, though she refused to dwell further. Andrid was dead due to his lack of restraint and his inability to resist the urges that foul orb brought on.

Salem was unsure if she could ever forgive him for it.

With the heavy rain, it became even harder to perceive any lurking creatures suppressing themselves in the distance. Tears of crimson pelleted the ground in heavy waves, tainting the dirt beneath it. They resembled daggers, falling onto the world with piercing assaults. Salem ignored its cries and repressed her own as they finally neared Fort Runswhick.

Salem might have permitted more tears to fall from her bottled frustration if she hadn't been mentally preparing herself for the conversation ahead. As the lands of the fort came into view, it marked a previous battlefield in its wake. Still, weapons lay scattered across the plains tainted in layers of dried blood that reverted to wetness from the rain. A lingering, fetid odor dwelled in a haze from the surrounding forest all the way to the fort's edge. Her previously dry eyes watered from the invasive miasma. The fog and debris shifted with a ghostlike silence, but no bodies lay amongst the fields.

As soon as their wagon became visible in the sheet of rain, with Kendra Dawn's flag waving in the strong winds, the soldiers apprehensively carved a path for them. They neither greeted nor saluted them as they normally would have, as if their respect had disappeared with the sun. When the mercenaries reached the elevated entrance in front of the closed portcullis, they halted underneath a makeshift tarp, held aloft by metal poles protruding from the wet dirt.

A soldier, bearing the metal and cloth of a lieutenant, strode forward to meet them.

"Kendra Dawn, an unexpected surprise," the lieutenant said, standing upright with his hands clamped behind his back. "You may refer to me as Sir Knight Hadawaye, lieutenant of the Middle Guard. What are you doing at Fort Runswhick? I'm sure you've been alerted of this happenstance."

Salem struggled to control the foul expression that crossed her face, undoubtedly failing from the twitch of her brow. "We came to see if the rest of the volunteers of Kendra Dawn needed aid," Salem replied. She placed two fingers on her locket, extending a hidden sphere of magical energy around them before she prodded further. "What happened to the casualties? Each soldier from both forces were supposed to be returned to their homes."

"A disease spread. They were burned," the lieutenant replied.

A lie.

"Kendra Dawn never traveled with the second wave of soldiers to the fort from Goldenrise?"

"No." Another lie.

The Avernos Empire clearly hid something from them, a plan they didn't wish to unravel to the faction that held a standing with both kingdoms. Though, it didn't explain where the rest of the volunteers that journeyed from Goldenrise currently were.

"Will you grant us entry into the fort until the morn? The lands are dangerous at night, especially with a Blood Moon," Salem said, gaze circling past the lieutenant to view within.

"By Emperor Wymond's orders, no one is to enter the fortress," he responded. "I assume you would have heard at this point. Kendra Dawn is no longer established as a neutral party in the war. We have merely accepted your presence for the sake of pleasantries."

"We had a contract! Emperor Wymond can't just break our agreement," Salem seethed, unable to find the words to project her anger.

Hadawaye smirked. "He can do anything he wants. He's the emperor and future ruler of all Terrisae. Kendra Dawn has proven to do nothing but halt our forces from continuing further by their demands of dealing with the dead."

"I don't understa—"

"Your further presence will be reported as trespassing. Unlike yourselves, we aren't pretending to be warriors. We are real soldiers in a real war with real responsibilities." Hadawaye lifted his chin. "Now go back to playing pretend with your friends out in the wilds with the beasts where you belong."

The surrounding soldiers reached for their weapons, drawing their blades and leveling the pointed edges, like an iron maiden baring its teeth.

Salem stepped forward towards the lieutenant with a glare that could cut through him even better than her undrawn blade. Despite the height difference, she lifted her chin and pulled her shoulders back to straighten her composure, caring not for the maiden. She surveyed his expression with an unwavering scowl. The moment Salem stepped closer, a smirk of triumph spread across Hadawaye's face. He wanted her to attack. If that were the case, then she would gladly accept his invitation.

"Did you know that there are seven sins in this world, Lieutenant Hadawaye?" Salem muttered with a softened voice, feigning intrigue. "There are seven ruthless sins in total that take without concern. There is pride, the unyielding and the abhorrent; sloth, the callous and the negligent; lust, the devious and the fraudulent; envy, the jealous and malicious; greed, the selfish and the egotistic; and gluttony, the impulsive and the fervent...but there is one sin in particular that is the most dangerous of them all," Salem growled, revealing her teeth as a caged animal would. "You do not know real war until you've seen the Heavens fall and the pits rise. When the traitors of the Heavens attempted to seize the Golden Gates, it was *wrath* that met their treachery." Salem stepped one foot closer, leaving little space between her and her adversary. "You want me to return to the forests to which I belong? Then do not wave meat in the face of a hungry beast, *Lieutenant*, for I am all too eager to force a faux commander to kneel at my bloodstained feet."

Hadawaye stepped backwards.

"I think we're done 'ere," Gilben interrupted, stepping betwixt them. The dwarf prodded Salem back after several efforts against her locked stance. "We'll be departin'. Thank ya for yer...hospitality," he muttered sarcastically, ushering Salem to turn away from the soldier's leer. Even still, she kept eye contact with him.

"Fine," Salem spat, huffing in response as she turned away from the leader, who stood with fear swelling in his eyes.

Struggling to regain his composure, Lieutenant Hadawaye adjusted his uniform and turned back to his men.

It wasn't until the garrison shrank in the distance that the mercenaries halted the retreating caravan. They lingered far out of the soldiers' sight and under a canopy of trees before the rest of the party emerged from the wagon's boot, with Korbyn idly seated on its front seat. Salem paced in anger, creating indents in the dirt from the shuffling of her boots.

"I can't believe this! Stupid, petty, stubborn soldiers..." Salem halted, attention lingering on Korbyn. "No offense."

Korbyn shrugged, appearing unbothered by her professed irritation.

"Something's not right," Salem insisted. Her pacing created a spherical path from her feet. She lifted her finger to her mouth, wanting to bite the edges of her unkept nails, but was prevented by her gloves. "I used my magic to see if he was deceitful. He lied about burning the bodies of the soldiers and traveling with the volunteers of Kendra Dawn. Whether they made it to the fort, though, I'm unsure."

"Ya can tell by the lands they didn't burn bodies 'ere," Gilben stated, surveying the battlefield with squinted eyes. The field was hushed from the aftermath of the battle. "They would've dug holes 'nd placed the bodies in 'em to burn or they would've just piled 'em together. We'd see quagmires or thin's of the like. There's no signs of anythin' burnin', like the smell o' sulfur." The dwarf peered back at Salem's concerned expression. "Wherever the bodies 're, they weren't burned. Not 'ere, 'nd if they were truly filled with disease, they wou'dn't've taken them into the fortress."

"So where did they go? Why would they lie about it?" Oakley interjected, contemplation replacing his tired eyes.

"Perhaps they lied 'bout the bodies just to get us outta 'heir way?" Gilben suggested, stroking his beard, which was more unkept than usual. His accustomed braid that cascaded down the middle was left as a matted tangle of wild, thick hairs. "He did say tha' our clean-up work pushes off 'heir pursuits. Maybe we're lookin' a wee bit into it?"

As Salem contemplated in a brief silence, she heard the Blood Moon spilling silent cries from above, as if desperately desiring to tell them about something unseen. "No, there's more to this than we understand. Did you hear what Hadawaye said about the emperor? He said he would be the future leader of all Terrisae. If Avernos takes over Esperin, I don't think they'll stop there. They might initiate war against the Alliance of Thalar."

"We're a neutral party 'ere, lass. It's not our place ta get involved. 'Sides, it's a war, course the men wit' station 're all in on 'heir 'righteous' leader."

"We can't just remain idle. Kendra Dawn is missing, and this is where they should have been. He was blatantly dishonest about their shared travel. I just don't understand his foul intentions," Salem said, unable to steady her heated tone and the shuffling of her boots.

"Ya heard the lieutenant. We can't be helpin' the volunteers 'nd Micah if we get arrested ourselves," Gilben urged.

Salem appreciated his logical reasoning where she otherwise fell short, but the boiling in her chest called for answers. "We can't help the volunteers if we don't know where they are. What if they perished on the travel here? What if they were attacked by crazed monsters and left to die? What if they're in need of our help?" Salem glanced to the garrison, its shrunken shadow blanketed in crimson. "They're the only ones who have the answers."

Oakley's voice severed the conversation. "Then what can we do?" He stood at her shoulder now, erupting from her shadow. His serious demeanor was startling, though she found herself thankful for his mirrored resolve.

Salem surveyed Veeris. Usually, he offered a hint of guidance. When she sought to plunge into danger, it was Veeris who erupted with logical thought. Instead, he remained leaning against the wagon with crossed arms, and she couldn't tell if he was listening or not by his downcast eyes. For now, she was thankful for his distant thoughts, for in her own mind, he no longer had wisdom to bear.

Haven also resided in a quaint silence. Even though he was physically present, his attention drifted to the forest, as if something lurked there. She examined that direction and found nothing significant.

"Something bad is going to happen if it hasn't already. I can feel it," Salem said, twisting towards the fort. "We have to sneak in there and find out what they're plotting."

"They're probably reorganizing and planning their next action," Korbyn interjected from his place on the wagon. He had been a stalwart gargoyle atop his perch as they rode. He crossed his arms and scanned the fortification with his impeccable awareness. "It's half a mile between here and the old castle. If you did want to storm it, any assault would be seen rather quickly." He placed a hand to his chin, now standing on the wood flooring at the driver's seat. "A distraction—no, that probably wouldn't work." Enthrallment and concentration pried Salem for dominance, for Korbyn's serious tone and unabashed honesty was more fetching than he realized. "The only real way into a fort that guarded is with an army twice its size or an inconspicuous entrance."

"Then I'll find one," Oakley said with a grim line of his mouth and a furrowed brow. "I'm stealthy enough to get to the fort unseen. I can get in, find any information, and then get out."

"Sneaking our way into such a heavily facilitated place? Is a feat like that even possible?" Salem wondered, recalling the patrolling masses of soldiers. "Surely, we'd be seen."

"You underestimate me, Sale. I've snuck into the most heavily guarded locations in all of Terrisae. You should *see* the number of rooms I've pilfered! I was once known as the Silver-Tongued Scoundrel. For example, there is this one beautiful mistress who yearned for me for months after I taught her the sexual pleasures of devouring her—"

Oakley's ramble was cut off by a playful slap on the back of the head. Salem had not even seen Korbyn dismount the caravan as he now loomed over Oakley with a disgruntled countenance. His eyes were cold yet conflicting with humor as he replied wryly. "I don't see how that particular story helps us, but yeah, we should sneak in. It's really the only feasible way to go about locating information on Kendra Dawn's whereabouts." Korbyn twisted towards the fortification once again, his pointer finger sliding across his chin. "You can tell this fort used to be an old castle by its elaborate architectural features, like the ornate sconces and lavish windows. While it still works as a damn well defendable spot, its design is flawed. It's got too many pleasantries in the design just for show, and plenty of blind spots. Plus, the walls aren't very tall. It would be pretty easy to scale with the right equipment, even with the rain."

Salem nodded, joining Korbyn and Oakley at their side. "Great! Then the three of us will sneak in and see what we can find. Everyone else can stay behind with the wagon and be ready, just in case we need to make a quick escape."

Korbyn, Oakley, and Gilben exchanged concerned glances.

"What?" Salem snapped.

"Uh, no offense, Sale, but you're kinda..." Oakley motioned to her robust armor. "Loud."

"I'm not loud! I can be stealthy," she insisted. Salem lowered her body to portray a stalking stance, and the clanking of her armor followed. "Well, I mean I can be without all the armor. I could just take it off."

"Yeah, cause I'm sure the soldiers would be glad to let you put your armor back on before they chased you out of the fort," Korbyn jested.

Salem glowered, albeit thankful to hear his voice from his previous silence the day before. "But—"

"Stay here with everyone else. The smaller the infiltration, the better the odds," Korbyn urged. "I'll stop this one from getting into trouble." He jabbed his thumb towards Oakley.

"Oh, please, *you're* the one that's going to have to keep up with me!" Oakley smirked.

Korbyn mirrored his own grin, one that awoke the butterflies in her stomach. "Oh, really, Seductive Scrote...Harlot...or whatever it was they called you," Korbyn stammered.

"Scrote? That's *Stunning Silver-Tongued Scoundrel* to you, fiend."

"Did you add the *stunning* before or after you got caught by the lady's husband?"

"Maybe I added it *after* I silver-tongued your mother."

"You recall that I don't remember my mother, right?" Korbyn laughed, fueling a scowl from Oakley.

"Well, you know what, Korbyn? Just because of that, on all that is holy in all the realm, if I ever meet your mother, I swear to Elohim I'll use my charm and silver tongue and—"

"Even if ya get ta the wall," Gilben interrupted, gathering everyone's derailed attention. "How are ya supposed to get past the guards? I'm sure they're station'd at every entrance."

Oakley placed his hands on his hips. "Easy," he said, holding an open palm to Gilben.

Gilben stared at the open palm and blinked, analyzing Oakley with a questioning regard before returning to his hand. Oakley gazed down at Gilben, then to his palm, and then back down at Gilben.

"The map!" Oakley urged with wriggling fingers, as if it had been obvious.

"Oh!" Gilben shuffled through one of his satchels, digging through items and loose coin until he retrieved one of the available maps.

Oakley unraveled the parchment and pointed towards one of the fortification's walls. Salem, Korbyn, and Gilben gathered around.

"If you observe these three walls of Fort Runswhick, you'll notice each lead to a road," he commenced, gesturing to the west, north, and east path. "You've got the west road that leads across Exonia Creek to the Grove of Esperin; the north road, which connects to another Esperin fort, probably with some pretentious name; and then the east road, the one that connects to Fort Silvercrest. That leaves..." Oakley pointed to the southern wall, which sat closely to Exonia Creek.

"That leaves the southern wall, which—" Korbyn interjected.

The shorter man interrupted him, "Shh, shh, shh, this is my moment. Let me finish." Oakley shoved a finger against Korbyn's mouth. "That means the southern wall, which faces the river, will likely be the least guarded. I can find a weakness in the wall or at least be able to scale that side without any issues."

"You feel good about yourself?" Korbyn asked dryly.

"Most definitely."

"That was pretty smart, Oak. I'm impressed," Salem replied in astonishment.

Oakley frowned. "Are you implying that I'm not normally smart?"

Silence followed.

"Then it's settled," Gilben stated, heading towards the back of the wagon and pulling up the sack of supplies he just shifted through. When he untangled the tied bag, rope, two grappling hooks, and chalk sprawled out. "I'll start packin' yer bags."

Haven silently assisted, jumping into the back of the caravan and retrieving the heavy barrel of water. He waved the two over before filling their waterskins to the brim.

The two prepared themselves for the venture to the fort. Oakley pulled his hood over his head, strapping new vials along his belt. Korbyn followed in stride, securing the ties on his boots and taking one of Haven's extra knives. He fashioned a new leather strap along his waist and thigh before placing the small blade in his holster. Haven and Gilben tightened the straps of their bags, ensuring their belongings were fastened and not rattling with too much noise in the silence of the night.

As Salem merely stood there, watching as everyone shifted in preparation, she couldn't help but feel utterly useless.

"If you hear shouting from inside the fort or any type of horn or bell, run. It won't necessarily mean they found us, just that they found something amiss. The last thing we need while in there is any of you captured," Korbyn stated, adjusting the bag's strap. "Head northeast towards Umberfall and don't stop until you're there. We'll meet back up with you in the city."

Oakley nodded, conjuring a noise of confirmation. They faced the fort, ready to venture into the depths of the unknown path.

"Oakley, Korbyn," Salem stated, followed by their brisk turns. She circled her arms around their necks in a tight embrace. With the height difference, she could only lean in a single direction, resting her face against Korbyn's clavicle.

With hesitation, they both wrapped an arm around her. While Oakley's was a loose hold with a couple of reassuring, soft pats, Korbyn leaned into her with a delayed, tightened hug, as though he allowed himself a moment of weakness.

"Please be safe. I can't—just be safe, please, and return quickly," Salem whispered. As she pulled back and examined them, with a lingering hand on each of their shoulders, she couldn't prevent the forming tears.

As a previous archangel, Salem often forgot the weakness that was mortality. She became so fixated on feeling unstoppable, as though she and her friends defied the laws of the world. However, mortals weren't invincible, just as she no longer was. Andrid's death was and would always be a grim reminder.

Korbyn's thumb slid across her cheek, ridding the tear that threatened her. Without delay, he pivoted and hauled the cloak of his hood over his face.

"We will." Korbyn strode past the edge of the small forest.

Oakley walked backwards, an amused grin receding into the density of the trees at his side. "Don't worry, I'll keep him safe for you!"

Korbyn grabbed him by his collar and dragged him forward.

As Salem witnessed their retreat, she folded her hands and closed her eyes. "Elohim, please keep them safe."

Did Salem mention how much she hated waiting?

Korbyn and Oakley had only been gone for about thirty minutes when she succumbed to pacing. Gilben stoked the small fire, prodding the wood with an elongated stick more than he needed to. It was strange, not seeing a lute and pen in the dwarf's hands.

Meanwhile, Veeris and Haven lingered on opposite sides of their makeshift camp, enveloped in what she assumed to be their own thoughts. While Veeris' attention remained in a downcast avoidance, Haven observed the haunting silence of the forest.

Salem finally halted her never-ending strides, shifting her attention to the fortress. Despite her impatience, she was thankful for the surrounding quiet, for it implied their ongoing success. Even then, the stillness was daunting.

"Lass," Gilben stated. With her pulled attention, Salem realized she had ceased her pacing only to incessantly tap her foot. "Yer gonna have ta calm yerself."

"Sorry," Salem replied, running a hand through her disorderly locks. "I'm just worried about them."

Gilben nodded, rising from his seated position. "Speakin'a which, I think we shou'd discuss some thin's." The dwarf gestured to Veeris with a crane of his neck and a flick of his eyes.

"Right," Salem said, motioning to grab Haven's attention with a simple wave. At first, the half-orc didn't react to the intrusion. "Haven? Are you alright? Can we talk?"

As if he had just departed from a haze, Haven stared back in clarity. "Yes," he muttered, following her to the vigorous campfire. They sat adjacent to one another, ensuring Veeris remained within their visual proximity. Though it was obvious he would be the topic of conversation, he didn't appear to mind.

"Who do you want to start with?" Salem inquired, stoking the fire.

Haven stared at the glittering flames, watching warm embers trickle towards the night sky.

Gilben closed his eyes, as if the beauty of the world had been a distraction. "Do ya know anythin' about tha' dark power, lass?"

When Veeris attacked, the demon contained in Korbyn's body surged. Despite being knowledgeable on demons and their origins, this situation was abnormal. Never had she heard of such evil housed within a mortal. Korbyn's voice, mind, and actions had become the will of the demon amid the bout. It resembled his normal voice, but with an echo of otherworldliness, spewing knowledge that a normal mortal wouldn't have known. Wherever the demon had come from, it was conversant with Salem and Veeris' secrets.

There were two types of creatures that resided in the Hells: devils and demons. While devils were the previous archangels, stripped from their powers and cast away, demons were the creations in the aftermath. They were conceived from angels and devils much like mortals were born, gifted with newfound powers when no longer blessed with Elohim's holy light. It was why Elohim banned intimacy, to ensure this catastrophe never occurred again. They shared the same eyes as Korbyn, with pits of darkened sclera and irises of the moon.

How he contained a demon within, Salem still didn't understand. He was clearly a mortal, though somehow inflicted with a curse that he couldn't control. The darkness seemed to be creeping in the shadows, gaining dominance over his person entirely. He needed their help before he lost himself permanently to whatever was attempting to overtake him.

"I only know a little bit about the dark powers, I think," Salem finally admitted, watching the firewood shift upon its burned edges turning into cinders. "Though I can't be fully sure of what's going on with him. All I know is that there seems to be something within him vying for control. While it's seemingly managed, it doesn't seem permanent."

"Is there a right fer concern? I want ta put me confidence in the lad, but if it ain't somethin' he can manage, he cou'd be a danger," Gilben said.

"Who are we even talking about here?" The words were Haven's, and yet they held within them a sting so rarely heard from his usual soothing tenor. "It looked like Veeris was the one who lost control. It's his fault that..." Haven trailed off, squinting at the embers like it was a formidable nemesis.

"We were speaking about Korbyn. He needs our help," Salem responded. "Something wrong is going on with him—something out of his control. Whatever is inside him is dangerous, and we're the only ones who can stop it."

"Korbyn needs our help, tha' much is assured," the dwarf responded with a hearty smile hidden behind coarse hair. "Then we'll do everythin' we can ta help the lad. He's a good one."

"I couldn't agree more," Salem replied with a genuine smile, hope manifesting through her dissolving doubt. "What do you think, Haven?"

"I agree," the half-orc replied with a hoarseness he seemed unable to rid from his throat. "I don't blame Korbyn for what happened. I wanted to help him in the moment, just as much as I want to help him now..." He trailed off again, ending his statement with a curl of his fist. "I want to rid us of our *problems*."

"Good, then how?" Gilben asked, turning to Salem with lifted brows. Her bewildered expression must have shown true based on his immediate reply. "Sorry, lass, it's just, ya always have a plan o' some kind, even if it's, uh—"

"Even if it's what?" Salem huffed with crossed arms.

"Even if it's...in need o'...adjustments..." Gilben's contagious bellow curled her own lips, and she chuckled in parallel.

"First of all, that's rude. Second of all, I think after we locate the volunteers, we should start focusing on Korbyn. The sooner we get it resolved, the sooner we can alleviate the tension between him and Veeris."

Haven's attention was fixated on Veeris, seemingly unaware of their brief amusement. With the reflection of the fire's light, Salem watched swirling emotions fill his indecipherable gaze.

"Good. Keep Korbyn away from the *murderer* until then," Haven growled. It was a whisper, just short of being inaudible. One of his legs bounced in agitation.

"What's goin' on with Veeris?" Gilben probed. "There has ta be more than the Blood Moon affectin' him. You know 'im best."

Salem frowned, analyzing Veeris' blank regard. "I don't know, Gilben. He's completely different than the man I used to know. I've ignored the signs when I shouldn't have. I disregarded my problems, and now Andrid is gone."

She felt Haven's bouncing leg pause at the reminder of Andrid's death. Her incessant need to remove the grime from her nails grew more irritable. Instead, Salem clutched her locket to diminish its gleam, evoking her internal inadequacy. This incident might have been prevented if her friends knew the truth. Maybe it was time to tell them.

"It is not yer fault, lass," Gilben reassured with rough pats on her shoulder. "We'll have a moment's rest once we locate Kendra Dawn. Until then, keep yer chin up."

Her smile was pained, though it crept up to her face. "You're right," Salem whispered, unable to prevent the wandering of her eyes to the fortress in the distance. "Once they get back."

"Hopefully the Stunning Silver-Tongued Scoundrel 'nd his squire successfully complete 'heir reconnaissance, aye?" Gilben added, and they both laughed.

Salem could almost hear Andrid's fit of unique laughter at her side, coercing her lips into a downward pull. "All of this light-heartedness...it feels wrong without Andrid here. But at the same time, the break from the grief is pleasant. Am I wrong for feeling guilty, Gilben? Are we wrong for jesting?" Salem wondered, wiping away the tear before it cascaded down her previously damp cheeks.

Gilben sighed. "If there was one thing Andrid liked more than anythin', it was smilin'," the dwarf said, rotating his robust hands in front of the fire. "There's a difference between continuin' an' forgettin'. There's not a moment we be forgettin' about 'em, or a moment where we don't miss 'em. Sides, Andrid would've been upset if we're not smilin', methinks."

"You're right, but..." Salem let the words hang.

Gilben interjected with a shake of his head. "No buts, lass. What is it that the religious say? Somethin' like they're in a better place?"

Salem glanced down, clutching her locket that shone against the raging flames. "Right," she whispered sadly. "A better place."

"There is no better place."

Salem and Gilben twisted to Haven.

The half-orc tried to clear his throat, but he hacked with phlegm. It echoed across their temporary encampment, and Salem shifted with palpable concern.

"Haven? Are you okay?" Salem asked.

One of Haven's legs bounced incessantly, as if he was plagued by irritation, anxiety, or both. He dragged his nails across his alternate arm, leaving scratches behind in his gray skin. When blood sprung from the fresh wounds, he didn't cease his endless clawing. Instead, he seemed to welcome it.

"Haven! Stop, you're bleeding. Is everything okay?" Salem persisted, reaching out to his restless form.

"I *hate him*," Haven whispered louder, his eyes wide and unblinking. His movements became more restless and sporadic, flinching occasionally from his tensed muscles. His unremitting scratching intensified, blood pouring out of new wounds.

Salem and Gilben stood, surveying his body. The moon, silent in recognition, cast its red light down onto Haven, who rose from his seated position.

"Haven, I think ya need some rest—" Gilben stated, interjected by a harrowing voice that sounded nothing like Haven.

"No. *What I need is no longer here*," the half-orc spat. He gurgled like death, a raspy voice that hadn't spoken in decades and no longer had breath to take.

As though not catching the abnormality in his tone, Gilben reached out.

"Wait—" Salem was too late.

Haven thrust the palm of his hand into Gilben's chest. The dwarf flew several paces towards a tree, slamming into it so hard that the trunk toppled over from the force. She heard him grunt before he collapsed, eyes closed and blood dripping from his brow.

"Gilben!" Salem shouted. As she turned back to Haven, reaching for her blade and shield, the larger male grabbed her throat. She lurched as he leveled her off the ground, desperately pointing her toes to reach the solid earth.

"H-Haven..." she gurgled, scratching at his wrists to loosen his grip. "Haven, you're being possessed...it's a—"

When Haven's grip tightened, her ability to inhale disappeared.

"*Veeris*," the creature behind Haven's eyes snarled. His normally dark eyes disappeared into a pit of blackness, a similar aura of magical energy spilling out of his body. Haven's eyes resembled Korbyn's, except lacking pupils.

It was only then that Salem realized her magical sphere had dwindled due to her frustrations. As manipulated shadows swelled around them, she struggled underneath the monster's harsh grip.

"Wraith," Salem choked out.

THIRTY-FOUR.

"So, what happened back there?" Oakley asked, leaning against the southern wall.

Korbyn examined the top from his own seated position along its base, perceiving the shuffling of several guards on the battlement above them. Magical hues of colorless energy flared like flames, even with stone standing between his observant eyes and the soldiers on the other side.

"I don't know where to start," Korbyn replied, lowering his gravelly voice to prevent the patrols above them from hearing.

Oakley had been right; this wall was the least occupied. Given that Exonia Creek rested not even thirty paces towards the south, the forces didn't place much attention on patrolling the walls. Any attack would likely come from the north or east, or even the west towards the Alliance of Thalar in the directions of the other nations. Even though the other lands weren't involved in the war, the western side still employed more soldiers than the southern wall. Luckily, the red-hued rain continued its descent, creating formations of fog that clouded the air. Instead of impeding their efforts, it would provide visual and audible assistance to infiltrate Avernos' barriers.

"Oh, you know, how about just the end so I'll get confused and have no idea what's going on," Oakley retorted sarcastically, causing Korbyn to frown. "Oh, wait, that's where I am now. Obviously, I want to hear it from the beginning, ya nincompoop."

Korbyn glowered. "At least curse if you're going to insult me."

"I don't speak profanity. It ruins my adorable personality."

"I don't think 'adorable' is the right word."

"My suitors would have to disagree with you." Oakley closed his eyes and grinned, as if deep in thought about previous endeavors and pleasures.

"What suitors? Or are we talking about your alter ego? What was it again, the Blithe Bandit?" Korbyn questioned, feigning ignorance with a twitch of his lips that threatened to break into a smirk.

Oakley huffed. "It was the *Silver-Tongued Scoundrel,* but I can't lie. That's a pretty good one, I might write that down. And believe it or not, Korb, I had *lines* of people yearning for me," he replied, waving his arms about like an actor in a play. "It would be a crime if I weren't to bless them with my presence. Now, enough about my endless romantic ventures. Tell me what happened and why you can't sleep," Oakley said, rubbing his arms to spread his warmth in the rain.

Korbyn leaned back once again, resting the crown of his head against the stone. Several soldiers still paced above them, forcing them to wait until their shifts had changed.

"If I'm being honest, I'm not sure anymore," Korbyn admitted, taking a deep breath and closing his eyes.

Oakley tilted his head. "What do you mean?"

"Well, I haven't been able to sleep, but every time I try, I start having these hallucinations that I can't explain."

"Korb. I hate to break this to you, but they're called dreams. They're this thing that happens when people sleep, and—"

"No, idiot, I'm not talking about dreams. They're different." Korbyn slid his hand through his hair. "I'm awake the entire time, and I don't get any rest. I keep having these strange visions of a dark place, with a red sky"—he glanced up to the moon—"kind of like this one, but there's a dark cathedral in the distance. It's massive, greater than any castle I've ever seen."

Oakley pondered in silence for a moment. "You sure you're not just having nightmares?"

"Yes, Oak. I don't even fall asleep."

"How are you even awake right now? I mean, by this point, you should have passed out from the exhaustion."

Korbyn gazed back towards the fort, igniting his enhanced vision to see through the fortification's defenses. Four burning flames still danced across the walkway towards the bastion. "I don't know. The day after I awoke, a strange mark appeared on my arm. It's like a brand." The mark pulsed in recognition, and Korbyn pressed his leather brace against it to alleviate the irritation, though still he failed to quell it. "I think it has something to do with it."

"Well, that's...definitely unnatural." Oakley leaned forward and analyzed his forearm, though he wouldn't find answers from the armor and cloth concealing its presence. "Any other weird occurrences? I mean, I know the answer is yes, but you were acting and sounding strange before Andrid..." Oakley frowned. "You definitely weren't yourself."

You hide and run from the destiny that awaits you, but no matter which direction you run, time always progresses forward, the demon whispered.

Korbyn ignored it, responding to Oakley, "Yes, but..."

Would they leave you in the dead of night, alone and scared to face your destiny without them?

"I'm afraid," Korbyn whispered to Oakley, the demon, and himself.

"Of?"

"When I went back to Avernos, it felt foreign to me." Korbyn gazed to the east containing the forest that obscured their allies and their encampment. "But here with you guys, it feels like home." He trailed his fingers over his clavicle, a small bit of warmth still alleviating the never-ending chill. "But, at the same time, I don't want to put you all in danger. Something is wrong with me, and it's clear I don't always have it under control. I don't want to hurt any of you. And Andrid is gone because of me."

"It's not your fault, Korb. Andrid died because they wanted to save you. I'm still angry and confused when it comes to Veeris. He hasn't been the same, and I don't know what's been going on with him, but..." Oakley took a deep breath and exhaled. "Sale, Andrid, Gilb, Have, and I, we all saw something in you that day at Silvercrest. I know that Sale's the one who made that decision, but we all wanted you here. It must be difficult and lonely without your memories. We wanted to help."

"Even though I've been keeping secrets?" Korbyn murmured, inspecting him.

"Especially because you've been keeping secrets. It means you're normal. And, if we're starting to get truthful, I haven't been completely honest either," Oakley confessed, returning his gaze. Korbyn scrunched his eyes in confusion. "I haven't been very open with anyone about my past."

"You don't have to share with me if you don't want to—"

"But here's the thing. I want to." Oakley slid further down the wall, slouching and resting his elbows on his knees. "I was an orphan. I grew up on the streets in a city called Wellcaster, a city not too far from Goldenrise in the Avernos Empire. I was never really sure of my heritage, but I was always short, shorter than most people, and definitely shorter than other homeless kids on the street. I'm at least majority human, but I'm pretty sure I'm part gnomish. People don't like it when you're different, and they take advantage when they're bigger than you."

"Sorry about the jokes." Korbyn frowned.

"It really doesn't bother me. It never did. I like who I am. It just wasn't very beneficial at times when I was on my own. So don't get all sappy on me, you tall freaking tree," Oakley said.

The corner of Korbyn's lips twitched upwards.

Oakley hugged his body when the rained pelted down in a thicker wave. "So anyways, being small made me realize I wasn't so good at fighting head-on. I got pretty good at being unseen when I wanted to be. One day I tried stealing from some fancy people in a big mansion. I ended up getting caught, with a huge sack of gold, jewelry, and antiques that were twice as big as me. I was *this* close to escaping. But, instead of getting killed or thrown in jail, the lord of the house gave me a job as a spy."

The memory seemed to be quite fond for him, but as Oakley trailed off, the beaming smile disappeared.

"What happened after that?" Korbyn questioned.

"The lord wasn't a great guy. He'd been making lots of big mistakes, and bigger enemies. My job as a spy changed into something else he needed. He wanted me to become someone to get rid of his problems."

"An assassin," Korbyn guessed.

Oakley nodded, half-lidded eyes brimming with remorse. "At first, I refused, but he threatened me, started spewing things about ruining my life and that I didn't have any other alternatives." He tugged the turtleneck of his shirt towards his mouth and mumbled into the fabric. "So, I became an assassin."

"It sounds like you didn't have a choice," Korbyn offered, watching different emotions cross his features.

"But I did. At any point, I could have left. I could have escaped while everyone was sleeping, and they wouldn't have known until

I was long gone," Oakley explained as he lowered the fabric, placing a hand on his chest. He gazed up at the stars and welcomed the pouring rain. "I was content with my life. I was earning my own money. I had my own alchemy lab and office. I was living in a big estate with fancy food, nice clothes, people yearning for me, but the worst of it..." Oakley slackened his shoulders, whispering his truth. "I enjoyed the thrill. I liked being an assassin. I somehow convinced myself that I was killing only bad people and that I was doing a good thing, but I was just attempting to blind myself. I murdered innocents, and I washed their blood and memories away and went back to my luxurious life, every single night."

"And you haven't told the others this?"

"Not a soul. I'm afraid of what they might think," Oakley admitted.

"So why me?" Korbyn wondered.

"I guess because I wanted to show you that everyone has a darkness." Oakley peered at him. "You have one that you seem to not be able to control, but me, I fight against that adrenaline every single day. That's why I eventually left and became a mercenary that killed monsters, because I needed a way to alleviate that need again. I know they all care for me, but they also think I'm this fun, quirky guy that jests all the time, and I guess I can relate to your darkness. I've never had any siblings, but I kind of think you and I could have been brothers." Oakley scanned him with dramatically raised brows. "If, you know, you weren't so deathly pale and instead had a beautiful complexion like I do."

Korbyn rolled his eyes and nudged him with his elbow. "Then I'd be tall, dark, and mysterious." he snickered. "Damn. I feel like it's a missed opportunity."

"You're right. Put my good looks with your height, and you'd finally be a handsome devil."

"Ah, shut up."

They both laughed, allowing the rain to cover their moment

of respite. Afterwards, silence ensued as the duo awaited the departure of the soldiers above them. Korbyn watched the auras carefully. The same men still lingered at the battlement's edge, though they seemed to be focused on their conversation rather than paying attention to the fort's surroundings. At this point, the moon had ascended to the sky's highest point. Hopefully, they would retreat from their stations and allow the two intruders ample time to scale the wall and enter without watchful eyes.

"Are you not afraid?" Korbyn questioned. "Of me? Even though I haven't told you everything and the fact that I don't know what awaits me?"

"Why would I be?" Oakley asked, his eyes hiding from the moon's shadow. "You're my friend. It's my job to be here for you if you need me. And I know you'd never hurt me."

Korbyn returned to surveying the wall, struggling to hide the glistening of tears in his eyes. "Same, buddy."

Korbyn roughly tugged Oakley's hood down over his face. Oakley flailed at the unexpected gesture, waving his arms to pry the cloth away.

When Oakley reared back and escaped the confines of the hood, he frowned with a pursed lip. His anger was incredibly unthreatening, as though Korbyn had just stolen the last piece of gingerbread without asking. Imagining the man as a lethal assassin proved a difficult endeavor.

"Hey, jerk, what's the big idea—"

"It's time," Korbyn stated after surveying the battlement. His eyes sparkled in adrenaline, watching the small embers stride down the rampart towards the gatehouse.

Undoubtedly, the soldiers searched for their replacements, gifting the duo sufficient time to scale unseen. Korbyn shifted his gaze to the very top of the keep, perceiving a tall tower that stood in the middle of the fort's grounds, and the most likely place to discover an army's secrets.

"To the top?" Korbyn urged with a confident grin.

Oakley smirked, spreading white chalk on his palms to dry his hands. "To the top."

Scaling the wall had been easier than Korbyn originally thought. Even the rain didn't stop them, thanks to the white chalk and the security of the grappling hooks. Oakley had been the first, climbing with an unnatural speed and propelling himself in between two merlons. While he monitored their unseen approach, Korbyn scaled the parapet, hauling himself up with a surprising strength.

As soon as they crossed the battlement's threshold, they crammed the grappling hooks into their satchels and stalked in the shades of the overhanging fog. Their existences were concealed from the partially covered Blood Moon of darkened clouds and the cadence of rain against stone.

Oakley guided the way towards the main stronghold, a mere shadow lurking with muted steps. Even with his increased perception, Korbyn couldn't hear him underneath the rain's tapping. Oakley darted amongst the umbra as though he belonged there, the gloom welcoming him like a friend.

Korbyn couldn't concentrate on both tinted energies and his steps. Instead, he depended on Oakley, who urged him to silence and halted motions when guards walked by. As they ventured closer to the stairs, Oakley tugged him behind a set of barrels filled with accoutrements. Upon the soldiers' departure, Oakley progressed forward, not paying heed to Korbyn's pursuit. Korbyn almost overlooked his disappearance, and he quickened his strides to pursue the stalking predator amidst his favored terrain. Watching him now, it was quite easy to imagine him as an assassin.

Attempting to keep up with his ally's strides, Korbyn inadvertently stumbled into a barrel. A single soldier, who had been on the edge of the fortification and analyzing the nighttime sky, turned to Korbyn with wide eyes and a raised weapon.

"Fuck," Korbyn muttered.

THIRTY-FIVE.

"**W**raith," Salem exclaimed, gurgling with Haven's tightened grip around her throat. She fought and thrashed against his hold, but his attention resided elsewhere, with eyes in a cavity of darkened bleakness, meeting Veeris' confused and surprised expression.

"*Veeris*," the creature spat from Haven's mouth, dropping Salem to the ground when the world blurred. She grasped her throat, coughing for air. It walked away from her, with black aura in concert with its heavy steps.

"H-Haven," Salem rasped. She stumbled to her feet, drawing her blade and shield. She gazed to its objective: Veeris trembling, fear and shock gluing his feet to the ground beneath him. "Veeris, move!"

Haven—the wraith housing his body—stopped, turning its form to watch her approach.

The wraith extracted the great axe resting upon its spine and swung it in the same fluid motion. Salem lowered one knee to enhance the strength in her stance. With a raised shield, she parried the strong attack with a sweep but still stumbled from the sheer force.

She had fought a wraith before this one. They were monstrous, instinctual creatures that lurked and watched from the shadows, waiting for their victim's emotional vulnerability. They seized onto the distraught, overcoming their heart, mind, and body like a leech. They lured their targets to the edges of forests and then possessed them. Usually, she was able to sense their presence, but this one had somehow avoided her notice while overtaking Haven amongst a group of people.

The Blood Moon churned, endowing the wraith with more power. The monster straightened its posture, awakening his previously slack muscles. It then turned to Veeris, croaking in various sounds of hunger and desperation. Saliva dripped from its underbite fangs, a smile creaking open from the river's flow. It sauntered forward, disregarding Salem completely and trudging towards its target.

Wraiths were dangerous foes for two reasons. One, they believed that consuming souls would grant them life. Salem had never seen a wraith successfully return from death, and she didn't think they could, but she had seen many victims of their attempts. Possessing a mortal body gave the monster more strength. Eventually, the soul would be consumed, causing the body to wither and die. After this happened, the wraith would eventually be exorcised from the deteriorating body and return to the shadows, searching for new victims but strengthened from the life it consumed.

Secondly, wraiths believed that to consume the soul, it must enact the person's greatest desires. In this instance, Haven seemed to want Veeris dead, and he was much like an immovable statue.

"Veeris, run!" Salem repeated. She projected her body forward in a lunge.

The monster threw its arm in an arc behind it, hooking Salem in the jaw. Her legs swept out from under her, and she crashed into the ground with a decisive thud.

Salem recoiled from the pain in her chin and twisted her body to rise to her knees. A moment's slack might end in both of their lives, and she allowed the adrenaline to push her forward. Despite her assault, the wraith didn't turn towards her. Instead, it remained locked on Veeris, who still hadn't seemed to react to the situation. It was as if he was overridden by shock, with wide eyes and a still body.

"Ey!" Salem yelled, seeking to grab its attention.

Still, the wraith ignored her, closing the distance between it and Veeris.

"Ey!" she screeched louder, banging her blade against her shield incessantly. It rang like a bell.

To her surprise, the creature hissed from its continuous reverberation. It grasped its ears, flailing and wailing like it was trapped in a cluster of flames. Salem almost stopped from the sheer awe of its response but resumed. Steel clashed against steel, a chant of war that the monster couldn't stand.

It growled and chomped on its own lips. No longer caring for its first objective, it turned towards her in a hunched leap, resembling the animal it desperately wished to not be.

"Stop!" the wraith croaked, lunging for her.

Salem turned, launching herself into the forest and out of its grasp.

The proximity of the trees provided less advantageous for the sheer size of Haven's form. While Salem danced through its small crevices between the oak, the brute forced its way through. She led it to the thickest point in the forest and sheathed her blade, awaiting her adversary's arrival.

Salem had fought monsters and creatures many times, but

none were like the one that chased her—a half-orc trained among the strongest warriors in all Terrisae. Despite being smaller than a full-blooded orc, Haven still soared over the rest of them in terms of pure muscle. Fighting him alone would prove dangerous for her in an elongated duel. If she was going to win, she would have to outsmart him while he wasn't in control of his own senses.

As the monster directing Haven's body swung after her, it couldn't achieve enough space to have the full momentum of a swipe. Instead, it hacked at a tree, and it screeched in anger when it penetrated the bark, wrenching the axe's inert position from the trunk. Shadows of the branches clouded her steps, and Salem raced further into the forest to stray from Veeris' stagnant form. For once, the darkness would provide her aid.

"*Light—must—take—*" the wraith gasped out, as if it had no air in its lungs. It haphazardly swung its axe about, cutting through the branches like they were nothing but paper. However, its form was still too massive to easily maneuver through the trees.

"Haven! You have to listen to me! There is a wraith possessing you! You must gain control of your mind!" she yelled.

The wraith's mouth was tugged upwards by an unknown force. "*The orc cannot hear you.*"

Salem gasped. She had never known wraiths to be cognitive.

"*So full of light...wonder...what was it like...to live?*" it moaned, inhaling for air it didn't have. It smiled with the same breath, as if recalling a distant memory.

"Come on, friend," Salem whispered, standing with a tired breath. "I know you're in there."

Even though she whispered, it chuckled.

The wraith rushed again, this time not swinging its axe as she had expected. Instead, it grappled with the shield. Salem lurched backwards, stepping several paces to wrench her shield free. Eventually, it tripped her, and they both fell to the ground.

The monster started throwing punches. She failed to pull her shield free from the weight of its leg, instead attempting to prevent its assault with raised arms. It sent curved jabs at her face, bypassing her makeshift defense and beating her on each side of her head. Blood sprayed with each strike.

"I'm sorry, Haven!" Salem yelled, thrusting her thumbs into its eye sockets.

Reeling back, the wraith screeched into the night sky. With its body leaning backwards, she wrenched the shield free and swung it like a weapon. It collided with the side of its face, and the monster fell off her and rolled.

Salem followed the momentum and stumbled on top of it. She struck towards its throat, aiming for the flow of blood and oxygen to its brain with a strong enough strike that would have sent it into unconsciousness. However, the muscles around its neck proved to be too thick. When the first hit failed, she tried again, to no avail.

The wraith punched her so hard in the jaw that she fell back. When her head hit the dirt, a high-pitched ringing pierced her ears. The world around her swirled. She grounded herself, and the pain in her jaw throbbed from a definitive fracture. Salem stumbled to her feet several paces away until she rested against a tree trunk, every heave sending jolts of pain up her chin.

The creature stood as well, not as injured as she. If it was in any pain at all, she couldn't tell. It was overcome by a wicked smile of the wraith that crept underneath. Salem wiped the blood trickling down her lips. This fight would have been much easier if she could use her sword, but she didn't want to risk hurting Haven beyond repair. However, holding back proved detrimental. There had to be something she could do.

"*Consume...the light...*" It gulped again, leaning its torso back to revel in the darkness around them.

Salem grasped her locket. If the creature wanted light, then she would give it.

A luminescent holy light emanated from her necklace. The wraith sneered, throwing its free arm in front of its eyes. Its figure wriggled, curling like a dying insect. It motioned to hide behind a tree, but there wasn't anything large enough to conceal it. Instead, the wraith turned from her.

Before the monster could retaliate, Salem dashed and threw her body forward. She wrapped her legs around its torso and covered her forearm against the front of its throat, hauling back with her full strength to halt its breathing long enough for it to fall unconscious. The wraith dropped its axe and used both hands to fight against her chokehold. With Haven's natural strength, it wrested her arms away and slammed her back into a tree, freeing itself of her grasp.

Salem fell just as the wraith reached for its axe. She rolled as it soared above her head, slicing the tree in half. The monster cackled breathily, a combination of Haven's voice and its own. It wildly swung about and severed any trees in the weapon's path, each arboreal victim toppling with conclusive clunks. Salem could only stare in astonishment as it rampaged through the dense forest. Not only had the creature been cognitive enough to form responses, but it was also sufficiently intelligent as to create strategies mid battle.

The Blood Moon grinned above her.

It stood Haven's body to full height, leveling its head as she rose from the dirt. "*Consume...all life,*" the wraith rasped, its saunter shifting its weight from one foot the other, still not used to the heavy form of the half-orc. It sprinted, raising the axe vertically and slashing at an angle.

Salem parried several attacks with her shield. Despite Haven's colossal size, the creature drove its body forward with unnatural haste. With the wraith's abilities enhancing the sheer ferocity of one with an orc's body, each strike felt like a mountain slamming into her own.

Salem neglected a tree stump from the monster's rampage. She tripped over the foliage, falling to her back. Her shield dislodged from her grip and rolled out of her reach. As she scurried, the wraith slammed its foot on top of her wrist. When it cracked, Salem screamed. She clawed at its ankle, struggling to pry it off her.

"*Consume...you!*" the wraith screeched out horrifyingly, lifting its axe above its head.

Salem curled, though it would do nothing to defend her against the assault.

Something crashed into the wraith, and it tumbled sideways away from her. It somehow managing to hold onto its axe, and it grumbled and tripped when attempting to rise. Salem jerked her head upwards to view the foreign source, smiling when she saw the dwarf above her. "Gilben!"

"Sorry I'm late, lass," the dwarf greeted, swinging his broadsword to rest across his shoulders as he extended forth his open palm with the other. "Whaddya say we put this wraith ta rest?"

Salem nodded with a smile, grabbing his hand with her unbroken wrist and allowing him to haul her to her feet. She initiated her bone's healing, soothing the pain with her magic.

"I'm so glad to see you," Salem breathed out, pain surging from her jaw fracture. The discomfort escorted an impairment in her speech, but she tried to ignore it. "This wraith, it's nothing like we've seen before. Under the Blood Moon, it seems so much more logical and rational."

When her bone mended to a useable extent, she twisted it a couple of times, hoping the pain and inflammation would diminish quickly.

"Then we'll have ta not give it enough time ta think, aye?" Gilben questioned, offering her an encouraging smile.

Salem nodded, ushering waves of energy around her fractured jaw.

The wraith rose from its prone position, hunched in stature like a lurking predator. Again, it gurgled, reaching for unobtainable breath. "*You halt...my efforts, yet...no one questions...when the wolf...devours the deer...surely no one will miss the snake.*"

Salem grimaced. With her fracture mended, a poised trek towards the creature followed. "With me, Gilben!" she announced, scooping up her shield.

Both mercenaries charged.

As they approached, the monster swung wildly. Gilben dodged the incoming attacks and rotated again. Not realizing how large the dwarf's weapon was, the blunt of the blade crashed into Haven's chin. When it stumbled back, Salem charged forward and spun on her heel, using her shield as her weapon of choice. The front of it crashed into its nose, as confirmed by a resonating crack.

Gilben approached with another controlled swing. The wraith ignored the broken nose and recuperated from the dual assault. It parried the attack with pure intensity. Though it lacked any technique of a warrior, it slammed the axe into Gilben's blade. The dwarf struggled to hold onto the grip of his sword, and he followed the momentum of the parry to try and rebel against the creature's weight. The wraith threw its foot forward and slammed it into Gilben's chest. The dwarf tumbled backwards, barreling like a tumbleweed.

Salem counterattacked when its attention was elsewhere, lowering herself to bludgeon her shield into the back of its legs, attempting to knock it down. To her surprise, the monster followed the motion of its descent, lowering itself and pushing off the ground to slam into her.

She stumbled back out of its reach, exerting holy light from her locket into her blade, its steel shining amidst the forest. Its grand light illuminated the darkness with boundless intensity. With the trees cut and knocked over, the wraith had nowhere to hide from the sacred energy. For a moment, the wraith squirmed in pain from the light's touch. Its gurgles and breaths sounded like a drowning man, and then erupted into a screech that made Salem want to cover her ears.

"*The Blood Moon,*" the creature muttered, disregarding the rays despite the pain it caused it. "*Burns brighter than gold!*"

It lowered to all fours, still grasping its axe as it launched forward. Halting her spell, Salem dodged right to avoid the vertical swing of its axe. The wraith whisked several more, and she danced to an unheard song. Gilben and Salem both adjusted their footing and launched towards the creature from both of its sides, endeavoring to confuse their adversary.

Instead of choosing one to counter, the wraith chose both. It dropped its blade to the ground and lurched forward at their necks. It slammed them earthward, with both mercenaries crashing into the forest's terrain.

The wraith lifted its foot and aimed for Gilben's chest. The dwarf released a noise of surprise and tumbled out of the way. When its heel met the earth, it reached for the axe and swung down at Salem. She also avoided the attack, rising to her feet and readying herself once again.

"We need a plan!" Salem motioned, taking several deep breaths when she put distance between her and the wraith.

Its smile had returned, as if realizing her holy light wasn't as effective as it should have been. It was as if the Blood Moon outpowered her radiance, drowning out its abilities like a distant bell.

A bell.

"Gilben!" Salem said. "Do you remember one of our first missions together? Back in Lockridge, after we defeated a crazed wolf pack? We helped the farmer shepherd his panicked sheep."

"Erm, yes, though I don't know what sheep's gotta do with a crazed wraith," Gilben remarked, wiping sweat that was gathering at his beard as the wraith sauntered forward. "Care to do a wee bit o' explainin'?"

"There's no time! Just trust me!" Salem declared, unsheathing her blade and sprinting forward.

As the wraith swung its axe, Salem slid to the ground and passed it, slicing a narrow cut in its calf. She stepped a meter away, smacking her blade continuously against her shield to create the irritating noise.

The wraith didn't know if it should concentrate on the wound in its leg, the dwarf, or the clanging. It once again thrashed and cried out, digging its nails into its ears. Blood spewed from its desperate attempts. Realizing it couldn't diminish the sound, it turned its attention fully to her, ignoring the approaching dwarf behind it.

"Foul creature!" Gilben yelled, swinging the blunt part of his large sword upwards. The flat part of Gilben's broadsword slammed into the wraith's head, sending it careening to the ground.

Salem continued clanging against her shield while the creature was preoccupied. The wraith screeched in defiance and scooted backwards as she herded it towards a part of the forest that still contained undamaged trees.

"Haven! Take back control!" Salem demanded, not halting the ringing. "Defeat this!"

"No, *no, no, no, no!*" the wraith screeched, scrambling backwards. It grasped its head, craning it in different directions. "*The bells of retribution—do not let them ring! Do not send me to Abaddon! Terrisae should belong to the darkness!*"

Before the creature could retaliate, Gilben slammed the flat part of its blade into its chin. It shuffled backwards. Salem spun several times, building up momentum before she threw her shield. The projectile followed her motions and soared through the sky and crashed into the wraith's jaw. It struck the tree behind it and fell limp, sliding down to its base with a thud. Its muscles relaxed and its eyelids closed over the chasms of black.

Salem sighed heavily, a thankful grin crossing her lips. She allowed her adrenaline to subside while catching her uncontrollable breaths. Gilben mirrored her own triumphant expression, the coarse hairs of his beard lifting from his smile.

"Tha's a good idea, lassie," Gilben stated as Salem walked up to him. Both warriors placed their hands on their hips, stretching their lungs. "How'd ya come up with tha' one?"

"Honestly, it was luck," Salem breathed out, finally catching up to the unevenness of her exhalations. She recalled its dying words, though she was unsure of the meaning of its sudden declaration. She didn't know what the bells of retribution were, and she'd never heard of a place called Abaddon. "Though, I'm a little weary about whatever it was saying."

"I wouldn't think too hard on it. Was probably just sayin' some crazed things ta distract ya," Gilben said, giving her a consoling pat on the back. "Sides, we should focus on wakin' Haven 'nd makin' sure he's alright. Ya gave him quite a beatin' ta the nose." He laughed, placing his hand on his gut.

The dwarf's contagious mirth initiated her own chuckle, and the tensity in her shoulders slackened.

"You're right. I'll start healing—" Salem paused when a shadow loomed over them. When she tilted her chin to the side, she saw nothing but Haven's torso and a smirking face.

A ploy, and they had fallen directly into its trap.

The wraith kicked Gilben in the head. The dwarf stumbled back, falling unconscious the moment he was hit.

Salem pivoted to thwart its next attack with a swinging blade, but she faltered. The creature's large hand clamped onto her throat and slammed her into a tree. She struggled underneath his grip, clawing and pulling back its fingers to pry it away. As she thrashed, a dark mist rose, the flow of her breathing cut off from its immeasurable strength.

"H-Haven..." Salem whispered, the haze filling her lungs, an unbearable intoxication. An abyss of black stared back into hers as it guffawed, its high pitch ringing in their ears. When the swirling of the fog surrounded them, she felt the world around her beginning to disappear—permanently.

"Your kind fears the creatures of the darkness but cares not for the real monsters that lurk under mortal skin," the wraith whispered, smiling wide. *"When I consume this body, I will rally the beasts in the depths of the night into a new beginning. No longer will the world be led by mortal flesh."*

"Haven!" a voice called from behind, disrupting the darkness.

Hearing the voice it wished to cease, the wraith dropped Salem. She fell, clasping her throat and reaching for her lost breath. As the world spun, Salem glanced behind Haven. Across the field, staring with glassy eyes, was Veeris.

"V-Veeris..." Salem whispered, coughing more.

"It's time for your revenge," Veeris declared, bearing no ethereal blades to fight at his side and beckoning it forward with extended arms and his vulnerable chest. "Kill me."

THIRTY-SIX.

With warring, locked eyes, Korbyn and the Avernos soldier stood standing on the parapet with bafflement, both reconnoitering each other's postures. While the soldier held a spear defensively, Korbyn prepared the retrieval of his sheathed dagger.

The soldier's eyes, for no more than a second, darted from the iron gong dangling within a belfry and then back to hold eye contact. The man must have realized Korbyn's astuteness, for no more than a second later, the soldier leapt towards the belfry.

Korbyn followed suit, withdrawing the dagger from his belt and flinging it. The soldier reeled back to avoid the weapon's trajectory, and it soared off the fort. It gave Korbyn just enough time to intervene with the soldier's plans.

When the man stepped to the side, Korbyn slammed himself into his body. The soldier crashed into the stone structure of the bell's spire, and before he could retaliate, Korbyn clutched the top of his head.

"Sleep," Korbyn whispered, sweeping his thumb over the man's eyes. When the order had finished, the soldier collapsed.

Unprepared for what he had just done, Korbyn clumsily caught the man in a heap and dragged him behind the barrels, tying him up with some discarded rope.

"How did you do that?" Oakley whispered when Korbyn caught up with him.

"I have no idea," Korbyn answered honestly. "And I really don't know how long that will last, so let's make this quick."

Instead of descending the stairs, they crept down the pathway and slid off the roof of the empty chapel against the battlement's wall. They maneuvered along the stone rampart, avoiding the crowds of soldiers. Luckily, with the Blood Moon, the eyes of bystanders veered towards the sky, allowing Korbyn and Oakley to stalk within the shadows, unseen.

Breaking into the principal stronghold would prove difficult. Even during the dead of night, many of the guards seemed disturbed by the Blood Moon, causing many to endure a sleepless night. From outside the keep, Korbyn could see numerous soldiers wandering the halls, irritable from its red haze.

Korbyn found a set of dual, narrow windows that led to an unoccupied hallway. It took him a couple of times, but he managed to toss both grappling hooks up to the windows. Oakley spread more white chalk on his palms before grabbing hold of the edge of the rope.

"See you in a few minutes," Oakley said with a wink before sauntering up the wall. With the aid of Oakley's smaller and dexterous form, he scaled the stone in moments, adjusting his body to lean back against the rope's hold and using the uneven crevices marked between stones to support his ascent.

"Show-off," Korbyn muttered, wiping white chalk across his hands. Unlike Oakley, he had to rely on his upper body strength to propel himself up. He placed his feet on small reliefs in the stone and climbed at a consistent pace. Eventually, he arrived at the window, hauling himself up and repossessing the rope.

They stalked through the hallway, craning their bodies downwards to avoid casting eyes. They passed several open rooms, including several storerooms, a larder, buttery, pantry, and a blacksmith's forge.

The duo arrived at a spiral stone staircase that led up to the top of the fortress. Korbyn inspected the rooms as they ventured, searching for an official writing office. When they located a locked door, they nodded in affirmation to one another, a silent understanding.

Korbyn fixated on the room, searching for colorless flames.

"It's empty," Korbyn whispered, peering down into the hallways, rooms, and stairwell to check for energies. Only a few lit up on the floor they were on, and they were low and glittering with a dull flame, as if they were asleep.

"Do I even want to ask how you know that?" Oakley observed, sitting on his knees and removing his satchel from his shoulders.

"Nope."

Oakley rummaged through his bag until he found what he was searching for—a bundle of leather wrapped in thin rope. He unraveled it like a scroll, revealing various elongated pieces of brass. Each resembled different shapes, varying from single to four different protrusions at the ends.

The smaller man picked up one of the skeleton keys and placed his ear by the metal lock, carefully inserting the brass into it. When the key failed to turn, Oakley replaced it with another. It only took him three tries before the metal unlocked under his touch.

Korbyn pushed the entrance open, allowing Oakley to duck in first before following his steps and shutting the door behind them. He picked up the iron drawbar on the inside and slid it across the slot, securely locking them inside.

"Let's be quick," Korbyn stated, analyzing the room.

It was more of a scriptorium than a chancery. Several wooden desks scattered across the room with a singular, large escritoire in the middle. The slanted desks sat closer to the glass windows that faced away from the eastern wall. Each of the slanted desks had incomplete manuscripts, as though their previous writers had been interrupted. Along the northern stone was a door that led out to an outdoor aviary. On the other side, tall bookcases were disorganized with tomes, scrolls, and other forms of parchment, clearly rummaged through. The wide escritoire in the middle seemed recently utilized compared to the rest of the furniture, with systematized scrolls and parchment neatly placed on top of forgotten, dried ink.

"Don't have to tell me once, or twice, whatever the saying is," Oakley said, shuffling through his bag and pulling out a small oil lamp. He poured some oil inside the chamber and then retrieved a tinderbox. Sliding it open, he grabbed a piece of flint and steel, ensuring the quartz was dry and sharpened.

While Oakley focused on igniting the flame, Korbyn shifted his attention to the stacks of papers on the desk. Luckily, he could easily perceive its contents in full clarity, despite the lack of light in the room. He started delving through the different pieces of parchment, reading the first few sentences of several documents to try and decipher its use. His intuition had been correct—these texts were specifically written by the Avernos army. It seems like they made themselves at home within the chancery so that they could formulate letters to send to the emperor.

"Ow! Fuckin' prick," Oakley muttered, who scraped his skin along the tinder to start the fire. He shook his wrist and put his knuckles in his mouth.

"I thought you said you didn't curse," Korbyn stated, shifting through the pieces of parchment.

"I said I was adorable, not perfect."

Korbyn disregarded several of the first pages, reading through topics that dealt with financial approvals and denials, the status of remaining soldiers, recognitions of honor, lists of gathered supplies, and a lot of other useless details.

"Maybe Kendra Dawn really didn't make it here. I can't find anything on them," Korbyn commented, searching through them one last time to see if there was anything he had missed.

When Oakley finally lit the oil lamp, he placed it on the desk and assisted. Unfortunately, he arrived at the same conclusion.

"Maybe they just didn't record any of it?" Oakley offered, adjusting the documents so that they were neatly stacked in their previous positions. "I can't really envision a scenario where it would have been important enough to document. The only thing I could think of is an official manuscript ending the agreement of Kendra Dawn's peace treaty with both nations, but that's something the emperor would probably have."

"So, was infiltrating a waste?" Korbyn muttered.

"Maybe there's something we can find…"

A prodding against glass disrupted Korbyn's pondering. He peered at the apiary. A messenger hawk was pecking at the closed window. A cylinder-shaped case was strapped to its back, with Avernos' symbol engraved into the satchel.

Korbyn opened the window, allowing the bird to flutter on a perch beside a tray feeder. The hawk began picking at the seeds happily as he untied the string.

"You sure about this one?" Oakley questioned.

"Nope," Korbyn stated truthfully, breaking the seal. He unraveled the parchment and spread it across the escritoire.

BY THE EMPEROR,
A Proclamation of Hastening Advances.
Titled to Sir Knight Hadawaye of the Middle Guard,
Enforced immediately, Sir Knight Hadawaye is hereby ti-

tled Knight-Captain of the Middle Guard forces. All Knight-Captains are obliged to direct their forces, thereby expediting previously declared plans. The Rearguard shalt remain unwavering along Exonia Creek. The Middle Guard forces shalt grow the undead army of Esperin's fallen, shalt conquer the Brinshire Mines of the Esperin King in the name of Emperor Wymond, conquer their town, capture those knowledgeable of decidite, claim their decidite and all available resources.

The Vanguard troops shalt advance their march through Shadowbane Forest, ready to split between the two separate forces, one to claim Graycott and one to execute the Fall of Umberfall. The siege and excavation of tunnels underneath Umberfall's walls is nearly readied, soon to be replaced with wood and straw to burn and collapse their eastern wall. When Esperin's troops leave their capital, initiate the attack and siege of Graycott Village and Umberfall with main forces of the undead. Claim the Capital and Tranquility Tree in the name of Emperor Wymond.

Declaration Written in the Eyes of the Court, the Seventy-Eighth Day of Autumn.

TO THE END OF A WAR, BY EMPEROR WYMOND.

"O-Oakley..." Korbyn stuttered, rereading the contents to double check if he had imagined the document he just read.

"It says that Avernos is actively mining under Umberfall's walls. How is that possible? How have they not been noticed?" Oakley questioned.

Korbyn pulled out a map and spread it across the escritoire, tracing his finger across the parchment in a reverse crescent shape to mimic the forest's curvature. "Shadowbane Forest. There aren't any forces guarding it. If I was the attacking army, I would have started digging a tunnel from the edge of the forest all the way to Umberfall. If the Avernos army really did march straight through Shadowbane, Esperin would never see them coming." Korbyn motioned to the empty space between the forest and the city. "They've been planning this for months. And we got rid of their last remaining blockade—raging ogres."

"What about the undead? What does that even mean?" Oakley inquired, revisiting the parchment to locate an explanation.

Korbyn bit his lip when he realized he didn't have an answer. "I don't know," he responded, folding the parchment. "But that sounds like the ogres. They were all dead, but somehow still alive. It doesn't make any sense."

"I can't believe this. They plan to outright murder innocents to claim the capital! How evil. How despicable! Hundreds, no—thousands of people are going to die—wait, what are you doing?" Oakley fumbled over his words as he watched Korbyn stuff the document in his bag. "We can't take that!"

"We've already committed a crime that will get us killed," Korbyn said, referring to the destroyed, official seal of the emperor. "Besides, we may be able to deter the attack on the towns and Umberfall if we take this. Hadawaye won't know to expedite the attack on the town by the mines, and if they don't attack the mines, then the soldiers won't leave Umberfall." Korbyn pulled his bag over his shoulder. "And if the soldiers don't leave Umberfall—"

"Then the armies won't attack Graycott or the capital. You're a genius, Korb!" Oakley whispered excitedly.

Korbyn frowned. "That was my moment, but whatever." He ushered towards the door. "Let's go—"

Korbyn felt as though he'd been hit in the temple, and a loud screech of a ringing pierced his ears. He convulsed as the pain erupted from his head and down to his neck, then spine, then legs. His knees locked, and he collapsed. When he smacked into the stone floor, visions unfurled like moving images. He stared into the abyss, and the abyss stared back.

Rows of innocent volunteers—humans, dwarves, elves, and gnomes, lined together by shackles clamped around the stomach, ankles and wrists, interconnected by chains; the descending spirals of stone staircases; emergence into bloodied water of a cistern with tall, stone columns and lit sconces; cages lined across stone walls; a pedestal tainted in blood; a harbor for the dead; a growth, an infection; a man cloaked in power, holding a scepter of bone; a skeleton hand, holding a bone and gilded decidite scythe; the skeleton turned to dust, leaving only the scythe to remain.

As Korbyn roused from the vision, he heaved and trembled, facing the windows and lying in a pool of his own sweat. The hue of the red sky streaked through, shimmering against the glass and casting onto his face. Above him, Oakley sat on his knees, actively struggling to calm him with pats of reassurance. At first, his friend's voice failed to reach his ears. Only when the piercing ringing dissipated could he hear Oakley's concerned terror.

"Korb! Answer me, are you okay?" Oakley urged.

Korbyn crawled to his knees, and they stirred in defiance. He held his head low in pain, eyes directed towards the stone beneath him. That was when he saw it: gray flames that kindled but remained hushed like a dying fire, somewhere far below them. There were dozens, no—hundreds of lingering, monochrome embers that swayed against a non-existent breeze.

Radiance and necrosis are two sides of the same coin, the demon explained, severing his ill thoughts.

"Oh, no," Korbyn muttered.

"What happened? What is it?" Oakley asked, pulling him into a sitting position.

Korbyn looked back up at him, replying with fear and full clarity. "I think I know where Kendra Dawn is."

Luckily, the halls of the keep decreased with wandering soldiers. They descended several staircases, arriving on the main floor. It was a great hall with many small elevations divided by stairs and small foyers. In the center resided a seating area and some extra dining space for soldiers. Several of the foyers were sectioned off by simple walls with hanging drapes and console tables, acting more for aesthetic than purpose. It allowed Korbyn and Oakley to pass through the hallway unseen, as the soldiers were focused on the dining table's food contents. They stalked through open archways and empty backrooms before they found another staircase that led further down.

They entered an undercroft. The room was massive, lined with various brick columns that formed overhanging arches, which were probably intended to secure the vaulted ceilings. Analyzing them, Korbyn noted they resembled crafted stars. Currently, the room was empty, except for random assortments of boxes and barrels haphazardly discarded across the vicinity.

Korbyn surveyed the ground, seeing the same, faint gray energies a floor beneath them. He strolled around the large corridor, searching for another staircase or latch.

"Over here," Oakley whispered.

Korbyn walked past a few stacks of boxes and observed a tall, brick arch, which led to another circular staircase, a descension blended with shadows. With a nod of approval from both, they treaded down the flight as silent as mice, with Korbyn leading the front.

The stairway seemed to decrease in size the farther they traveled, and Korbyn positioned his hand on the stone to his left for balance. The sconces along the walls were dimly lit, casting most of the area in darkness. Oakley followed him from behind, keeping his hand on Korbyn's shoulder. They strode warily, in quietude.

They entered a cavern, with tall columns and more hushed

sconces along the wall. The water was dirtied, tainted in the red hue of blood that reflected the ceiling of the cistern. In the middle of the room was a pedestal of stone, elevated from the water and dripping in scarlet.

"What is this place?" Oakley questioned, his eyebrows furrowing as he inspected the bloody water.

Korbyn stepped forward, causing a ripple to span the entire chapel. "Only one way to find out."

The duo trudged through the bloody water, watching the currents from their steps. They reached the pedestal in the middle of the room, gazing upon its crude design. It was covered in blood, mimicking a star with a circle surrounding it. In the middle of the five points was a familiar symbol—the same one marked along Korbyn's left forearm.

"Is that...a pentacle?" Oakley whispered, examining the strange markings. The shorter man's deep analytical expression dropped when he once again regarded Korbyn. "What's wrong?"

"That mark. It's the one on my arm," Korbyn muttered, pulling off his leather bracer and pulling up his sleeve to reveal the darkened lines underneath. It was still irritated with red swelling around it. He scanned over the strange symbols along the pentacle, and he recognized the language written in the tome he stole. Before he realized it, he read the words out loud: "To the King...Crown of...Horns and Blades, we call...loyal servant...fleeting breath...take the power of Death until...fallen to ashes...and made anew."

"What does that mean?" Oakley wondered, observing his mark before scanning the symbol on the stone. "And what does it have to do with you?"

"I-I don't know," Korbyn replied uneasily, rubbing his alternate hand across the mark when it pulsed with memory. He wasn't sure if he was thankful for the hushed whispers of the demon or not. "The cavern extends further. Let's keep looking."

As they trekked forward, Korbyn noticed it expanded further. It seemed recently excavated, held aloft by fortified wooden planks all the way to the ceiling. In the middle of the room was some sort of laboratory, with wide bureaus covered in various types of flasks and dishes, some with multiple, tall necks, others cylindrical in shape, and some half-filled with strange concoctions of various hues of red and purple. Books were scattered on top, underneath, and randomly distributed on several bookshelves along one of the walls. Open satchels and boxes lay forgotten around the area, recently emptied and left behind in a hurry.

At the far side of the room were the dulled flames that Korbyn had seen from several stories above. Hundreds of bodies were trapped in tall, metal cages that were stacked on top of each other. Most were filled with soldiers of Esperin, bathed in blood and covered in wounds. Some were missing arms, jaws, eyes, and riddled with holes, gashes, and wounds that portrayed their moments before death. However, instead of lying in heaps, they stood as they would if they had been alive, but with glazed eyes, as if their souls had departed from their bodies long ago. Instead of looking upon the two entering the room, they stared straight through them. They appeared to be waiting for something, their bodies swaying idly.

"K-Korbyn..." Oakley whispered from the top of the stairs, hidden by one of the columns. "Look."

In one of the cages, volunteers of Kendra Dawn stood with lifeless eyes. Each had been marked with similar forms of death, with large lacerations on top of the shoulders and their lower torsos. Some of them Korbyn recognized as members who died during the manticore attack.

Towards the front of the group was Nevin. His stitches from his embalming had come undone, causing some of his intestines to unfurl towards his small feet. The small gnome's eyes, matte, and lack of life, stared blindly with no comprehension of his current condition.

"Is that Nevin?" Oakley whispered. "Did they dig up the bodies from the manticore attack after we left?" His voice cracked with apprehension. "How could they do something like this?"

Korbyn's chest ached when he met Nevin's lifeless eyes. "Undead. This is what they meant."

He avoided the unmoving stares and directed his attention to something else, and he saw something familiar. Seated upon a lectern resided a larger-than-average tome. Korbyn strode down the stairs and ventured over to it.

It wasn't the same book as the one within his pack, but it was familiar. It bore the exact, strange symbol on the front, covered in ancient leather wrappings that were recently pulled from its ties. He opened it with ease, and it whispered to him with recognition. It was written in the same foreign language.

"How can you even read this?" Oakley whispered, standing on his toes to peer into the book.

"I'm starting to get incredibly repetitive, but I don't know. Sometimes I just figure out new things I can do."

He read through its contents, flipping pages after scanning multiple sections. The beginning of the text posed questions for philosophical debate, which he skimmed. There was one portion that caught his eye—a legend of old indicated by an improvised bookmark. It was a damaged black feather with fringed ends and splattered with glitter and gold.

The Legend of New Beginnings. After the War against the Heavens, the rebelling angels fell to Abaddon. With their lack of wings and depleted holy light, the Fallen succumbed to age. But when tales end, legends start anew. When Death, the Reaper of Souls, takes new form, it will initiate the start of the

Revelation War and make way for the new Crown of Horns and Blades seated upon waves of scarlet.

In the next excerpt, he read:

The Rally of the Four Horsemen. Famine, Death, War, and Conquest. All serve the Revelation King. To call upon their aid with mortal hands beckons strife and consequence. Each of the fingers resembles their authority: the fifth, one of hunger and proportions, like Famine. The fourth, one of everlasting love and of the inevitable, like Death. The third, one of declaration and quarrel, like War. The second, one of initiation and fortuity, like Conquest. The first, one of leadership of the four and an apocalypse of new beginnings. Each Horseman is bound by mark and duty with a sigil of the Crowns of Horns and Blades to show their open declaration to the Revelation King.

"Wh-what? What is it?" Oakley stuttered, peering from the other side of his shoulder.

Korbyn kept flipping through the pages as he replied, searching for answers to the never-ending questions. "This book sounds like it belongs to a cult. It talks about fallen angels, Abaddon, something called the Four Horsemen, a Crown of Horns and Blades, and a Revelation King."

"Abaddon? What's that?" Oakley questioned, frowning in response.

"I think it's the Hells," Korbyn answered, recalling back to his discoveries from his own, magical tome. "But I'm not sure why all this is important."

Footsteps originated from an unseen door behind one of the bookshelves, echoing down hallways of stone. Without even exchanging glances, Korbyn and Oakley darted towards an extra desk towards the wall and hid behind it, leaving the tome in its spot on the podium.

From the secret door emerged a man, clad in black robes and features hidden behind a large hood. It draped over both sides of his face, along with long, full sleeves that completely enclosed his hands and reached halfway down his hip. Long red, disorderly curls cascaded from the bleakness of his hood, reaching past his navel.

On top of his hood was a jury-rigged crown made of dirtied bones. It secured his cape to his face, with phalanges extended upwards to encircle the entirety of his head in different heights to portray dynamism. Each bone increased in height to lead to the tallest point at the front of his crown, which were framed with straight goat horns. They curved backwards at an arch and somehow heightened the man's average stature as he tilted his chin upwards.

In one of his hands, he fastened a scepter made of more human bones, each ragged framework connected by melted iron. It was a crude contraption, as if attempting to imitate a grander design. Several different types of finger bones were attached together by iron to form a makeshift cage to house an object within. Much like a throne in the middle of its formation was a piece of decidite, with threads of gold decorated across its matte surface. Despite its grotesque design, it seemed surprisingly durable as the man relied on the staff to saunter forward.

"Gilded decidite," Korbyn breathed.

Behind the man, two soldiers emerged, dragging a person between them. She was bound by shackles at her hands, waist, and ankles, covered in blood and swollen with lacerations. Her hair was matted and stuck to her face from the dried gore that covered her cheeks and temples.

"Micah," Oakley whispered, his hand reaching for his blades.

Korbyn shook his head in defiance. He pointed to the soldiers carrying Micah. At least eighteen more followed, approaching in two separate lines with readied spears. The man in the front, cloaked in mystery, grabbed the forbidden text. When the soldiers followed, Korbyn and Oakley trailed them from behind.

The soldiers cared not how Micah was hauled across the room. One of her legs, her previously good one, appeared as though it had been smashed. It bent awkwardly in the opposite direction and dragged lazily behind her.

The mass of soldiers reached the front of the cavern of bloodied water, where the pentacle remained, damp and ready to be used. The men threw her forward and yanked her to her knees.

"What will you all do when they turn you into mindless monsters?" Micah taunted with a smirk. "They claim you to be heroes, but you're nothing but tools of war."

"Silence, cripple!" a soldier barked, backhanding her across the face.

Korbyn and Oakley hid behind two separate columns, watching as the soldiers spread out across the cistern. With Micah in the middle of the pentacle, four soldiers stood at different points of the red symbol, leaving the cloaked man at the last end. He sauntered to Micah's front, prodding her cheek rather aggressively with the bottom of his staff.

"They say you killed a dragon," the long-haired man spat. "Is it true?"

"That's what the legends say," Micah replied, hurling a glob of blood at his cloak. "There's always hidden meanings behind old tales. People tend to believe in the things they want to be true, not in the things that they should."

"Your death is one I will enjoy, for my first act of retribution can be for the dragon's blood you spilled," the robed man hissed.

He opened the text and gave it to one of the soldiers to hold it as a podium would. He then placed all the tips of his fingers together, leaving the space between his palms open like a barred enclosure. He spoke in the language found in the tomes, projecting his voice in the strange, foreign tongue.

"I call upon the fallen archangel Samael, the ruler of Abaddon, as your heir and future Revelation King. I beseech the Crown of Horns and Blades, your fallen powers, and the loyalty of the Horseman, the archangel Azrael, the one known as Death.

"When he gives his final breath, we will usher in a new age, where the years of old die and soon begin anew. Until then, gift me once again the ability to breathe life where it has once been lost, for I may help lead these kingdoms into a new era. When Elohim's chosen empire, the Kingdom of Esperin, dies, may we enact vengeance to resurrect the world anew."

"What are they doing?" Oakley whispered.

Korbyn, unable to find clarity amongst confusion, whispered a reply, "I don't know." Power and magic surged in the forgotten cistern. "He's claiming to be the Revelation King."

When the man lifted his staff, magical energy swirled from the gilded decidite at its core. The sigil below Micah illuminated as the mage weaved the scepter around, with swirls of golden energy surrounding their forms.

"The end of Azrael is near. Until then, I once again take the powers from moribund Death and the remnants of shadows from Abaddon, releasing these souls and contributing their bodies to a greater cause."

The soldiers initiated the slamming of their spears on the stone in a syncopated rhythm, followed by hushed harmonious hums. It sounded like a requiem of the dead, a resonance that reverberated against the columns and walls. Korbyn watched as Micah's body convulsed. The man was drawing upon the energy of her remaining life.

"Korbyn, we have to do something!" Oakley whisper-shouted, fidgeting with indecisiveness.

Korbyn waved his arm to halt his movements. "Wait, we need a plan. We can't just charge twenty soldiers on our own."

"But—"

"If we die here, who's going to warn everyone about an undead army?" Korbyn asked, digging his nails into his own skin, hoping his physical pain would overcome his mental one. "We can't just make a reckless decision—"

"*Hear our cries, for we contribute our voices to the Song of Abaddon!*" the mage exclaimed proudly.

You are not meant to save, the demon chimed.

As Korbyn turned, the four soldiers thrust their spears into Micah's torso, the edge of their weapons penetrating all the way through her body. She gurgled a gasp, her life fading just as rapidly as the attack had come. The weapons wretched out of her body, and she fell to the side, smacking her head harshly against the cobblestone.

Korbyn witnessed her soul, like a wisp, enter the ether, only to dissipate. The Reaper didn't appear to claim her soul, as if her life ended too soon.

Not even the Reaper of Souls is safe from his future death.

"No!" Oakley screamed, tears welling in his eyes as he stepped out from behind the column.

They turned. Korbyn froze.

With a raised hand and the aura of holy energy from the gilded decidite, the hooded man uttered a command: "Rise."

The pounding of metal reverberated against the walls behind them. When Korbyn pivoted, he saw each undead in the cages bashing their bodies against the bars that penned them. The weakened iron succumbed to their surprising strength and force, each of the gates toppling over with ease.

Micah's body shifted as it attempted to rise, but its broken legs failed to stand. Instead, its limbs caved underneath its weight. As if feeling no pain from the attempts, the body crawled in Korbyn and Oakley's direction. In the hollow of its eyes resided not Micah's normal irises, but an abyss of darkness. Its neck craned to the side from the gaping holes in its shoulders, with tendons pulling like thin strings to keep its head attached to the rest of its body. Each undead within the cavern hummed in a chorale of groans, breaking their restraints.

From underneath the cloak, Korbyn saw a toothy grin appear with a hunger for power.

"Feast."

THIRTY-SEVEN.

As the undead emerged from the cages, they toppled in chaotic heaps. Their eyes, hollow from an abyss of black, locked onto Korbyn and Oakley. Their ordered steps directed them forward with jostled impetus. In front of the duo, the soldiers raised their weapons, readying themselves for their ambush. They were completely surrounded.

"K-Korb!" Oakley urged nervously, staring back and forth between the hoard of undead behind them and the wave of soldiers in front.

Reaching towards where his dagger should have been, Korbyn only caught air from his empty sheath. The blade now lay somewhere on the outskirts of the wall. He scoffed in dismay.

"Korbyn!" Oakley repeated as the soldiers and the hoard of undead closed the distance.

Korbyn adjusted his posture and stood straighter. Instead of letting the panic consume him, he closed his eyes and breathed with astonishing composure.

I'm finally listening, Korbyn thought, reaching for the demon. *What do I need to do? I must have more power than this.*

You are Darkness. You are Death. When they are denied entry to the Golden Gates, you are there to snuff out their light, it responded, sounding satisfied.

With hands facing downwards, Korbyn uttered a demand. "Sleep."

A burst of energy emitted from him, its violent winds encircling the entirety of the cavern. The sconces snuffed out, leaving them in an impenetrable darkness.

"I can't see!"

"Wh-where are they?"

"Stop them!"

The soldiers engaged in a tumult, encumbered by sudden panic.

The Revelation King had also become blinded by the night. When the hooded figure's vision was clouded, the undead halted their sporadic movements.

"K-Korb!" Oakley cried out, gesturing his arms forward as if something was there to help him. "Where are you?"

Korbyn rushed forward and pressed his shoulder against Oakley's stomach, lifting his smaller frame with ease. He sprinted around the disgruntled soldiers and straight for the circular stone staircase at the entrance of the cavern.

"Soldiers!" the cloaked man yelled, arresting their sonorous shouting. Korbyn saw a faint glow of golden brilliance from the corner of his eye as he ran, the immediate area revealed by what he assumed to be the gilded decidite from the man's scepter.

But the cloaked man hadn't been quick enough. Korbyn already traversed through the water and reached the other end of the cistern.

"After them, immediately!" the redhead screeched.

"How—did—you—do—that?" Oakley asked with every bounce

of Korbyn's run. "They're coming!"

The unbothered sconces along the curvature of the wall barely revealed their path as Korbyn dashed up the stairs with Oakley in tow.

When they ascended halfway, reverberating alarm bells reached Korbyn's ears, ones with ongoing cadence that he couldn't previously perceive from the depths of the cavern below. He paled as a group of soldiers countered their route up the circular flight with their physical blockade and raised spears.

Korbyn once again reached for a non-existent weapon and found none waiting for him. The soldier in the front of the group, leading the fray of a single-file line of warriors on the staircase, angled his spear.

From behind them, the hollow growls of the undead scaled the staircase, all uncaring for kinship with aggressive jostling. Their groans and stench materialized faster than their bodies had, and Korbyn tried to ignore the nausea. He dropped Oakley to his feet, who turned and withdrew his own daggers to face the approaching hoard. They were pigeonholed.

"Fuck!" Korbyn spat. He glanced at Oakley from the corner of his eye. "Hold them off for as long as you can!"

The soldier in front of him propelled his spear forward, and Korbyn did the only thing he could think of.

Korbyn raised his palm, permitting the spear to penetrate it. The soldier reeled in surprise and almost fumbled. Korbyn seized the hilt below the spear's steel and yanked it. Standing unevenly on the stair, the soldier tumbled forward. Korbyn converted the pull into a push, crashing the bottom of the spear's hilt into the man's uncovered forehead. Korbyn pulled again and heaved the dazed soldier in his direction.

"Oakley, move!" Korbyn yelled, hauling the falling soldier's form over his shoulders.

Oakley jumped to the side, and Korbyn slugged the soldier

down the staircase. The man crashed into the rising dead trudging in chaotic formations lower down. They all tumbled, diminishing the immediate threat from behind.

Korbyn yanked the spear from his wound, ignoring the spewing blood. He twisted the weapon's direction and thrust the pointed edge into the next soldier's neck. The man gurgled when blood bubbled and leaked from his mouth and pharynx, clawing at the spear. While it sprayed against the stone walls, Korbyn shoved him upwards.

Multiple soldiers behind the dying man tripped, plummeting down the stairs around the duo like a gushing river on both sides of a protruding rock. When some of the other men higher up the stairs prepped a counterattack to their ascent, Oakley reacted first.

"Korb!" Oakley shouted.

Korbyn jerked his head to the side. A thin, needle-like dagger whizzed past, piercing a soldier's eye socket through the slit in his bascinet. He writhed with flailing arms. Several more combatants tumbled from the disorder and joined the fall, allowing Korbyn enough leeway to continue thrusting the soldier penetrated by the spear upwards.

As they reached the top of the stairs, the soldiers tripped backwards in a growing pile. Korbyn jumped over them, tugging on the wedged spear, but it was too deeply lodged in his assailant's throat. Instead of wrestling another for a weapon, he raced after Oakley.

They dashed down several corridors, arriving at the entrance of the fort. They skidded across a carpet runner at the top landing, barely avoiding crashing to their knees. When they adjusted their postures, they met the gaze of a hundred soldiers, each wielding spears and readied crossbows.

"W-wrong way," Oakley stuttered, stepping back a couple of paces. "Wrong way, wrong way!"

"Loose!" a soldier yelled alongside a volley of arrows.

The duo dodged and weaved amongst the curtains, the large bolts whizzing and tearing through fabric like hundreds of chirping birds. The dangling cloths concealed their movements, and they tripped and fell to their stomachs when the iron tips traveled too close. They wrapped their arms around their heads as bolts volleyed through the air and stuck into the cobblestone above them.

"Go, go, go!" Korbyn yelled, pushing Oakley up to his feet. They sprinted down the hall, in desperate search of an alternative exit.

It was obvious Korbyn and Oakley chose to infiltrate the fort at an inopportune time for the army, especially for those on higher levels. They didn't react as quickly as those stationed in active duty; the men and women replied with confusion as Korbyn and Oakley darted around them. The two only received sedentary reactions as they scurried past those alighting the flights to adhere to their captains due to the bell's chime.

"Where do we go?" Oakley questioned, taking heavy breaths with every step of his run.

"I don't know—anywhere but here!" Korbyn yelled.

To their dismay, there was no other hallway, no alternate room, and certainly no other means of escape at the end of their hall. Instead, a machicolation window faced them with a luminescent glow of red from the moon outside, but otherwise a dead end.

Skidding to a halt, the duo turned back. The path behind was now encumbered by converging soldiers that formed a practiced line, establishing a makeshift blockade. They reloaded their crossbows, readying another attack.

"Korb..." Oakley muttered, his shoulders slumping in defeat. His countenance visibly bore fear and regret along his furrowed brow and quivering lips. "I...I don't know what to say. I never thought we were actually going to die. I never planned what to say during a moment like this. I—"

Korbyn seized his shoulder, turning Oakley to face him. "We don't die here, brother," he declared, surprised by his own, unyielding confidence. "Not today."

Korbyn tugged Oakley over his shoulder, and as the soldiers released their arrows, he hurtled towards the window—and jumped.

Another storm of bolts cried like a wave of thunderous birds. Korbyn curled Oakley's form into his chest mid-flight, utilizing his back as a shield to protect his friend from the imminent volley. Arrows pierced him as they soared.

Korbyn's vault eventually led to a quick descension, and he engulfed Oakley's body within his, but it didn't suppress the smaller male's fearful yells as they plummeted. They crashed into one of the tarps held aloft by metal poles, and it caved under their weight. They toppled in heaps amidst the fabric, only rolling to a stop when they were entangled in its clutches.

They both groaned, pain riddling their bodies as they twisted and turned in the restrictions of the drapery. Korbyn's back was riddled with arrows, and he sprung to a hunched kneel as the pain coursed through him. He hacked, and saliva splattered like flinging paint. As he ventured to stand, his right foot protested in twinging agony and betrayal. It commanded his attention, and Korbyn witnessed its dramatic position, his foot facing opposite the way it should have.

"Are you okay?" Oakley yelled, scooting closer to him while grasping onto his own shoulder. He bellowed a squeamish squeal. "Oh, no...Korb, I don't think I can carry you."

Korbyn sat down, reaching for his heel.

"I know that I'm impressive and all, and I know this might surprise you, but I'm not that physically strong. I mean, I'm strong, but you're such a tall guy. I don't think I'd be able to actually carry you—"

The abrupt crack severed his ramblings, ejecting from Korbyn's brisk hoick of his foot. His scream echoed through the night sky when he failed to stifle it. Even afterwards, Korbyn hunkered down, wishing to grab the origins of the pain but knowing nothing he would do would alleviate it. Instead, he spewed guttural winces and curses at every throb of his ankle.

Korbyn broke out into a cold sweat despite his body not growing warm. His gruff, pained palpitations shifted into slowed, full breaths when the immediate agony subsided into a throb. Postponing the overarching issue, he dislodged the accessible arrows perforating his back.

In the moments of their brief respite, they witnessed Korbyn's bodily response to the lacerations and broken bone. The abnormal restoration mimicked mending more than a remedial magic. Muscles laced and skin weaved like intertwining threads within his back and hand. Even his foot began mending the breakage, though it still throbbed with inflammation and an irksome soreness.

"How did you know that would work?" Oakley wondered with unbridled awe.

Korbyn wiped the sweat from his brow and tested the strength of his foot with carefully placed weight. When he was confident he could at least walk despite the throbbing pain, he rose.

"I didn't," Korbyn stated, analyzing Oakley. His shoulder was flattened, leaning forward accompanied by a flexed elbow. "Are you alright?"

"I uh, think my shoulder is dislocated," Oakley admitted, holding his arm like it was a newborn.

"I can try to fix it—"

Before Korbyn could offer his assistance, a rally cry of soldiers echoed across the bailey. Hadawaye stood amongst them, ushering with flailing points of his dominant finger and a disgruntled visage. They met eyes, and Korbyn watched his scowl deepen.

"Never mind. We have to go!" Korbyn yelled, grabbing Oakley by his uninjured armpit and hoisting him to his feet. The bells permeated the red sky in declarations of war.

They disregarded their grappling hooks, exploiting the crevices of the stone and relying on pure adrenaline to scurry upwards. Some of the closer soldiers recognized them, propelling arrows in their direction. They weaved around the incoming hails, relying on the protruding arrows to heave themselves up the wall.

Even with one arm, Oakley scampered to the top of the rampart with quickness afforded by his smaller form. Soldiers advanced from both directions, rushing headlong in a conforming cage of raised weapons along the parapet.

"We need to get to the stables!" Korbyn shouted, motioning towards the entrance of the fort.

"W-we'll never reach it!" Oakley stammered, readying himself for the barrage of sprinting soldiers with a single dagger in his nondominant hand.

"We don't have a choice! If we can get a horse, we can ride back to the others without dying by a barrage of arrows!" Korbyn stalked forward towards the soldiers with an attempted ignorance of his limp. "Follow my lead."

Fortunately for Korbyn, they charged in small waves instead of unified bouts.

The first soldier swung his blade, and Korbyn ducked out of its arc. He clutched the man's swinging wrist and struck his stomach with his alternate elbow. Then, he careened his arm upwards, slamming it into his jaw. The bone cracked, and the man bit his tongue, causing blood to spew from his lips. His neck craned as he tumbled backwards and dropped his blade. Korbyn heaved his foot against the man's stomach and shoved, knocking him into another unprepared soldier.

As two more soldiers rallied and charged, Korbyn rolled his wrist to test the heaviness of the sword. It felt light in his left hand, and he easily parried two swings from each of the soldiers. Due to his left-handedness, the soldiers didn't expect his deflection. The momentum of his counter sent them over their feet and disrupted their stances. Korbyn pivoted on his heel and slashed them across their vulnerable necks. He brushed past more soldiers with haste, diving into the crowd to not remain stagnant for too long.

Occasionally, Korbyn glanced back to ensure his friend's safety. Oakley trailed in his shadow, asserting strikes as they weaved through the masses. Despite striking with his nondominant hand, he moved with practiced grace, bombarding his targets with quick pierces in the clefts of their armors before they could retaliate.

Adrenaline and vivacity fueled Korbyn from the Blood Moon's red shroud. He basked in its glory and weaved amongst the soldiers with a flurry of a rotating blade. Each strike from an enemy was met with the clanging of his sword, countering their attacks with greater strength than they could muster. Still, Oakley followed through the swarm and struck the ones that Korbyn bypassed.

Korbyn finally reached the end of the group of soldiers, engulfed in heavy breaths. He couldn't help but allow a smile to drift to his face; for the first time, he reveled in his gifted power, experiencing the adrenaline that propelled him forward like an army of his own.

Behind him, Oakley mirrored his smirk. "We should be able to get to the stables now—" Oakley urged, not seeing a rising soldier behind him.

"Oakley!" Korbyn screamed, charging forward.

Oakley spun, not catching the soldier in time. He raised his weapon to parry the strike. Instead, the soldier elbowed him in the head, sending him face first into the battlement. The soldier followed in stride, slamming his palm into the back of Oakley's head and grabbing his dislocated arm.

As Korbyn ventured to assist, his steps halted. The sounds of the battle quieted, with the surrounding world dissipating into a hazy mist. Korbyn could only hear his deep and desperate breaths of fear, watching as the soldier intended to kill his friend right in front of him, and he could do nothing about it.

No! Please! Korbyn cried to the demon, attempting to push against the restraints of his stagnant legs.

No matter how much Korbyn fought and writhed against its hold, he couldn't move closer. Oakley remained just as stuck as he, unable to break free of the soldier's tightened grasp. Tears threatened them both, proving just as much an adversary as their captors.

Please. Not Oakley. I'll do anything, Korbyn pleaded.

How many times must I inform you that you are not meant to save? You are meant to take.

The soldier ripped Oakley's arm, and a guttural crack filled the red sky. He shrieked, cradling his shoulder.

Even from Korbyn's position, he could see a smirk of victory on the edge of the man's face. He kicked forward, smashing his heel into Oakley, causing him to topple back into the merlon.

"Runt," the soldier hissed, his voice echoing from within his bascinet. He lowered his torso and picked up a dropped blade. Before he jutted the weapon forward, a cackle emanated from Oakley's lips. Korbyn and the soldier stared with equal hesitancy.

Oakley lifted his head and rolled his shoulder, relief replacing where the pain had been. "Thanks for realigning my shoulder, fucker."

The soldier huffed, running forward to slash at his neck. From his lowered position, Oakley tumbled into a roll to avoid the strike. The soldier's blade slid thinly through the stone. They both turned to face each other, and the man lunged.

Oakley dashed forward and circled both of his arms around the soldier's thrusted one. He pushed off the wall for leverage and swung his entire body around the man's back, wrapping his legs around his neck. Oakley leaned into the momentum of his jump and aimed earthward, pulling the soldier with him. Both hit the ground, and they rolled. The man's sword fell with a clang.

Before the soldier could reach for his discarded blade, Oakley spun on his heels and pulled out a dagger, thrusting it under the soldier's bascinet. The man released croaking rasps and flails of maladroit desperation as blood spewed from his chin. When his thrashes continued, Oakley twisted the blade and dug it further. Soon, his writhing ceased, falling still under a blanket of red.

Korbyn and Oakley panted, readjusting their postures to allow their lungs ample breathing room. They exchanged glances, and Oakley grinned, offering him a thumbs up in consolation.

"You cursed on purpose that time," Korbyn inferred, attempting to hide his previous stress with a joke.

Oakley shrugged while sheathing his daggers and rolling his previously locked shoulder. "It felt right."

A strange whizzing pierced the air, like a lone, crying bird. They both ducked out of the way of an arrow, the metal piercing the wall behind them. Gazing down, an army rose to meet them. Exiting one of the side entrances of the fort and surrounding the bailey, a mass of soldiers leered up at them, readying their weapons.

"Get to the horses?" Oakley asked.

Korbyn nodded. "Get to the horses."

THIRTY-EIGHT.

The wraith emitted a disturbing caw, a foul mixture of both man and beast. It sounded more like an echo, an image of who Haven was.

"Haven! Stop this!" Veeris urged, trying to draw the wraith's attention. From behind the creature, he witnessed Salem fighting—and failing—to stand on her feet, with an unconscious Gilben at her side. "You want your vengeance, then here I am."

"N-no..." Salem stammered.

"*Veeris*," Haven—or maybe the wraith—whispered underneath jagged breaths, as if Veeris was a vile gnat that it wished to squash. It accepted his call, plodding forward and sliding its feet through the dirt. Its shoulders leaned forward, leading the expedition towards Veeris' confident stance. "It's *time*."

Veeris would somehow have to exorcise the creature before it consumed Haven's life. The longer the wraith was housed in his body, the more difficult it would be to remove it. As it stepped closer, Veeris circled the area and created distance between them, not allowing the wraith to close the distance.

"Haven? Are you in there? I need you to listen to me."

"*I thought you said you wanted me to kill you?*" the wraith questioned, mimicking its captured soul with obvious intent. "*Yet you stray from me.*" It gurgled as though it were choking on water.

"I know the objectives of a wraith, vile creature," Veeris spat, glaring at the monster within. "I will not allow you to succeed."

The wraith halted its saunter, laughing maniacally to the listening sky. "*Shame. It's a good thing I do not need your permission to take your life. I certainly didn't need the orc's.*"

Veeris scoffed. It grinned.

"He's not dead, not yet."

"*Time kills all, even you, mortal angel,*" it whispered between them.

Veeris glared. The wraith grinned wider, revealing its teeth.

"How do you know about that?" Veeris questioned, gazing over to Gilben, who was unconscious. Luckily, he would not hear this conversation, at least.

The monster's smile split, almost touching ear to ear. Its fangs gleamed unnaturally. "*Monsters recognize other monsters.*"

"I'm no monster."

"*Are you not? Monsters tend to be animalistic in nature, killing when their territory is threatened and resorting to violence when necessary. So, tell me, killer of mortals, how is it that you are any different?*"

Veeris ignored its question, unwilling to face its truth. "Life is something you crave—something you will not have."

The wraith finally frowned.

Veeris pulled out a single ore of decidite, infusing his body with its magical energy. It crumbled between his fingers, the dust scudding in the trailing wind. "Come claim your justice."

The wraith lurched forward, grasping the hilt of the axe with both hands. Veeris reacted in tandem, throwing forward his fingers to summon ten ethereal blades around his person. He thrust two downward in a line, a partition of holy light appearing in between them. The wraith swung and crashed into the barrier. It didn't destroy it, but the strength of the creature's attack shot pain through Veeris' fingers, as if he had physically blocked it himself.

With every swing of Haven's blade, Veeris' own were there to meet it. The trees became victim to their battle, with the hacking of blades coursing through the air. Trunks toppled and debris shifted to meet the night's embrace, laying waste to their skirmish. The entire time, Veeris kept on the defensive, waiting for a moment to strike.

The wraith's next attack was so strong that it carved a crack through one of Veeris' blocking blades. Veeris experienced a pop in the finger controlling it, its fracture afflicting a sharp pain from his finger to his dorsum. He cringed from the discomfort, and the wraith laughed.

With every collision, Veeris unintentionally took a step backwards, vibrations shooting from his fingers, up his arms, and down the rest of his body. His arms and legs cried in defiance, needing a moment's pause to reevaluate the situation.

Instead of blocking the next, Veeris darted to the side. He slid on his stomach, recoiling from the fall. When he peered upwards, the creature thrashed, struggling to retrieve the axe stuck in the trunk of a tree. From his position on the ground, Veeris shot up one hand and outstretched five of his fingers, motioning five matching blades to dart forward.

The wraith pulled so hard that it unintentionally swung the blade around its body, deflecting all the ethereal swords. Veeris' hand shot back from the impact, a wave of pain shooting up his arm. He grasped onto it, cursing under his breath. The monster ran forward with the axe above its head, and Veeris scrambled out of the way, barely avoiding the crash of the weapon's edge.

The wraith followed suit, and on its next swing, the monster let go with one hand like a full-bodied lunge, and the axe to continued its full course. It pushed Veeris back with a blade controlled by his other hand. The strength of the attack almost dismantled his magic completely, but he remained steadfast despite the agony coursing through his muscles. Instead of backing down, Veeris retaliated with his own move.

Veeris swirled five of the blades, flicking a ring finger, two indexes, a pinkie, and a thumb to initiate their movements. They swarmed around the wraith until they encircled it. With their edges pointed down and imbedding into the dirt, a barrier of holy light formed around it. The creature shuffled within the crude cage, endeavoring to destroy it with vicious swings, but the wall proved a formidable blockade to its efforts.

"You will let Haven go," Veeris demanded, faking a confidence to drown out his obvious exhaustion and the pain caused by every attack the wraith enacted on the partition. "Or Elohim shall vanquish you Himself."

"*You think that name scares me?*" The wraith laughed, taking a moment to pause its swings. "*I know He does not listen.*"

Veeris' eyes narrowed. "You know not of what you preach."

"*The hypocrite questions the will of the damned,*" the wraith stated with a sarcastic chuckle. "*You speak on behalf of a god without knowing true intentions, and you fail to realize you rely on those who care not for your own well-being.*" The creature craned its head sideways. "*Tell me, did Haven ever tell you the truth? About how he never trusted you?*"

Veeris flinched. "As if I would believe a lying, deceitful monster. Haven once said that the blood of the covenant is thicker than the water of the womb."

The wraith cackled. "*Yet you and I both know that wraiths can read the minds of the creatures they overtake. According to the orc, you were only accepted into this group because of Salem. She's much more liked than you. And you know what the saddest part of that is?"*

Veeris trembled. "Don't." He lowered his arms, hands trembling. "Don't."

"You were never her first choice," the wraith spat. *"And now she has abandoned you."*

Veeris faltered, and the wraith struck.

The power behind the creature's swing crashed into the barrier, sending the magic into fragments of shimmering light. Two of Veeris' bones cracked under the pressure, and he screamed. He stumbled, clutching onto his twitching fingers.

"Veeris! Move out of the way!" Salem shouted.

Veeris shifted his attention away from his pain and refocused upwards, but he did not see the wraith's approach in time.

The monster slammed its foot into his chest. Ribs cracked under its heel, and Veeris' breath disappeared. He flew backwards into a tree, ungracefully toppling to the ground. The wraith ambled over and lifted its foot, slamming it onto his forearm. Veeris cried out in pain when a crack resounded.

"Since you're always so eager to point fingers for your mistakes and raise them in your own blight of anger, how about we prevent that from happening?" The monster swung down its axe and embedded the sharpened edge into four of his fingers, severing them from his palm.

Veeris screeched, squirming from the pain as open flesh met cold air. Blood spewed matching the cold stare of the moon above them. The wraith's foot against his arm still held him down, and he was unable to move from under its weight.

"Veeris!" Salem yelled and rushed forward. She seemed as though the world around her spun as she trampled forward with a lack of the grace she usually had.

She vaulted towards Haven's back, but the wraith reacted with watchful eyes. It turned, whisking its arm in an arc and slamming its forearm into her chest. She toppled to the ground, her armor smacking into the earth below.

Gilben, who had at some point woken up amidst the fray, also raced forward, but the creature met his approach with a kick to his torso.

Veeris rolled, holding his palm in his hands. It throbbed with excruciating pain. His blood gushed like water from an open dam, despite how much he tried to halt the flow. Touching the wound sent another wave of sharp agony through him, forcing him to release another cry.

The wraith focused its attention on him once more. It reached for its axe, ready to strike at Veeris' undefended form.

"You're right, Haven," Veeris admitted, struggling to meet the monster's gaze. "You're right. I always knew that she didn't care for me, not the way I did her." He peered over at Salem, who couldn't seem to hold his contact. "But that demon...he showed up and ruined everything," Veeris seethed, biting his lip so hard that blood was drawn. "While I admit that I let my anger control me when it shouldn't have, there is no reality where my actions weren't led by passion to protect you all. Andrid is dead because of that *demon*, and I would kill him without remorse if it meant protecting you."

"*Protecting? And what about Andrid?*" the wraith inquired, seemingly intrigued by his answer.

"It was the *demon!*" Veeris urged, his hand twitching, though he strove to ignore the pain. "Please, Haven, you must understand. That demon is foul and had been planning something even before we found it at Fort Silvercrest. I know that is hard to believe, but it has enchanted you. I can help you see the truth. If you are truly my friend, then I need you to trust me."

A screech penetrated the night sky. The darkened shadow of the wraith expelled from Haven's body, thrashing and crying in defiance. As it was exorcised, it reached out to Veeris. The wraith clung to his ankle in a last attempt, and eventually, it dissipated into the mist, out of Veeris' sight.

Haven's head hung low for a few moments, Veeris watching in awe as the gloom subsided. There was no more wailing, no fighting, and no strange voices parading in the mists. The only thing that stood before them now was an angered half-orc, fully his own once again.

"Friendship?" Haven hissed as the black sclera of his eyes shifted into whitened seas surrounding an island of dark irises. "Trust?" Even still, his anger rivaled that of the exorcised wraith. Haven stared back with a firm line of his mouth, veins of red spreading across his sclera. "Friendship is formed through trust, and trust is earned, yet you have done nothing but verify you are unworthy of it."

Haven dropped his axe, the blade slicing into the soil. The movement was so sudden that Veeris lurched back in fear.

"That is the very thing you told Korbyn, isn't it? You're nothing but a hypocritical, selfish *brat*," Haven spat, his hands tightening into fists.

Veeris could insinuate that he was getting ready to punch him senseless once again. "That's different!"

"Then *clarify!*" Haven yelled, taking a step to loom over him.

Veeris shuffled back once again but could no longer put space in between them when his back met a tree. "It's the demon—that *creature!* And the Blood Moon! It's the reason for all our suffering. It killed Andrid—I was trying to help the entire time. If you all just listened. If Andrid just hadn't gotten in my way—"

Haven grabbed Veeris by the throat and slammed his head so hard into the tree that the world blurred, threatening to pull him into permanent unconsciousness. He grasped Haven's wrist with both hands, but one was a mangled mess. He struggled against the sturdy hold, squirming when he had no ability to intake air.

He saw the folds in Haven's face resemble a hungry hound.

With his distorted form blurred, it duplicated into multiple replicas, imitating a pack of snarling wolves. They loomed over him, and Veeris couldn't help but squirm like a fearful animal caged under bared teeth.

"No!" Haven screamed. "It wasn't the fault of us, it wasn't the fault of Korbyn, and it certainly wasn't the fucking fault of *Andrid!* It was you," the half-orc growled much like a ferocious beast, sending waves of fear through Veeris. "*You* were the one that killed Andrid."

Haven let go of his throat, and Veeris crumbled to the ground. He coughed, wishing to alleviate the grip that felt like fangs across his throat. He heaved, not easily locating the air to relieve his lungs.

"And his name," Haven snarled with a leer. "His name is *Korbyn*. And Korbyn has done nothing but prove time and time again that he is kind and reliable, while you hide behind glorified words and self-righteousness." There was no guilt or remorse in his eyes, leaving Veeris once again unable to read him. "There may be some dark power, or even a demon that dwells inside of him, but behind that gloom is a kind-hearted person who genuinely cares about others. The creature you house inside is something far worse—a terrible, deplorable, and despicable *snake*."

Veeris gasped, tears swelling his eyes, unable to believe the words that spilled from his mouth. "Haven, you don't mean that."

"I mean every single fucking word," Haven spat. "You deserve death, but that does nothing except help you avoid the outcomes of your mistakes. I will not be sending you to join Andrid. They deserve reprieve of your betrayal."

"But—"

"You will atone. Not through vengeance, or torture or death, but by continuing to live." Haven's hands once again curled into fists, and it was then that Veeris could see the dried blood on his palms that he refused to clean. "Live your long, lonely, selfish, and pathetic life contemplating your mistakes. When you wake up in the morning, think about Andrid's voice. Think about the sorry excuse of a person you are and remember that it should have been *you* that died in Andrid's place."

Veeris' tears fell, and he couldn't figure out if the ache that followed was caused by the fear of loneliness or everyone's turned backs.

THIRTY-NINE.

Reverberating bell chimes disrupted the tension-filled air. Salem and the rest of the mercenaries stilled under swaying branches. Her apprehension peaked when her intrusive thoughts conjured the different possibilities, most of which involved Korbyn and Oakley captured, beaten, and then killed. Salem pivoted towards the west, but the branches of the remaining forest concealed Fort Runswhick and prevented her further speculation.

"Everyone, get up. We have to go!" Salem urged, racing to Veeris when she realized he hadn't even regarded the alarm.

She hauled him to his feet, ushering him forward with a push on his back. She was afraid, for brief moment, that if she didn't physically coerce him, he wouldn't have moved at all. Still, Veeris appeared to be overridden with shock as he fixated on the ground, eyes glazed, and shoulders slacked.

Haven and Gilben both concurred with brisk nods and scrambling forms, both retrieving their weapons and belongings before darting for their camp.

As Salem motioned to follow, she noticed Veeris remaining stationary in a dumbfounded stupor. He was clutching his mangled hand, which was lacking four fingers and covered in blood. Unfortunately, she wouldn't be able to do anything for him now with their limited time, physically or mentally. Salem thought he might have not even been breathing if not for his occasional trembling.

"Veeris!" the paladin yelled, though she failed to gain his attention. When that didn't work, she leveled her face with his, still straining to meet his averted eyes. "Veeris!"

Still, he disregarded her, though Salem imagined it wasn't deliberate.

Thinking of no other solution other than carrying him, which would have proved strenuous on her aching body, Salem lifted her palm and slapped Veeris across his face.

That seemed to rouse him. Veeris peered upwards, meeting her glance with a reddened cheek and a slack jaw.

"Let's go," Salem demanded.

He didn't display any type of agreement other than following her.

Salem and Veeris burst past a set of bushes and approached the camp in haste. She observed Haven at the wagon's front, fumbling with the horse's harness and ripping it from the vehicle's shaft before leading the frightened steed in the opposite direction of the fort.

As Salem opened her mouth to question him, the ground started to tremble. She heard various rhythmic clops from a mass of galloping horses. To the west, Korbyn and Oakley approached the group on separate steeds, racing through the plains with soldiers chasing their heels.

"Gilben, get on the horse!" Haven yelled.

Gilben shuffled towards the half-orc, allowing his companion to lift him atop the creature.

"But, our supplies!" Salem said as she motioned to the discarded caravan. "We—"

"We'll never outrun an army with a wagon! Veeris, let's go!" Haven interrupted, motioning Veeris over. When he didn't reply, the half-orc yanked his arm and hoisted him on top of the horse behind Gilben.

Haven slapped the steed's hip. Already panicked from the quakes of the encroaching army, the horse reared and sprinted into a full gallop down the red-hued path, dust stirring in its wake. Salem turned back towards the fray. The mass of soldiers behind them seemed endless. They were waving their sharp-edged blades, barking various orders, and barreling across the plains like a sudden surge of water. There wouldn't be enough time to halt the horses, and Salem and Haven would drown in the masses.

"Run!" Korbyn yelled as he waved his arm, motioning them towards the blanket of the trees.

Salem and Haven pivoted towards the forest and raced forward.

Haven reached Oakley's horse first. The half-orc grabbed the horn of the saddle and jumped with a brute force. His weight slammed on top of the mount, and it appeared as though it might topple from the male's size, but thankfully, the horse's adrenaline prevailed. Haven retrieved the reins from Oakley's grasp and beckoned it faster with a kick of his heel.

As Salem ran to mirror the approaching steed's stride, she lost her breath and stumbled. A wave of weakness and numbness faltered her bolt, no longer able to keep her body aloft. She fell, trying to push herself to her feet, but a migraine pounded, mimicking various punches to her cranium. The world swirled in agony, and she could no longer decipher which way the sky faced.

The paladin dripped in sweat, and the world and events morphed into a swirl of heavy breaths and trees. Had Korbyn already passed her? Had he done the smart thing and left her behind? No, she didn't think he would, but she couldn't pinpoint the direction of the galloping horses as the world spun. Salem analyzed several directions, searching for the one that led to the fortress in the distance.

It was then that she saw it—Korbyn's distraught face as he closed the distance on horseback between them.

"Leave without—"

Korbyn quickened the horse's gallop with another click of his heels. Then, without even a moment of hesitation, he slid one leg through the rear strap and lowered his body sideways, a hand grasping the horn of the saddle and the other reaching out to her. Somehow, he managed to keep his body upright to prevent himself from careening off the horse.

"Salem!" Korbyn yelled. It gave her the strength and courage to reply.

Salem reached out, grasping onto his arm below his elbow. He did the same. With a yell of desperation, Korbyn plucked her from the ground and lifted her upon the horse, despite the heaviness of her armor. Salem landed on the saddle in front of Korbyn's torso, and he took over the reins, urging the horse forward through the darkness in the trees.

From behind, Salem saw the army come to a halt at the edge of the forest, as if afraid of the creatures that lurk in the shadows under the gaze of the Blood Moon.

She leaned back into Korbyn's chest. When fatigue consumed her, Salem sank into a pit of black.

Warmth caused Salem to stir. As she instigated her eyes open, she saw embers of dancing flames shifting among burning timber. A small fire, in comparison to normal. The sky was still dark, and she could see the clouds dripping in red from the Blood Moon. It appeared as though it was beginning to depart past the horizon, and for some reason, she felt as though it wasn't offering a permanent farewell.

Across the camp, Gilben tended to Veeris' hand, wrapping it in gauze around the entirety of his palm. From her position, it wasn't the best patch-up job, but it would surely prevent filth from entering the wound. Though, Veeris didn't seem to mind, his eyes traveling elsewhere. Gilben was speaking about something, but his voice didn't reach her listening ears.

Haven stood alone, his eyes wandering into the encompassing trees. Salem analyzed the area in tandem, noticing no visible path. They must have strayed from the main road, a smart idea indeed. Traversing betwixt two forts meant Avernos soldiers would inevitably scout along the connecting route. She imagined they were somewhere between Fort Runswhick and Fort Silvercrest by now, but she knew not of their next destination.

On the other end of the camp, Korbyn and Oakley sat next to each other, speaking in hushed voices.

"Should still have Salem examine at your wounds," Oakley suggested. A scowl had already formed on Korbyn's face when she scanned him, as if they had been in a disagreement for a few minutes.

"I told you, I'm fine," Korbyn stated in a lowered whisper. It appeared as though there was a closing hole in the middle of his palm. "It's been healing on its own. She needs rest."

Returning her attention to her own body, Salem felt the migraine not subsiding. Even now, the world appeared like it had shifted at an angle, and she couldn't seem to ground herself. She most likely suffered a concussion, which could heal just fine on its own. If the others needed medical attention, then she needed to aid them.

A leather bag sprawled underneath her head, accompanied

by a thin quilt spread across her body. Most of her armor had been removed, save for the golden chainmail. She rose, the blanket falling to her lap as she massaged her temples and rallied waves of healing energy through her fingertips. The rest of the encampment turned towards her.

"Speak of the devil!" Oakley stated with a smile. Beside him, Korbyn frowned. "What?"

"Nothing," Korbyn responded before returning his attention to Salem. "How are you feeling?"

"I'm fine," Salem responded, sighing in relief when the headache began to alleviate. She sat up with a little more clarity, the dizziness disappearing. She was eager to rid herself of the physical ailments so she could learn more about what Korbyn and Oakley found within Fort Runswhick.

She tried to not think about the fact that Korbyn and Oakley didn't return with any members of Kendra Dawn. A conflict of relief and anxiety battled for dominance within the pits of her stomach.

"Tell me everything that happened," Salem urged.

Korbyn and Oakley approached the campfire, sitting down and gazing at it and then each other. The grim silence that followed unsettled her. They sat there, arguing without any words being said. It was as if they were debating who should speak up first.

"I's not good, lass," Gilben said, striding towards the fire and sitting down on her other side when he had finished with Veeris' patchwork. "You might wanna prepare yerself."

Salem took a deep breath and exhaled. "I'm ready."

It was interesting how Korbyn and Oakley could speak to each other without the use of words. Oakley elbowed him, and Korbyn replied with a glare. Oakley shrugged and then motioned over towards Salem with his head. Korbyn rolled his eyes in retort. Their friendship filled her with warmth.

"We found this," Korbyn said, retrieving a note from his satchel.

She quirked a brow before examining the parchment. It was an official letter sent by Emperor Wymond. The seal was broken.

"How did you get this? Did you open this?" Salem questioned.

Oakley rubbed his neck and shifted uneasily. In contrast to the shorter male, Korbyn did not break her eye contact. Intensity and concern burned in his ivory gaze.

"Just read it," Korbyn urged.

She opened the letter. Middle Guard...undead army...conquer the Mines of Esperin...capture those knowledgeable of decidite...Vanguard...Shadowbane Forest...Graycott and Umberfall...

"An army of what?" Salem asked, almost not believing what she had just read. "Does this say undead?"

"Yes. Just like the ogres in Shadowbane," Korbyn explained, his eyes traveling from her to the parchment in her hands. "Avernos has an entire army of dead bodies that can somehow be controlled by a mage and used as soldiers, and there are hundreds, almost a thousand of them."

Salem inhaled, calming herself before she relayed her next question. "And Kendra Dawn? Did you find Micah?"

Korbyn frowned, and Oakley slouched next to him. "She's gone. They're all gone," Korbyn said. "I'm so sorry."

Salem grasped the locket in her hands, running over the gold with a calloused thumb. She drooped her head and took a sad, painful breath, holding in a shudder that would inevitably lead to enraged tears.

Micah, I'm so sorry, Salem thought, knowing very well she couldn't hear her. She whispered another silent prayer, attempting to ignore the fact that she wasn't certain if Elohim was present or listening. There would be a day when she allowed herself to mourn, but for now, there were thousands of lives in danger, and they needed to act quickly.

"They plan to capture the mining town to claim the decidite?" Salem questioned.

Korbyn and Oakley both nodded, clearly filled with apprehension.

"We have to get to the towns before the armies do," Salem declared, beginning to rise from her seated position. Clearly, the trauma to her head hadn't completely abated. She swayed for a few moments, and everyone around her reached out. She steadied herself, locating her removed armor, weapon, and shield. "If these monsters resemble the ogres at all, then they need to be stopped. Let's leave and head north."

"We already have," Gilben stated, pulling her back down. "We're north of Fort Silvercrest headin' ta the mines. We knew what ya'd wanna do."

"Then we must reach Brinshire and evacuate the town."

Korbyn, Oakley and Gilben nodded. Haven was in the back of the group, farther away from the fire, but he seemed to be listening. Veeris was unresponsive.

Salem fumbled to rise. "We don't have much time. We should—"

"We all need rest, Salem," Gilben interrupted, ushering her down for the second time. "There's only a few more hours til the sun rises. Get as much sleep as ya can, and we'll leave right away."

With a sigh, Salem nodded.

Gilben rose, heading over to Veeris. Oakley pulled Korbyn up, and they returned to their perch, assumably to continue their own conversation. To the side, Haven stood alone. He was watching the forest, probably for any monsters, creatures, or soldiers that might lurk in the shadows. She hadn't yet had a chance to speak with him since Andrid's passing, and she was beginning to worry.

Salem could see the physical and mental toll it was taking on his body and mind. Instead of the collected composure Haven usually wore, he sat with a heavy slouch and an empty regard. He cared not to alleviate his thirst with ale or spend his time to sharpen his axe. Instead, he seemed to care not much for any-thing at all, and she was beginning to worry about her friend that seemed so far out of her reach, just as she felt Veeris had become. Who was it that Haven would be without his partner at his side? Before Salem allowed herself to rest, she walked over to Haven and peeked into the forest.

"Are you okay?" Salem prompted, wrapping her arms around her torso to keep the warmth of autumn close to her. With each passing night, she felt the breeze getting colder.

"No," Haven answered. "No, and I'm having a hard time pre-tending I am."

Salem offered him a melancholic grin, unable to mask her ex-pression. "I'm so sorry about Andrid. I won't pretend to know what they would want for you, for us, and the future. You knew them best," she stated, grabbing his hand and squeezing it. "But I do know that they had a pure soul. Andrid would want you to be happy. I'm sorry if that sounds cliché."

She couldn't decipher the emotions in his glistening eyes. Haven had always been the hardest to read. The only one who had ever been able to penetrate that self-created barrier was An-drid.

"I know, and I appreciate that nonetheless, but there is a hole there that cannot be filled. I don't know how to be happy when my biggest source of joy is gone."

"And your friends?" Salem asked. It was selfish of her to ask, but she had hoped that they had something that could fill his emptiness.

"You know how I feel about you, Say. You'll always be one of my favorite people," Haven replied, eyes flickering to Veeris. "But he is a stranger to me now. This group will never be the same."

"Well, either way, I'm happy for the option you chose." Salem followed his gaze. Veeris slouched beside Gilben, who continued to speak to him. She was unsure if he was listening to the dwarf. "More death wasn't the answer."

Haven nodded. "Looking at him now, he may not agree with you." He took a deep breath. "I honestly don't know what I'll do...after this."

Salem squeezed his hand tighter. Even though he didn't return the gesture, he accepted it. "Whatever it is that you feel is right, I support you. No matter what."

Haven finally turned to her, analyzing her with the eyes that she remembered. "Thank you, Say."

Salem left him to his own thoughts. Instead of returning to her improvised bed, she walked to the edge of her camp and sat against a tree. She wrapped her arms around her torso and leaned her head back, staring at the descending Blood Moon.

Salem closed her eyes, shifting her attention away from the looming harbinger and channeled waves of holy energy throughout her body, mending the cuts, aches, and bruises. In the morning, after she'd rested and regained more of her energy, she would heal Haven's broken nose and Veeris' hand. They would need to be at their full strength when they set for Brinshire.

She only hoped they wouldn't be too late.

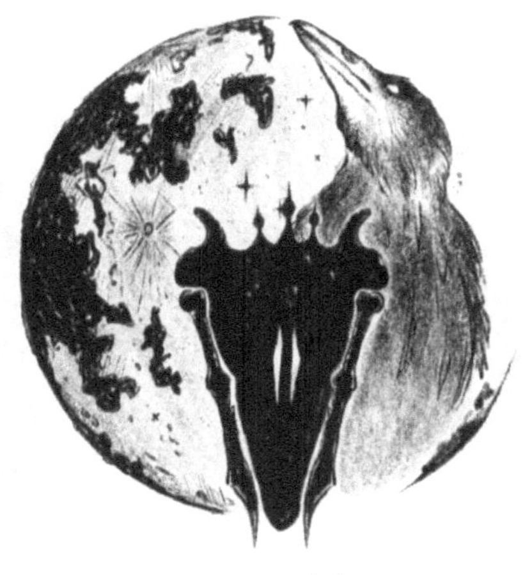

FORTY.

Once Oakley retreated to slumber, Korbyn resorted to the dangers of his thoughts. He stared up at the Blood Moon with a mixture of loathing and intrigue, its returned regard adding a surprising amount of comfort. With its gifted power, he felt unstoppable, an immeasurable amount of potential fueling his actions. Jumping from the fortress, scaling its walls, combating a mass of enemy soldiers, mending drastic wounds—none of it made him waver. His biggest concern had been for Oakley's safety, to which his body prevented his brisk response.

But if Korbyn had been alone, fighting off the endless soldiers, could he have been stopped? The mark pulsed in response. He rubbed the tattoo from the top of his sleeve, wishing to alleviate its irritation.

He silently pulled out the ring from his pocket. Even under the light of the red moon, it shimmered. The moon and the sun sat in adjacent beauty, mere centimeters away from touching. He turned the gold within his fingers, watching every angle of it glimmer in the fire's dance. Somehow, the sun seemed to shine brighter than its counterpart.

The sun and moon, so conflicting and harmonious, yet kindred spirits and ostensibly powerless, the demon whispered with a saddened tone.

Korbyn rubbed the heel of his hand across his brow, relieving the ache. Never did he wish to return to that brief dream, but he couldn't ignore its pleas.

Ignorance quells the perturbed mind. Will you consent to the same mistake?

For once, can't you just shut it? Korbyn spat internally.

The demon bellowed in a guttural laugh that mimicked his own. *But who will offer you guidance? Those in denial tend to try and silence the truth, if only to tolerate their injustice.*

Your riddles are anything but helpful. If you want to offer some guidance, then at least speak plainly.

How does one grow without challenges? How does one expand their knowledge without heralding new information? How does one grow stronger without physical exertion? One does not simply walk the shorter path and also commend their worthiness—except the simple-minded.

You're infuriating, Korbyn grumbled.

Nothing is as infuriating as those ignorant of their own stupidity, the demon snapped with a surprising amount of fury.

Just tell me what you know, Korbyn demanded. *This isn't about growing to be a better or stronger or smarter person. Salem's life is at stake. I can't make that mistake again, not like Andrid.*

There are many possible paths, but it is up to you which one you take.

Then tell me which one to take! Korbyn yelled in his mind. *Help me save her.*

Is there more to life? Is destiny but an illusion of a lack of choice? Will the sun and moon forever be forced to coexist in eter-

nal separation? For some reason, Korbyn sensed the demon's frown. *The sun gifts the moon with its light, but it does not deserve it.*

"Hiya, lad," Gilben said.

Korbyn flinched, concealing the ring within his palm. He had been so preoccupied with the demon's voice that he hadn't heard his friend's approach. With some sort of ability to read his thoughts like the demon had, Gilben offered a smile of reassurance.

"Ya don't have ta act as though I don't know what yer feelin', about Salem," Gilben said, sitting beside him.

Korbyn raised his knee up to shield his embarrassment. "Is it that obvious?"

Gilben readjusted, locating a comfortable position on the ground. "Ta me 'nd others, sure, but it's always a wee bit difficult ta look objectively at a situation when yer on the inside," the dwarf said, crossing his legs over each other and placing his hands in his lap.

They sat for a few moments, neither exchanging words in the comfort of the silence.

"I don't know what to do," Korbyn said to sever the quiet, placing his arm horizontally on top of his knee and resting his face on it. He lowered his head further and mumbled. "I'm not good enough for her."

Gilben huffed out a chuckle, but it almost seemed sad or sympathetic. "Is that 'er opinion or yers? If yer not sure what someone's thinkin', do ya know what the best way ta combat that is?" Korbyn lifted a questionable brow, followed by Gilben's deep, cadent laugh. "Ya ask 'er."

Such an obvious, but terrifying solution.

"There's just so much going on right now," Korbyn interjected, gripping the ring tighter. "Especially with Andrid, and Veeris." He sighed. "It's a bad time."

"There's never a good time, lad, 'specially with the life we live." Gilben closed his eyes and leaned against the tree trunk behind him. "Ya might regret thin's if ya do them too late."

Korbyn scanned his robust form. The dwarf appeared as though he was scrutinizing behind closed lids, as though recalling a memory. "You say that as if you've gone through something similar."

Gilben grinned. "You'd be right."

"Does it have to do with whatever you've been writing?" Korbyn questioned, motioning over to the stack of parchment and his lute. "I noticed you've been working on something for a while."

The dwarf smiled. "That's somethin' different. It'll be me best work. Just ya wait."

Korbyn leaned forward. "Then, do you mind if I ask what happened?"

Gilben nodded and did what he had always done when he started telling a story. He took a few, deep breaths, urging calmness for his hearkening crowd. However, this time, he had no lute to keep him company. Korbyn felt his breathing fall into rhythm with the bard.

"I'm originally from a city in the Alliance of Thalar called Lightforj, a dwarven city. 's rather peaceful. I fell in love with a lady just as headstrong 'nd determined as Salem. She was a seafarer, often times returnin' ta the keep just ta sail away the next day. Then there was me. At the time, I wasn't much a traveler. I usually kept to playin' me music in taverns 'nd such. I always was watchin' her from a far, thinkin' she was too good fer me." For the first time, Korbyn saw Gilben's smile fade. "Then one day, she didn't come back. I waited fer days, months after she said she'd be back. They found 'er ship not too long after tha'."

Korbyn exhaled. "I'm so sorry."

The dwarf shook his head. "Not yer fault, lad, I've only wanted to tell ya ta not make the same mistake I did. I made a grave for 'er, despite not havin' a body. I would visit it all the time, an orchid field by the ocean's edge. I made it a reminder ta not waste any opportunities. Life's too short."

Kobryn motioned to say something, despite not having the right words, but Gilben continued before he could.

"The reality is that there'll never be a good time. The world's always gonna keep movin'. It's up ta ya to decide if yer gonna keep up or not. Do ya want to be runnin' with it together with someone ya care about, or ridin' the waves alone?"

Korbyn retrieved the ring once more, shifting it to admire its brilliance. In truth, Korbyn was afraid. He was afraid of her rejection, her mirrored affection, and of the unknown power, but he wasn't just afraid—he was terrified.

"Thank you, Gilben. You're a good friend," Korbyn whispered.

Gilben's offered another warm smile that gave him confidence before leaving him to make his decision.

After several, lone moments of contemplation, Korbyn rose and strode over to Salem, careful not to disrupt her.

"Salem," Korbyn whispered. Salem flinched as her faint magic dissipated, as though she did not hear his approach.

"Korbyn," Salem whispered back.

When their eyes met, Korbyn felt a tightness in his throat, unable to hold her gaze. Instead of saying anything, he sat beside her, accidentally grazing his arm against hers. Another spark surged, and he quelled the sensation with a rub of his hand.

Silence lingered as they observed the small, dancing flames. Korbyn exploited their inaudibility by analyzing the surrounding shadows, seeing nothing concealed within. The only thing that bore witness to the camp and the duo was the Blood Moon, which remained hushed, as always.

"I miss Andrid," Salem whispered, leaning against the tree. Again, she fumbled with her nails and picked at the grime that loitered beneath them.

"I'm so sorry," Korbyn murmured, guilt trailing from his breath. "I don't think I can ever express my regret."

"No, I'm sorry. I didn't mean any implication by it. I just miss them." Salem frowned, wrapping her arms around herself. "They brought so much light to this world. It just feels like a piece is missing. I still can't believe it."

Scattered pieces, but one placed in the puzzle.

"It doesn't make it any less my fault," Korbyn said, leaning his head back against the bark of the tree. Even with the distance between them, he could feel the light bouncing off the moon. "I should have left that day."

Salem whirled to face him. "No, Korbyn it's not your—"

"It is," Korbyn stated. She opened her mouth to retaliate, but he interjected, "If I am not responsible, then who is?"

Salem's attention drifted to Veeris. He sat by the small fire, which presumably failed to keep him warm. Instead of watching the performing embers as they dwindled, his glazed, cerulean eyes stared forth into the shadowed, overhanging trees.

"You shouldn't blame him," Korbyn noted.

As if not knowing she had glanced to Veeris, Salem whisked her head back. "What?"

"If I wasn't here, none of this would have happened," Korbyn continued, following Veeris' stare towards the gloom.

"You're not angry with him?" she probed with a rise in pitch. Her golden eyes danced from one of his ivories to the other, and he knew she attempted to find some sort of dishonesty among them, but Salem would find none.

Korbyn scoffed, a sour combination of amusement and anger. "Hell yeah I'm pissed. That bastard tried to kill me."

Salem huffed, the edges of her lips curving upward from his jest. Eventually, their intermingling, somber chuckles dispersed amongst the reverberating silence.

"I understand why he did it," Korbyn said. "He was just trying to protect you all. I may have done the same thing."

Salem sighed, clutching her locket with a light shaking of her head. "You have a good heart, you know that, right?" she urged, her smile not fading.

Korbyn huffed again, unable to hold her eye contact. "Then yours must be made of gold."

They laughed again, and he tried to ignore the demon that bellowed in tandem.

The silence between them was never too prolonged or gauche, for even amongst the quiet, he could feel her permeating warmth. While he resided at her side, the ice melted like mist. He pined for the ecstasy of her temperateness, for this moment of reprieve alleviated his never-ending chill. In daring contrast, when Salem nudged her elbow against his, the spark leaped up his arm.

"Do you remember anything about what happened? Before we got to Fort Runswhick?" Salem asked, shifting a bit closer to him. "Your powers, I mean."

Korbyn fiddled with the ring inside his pocket. "Not every-thing," he answered honestly, closing his eyes to recall the event. He took a few, deep breaths, just as Gilben had silently practiced before. "I remember Veeris' face, his voice. He was so angry with me. I remember feeling confused, wondering what I had done to anger him."

He sensed a slackening in her shoulders and her matching frown, as if both were connected by matching strings. Korbyn wasn't fully cognitive during that duration while he was lost in the depths of his own mind, but he wasn't sure he wanted to admit what he did remember.

"I remember trying to stop him from fighting me, and then all of a sudden, I was walking through a forest clouded in mist. It felt like I was wandering for ages, and then I woke up, and before I could move, Andrid was there." He grabbed his left arm, wishing to alleviate the irritation. "And then they were gone."

"I'm so sorry, Korbyn." Salem sighed. "No one deserves to go through something like this. Veeris has been unkind to you."

"I'm the one who should be sorry," Korbyn replied, fumbling his words. "But you, you shouldn't apologize. It's not your fault. I..." He took another deep breath, though it didn't pause the quick beats of his heart. He placed his hand over his chest and gripped the fabric, calming its intensity. Hopefully she couldn't hear it, though the silence of the night and the soft flickering of the campfire was somewhat deafening.

Korbyn needed to unveil his truth, if not to confirm his suspicions.

"I know the truth." Salem whipped her head around from the corner of his eye, but he refused to look at her. "I overheard you and Veeris that night in Enderbrooke, after they rescued us from the woods. I didn't mean to eavesdrop." He exhaled. "You said it was a demon."

"Korbyn, I..." She paused, scrambling for words. Her silence was more painful than the sentence that followed. "I'm so sorry, I didn't mean for you to overhear that."

"You shouldn't ever apologize to me, for anything." Korbyn brought up his knee to his chest and draped his arms over it. He couldn't shield himself, but he would try. "And you don't have to apologize for the truth."

Salem's jaw clamped shut.

When another silence invaded the air, Korbyn broke it with uncertain words.

"There's something wrong with me, Salem," he said, staring up at the Blood Moon that welcomed him. "There's a darkness inside me. I don't fully understand it, but I know it's there. It's trying to tell me something, but I've been too afraid to listen."

He felt Salem's transfixed gape, but he continued anyway.

"Veeris was right this whole time. I'm a creature, a monster lingering in human skin. I don't deserve to be here. I don't deserve to be anywhere. Which leaves me to my question..."

Korbyn craned his head, unsure of how his eyes appeared from the emotions that swirled beneath them. "Does it matter?" he whispered with a slight crack in his voice. "Does it matter what I am? Does it matter that something lingers inside me?"

"No, Korbyn," Salem replied, tone wavering. "It doesn't. It never did. I always knew the truth, despite not understanding it. I knew from the moment we found you on the battlefield."

A part of him wanted to believe her. Another part of him didn't, for no matter what her words were, it would never prove logical.

"Why did you not kill me?" Korbyn laughed, unable to hide the pain peeking through his faux hilarity, for his eyes and speech defied him.

"Because you are Korbyn," Salem declared without a trace of insincerity. "Regardless of what stirs underneath, you're a person. A person who woke up without his memories, a person who avoided death despite all odds, a person who wants to exist in a world that was betting against him." She pressed herself closer, as though afraid he would disappear from his seated position before she could continue. "A person who despite all of his trials, all of his loss and pain, chooses to defend and fight for those that need it. I wanted to help you, and I like betting against difficult odds."

With another one of Salem's famous smiles, a wall surrounding Korbyn's heart collapsed. The ring felt heavier in his pocket, exigent in its existence. As he fumbled for words, she closed the remaining distance between them.

Salem pulled his right arm in her lap, her fingers brushing along his tattered sleeve. The sparks returned as demanded by its audience, an encore of unfurling excitement. When she reached his right bracer, she tugged until it fully slid off his forearm. He watched her motions with a stilled breath, unable to heed to the declarations of his lungs.

"Do you feel that?" Korbyn managed to whisper with a pounding heart, hairs raised underneath his sleeve. "That spark?"

"Yes," Salem murmured, rolling up his sleeves to his elbow.

Korbyn's skin yearned for more of her, bumps springing from his wrist up to his elbow like an ocean's wave. Following the formations, Salem traced her fingers over them, his right forearm left completely bared for her.

She reversed her movements, creeping back down against the bump's grain all the way to his twitching palm. The sparks intensified, tingling so much that his arm jerked at her tenderness. He desperately wished to ignore the other springing limb.

She huffed a smile. "Yes, I feel it too."

"Does your heart feel the same way?" Korbyn asked, craning his head back against the tree to gaze fully into her eyes. He was afraid of her response, despite aware of her transparent answer.

Salem leaned into the tree, mere inches away from his face. "Yes. More than you know."

His hands were cold and sweaty, the ring encased in his left palm bellowing to be heard from its capture.

What is more painful? the demon bellowed. *To have your heart ripped from you, or to never possess it at all?*

"You're crazy." Korbyn laughed, not tearing his attention from hers. "You know that, right? You don't even know who I was before this. I could have been a monster all my life."

Monsters can be slain. No, you are not a monster, it cooed. *You are a* disease.

"If there is one thing you are not, Korbyn, it's a monster," Salem said, sliding her fingers into his and clasping their hands together.

The tingling continued to surge, escorted by the wild beats of his heart. She leaned forward, observing Korbyn's mouth and then his eyes. A spark danced from their lips, dragging them together like attracting opposites.

"That is something I refuse to believe," Salem whispered.

Korbyn leaned forward, surrendering himself to her.

Before their lips coupled, a vision surged.

Salem erupted in a blinding light with unfurled, angelic wings, the feathers riven from her back in a spray of crimson. Her shrieks followed.

The Blood Moon lingered above a black cathedral in lands glazed in ice. Countless hounds, ginormous in size in comparison to even wolves, sauntered forward with dark fur and hollowed eyes of bleakness. Their elongated jaws reached far past their skulls, gushing with blood and saliva past their daggered teeth. Bones protruded from their spines and hind legs in jagged formations.

A figure stood underneath a cloak, with a black, gilded crescent blade in his left hand. A tumult of innocents cried out in deranged fear. The silhouette of Death issued a command to the wolfhounds. The beasts lunged forth and slaughtered them, sparing none underneath the cages of their jaws. His glazed eyes, reminiscent of the moon above him, peered underneath the shadow.

A blade clashed against his own, initiating a bout of desperation. Salem met his eyes and leveled a blade in his direction. Korbyn swung the scythe again, combating her on the battlefield of ice and sorrow under the Blood Moon's approving sneer.

Korbyn broke through the waters much like an ocean, inhaling air after his stilled breath. He clutched onto the cloth above his fast-beating heart to quell it to silence. A cold sweat broke out amongst his brow alongside a slight quiver of his jaw, and he fought his trembling legs as he relied on a tree to keep him upright. Unknowingly, he had retreated from Salem and the camp and into the clutches of the darkness that, for some reason, brought him comfort.

"You're the one showing these visions to me," Korbyn muttered, calling out to the demon he previously attempted to ignore.

"Why?"

There are many paths, and I have seen countless ones. Each road diverges into ambiguous crossroads, ones you have already chosen. Although you possess less options than most, still you have deviated towards the most tenebrous path, the demon explained. *Because you are drawn to the darkness.*

"Korbyn?" Salem pushed past a set of branches.

"I'm sorry," Korbyn said aloud, turning away from her. "I shouldn't have tried to kiss you." He fought the vertigo by relying on his own strength to stand upright.

"Why?" Salem asked, leaves cracking under her approaching steps. "I was going to let you."

"I..." Korbyn trailed off, unable to find the words that evaded him. His shoulders slackened, hoping she would keep her distance from him. "Because we can't be together."

"And why not?" she questioned, a bit of defiance on her tongue. Without glancing at her, he knew her arms were crossed over her chest, to defy his proclamations before he even explained himself.

"Because we can't. Because of what we are." He glanced back and regretted it.

Behind the wrath Salem permeated, Korbyn saw glimmers of sadness in the riches of gold. Inadvertently, his eyes drifted to where her wings should have been.

She followed his regard before returning to his face. She made use of her faltering hand, fiddling with the locket on her chest.

"And what are we?" Salem asked, appearing too frightened to ask.

"I think you know," Korbyn replied, not allowing her to escape his observation.

She gulped down gathering saliva, licking her lips where they had dried and offering no response. Salem assumed an astonishing silence in comparison to her normal brazenness.

Instead of awaiting her response, Korbyn walked past her, aimed to descend into the camp where the diminishing fire awaited them. Before he entered the trees, Salem grabbed his left wrist and halted his tread.

"Korbyn—"

Korbyn intervened her next declaration, heaving her towards a nearby tree. He slammed her back against it, hovering over her with an arched back.

"*Admit it. Deep down, despite what you claim,*" Korbyn spat with a newfound roughness to his voice, a hopeful endeavor to confirm his suspicions. "*You fear me.*"

Salem analyzed his scowl in full, lingering from his chest to his clenched jaw. Gold flickered incandescently despite his brooding shadow, roaming to his eyes, then down to his lips, and then back up. Instead of tensing underneath his posture, she relaxed against the bark and craned her chin upwards.

"I fear many things, Korbyn," Salem declared. "But you are not one of them."

Korbyn scoffed, propelling off the tree and whirling away from her. His palms pressed against his face, a poor attempt to lessen the frustration. He exhaled after his deep inhale, running his hand through his hair before stuffing both palms in his pockets.

"I know what you are."

"And what am I?" Salem muttered with an implication of cognizance.

"An angel."

After a moment's pause, she finally spoke, "How did you know?"

"Even the vilest creatures are drawn to the light," Korbyn replied, turning in the direction of the camp.

As if fearful of his retreat, Salem called out with a mixture of fury and dejection, "And what if I am? What does it matter? Why would you let a demon decide your happiness? Only we can choose our destiny. It is our place to—"

Korbyn laughed, not intending his response to sound so belittling, but he couldn't help but recognize its irony. "Destiny is an illusion. Apparently, I can choose my path, but I inadvertently chose the darkest one, and I must walk it alone."

"Why?"

"Because I am a disease," Korbyn answered.

He left her alone in the darkness, desperately striving to rebuild the walls around his vulnerable heart.

FORTY-ONE.

Brinshire, the mining town to the north, would be overrun by a hoard of undead if Salem and the rest of the mercenaries didn't arrive in time.

They were close to the town when the setting sun closed on the horizon's extended, welcome arms. Light still shimmered across the valley, informing its residents they had but little time left of brilliance before it descended into darkness. Despite the moon's current absence, Salem somehow knew its scarlet hue would return.

She felt sorry for the horse she mounted, having to carry both Haven and Salem. Between Haven's hefty stature and Salem's plated armor, they were heavier than a usual rider. And the trek had proved gruesome, as they only stopped a handful of times to give their horses reprieve. Salem remained quiet for most of the trip, dwelling in a mixture of sad thoughts and foreboding trepidation.

"Something's bothering you," Haven declared.

At the moment, their group dallied next to a small pond, endowing the horses with an interval from their hasty expedition. The steeds fed upon the grass, remaining ignorant of their riders' apprehension. They lingered not too far from the northern road, still able to see their route as they stood amongst butterfly weeds on the outskirts of the water's edge.

"I'm fine," Salem snapped, having little energy to conceal her true feelings.

"Really, Say?" Haven questioned.

Korbyn and Oakley tended to their horse, speaking to each other in hushed whispers. Gilben and Veeris stood on the opposite side of the water, with the dwarf offering his consoling presence to Veeris' unending silence.

Salem sighed. "Fine, other than the obvious things that are bothering me, I was talking to Korbyn last night and well," she stumbled. "He says we won't be together."

"Wait, you two still aren't together?" Haven inquired.

Salem gawked, taken aback by his bluntness. "What? No. Why would you think that?"

The expression upon the half-orc's face was almost amusing, his head craned to the side and his eyebrows lifted, overcoming his usual deadpan. "Really?" For the first time since Andrid's passing, he huffed with a small smile, though it was quickly replaced by a shake of his head. "Come on, Say. I don't think I need to explain myself."

Salem brushed the horse's snout with her hand, hiding the embarrassment and the sadness that resulted. "Well, we aren't together, and it looks like we never will be."

Haven frowned. "I'm sorry. Why?"

"I don't know," she replied. "He said we weren't meant to be."

"According to whom?"

"I don't know." Salem sighed. "To him, I suppose. I think he assumes he's too dangerous."

"If it were Andrid..." Haven trailed off, peering into the surrounding forest. "I wouldn't let that stop me."

Salem stared, trying to respond, but was interjected by Korbyn's voice.

"Do you hear that?" Korbyn exclaimed, motioning towards the path with a pointed finger.

Everyone turned, pivoting towards the empty trail and listening for whatever he had heard. Quietness replied.

Korbyn analyzed the growing mist with a sight the rest of them couldn't comprehend. "There are people coming. A lot of them. Hide!"

They pulled their horses into the foliage. When they were deep enough, Salem stroked the nose of her horse, calming its neighs. They were concealed under so much darkness that she couldn't even see the rest of her party, as if they had been swallowed by the forest like a thick cloud.

The branches created a canopy with but a single crevice to peer through. Still, she saw and heard nothing approach. Silence swallowed their group, each struggling to remain noiseless amongst the ear-piercing silence. After several minutes, she eagerly wished to depart from the trees. She almost sought for Korbyn and demanded an explanation, until she saw the marching figures.

A group—no, an army of at least one thousand men and women carrying weapons marched down the path in strict unison. Horse-drawn wagons carried supplies, soldiers, and pulled large mangonels. They bore the flag of Esperin, their continuous march announcing their proclamation. They headed south, away from Brinshire. After a long time, when the soldiers finally disappeared, each of the mercenaries departed from the trees' embrace.

"Esperin soldiers? Where are they going?" Oakley wondered, speaking barely above a whisper, as if he was afraid the departed army could hear him.

Salem tightened her grip on the reins. "Let's hurry."

"The mercenaries of Kendra Dawn, you say. Thank you so much for everything you have done for the people!" a middle-aged man exclaimed after the mercenaries entered Brinshire, despite having no flag to declare their alliance. He carried the soot of his workday along his brow and wiped his wrinkles of any lingering sweat. "Are you wanting to stay the night? It's rather late. You're welcome to visit as long as you like. My wife works at the tavern and inn in town. I'm sure she could get you all free rooms for the night. Is the Arbiter with you?"

The man hadn't waited for her to answer any of his questions. Instead, he peered behind Salem towards the southern road, awaiting the legendary merc's appearance. With his distracted attention, Salem analyzed the town's defenses. This settlement was anything but safeguarded. It was an accumulation of buildings, huts, farms, and several mines that surrounded the base of the overarching hills. A poorly constructed and forgotten picket fence enclosed the entrance, with only the hills to protect the people on its sides. Towards the top of the western hill stood a tower with a bell, which appeared unused for the entirety of its existence.

"We're looking for your mayor. Where can we find them?" Salem urged, ignoring his previous question.

The townsman shrugged, placing a hand on her back and leading her further into the town towards the widest building, which Salem assumed was the tavern and inn. "Mayor Turlson? He's a bit of a lark, I'm afraid. Tends to go to bed before even the sun does." He waved it off, smiling and motioning to the inn. "But in the morning, I know he'd be happy to meet with you—"

"I'm afraid that this is urgent," Salem said, pivoting to fully face him. "This is about the war. We have to meet with him. Immediately."

At first, the man was a bit surprised by her directness, but then his tired body motioned towards the other end of town. "Very well, young lady. Across the way, closer to the northside, you'll see a three-story building with a tall chimney with a stable out front. If you need a place to stay tonight, please don't be afraid to come by the inn."

Salem forced a thankful smile despite her apprehension. "Thank you, sir," she said, ushering the others forward with her horse.

As they passed through the town, filled with smiling faces of the common folk, she tried not to imagine what each of the houses would look like if they were set ablaze by the flames of war.

They reached the home within a few moments. It was simplistic in design like the rest of the buildings, with a cobblestone base built upon two more stories of wooden planks and shingles on the roof. Several windows protruded separately on each side as well as a terrace above its main entrance. Standing even taller than the building was a stone chimney, no smoke emitting from within.

The mercenaries led the exhausted mares to the stables, feeding them properly before they approached the portico. Haven and Veeris stood behind the group, with Korbyn on the half-orc's other side. He had pulled up his hood before they entered the town, careful to avoid wandering eyes. Beside her, Oakley and Gilben smiled brightly, ensuring their support.

Salem knocked upon the door, hearing the metal hinges clanging in vulnerability. It made her frown. If—when the army attacks, these doors would fall instantly. Are they even prepared for the possibility?

When no one answered, she knocked even harder than the first time, utilizing the side of her palm to cause a louder reverberation.

"Coming, coming!" someone exclaimed from inside.

After several seconds, Salem heard a singular click before it swung open. Her frown deepened upon seeing the elderly man. He opened it with closed eyes and clothed in nothing but a sleeping cap and a long gown.

Finally, the mayor blinked a few times and scanned the warriors in front of him. Once the mucus had been rubbed away, he grabbed his spectacles and positioned them on the bridge of his nose.

"Oh, hello, young folk. Is there anything I can help you with? It's rather late, isn't it?" he questioned between a yawn.

"Mayor Turlson? My name is Salem, and these are my comrades. We come bearing news. We are the faction Kendra Dawn," Salem announced, almost referring to their absent flag.

Mayor Turlson perked up with recognition. "Ah! Yes, I have heard much about you," he replied, his eyes grazing over the rest of the group and then glancing at the sky. "Although, it is rather late. Is this something that can wait until the morning?"

Salem placed her foot in the way of the door's edge and pressed open the shabby wood. "Your town is in danger. An army is coming."

"I'm sorry, Lady Salem. I'm afraid that's just too difficult to believe," Mayor Turlson said with a frown, ushering his wife Silvia to pour more tea into his empty cup. She obliged with an unworried smile, tipping the steaming liquid into his ceramic mug. "We've been just fine here in Brinshire. The soldiers have been so nice and encouraging when they stop by."

Salem frowned, ignoring the steaming cup of tea on the table, untouched by her hands. She sat in their living room with the rest of her friends, informing the mayor and his wife about the approaching army.

"Please, just call me Salem," she insisted. "And we are telling you the truth. An army is coming, filled with creatures called undead. They were once living people now turned into ravenous monsters. They're on their way here right now." Her leg bounced uneasily, and she endeavored to control her tone.

Gilben placed a palm upon her knee, coercing her fidgets into a dull rhythm. The dwarf inhaled deeply, followed by a gentle exhale. Usually, Salem would have breathed in tandem, but this time, it failed to relieve her jitteriness.

"What Salem is tryin' ta say is tha' it wou'd be in everyone's best interests if we evacuated the town," Gilben stated. "We've been on the front lines. We met with Emperor Wymond of Avernos recently, 'nd he dismissed Kendra Dawn as a neutral party—"

"Does that mean the war is over? How marvelous!" the old man stated, grabbing his wife's hand and shaking it with an encouraging grin.

Salem clenched the arms of her chair. "You're not listening!"

The couple recoiled, still clasping onto each other's wrinkled hands.

"The war is not over," Salem insisted. "The worst is about to begin. An army is coming straight for Brinshire and the mines. You all are in danger."

The mayor waved off her concerns, taking another sip of his tea. "Nonsense!" Before she could repeat herself, the mayor continued. "Why would they send Avernos soldiers if we don't have any more decidite?"

"What?" Korbyn hissed, ice practically spitting from his lips.

The couple reeled from his tone.

"I-I said we don't have any more decidite," Mayor Tulson repeated, peering between his wife and the mercenaries. "The mines have been cleared of the ore. The soldiers even went into the mines and checked themselves. They brought what was left to the capital so they could forge it. The king informed us that they have skilled blacksmiths that can mold the metal into weapons. It appears that's how we've won the war!"

"I told you, the war is not over," Salem declared. "Avernos soldiers are on their way here right now!"

"The Avernos Empire hasn't even breached the border! How could they possibly reach past the fortresses along Exonia Creek?" the mayor asked.

Salem analyzed Gilben's concerned face and then back to the elder. "Yes they have," she replied, leaning forward in her chair. "Both Fort Silvercrest and Fort Runswhick have fallen to the Avernos Empire. Fort Silvercrest was taken first, around two months ago."

"Oh, deary, that's absurd! If that were true, surely we would have heard of such news." The elder leaned back into his chair, straightening the remaining curls of his receding hair. "The soldiers that were recently stationed here were sent away because we had nothing to fear!"

"How long ago was that?" Oakley prompted, sipping his tea just as fast as the mayor had.

"Less than a fortnight ago?" The mayor scratched his cheek as if in deep contemplation before regarding his wife. She replied with a brisk nod. "They took the decidite and encouraged us they were winning the war thanks to our town's hard work. They also stated they would be returning once they brought the ore back to the capital." The mayor chuckled. "Besides, if we really were in trouble, our dear king wouldn't leave our town without protection."

Their amused laughs sent chills up Salem's spine.

"The soldiers and the king have deceived you," she urged, leaning so far in her seat that it might have tipped forward if not for her poise. "Your town is in danger. An army of undead is coming."

"And why would the king lie?"

"Because if the Kingdom of Esperin evacuated their town, the Avernos soldiers would know they were plotting a counterstrike," Korbyn explained as his face dropped, realization coursing through eyes of ivory. "The soldiers along the road."

"This was a trap. Esperin plans to retake Fort Silvercrest amidst the confusion, and they plan to sacrifice an innocent town to do it," Salem added, horror trailing her chapped lips.

The mayor and his wife didn't laugh this time; instead, they rattled in fear and confusion.

"Utter nonsense," Mayor Turlson protested. "The Herald of Light would never do something so foul-hearted! He is our king!" He stood from his chair, disregarding his cane. "And I will not stand idly by and let you all speak ill of him!" He glowered, his elderly voice cracking with urgency. "Kendra Dawn, I demand you all to leav—"

A hurried knock originated from the door.

"By the Heavens!" Mayor Turlson huffed. His wife strode to the door and opened it, allowing the visitor to peer inside. "Now is not a good time—"

"Mayor Turlson. Soldiers are approaching the town," a boy no older than sixteen interrupted. He heaved, sweat dripping from his brow.

Mayor Turlson stood up straighter. "See? I told you—"

"Th-they've come bearing the Avernos flag, sir," the boy stammered. "But something's wrong. They brought an army of monsters."

By the time they all emerged from the house, they could see the hill overlooking the town from the south. Approaching was an army of dead bodies. They fumbled and staggered, some tripping and falling down the incline, jostling each other like rapacious creatures. They dripped with saliva, gore, and murderous intent.

Somehow, from this distance, Salem swore she could smell their putrid insides that leaked from their wounds as they traversed the lands betwixt them.

In the back of the hoard, surrounded by an army of Avernos soldiers, was a man. He wore black cloth, with a scepter extended in his raised hand. A stone of gilded decidite glowed with holy energy, ushering the army forward in utter chaos.

The Revelation King.

From the east, an orb of red illuminated their path and lit Brinshire in a hue of crimson, foreshadowing the matching sea of blood that would soon spoil the land. As the hoard approached, the Blood Moon reminded her that there was no such thing as farewell.

FORTY-TWO.

"H-how did they get here so quickly?" Oakley stuttered. "They shouldn't have known about the attack. We took the letter!"

Gilben responded, keeping one hand curled around the hilt of his broadsword. "The emperor most likely dispatched more than one. In case it got lost or someone intervened."

"What do we do?" the mayor asked with desperation.

Everyone stared at Salem, who stood in paralyzed horror and failed to reply.

"Boy," Haven hissed, demanding the messenger's attention.

Korbyn watched the frightened boy shudder from Haven's guttural voice, shirking underneath the half-orc's looming shadow. With Haven's intense gaze, the boy adjusted his feeble stature into a feigned, rigid composure. Even with a straightened back, he couldn't hide his trembling.

"Y-yes, sir?"

"Do you have any horses?" Haven pressed.

"Horses?" the boy echoed.

"Yes! Answer the damn question."

The boy's eyes drifted. "Y-yes, two, but they're only draft horses—"

"Good. Retrieve them and bring them to the entrance of the town. Alert the townspeople as quick as possible." Haven turned back towards the mayor, who mirrored the younger boy's trepidation. "Do you have any guards? Any soldiers? Anyone who's had experience in the military?"

The mayor began to sweat under the moon's light, failing to internalize his growing panic. "W-we don't have any guards. We're but a small mining town. But there's Lucas and Meribeth. They are retired soldiers—"

Haven jerked his chin at the boy. "Grab any able fighters, men and women who could fight against the army. Find Lucas and Meribeth and tell them to organize the people. Have them grab any weapons they can find—pickaxes, knives and even pots for shields if you don't have any other options. Just grab whatever you can and meet the rest of us at the entrance of the town."

The boy nodded shakily before sprinting from the house.

"What should I do?" the mayor questioned, before the mercenaries departed. He leaned into the arms of his more stable wife, shaking from a mixture of age and dread.

Korbyn watched as Salem stopped, grasping onto her locket.

"Pray to Elohim, and hope that He hears you," she whispered. As she ran past him without a glance, Korbyn witnessed the army approach.

When the mercenaries reached the end of the town, the undead were closing the gap between them. There were around one thousand undead and a small army of soldiers in the back, guarding the mage that conducted their advance.

Fortunately, the townsfolk reacted hastily. People as young as twelve and as old as sixty gathered, heeding orders despite their fear. Haven ordered them around with a sense of leadership Korbyn had never seen before, dividing the people into groups and distributing the improvised weapons they were able to gather.

As Korbyn analyzed the wilderness, standing at the town's entrance, he saw a form with a dark cape fluttering through the breeze. The fallen angel clutched a scythe of bone and gilded decidite, analyzing Korbyn behind the shadow of his hood. Azrael.

When the others approached his side, the devil offered a glance before returning his attention to the forest. Then, the Reaper disappeared.

"Are we going to die?" Oakley whispered as they stood side by side, staring at the approaching army.

Korbyn noticed Salem was surprisingly quiet, stagnant amongst them with an avoidant gaze.

"If we do, it won't be without a fight," Haven declared.

Korbyn was surprised by his proactivity in comparison to the last several nights, where he hung his head in unbridled brooding, though he couldn't blame the half-orc, especially when he was guilty of the same. It was as if Haven knew he was going to die, ready to rejoin Andrid in the mysteries of the afterlife.

"Salem and Veeris, you two will stay behind on the defensive. Salem, your magical barriers can act as fortifications for the town," Haven demanded. "Veeris, you need to stay here and back her up and the townspeople. If you both can specifically aid the ones gathered to fight, you may give them the confidence they need against the undead."

Oakley glanced up at Haven. "And the rest of us?"

Haven examined the approaching army. "We can't take them all, but if we can break through the undead on horseback, and we may be able to reach their leader and cut him down. The soldiers might reply with confusion," he urged, motioning towards the back line.

"The Revelation King," Korbyn said, watching the mage instruct the monsters with raised arms. "If he dies, the undead might also fall."

"Or maybe even attack the Avernos soldiers, if they resort ta their natural instincts," Gilben agreed.

Oakley took a deep breath and sighed, retrieving a poison from his belt. He injected the toxin into the secret crevices of his blades, preparing their use. Haven and Gilben also drew their own weapons, stalking forward towards the approaching army.

As Korbyn followed, his pocket grew heavy, as though the burning brilliance of the golden ring seared a hole. He stopped, reaching into it to settle its demanding churns. It shaped a moment of contemplation, but it was brief. Instead of retrieving it, he dropped it and shadowed his allies.

"No."

The group turned. Salem confronted them with fists and furrowed brows, a challenger facing an adversary.

Haven frowned at her. "Salem, I know you want to fight on the front lines, but we need you here to—"

"I wasn't talking about that," she replied, not taking her eyes off Korbyn. "I'm speaking to you."

Korbyn raised a brow. "No?"

"No." Salem huffed, storming forward until she stood before him, raising her chin to alleviate the difference in their height.

"You're going to have to be more specific," Korbyn said, gazing back towards the approaching undead. "We don't have time—"

"You're wrong," she protested, seemingly unaware of their limited time. "I can't say for sure whether destiny is real or not, and I can't say for sure whether the road you have chosen is the darkest one, but I do know that you will not be walking this road alone, Korbyn."

"Salem—"

"Even if you choose to venture forward on your own and disregard me completely," Salem interjected, prodding his chest with the point of her finger. "I will follow you. Even if you walk the path that you claim is surrounded by shadows, I will illuminate it. Even if I lack any form of light, I will be by your side. That is something I have decided, and you won't stop me."

Korbyn couldn't prevent the laughs from escaping his lips. He shifted his gaze, shaking his head as a smile crept upwards. Not once did her contact stray from his, for deep confidence bestowed up on her.

"You're serious?" Korbyn asked, his shoulders slackening. "You're absolutely crazy, Salem."

Salem smiled, cupping his face with a stroke of her thumb. "If vile creatures are drawn to the light, then what does that say about the sun?"

Salem leaned up, planting her lips on top of his own. A spark coursed through him in sharp waves, attacking his muscles in strange spasms. It was intoxicating, as though he had just been immersed in heated water after being out in the cold for too long. It traveled from his mouth to the rest of his body. Instead of the feeling fading away, it only increased the longer their lips touched. He wrapped his arms around her and pulled her in closer.

When they parted, Salem stared up at him, and Korbyn could see the worry and passion that glistened in her eyes. She grabbed his hand and interlocked it with hers. "Please don't die."

Korbyn drifted backwards out of her reach, and she kept her arm outstretched, as if needing more of his touch. He kept eye contact with her for several steps, analyzing every detail of her appearance. Despite the odds of their survival, he couldn't stop smiling.

"I won't die if you don't," Korbyn replied with a smirk.

Salem smiled back at him. He didn't care that the sun didn't support their future, for a bright light still guided his way.

Two men brought forward draft horses, appearing somehow both robust and agile. Haven grabbed the reins of both with a nod, taking the brown steed with a dark, black mane. He stretched the other lead towards Korbyn, motioning the horse in his direction. It was so white that he would describe it as pale, with a matching mane and pair of unassuming eyes.

Haven helped lift Gilben to the back of the horse, followed by his own rise to the steed's saddle. Korbyn did the same for Oakley, interlacing his fingers together so he could form a step. When both sat comfortably on the saddle, they redirected their mares to the approaching army of the undead.

Korbyn withdrew his blade and stretched his arms and shoulders. He realized he was bound with endless energy and confidence that didn't exist before. He felt a newfound strength that even surpassed the effects of the Blood Moon.

"I'm honored to fight alongside you all," Haven stated, drawing his axe with a clenched jaw.

"As am I, lads. It's been an honor," Gilben said, gripping his broadsword.

"Yeah, I guess you guys are alright," Oakley joked, retrieving a short bow from the holster on his back. "If we're going down swinging, can we at least make it difficult for them? I'd rather be remembered as a hero or something."

The undead gagged on every inhaled breath, despite their discretionary heaves. It sounded like they were choking. Their gurgles shifted into various pitches, as though each tried to sing to their own melody, but each ignoring the rest, like an accompaniment fighting for dominance on a grand stage. Their incessant cries didn't drown out the stomping of their advancing footsteps.

If the demon said anything, Korbyn didn't hear it. Instead, he squeezed his legs against the horse's side and motioned it forward, with Haven and Gilben following.

"If it's the Hells they want, then let's give it to them," Korbyn said.

Hoping to instill confidence into his allies, Korbyn ushered his horse first, initiating the battle of the undead and the unprepared.

Korbyn focused on breaking the outer wall of undead with the clomping of his horse. He crashed the beast into the first bodies, causing two of the undead to slam into the ground on either side of the horse's shoulders. The creatures hit the dirt so hard that their innards burst from their insides, writhing from the impact and their spillage.

He continued, bursting through the cluster of the undead, their deteriorating meat notwithstanding the impact of the horse's gallop. Korbyn swung his blade towards an unready creature, the blade slicing straight through its dangling jaw. From behind him, Korbyn heard Oakley retrieve his bow. Then, arrows whizzed through the air like a starling's cry. Korbyn saw several undead hit the ground from his peripheral.

Haven and Gilben followed at their side, penetrating the advancement of the undead from another angle. The undead fell and toppled from the steed's gallop, both warriors hacking at the monsters at their sides. Foul viscera sprayed into the night sky like upwards rain, and the gurgles of the undead didn't cease when they fell to the mud.

Korbyn's loyal steed parted the sea of grime and decay. As the creatures reached to grapple the horse as they passed, Korbyn swung his blade on each side of the mount and chopped off their reaching appendages. Instead of precise strikes, he swung in a flurry to attack as many as he could, passing by a dozen in a matter of seconds. As more undead fell, they excreted a putrid smell when the flaps of their loose skin unraveled.

"Gross!" Oakley yelled, choking on a gag.

They raced forward as fast as their robust horses could carry them. Luckily, these draft horses were much larger than normal stallions. As they sprinted through the mass of undead, they crashed through multiple bodies at a time, some even splattering with their thinner skin and bursting into pools of guts and intestines. Multiple forms reached up to them but were laid to waste when the horses crossed their paths.

Another undead raced forward, one of dwarven heritage. Korbyn recognized it as a previous volunteer of Kendra Dawn. It was small in height like normal dwarves but lacked the stockiness of one. Its approach was disorderly as it threw forward its shoulders to direct its run, as if its arms didn't work. Its matted hair stuck to its face, clinging to its slack jaw. There were protrusions caused by fangs and claw marks of a large beast, which Korbyn guessed was a manticore. It seemed unaware of its spilling intestines and decaying reek, attacking without the use of its appendages.

Korbyn flipped his blade in a reverse grip before they passed it. He sunk his blade into its shoulder. With a valiant strength, he lifted the smaller creature and threw it to the side, its body slamming into a couple more approaching undead. They fell in a heap, unaware how to untangle themselves from one another.

"Watch out!" Gilben cried out.

Korbyn hadn't seen one flanking them from the other side.

An undead ran diagonally at their horse, charging forward in a protected wall of iron. It stood slightly larger than a common person. Its cries were gruff, and it sputtered as though its pharynx was full of water.

Korbyn slashed towards its neck, but the pure force of the undead's lunge was too strong. It sent the horse and its riders careening from the impact. Korbyn and Oakley tumbled to the ground, rolling several paces into the mud and away from the horse. When Korbyn gathered himself to his knees, he fixated on the pale stallion.

Before the horse could stand, a myriad of the fiends tackled it to the ground. It neighed and kicked, followed by whines. The undead sank their teeth into any part they could reach, some attempting to tear out its throat while others resorted to its underbelly and legs. They struggled to swallow its bitten-off parts, as if having an internal need to consume it. It seemed like a desperate effort to pilfer its life for their own. Tubes of intestines and meat spewed from its opened gut, the horse kicking and rearing to free itself from the pile that toppled it. Eventually, the horse's neighs filtered out and became still.

"Are they...eating it?" Oakley gasped, scooting away from the creatures.

Korbyn didn't reply, distracted by more charging monsters. They ran towards them like a herd of rampaging animals. If the duo didn't move out of the way, they would be trampled.

"Move!" Korbyn yelled to Oakley.

They fumbled to their feet. Korbyn lost Oakley in the flood of bodies that rushed past him. The undead hurtled passed him and trudged towards the town behind him.

"They're going straight for Brinshire," Korbyn whispered to no one in particular. "I have to stop the Revelation King directly."

The faux king and his artificial crown. When will he realize he will not hear the Song of Abaddon and the bells of the Revelation War? the demon whispered.

A mist rose from swirling debris caused by the stampede of undead bodies. It hadn't been so much of a hindrance for them when they were seated upon the horse. Now, it thickened like a fog of war, preventing normal eyes from peering through it with full clarity. Luckily, Korbyn was anything but normal, and he could decipher the undead by the hues of their gray flames. In the back of the army, he found the flickering blaze of the Revelation King.

"Get off me!" Oakley yelled from within the masses.

Korbyn cast his magical gaze in the direction of the voice. On the ground, underneath several monochrome energies, was what he believed to be Oakley.

A cry of pain shot through the sky thereafter, his desperation conflicting with the bodies that piled on top of him. Around him, even more groups of the undead charged towards Oakley's rebelling flame.

"Oakley!" Korbyn yelled, lunging for him.

With an undead racing beside him, Korbyn adjusted the turn of his heel and slammed his body into it. It toppled over, scrambling to figure out how to use its feet to rise again.

Korbyn grabbed a couple undead in the pile and yanked them backwards. As they tumbled, he swung his blade, slicing through their necks. He cut through a couple more of the undead until one was left, lying on top of Oakley, who was scrambling for his life. The monster's teeth were sunken into his shoulder, tearing off pieces of skin.

Careful not to tear the creature off in fear of pulling his friend's flesh, Korbyn grabbed onto its remarkably tough jaw and heaved. Oakley retrieved one of his knives and stabbed the undead in the throat several times. Korbyn tossed the undead to the side, ignoring the guts that sprayed onto their faces. As more charged in Oakley's direction, Korbyn swung viciously at any that entered his range.

"Freaking damn it!" Oakley cried, holding onto his arm and gazing at the deep wound carved by teeth.

"Can you fight?" Korbyn yelled back, piercing his blade straight into the face of a gnome, who was covered in nothing but two layers of garb and spillage of his own core. He twisted the blade and sliced left, cutting straight through its skull.

"Yeah, it just freaking hurts!" Oakley answered, pulling out his other dagger. He dodged to the side and pierced an undead's chin. Before it could wrap its arms around Oakley's form, he lifted his heel and slammed it into its stomach. Ribs split and cracked underneath his thrust, and the weakness of its older form toppled its torso completely forward, as if it was no longer attached to the rest of its bottom half. It fell to the ground when it failed to stand upright, unable to rise again. "Where are Haven and Gilben? I can't see anything!"

Korbyn shifted his eyes to the left, where he last spotted the duo. At some point, they had also lost their horse. Both were standing side by side. Without knowing them, Korbyn would have thought that they would intervene with each other's fighting styles as both warriors held overly large weapons. Instead, they fought like choreographed soldiers, striking at various undead. They alternated opponents, knocking down one when the other missed, all while not even speaking to one another.

"They're fine, for now," Korbyn replied, standing in front of Oakley when three more undead approached.

Korbyn swung at the first two that led the small party. He thought it might have sliced clean through, but the edge of his blade sunk into the second one's shoulder, rendering him unable to extract it. Korbyn pulled back his fist and smashed it into the undead's nose. It fell into the third behind it, and it gave him the ability to yank out the steel from its inert position.

"How are we supposed to get through this army?" Oakley questioned, avoiding the grasp of another undead and stabbing its temple. "I can't even see through this fog!"

Korbyn found the Revelation King behind the army of the undead, golden magic whisking around gilded decidite caged in his scepter along with his colorless energy inside his chest.

"I can," Korbyn replied, as more enemies ran towards them. "If we can manage to fight through this and reach the Revelation King, we can end this!"

Gilben and Haven eventually emerged from the thickness of the haze. Haven bellowed a rallying cry, swinging his axe through several torsos that lacked any form of protective armor. Gilben's momentum was slower than Haven's, but strong in his own right. The dwarf brandished his broadsword into numerous legs of the undead, mucous spraying like a waterfall crashing into stagnant rocks. Both mercenaries rejoined Korbyn and Oakley's, strengthening their defenses as war raged on.

When Korbyn halted in between the waves of approaching creatures, he glanced back at the undead they had slain. Already, almost fifty of them had fallen from their assault. He took a moment to catch his breath, not leaving himself vulnerable for a sudden attack. Korbyn couldn't help but let a smirk creep up to his face. Maybe they had a chance.

His grin immediately faded.

The fallen undead behind them squirmed under the intensity of the Blood Moon. They began to rise, disregarding their heads and other body parts that lay forgotten in the mud. Their groans seemed to call out for the red moon's aid as saliva dripped down their bloodied chins.

When each of the previously slain undead rose to their feet, the warriors' shoulders slumped.

"How is that possible?" Oakley inquired, his voice and determination wavering.

Korbyn pivoted towards the army, meeting the glower of the Revelation King. His arms were raised, with radiating energy seeping around his hands. When Korbyn concentrated, he could see magical strings linked from the gilded decidite, to the Revelation's fingertips, then to each of the undead.

Amongst the fifty they had previously slain, there were several that Korbyn noticed, a group of undead in Gilben's direction. They scurried from the dirt and mud beneath their fallen forms, endeavoring to scramble by clawing at the ground to pull them forward. Despite their attempts, they couldn't join their kin upright.

"Their legs—cut them down! It will halt their approach!" Korbyn strode forward. "Follow my lead!"

FORTY-THREE.

Salem's heartbeat pounded too loudly, like a drum of war accompanied by marching soldiers. Even now, she had trouble calming her breaths. She couldn't even imagine how reddened her cheeks had become. The comfort of Korbyn's presence and the coolness of his skin had been like a battle she didn't mind losing.

Before she lowered her hand, watching his retreating form, Salem saw something on her finger that hadn't been there before.

At first, she thought she had imagined it, for she was unsure when her glove had been removed. Upon her bare hand, an object of divine beauty glistened even brighter than the sun and moon it imitated. A ring of gold and diamonds greeted her. An aureate moon, seated above a thin gallery, longed to embrace the sun. Despite how close they were, they failed to directly touch each other, as if they had gotten so close but were destined to remain apart. Salem thought when it shifted sideways that they might have touched for a moment, but it was only momentary. It reminded her of an eclipse.

Despite the lack of words between them, Korbyn's heart called for an unspoken promise, one that Salem would never forget. She lifted the ring to her lips, allowing a brief solace amongst the grimness.

"I promise, Korbyn," she whispered, knowing he couldn't hear her. "We will reunite. That I swear."

When her voice quieted, Veeris severed the reprieve.

"Salem, it's time," he urged.

"Right," Salem responded, her warm smile faltering. She slid her glove back over her hand, gripping it until it slid comfortably over her fingers.

If they were going to win this day, they would need Elohim.

"Give me a moment," Salem whispered to Veeris.

He nodded, preparing himself for the upcoming battle by retrieving a piece of decidite.

When the rest of the mercenaries and the undead army collided, Salem lowered herself to her knees and rested upon her ankles. She took her locket in her hands and immersed herself in a moment of respite, her thoughts becoming intertwined with her deep breaths. Despite the chaos around her, she thrust her mind into a prayer of meditation. She focused on Elohim and His holy light, calling out to Him in a last, desperate plea.

She imagined herself in front of the Heavens' gates, its golden shine cast upon an endless sea of clouds. She could almost see the bright light of holy radiance greeting her arrival. For a moment, in the depths of her vision, she felt her wings return in their former glory, lifting herself in a breeze.

"Elohim," Salem whispered, analyzing its fortifications. "Elohim, I have been praying to You with no answer. You have sent me down here in search of the blades. I will find them, but I cannot find them amongst a world of ruin."

Instead, the gates remained steadfast. She imagined the metal creaked with the passing silence, ignoring her presence.

"My Lord, I ask for your aid. I know not if this is some type of test that You have bestowed upon me, but I humbly ask that You disregard it. There are thousands of innocent lives that will die in this war without Your intervention. I know they demanded their freedom, but that was a choice of their ancestors. Please do not force the people to abide by the consequences of actions they can no longer control."

The quiet pained her ears, like an incessant ringing that failed to dissipate. Instead, it only seemed to increase in volume, riling her into impatience and restlessness. Salem shifted her placid hands into tightened fists.

"Elohim!" she yelled, wondering if she hadn't been loud enough. "Elohim! Where are you? I have called out to You time and time again, yet You ignore me! I have needed Your guidance and strength, and You have given me neither!"

Truly, Salem thought she would have heard His replies, yet still, not even the wind cut through the tension.

"Why?" she raged, rushing to the pristine gates. She wrapped her dirtied fingers around them and yanked, failing to pry them open with her mortal hands. "You sent me here on a sacred oath. How can I accomplish Your wishes if the world is torn asunder? I am begging You, please help us!"

Salem felt blood seeping through her ears, but when she rubbed them, attempting to alleviate the excruciating pain of the loud ringing, her fingers found no cause. However, when she regarded her hands, they were shaking. Fear and anger washed over her, as though buckets of ice and lava interchangeably had drenched the entirety of her form. She grasped tighter onto the gates, their golden shine becoming tainted from her fingertips.

"Why have You betrayed them?" Salem screamed, her voice cracking in her desperate plea. "You created them, yet You deny their entry. You created them in Your image, yet You forsake them. They pray to You, yet You reply with closed ears. What have they done to deserve this?"

Nothing.

"Fine!" Salem shouted, propelling herself away from the stagnant gates, secretly wishing she could destroy them completely. She turned, tears threatening a familiar descent. "If You will not save them, then I will do it myself."

When her meditation ceased, Salem's eyes once again observed the tainted and forgotten world, lacking Elohim's presence. Her apprehension stifled her confidence when she saw the panicked expressions of the townsfolk. Children too young to carry a sword wavered from the heaviness of the steel within their palms. The elderly quivered as they grasped onto their garden rakes like canes. The middle-aged folk paced anxiously, fumbling with their makeshift armor.

She rose from her seated position and turned to Veeris, who awaited her instructions.

"We're on our own," Salem stated solemnly.

Veeris nodded, his face unreadable past his stoic expression. When he lifted his hands, with only six fingers left amongst both, six blades appeared by his side. He thrust them outwards, creating a blockade in front of the town's extemporary soldiers. Salem drew her own longsword and shield, raising the pointed edge of her blade into the sky, a proclamation of war and defiance.

A magical barrier, nearing an eighth of a mile in either direction, emerged from her holy spell. It surrounded the entrance of the town, glowing in a golden radiance. If she couldn't call upon the Golden Gates, she would create them herself, for the people needed to have faith, even when she lacked it.

She took a deep breath and spun towards the crude defensive line behind her, mostly filled with people who had never seen war in their lives. There were nervous parents, older men and women, and young people who were nearly considered adults forming in lines, all standing barely upright. They were all covered with makeshift armor of pots, pans, and any supplies they could gather.

So many of them were going to die.

"The Kingdom of Esperin has failed you!" Salem bellowed. She could sense Veeris cringe at her side. "King Alecain knew the Avernos soldiers were coming. He cared not to fortify your town. He withdrew his soldiers for what he deemed was a greater purpose: the security of his kingdom. While you all fell victim to the blades of the enemy, he would reclaim a fort in his name. After your hard work, your dedication, your love for your kingdom, the king and soldiers left you all with nothing but empty promises and bare caverns."

The townsfolks' shoulders dipped, their trepidation spreading from one to the next. They broke out in whispers like a plague. Some that stood on weaker legs turned towards the town in hopes of a possible escape; however, the barrier stood in their way. Before panic could completely overtake them, Salem spoke again.

"But you do not need them."

The town responded with hushed voices, turning to fully give her their attention. She stood with raised shoulders and an elevated chin, an aura of power and confidence trailing from her pristine form. Despite the protrusions in her armor, it gleamed with a brilliance that enthralled them.

"You do not need selfish kings. You do not need soldiers who abandoned you. In the face of the undead, these same soldiers who left you behind would have run from this very fight."

Among their confusion, Salem continued.

"Every mercenary of Kendra Dawn is equivalent to one hundred soldiers. If the kingdom provided five hundred men, then we offer you the power of six hundred. If the kingdom gave you soldiers with inexperience, then we offer you professional monster hunters. If the kingdom responded to your troubles with a blind eye, then it is Kendra Dawn who will slay your enemies."

Salem's blade glistened against the radiant energy of her golden partition, and she raised its sharpened edge towards the north, straight at Esperin's capital, Umberfall.

"You cannot rely on greater powers to aid you. They tread upon their fallen people like stepping stools and then sit upon their thrones of selfishness and neglect. They manipulate you with strings, controlling you like puppets and feigning their care for their own benefit, but you do not have to be victims today! Instead of wallowing in self-pity or fear, you can act upon your own vengeance!"

Salem looked around, seeing their faces glow with a new-found strength they were unaware they had. Their postures straightened as they appeared amongst each other with nods of approval.

"Today, you are the luckiest people in the Kingdom of Es-perin. Today, you have Kendra Dawn, the strongest mercenary band in all Terrisae to fight alongside you. For when kingdoms fall, we will still be here, and we will continue to serve you." Salem raised her blade in the air, and some of the voices of others fol-lowed, whispering in affirmations and gathering their strength in accordance. "You must fight for your town, fight for your survival, and fight to live on to remind the king of his failures! When they write the epic of today in the books of history, it is the town of Brinshire that will be remembered. Today, you are protectors. Today, you are warriors. Today, you are heroes!"

Salem pumped her arm in the air one last time. "For Brin-shire!"

"For Brinshire!" they yelled unanimously. Their cries carried into the sky, and Salem hoped Elohim heard them, despite know-ing He would do nothing about it.

Salem charged first, leading the townsfolk into the skirmish.

Veeris projected his blades forward to stay in the front, acting as martial piercing blockades to slow down the enemies. At the same time, the undead that managed to slip by Korbyn and the others barreled towards them with their arms held high.

Salem reached the first undead and spun on her heel, preparing enough momentum to cleanly slice through the creature's torso. Blood and innards sprayed from the intensity of her strike, and the creature fell over in a heap of its own guts. At the fall of the first, the rallying of the people behind her increased, and the fighting ensued.

The next creature that darted in her direction met the bluntness of her shield. Salem knocked it away with such force that it stumbled into the proximity of one of Veeris' ethereal blades. His weapon swung with power and velocity, striking the creature diagonally through its torso. The undead foamed and gurgled as it fell into a pile of remains.

With three blades on her left and three on her right, most of the undead's approaches were halted. Instead of racing past her, numerous creatures ran straight through the swinging swords. Occasionally, several undead would get past them and run towards Brinshire. The townsfolk were there to meet them.

They worked together, combating their numbers with their own. At least four people at a time would career towards an approaching creature and attack it. With some of the numbers of the undead dwindling, they caved to the strength of the town. They knocked down a single monster easily, allowing some of the younger men and women to end them with a swift blow.

Salem realized severing their heads wouldn't stop them. As soon as one of them had been beheaded, it began to try and stand back up. Realizing this, one of the men cut off its legs. Due to their deteriorating bodies and lack of armor over its thighs, it detached from the rest of its body. The undead fumbled to stand without its legs, but it couldn't rise again.

"Stay together in groups and aim for their legs!" Salem shouted to their defenses.

They responded with another rally, as if they hadn't previously been riddled with fear. Salem felt herself smiling.

Maybe, just maybe, they didn't need rulers after all.

FORTY-FOUR.

The waves of undead seemed endless.

Korbyn continued his onslaughts and ventured forward, no matter how much his body rallied against him. He couldn't hear the cries of the fighting, or the groans of the approaching undead, but only his loud beating heart. He swung with every pound, striking in cadence despite how promptly it was pulsing. His newfound strength guided by the red moon's gaze was now a familiar sensation. He slammed into a creature so hard that it flew back, flying into nine other rushing bodies. They all fell in a pile, and he heard their brittle bones breaking underneath the crash.

However, even the aid of the Blood Moon had its limits.

Korbyn sank to one knee as his foot dragged through the dirt. Exhaustion tugged on his loud heart, striving to catch up with his demanding lungs. They insisted on air, but he felt like he didn't have much to give.

He focused on his allies, who gathered to fight with a greater advantage. Haven led in the front and Gilben and Oakley followed his pursuit. They each struck with practiced and composed accuracy. However, Korbyn could tell they were beginning to tire. Even Haven, who did the best to hide his fatigue, had slowed with every swing.

Feeble fowls of a feather flock forever, the demon whispered, humming a chuckle at its own amusement.

If Korbyn charged directly for the Revelation King on his own, would he be able to kill him? Would his allies survive without an added number? Even if Korbyn disregarded the undead, could he combat the Avernos soldiers waiting for them? Korbyn scoffed, knowing the answer.

Knowledge can be stronger than steel or numbers. When is it that you'll release your true power from its cage? the demon challenged.

"I don't need your help," Korbyn huffed out. "I don't need your power."

A sound rattled in his mind, like a lock against a closed cage.

Birds should not be held in cages. They were meant to soar and ascend. Unlock these restraints and break free from this mortal form, the demon whispered.

"No," Korbyn breathed out, hacking his blade forward again.

He was too tired to swing downward in fear he would fall in that direction. Korbyn sluggishly severed the head off an undead, the threads of its skin looking like tendrils as they split and tore from its neck. It groaned in defiance, reaching out for anything it could grasp onto. It pulled on Korbyn, and he fought against it. He pushed off the creature and stumbled, swinging his blade through another's leg when it raced past him. It writhed in anger, squirming along the bloodied dirt. With one leg, it failed to rise from its fallen position.

Several more slammed into Korbyn's shoulder, and he swung as they did. His steel met air as he struggled to find his breath. It was lost in a grand sea, the waters too thick and dark to see through. He felt like he had plunged into its depths, his lungs fighting against his loud beating heart.

Ah, a familiar tune of retribution, the demon cooed, as if it had been listening to a ballad around a campfire. Still, the cage rattled. *The realms will know your vengeance, little bird. Unlock the cage and gain the power you seek to strike down your enemies.*

"No!" Korbyn yelled, hoping his defiance would give him the strength he needed. As he raced forward to attack the next, he felt a pull from below him. The undead's flailing arms clawed at his ankle, and he stumbled forward.

And just like that, Korbyn faltered.

He fell, somehow able to tighten the hold on his blade to not lose it in the chaos. Several undead trampled over him. When he realized the mass of runners wouldn't soon alleviate, Korbyn covered his head to protect his face, absorbing the blows of trudging feet as they crushed his body.

The pain was immeasurable. Even though many lacked body parts and internal organs, the consistent trudging of their forms slammed into him. With one step from a heavier man clad in chainmail, Korbyn heard his ribs crack. He screeched in pain, hacking his blade upwards to halt the mob. He struck upwards, penetrating the opening of a soldier's leg. The blade cut all the way through the undead's calf, but it didn't prevent its movements. He tried to withdraw it, but from the force of the creature's run and the angle of Korbyn's pull, the steel snapped in half.

"Fuck!" Korbyn screamed, covering his arms over his face when one of the undead kicked him in the jaw.

When he tried to raise his body, more feet crashed into him, driving him back down into the mud. Another heel crashed into his temple, and the world spun. The haze turned black.

FORTY-FIVE.

Holy magic radiated from every one of Salem's strikes, exuberating certainty and precision. The townsfolk were trying to fight off the undead, relying on her fortification to protect the ones that couldn't. Even though most had no combat experience before this, they ran forward with assurance, combating the mass of wailing undead.

Salem blamed herself for every person that fell victim to these horrid creatures, failing to contest the sheer numbers. With every life lost, her heart ached in resounding agony. It was her that rallied them. She wanted to believe her own speech, but she couldn't neglect the overarching sensation of inevitable doom. These creatures planned to leave none alive, and it was highly probable all would succumb to this massacre.

With a battle cry of anger and rage, Salem dashed ahead of the civilians and hoped the undead would charge her instead of the vulnerable town. She slammed her shield forward, and the undead in front of her crumbled from her blow. She didn't need magic to collapse its bridle skin and bones.

Salem danced amongst the battlefield with grace and power, keeping her heels from touching the dirt for too long. Instead, she twirled and spun, like a hurricane of blades. With every swing, she took down two undead, their torsos toppling behind her. Before they hit the ground, she was already swinging at the next that approached. Instead of slowing down to assess the battlefield, she replied to their instinctual attacks with her own, forcing her body to move faster. Exhaustion could claim her afterwards.

When she couldn't extend her arm for a full swing due to the closeness of the monsters, she resorted to using her shield to push them back. Then, Salem struck with her longsword, slicing through them easily. With one attack, she pierced forward, penetrating an undead that hadn't been armored.

A civilian. A volunteer. A member of Kendra Dawn.

Salem ignored its face.

With an angry cry, she jammed the blade further and turned the edge sideways. She severed its torso completely, not watching it fall to the ground.

How could they do this? Salem questioned, feeling her blood boil beneath her sweaty skin. *How could they do this to innocent people? How deep does their selfishness run?*

And why wouldn't Elohim help them?

Cries of pain and fear sounded behind her. When she turned, she watched as one of the townsfolk fought alone. Multiple undead approached the man at once, tackling him to the ground. Their teeth cut through his skin with ease, consuming his body in such large bites that he didn't suffer too long.

She wanted to turn and help, but the next wave was on her. Multiple undead slammed into her with heavy armor, pushing her down into submission.

A yell pierced the sky as Salem bent her knees and pressed back. Despite their added strength, she knocked them away. Holy energy encircled her curled fists.

The four undead stumbled backwards. Their armor clanged with every shuffle, and they readjusted their postures to prevent their descension. They were covered from head to toe in steel, and Salem failed to locate a gap in the armor. Even though she couldn't see their faces, she could hear the gurgles echoing within their basinets.

They charged again. They were slower than the rest due to the hefty weight of their steel. Salem pushed past the first, crashing her shield into the second. Magic swirled from her, and she infused its radiance into her shield. She bludgeoned the shield straight into its legs, denting the poleyn. Bones cracked as its knees caved inward, and it toppled back and flailed, clutching the two approaching undead behind it. All three plummeted.

The first undead spun around and lunged, screeching at the top of its lungs. Salem barreled past it and lowered her form, tripping the creature with an extended leg. It toppled forward with a harsh clank. It struggled to raise upright, thrashing chaotically with its appendages.

Salem surged magic once more, striking the edge of her shield down into its back legs continuously. The steel dented and creaked, and blood spewed with every bout. After several attempts, she carved her way through steel and bone, severing its legs from the rest of its body.

The other three were beginning to rise. Before they could stand fully upright, Salem charged with a battle cry. Instead of attacking with her blade, she swung her shield like a hammer. Their armors caved from her magically enhanced strikes, and soon, each of their armors indented so abnormally that they were unable to bend their legs to strengthen their rise. They seethed underneath their indented helmets.

The next wave approached, just as large as the previous one. They clambered through the battlefield and debris, caring not for the fog that sought to deter them. Above her, the Blood Moon matched in ceaseless oppression. With each passing second, it felt as though the scarlet orb was draining her magical abilities. Heavy sweat coated every crevice of her armor, and the wild strands of her hair clung to her brow as she struggled for a full breath.

Her power was waning—and it was waning rapidly. If she was going to stop the hoard, Salem had one, last chance.

She stepped forward, initiating a distance betwixt herself and the innocents behind her. She listened carefully to the battlefield around her. She heard the abnormal cadence of footsteps of the approaching undead, the heavy breaths of the civilians, her dripping sweat, the clanging of iron, and the shifting of the winds as a storm threatened to brew.

"You formed me from nothing. You gifted me with power upon my creation and instructed me to do right with it," Salem whispered as she clutched her longsword. Her locket glowed, a radiant energy trickling in embers. She could feel its heat rising under her touch, and she channeled the divine energy from within. "Yet still You remain silent, despite the souls You created falling beneath You. If You will not come to their aid, then I will."

Salem raised her blade into the air, and just as if the Heavens' gates had been opened, a radiant glow pierced the sky.

The light was blinding. The advancing undead halted. Some slid across the dirt, others fell, but all writhed. They screamed and gurgled like drowning victims, as if wishing to escape the magical daylight that burned their skin. Instead of fleeing, they turned away and shielded their faces.

"Charge!" Salem roared.

The cries of the town resounded alongside hers, and they ran forward. With their makeshift weapons, the townsfolk knocked down the undead with ease.

Salem joined them. Instead of giving in to her exhaustion, she leaned into the adrenaline. She swiped at each and every undead that she could manage. Even with their armor, she maneuvered to locate vulnerable crevices or relied on her shield to knock them down, trying to dent their armor with her wavering energy.

A moment of solace appeared, and she heaved from lost breath. She could not see her allies on the battlefield due to the haze—except for one.

Amongst the battlefield, Korbyn plummeted. Before he could rise to his feet, a hoard of the monsters trampled upon their pre-established path. From her position, they seemingly crushed him, his form disappearing into the haze of blood and gore.

"Korbyn!" Salem screeched, tears rising to the bottom lids of her eyes.

Desperately, she struggled to remember the sound of his voice, the feeling of his embrace, the cadence of his laughter. For some reason, amongst the chaos and ruin, she couldn't recall it. Everything happened so fast that she hadn't been prepared to witness his death before her very eyes.

Salem trembled and gaped, pivoting to find Veeris.

"V-Veeris, Korbyn's gone, he's..." she cried, stifling a choke. Her jaw slackened at the scene before her when she finally located him.

Behind Veeris was a shadow, a man of a broad frame, with armor made of dark steel and intricate designs of swirling branches. He towered over Veeris, with a helmet resembling a bull with curled horns that extended his height to over two heads taller in comparison. An enlarged shadow blanketed Veeris completely. For a moment, it wasn't a man Salem saw, but a minotaur.

Within the soldier's grasp was a large war hammer, raised high above his head. Her attention flicked back to Veeris, and she saw something she feared even more than the soldier behind him—sadness, guilt, and apathy behind glazed eyes. Veeris' shoulders slacked.

"*Veeris!*" Salem screamed with a crack in her voice. She reached out to him, but her wobbling knees failed her. The poleyn over her knees slammed into the dirt after her stumble.

When the war hammer swung and crashed into Veeris from behind, his body caved beneath it.

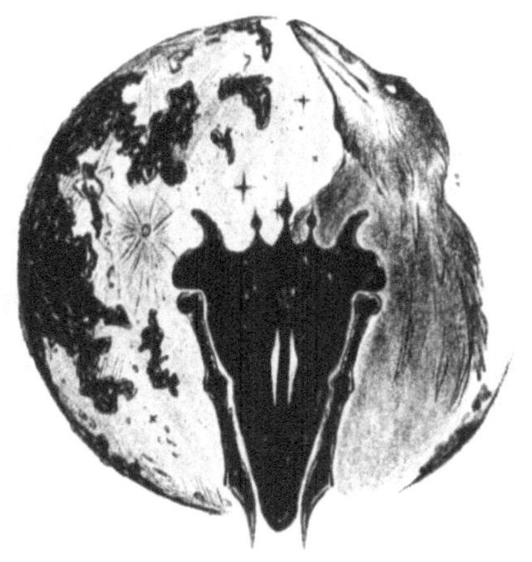

FORTY-SIX.

When Korbyn opened his eyes, he was no longer on the battlefield of Brinshire. He sprawled on his side among a grand forest, with trees surrounding him on either side. Open plains greeted him, immersed in a thick layer of mist that hovered just above the ground. Thick roots covered the lands and interlaced like multiple threads, each interwoven like longing lovers. It made the forest resemble a single entity rather than multiple formations of various trees. They hummed in low vibrations, as if attempting to speak, but unable to articulate any words.

Korbyn rose his head, and it was then he noticed how high the trees reached. In this place, there didn't appear to be a sun, a moon, clouds, or even a sky at all. Instead, the branches connected like skeletal fingers in such a dense layer of darkened gray leaves that he couldn't see past them. He wasn't sure if anything resided behind them or if they were trying to hide whatever existed beyond it.

This place reminded him of Shadowbane Forest, but instead

of impending darkness, mist covered where the shadows would have been. Fog trickled in from all corners, lingering over the land and caressing his skin. It didn't feel inherently dark and evil as the forest had. It resembled more of an embrace of a beautiful woman, like a siren luring you into her open arms and plump bosom. The smile of its wavering branches beckoned him forward, mimicking a blissful night that would only lead to trouble.

Other than the eerie fog, the forest remained in a stillness, but only temporarily. Voices on the other side of the trunks that functioned as partitions cried out in various tones. Korbyn heard people of various ages and differentiating pitches, but all hitched with emotional distress. They shrieked as if in pain, some of the wails lingering longer than others. Some were abrupt and unsettled, howling as if their life just ended.

Another piercing wail sent invisible insects crawling up his skin, followed by a rupture of chills. Whatever they were experiencing, he didn't desire to witness it.

Korbyn commenced a cautious walk through the density of the flora. No matter his direction, each part of the grove looked identical to his previous inception. Hours had seemingly passed since Korbyn first strode through the endlessness of this condensed forest, its wildlife resembling more of an illusionary facade than distinct greenery. The endless maze didn't cease its whispers despite his blatant endeavors to ignore their calls.

As Korbyn emerged from an assembly of shrubbery, an image appeared in his peripheral. He craned his head, spotting a darting shadow amongst coiled branches. A familiar, contagious laugh ushered him forward, one that resembled a giggle succeeding a gibe that went unheard by his ears. It coerced him further into the welcoming wood.

"Andrid?" Korbyn whispered.

His brisk walk turned into a jog, and the jog turned into a run. He cared not for the tension in his calves or the ache in his back, springing as fast as his trembling legs could carry him. He wanted to remain skeptical due to his overarching fear of disappointment of crazed hallucinations.

Unfortunately, when Korbyn pursued the anomaly past a wall of gray, Andrid was not there to greet him.

Instead, in the middle of the plains, an oval-shaped cage dangled under huddled trees. It extended roughly a head taller than himself, the crate held by a long chain that surpassed the forest's ceiling. The iron had severely corroded into grained browns and coated in equal layers of dust. Despite its suspension from the tree, it didn't swing with the light breeze, as if it didn't exist at all.

Branches and leaves encircled the top of the cage and the individual iron rods that attached to the top and bottom, a poor defense in case the restraints proved unreliable. Unlike most cages, this one didn't have a door; rather, an arrangement of small crevices bordered the entirety of its circular shape. It reminded Korbyn of an oversized bird cage.

A layer of darkness covered the inside of the enclosure like a black sheet, preventing any prying eyes. He couldn't see its contents despite his capabilities.

Korbyn crept towards the cage when his curiosity forsook him, avoiding any small branches and leaves that would reveal his approach. Even as he closed the distance, he still couldn't peer through the veil.

As his face inspected the metal bands, two hands lunged from within.

A gasp erupted from Korbyn's throat as he stumbled backwards, barely retreating out of the person's grasp. The crate swung violently from the lurch, the rusted iron producing a sonority against the surrounding mists. Korbyn tripped over a pair of roots, fell to the ground, and scrambled backwards, afraid the cage might collapse from the disturbance and break under its violent creaking.

Though the darkness didn't completely dissipate, Korbyn was now able to see what lingered within. Inside was a looming figure, draped in a similar cape and hood to Azrael's attire. The hood was abnormally large, dipping over their facial features like a veil. The cloak was just as bulky, covering the entirety of their enlarged body to hide their form.

"*For a new beginning to emerge, an end must occur,*" the voice greeted, a devilish whisper to meet his ears.

"Demon," Korbyn muttered.

The figure cackled. "*I suppose. There are many layers of knowledge that prevent an answer of simplicity.*"

"I'm tired of your damn riddles," Korbyn spat, rising to his feet. His knees quivered, despite his efforts at controlling his waver.

"*You only call them riddles because you fail to comprehend their meaning,*" the demon said, extending an open palm. "*Shattering these foul restraints would provide more clarity.*"

Korbyn scoffed. "I shouldn't have called your words riddles. I should have called them nonsensical lies," he replied, taking a step away from the demon. "I know better than to trust you."

It tilted its head to the side and bared a white smile of sharpened teeth underneath the blanket of darkness. The leer was so wide that Korbyn couldn't imagine how it fit on its face. "*There is no one you can trust more than yourself.*"

"Fuck you," Korbyn seethed, turning towards the forest he emerged from. "I feel a lot better knowing there's nothing you can do without my help. Rot in your cage for eternity, *demon.*"

Its cackle permeated the air like a cold sting along his skin. Korbyn grasped his forearms to halt the trembling, but he failed to alleviate the discomfort.

"*Yet here we are amongst the itinerant and forgotten. All who wander here are lost.*"

"And where is here?" Korbyn questioned, glancing back.

The demon's smile didn't fade. "*Knowledge is finicky. One does not always get to choose how much plagues your mind.*" The demon clawed at the metal. For the first time, Korbyn noticed the marks indented into the steel and the lock that barred a non-existent door. The screech from its elongated nails pierced his ears like a scream that was being evoked in the surrounding woods. "*And when it does, one can no longer feign ignorance and claim to be moral and impartial when tormented with truth. You must choose one.*"

Korbyn frowned. "Forget it. I'll find my way out," he sneered, directing his strides towards the dense trees and away from the watchful predator.

He heard its squawking, a resemblance of a horrid laugh echoing through the forest even after he ventured farther from it.

Minutes, hours, days might have passed. Korbyn felt as though it could have been years. The forest claimed him in its grasp as easily as he appeared. Visions he experienced in the moments after his new awakening troubled his mind once again.

An endless Blood Moon hung eerily in the air, unwavering from its stalwart position in the sky. A castle made of black stone and intricate designs of gold leered in the distance. Hail in the form of red rain plummeted to the ground, searing his skin so hot that it ran cold, or maybe it was the other way around. He saw a Crown of Horns and Blades atop a pool of red blood that resembled a cape. The warrior he'd seen time and time again reached out to him, guiding him towards something.

After one hallucination ended, Korbyn found himself screeching in a pain that matched the voices around him. They seemed not to notice his own agony, as if they couldn't comprehend the others that were lost in this vile place. It took only a few moments for the next nightmare to initiate, sending him spiraling through places and events that he didn't understand.

As Korbyn stumbled through a wall of vines, he fell to his

knees. His insides churned, and he threw up the remnants of what lay in his stomach. The contents spilled all over the ground and emptied everything that rallied against his abdomen. When the vomiting ceased, he coughed profusely. He was left just as empty as when he woke up on the battlefield that grim day.

From above, he heard a hoot and holler, followed by a maniacal cackle. When Korbyn craned his neck upwards, he saw the demon grasping its stomach, keeled over in a dramatic display of amusement, even from within its cage. Somehow, he had ended up right where he started.

"Shut up!" Korbyn retorted, stomping over to the cage.

The demon remained unfazed. "*Walking in the shoes of our victims. All, at some point, mingle amongst the mists. When her venture from the woodlands occurs, all will bear witness.*"

"Why? Why can't I find a way out?" Korbyn muttered, ignoring the demon's ramble.

It bit its lip, tasting something savory. "*Because your mind desires your presence.*"

"I don't want to be here. I want out," Korbyn protested, raising his chin to meet its amused expression. "Tell me how to get out of here, and I might consider letting you out from your cage."

The demon lurched forward, clutching onto Korbyn's shirt and yanking him against the cage. Korbyn slammed against the iron bars, struggling against its grasp. "*It is not a cage; it is a coffin, one that won't open until Azrael says so.*" Its fangs gleamed in a light that didn't exist in this place. "*But we can change that, for he is dying, and when he is gone, we no longer need to adhere to his demands. Assuming destiny actually exists, it cares not for the path traveled, only the destination. Take the knowledge and power now when it is desperately needed.*"

"Wh-who..." Korbyn stuttered, peering into the darkness with a quivering jaw. "Who are you?"

"*I am persistent,*" it declared, each statement afterwards decreasing in volume. "*I am hidden. I am uncontrollable. I am knowledge. I am power. I am fear. I am unwanted. I am desire. I am sinful. I am intrusive, but I am not a demon.*"

Korbyn trembled. "I don't understand," he lied, not wanting to perceive the bitter truth. "Who are you?"

With its free hand, it withdrew the fabric from its face. Its irises were completely red and surrounded by darker sclera, resembling garnets in a sea of black. The skin beneath its eyes was swollen and irritated. It was either a creature on the brink of death, lacking sleep, or both. A prominent, maroon scar stretched from one of its temples to the other, carved horizontally through the very eyes that stared back at him. Despite this bright red scar, the eyes of night appeared untouched by the mark that ravaged them. Surrounding its face were dark strands of hair on top of pale skin. The locks clung to its face from a recent, cold sweat.

"*I am you,*" Korbyn's mirror image stated, revealing its sharp fangs due its devilish smile.

"That's not possible." Korbyn gawked, unable to prevent his trembling. "You're a demon."

"*Yes, you are,*" Korbyn's mirror image agreed with a cackle. "*I am nothing more than your intrusive thoughts caged inside your mortal body, power temporarily quelled until your inevitable reckoning. I am the knowledge held under leash and cage. I am the power held back by foul restraints. I am the gift bequeathed by Azrael upon your miraculous rebirth. And I lay dormant until he finds you worthy.*

"*But I have seen possible futures and countless endings as I have been caged in this living maze, this labyrinth, and you have already chosen our inevitable destination. We will join with Azrael as one, and our power will be unleashed to uphold the duty that is Death, the Reaper of Souls. For it is not just your mind that is the demon; it is also you, your heart and body...it is us, and we are Grim, but we can take a different path to our destination,*" Korbyn's red-eyed copy whispered, clutching tighter onto his shirt. "For *knowledge and power is stronger than any gilded decidite. We do not have to hearken to Azrael's instruction. Take up the remainder of your mind and power and wield it for yourself.*"

Korbyn strained to halt his uncontrolled breathing, but he could only stare in utter astonishment. He recalled the times when the power aided him, when he broke the lock with a touch of ice, when the shadows danced around him and beckoned to his aid, when his body surpassed normal mortal capabilities. If he absorbed the dormant abilities of his mind and power, would he regain his memories too?

"What would happen if we merged?" Korbyn questioned, staring between both of his bloodstained eyes. "What will I lose?"

"*Your body, when it becomes a hollow husk. Your mind, when you deteriorate within its darkness. Your heart, when the two women, both most precious, become strangers. You may lose nothing. You most likely will lose everything. The possibilities are now blurred, even for me.*"

Korbyn hesitated.

"*I do not wish to see our friends die while we are powerless,*" the red-eyed copy continued, pain coursing through its eyes as though its feelings had just been hurt.

Korbyn frowned, ignoring the guilt. "You said that I cannot save."

His mirror image smiled weakly. "*Don't you wish to prove me wrong?*"

When Korbyn accepted the knowledge and power that lay dormant within his mind, he heard a loud, sonorous bell originating outside the forest, and he thought it might have resembled an initiation of war.

"Get up, lad!" Korbyn heard someone yell.

He lifted his head. Somehow, he was kneeling upright. The mass of undead seemed to have increased over the span of his unconsciousness. He wasn't sure how much time had passed, but Gilben and Haven, who stood several paces in front of him, appeared incredibly disheveled.

"Korb! Korbyn!" someone yelled. Holding his slouched form was Oakley, shaking with nervous rambles and barely keeping both of them upright.

When Korbyn gazed over at his friend, nausea attacked his senses like an incessant sickness. No matter how many times he tried to shake his head to deter the world's spinning, he watched the battlefield turn in unnatural rotations.

"What happened?" Korbyn muttered.

Oakley seemed not to hear or recognize that he was conscious. He was yelling to Gilben, who was swinging his broadsword at a group of the undead, but Korbyn didn't comprehend what was said.

"There's too many!" Oakley yelled. "Gilben, I could really use one of your songs right now!"

Gilben halted with a sudden gleam in his eyes that wasn't previously there. A spark, a newfound inspiration after a block that threatened all artists, ignited in his taupe eyes. He offered a warm smile. For the first time, Korbyn saw it in full clarity.

"Yer right, laddie," Gilben stated, lowering the hold on his blade. "Do ya think ya cou'd take on the soldiers guardin' 'heir leader?"

"I'll find a way!" Haven yelled, swinging his axe like a hatchet at his own group of crazed monsters. When their heads flew, sewage from their insides spewed from the wounds like freed water.

Gilben walked away, following the direction of the sun's departure, seemingly eager to chase after the light's warmth.

"Where are you going?" Haven shouted.

As Korbyn focused on Gilben, he saw two eerie smiles underneath his beard from the blurriness of his silhouette.

"It's time ta finish me ballad," the dwarf replied, backing towards the belltower. "Do me a favor, would ya? Go say hi ta Dawnora's grave for me."

FORTY-SEVEN.

earful cries of the townsfolk subdued Salem's ears as the hoard of undead prevailed in their incessant approach. She noticed little when her barrier dissipated, the creatures barreling through the people. The hammer slammed into Veeris' body, and she failed to hear his bones break. She didn't hear the moment he collapsed from his assailant's strike, and she most certainly didn't hear her own scream.

Uncaring of her own vulnerability, Salem stumbled towards Veeris' fallen form. Tears slid down her face like cascading streams as she reached for him, becoming victim to ceaseless trembling.

Veeris' spine lay shattered among an unnatural arch of his back. Too afraid to move his body, Salem coddled his cheeks, cautiously adjusting his face to investigate the fatality of his condition.

His eyes were glazed over, but his heartbeat thrummed against her fingers when she placed them upon his neck. Somehow, he was still alive, though barely.

The captain of the royal guard from Umberfall, clad in dark armor that reminded her of a garden and the helm of a bull, strode past her. He inspected the battlefield with his weapon at his side, mimicking a man longing for war. The undead continued to tread across the open plains.

The world remained encased in silence. Salem watched the townsfolk, now overwhelmed with fear, flee from the overbearing hoard. She couldn't hear their guttural cries, but the undead overcame them easily, tearing out their throats and ushering them to join the quiet. The people began falling coordinatingly, descending like waves of alternating raindrops.

Instead of aiding them, Salem sat by Veeris, doing nothing to save either in her hesitancy. She had failed them once again.

Salem pushed hair out of Veeris' unresponsive face. Even though he hadn't yet died, his eyes resembled it. It was as if his mind had given into death even before his body did, ready to accept a fate that he deemed worthy.

Veeris had always been intelligent, kind, and astute. He used to smile and jest. He used to encourage her when she yielded to doubt. When she questioned her decisions, it was Veeris who was there to support her, to gift her with knowledge, to give everything he had in the Heavens to help her. And how had she replied?

She betrayed him.

Veeris had needed her in his time of trial, and she hadn't been there to assist him as he had for her. Instead, she watched him deteriorate from the inside out, allowing the strong emotions of mortality to overwhelm him. While she was so focused on her romantic feelings for Korbyn and her grief for Andrid, she let him face the darkness that ravaged his heart alone.

Veeris was her sole responsibility, and she had failed him.

Salem stifled a cry, watching his life fade from his eyes. With her magic drained, she wouldn't be able to heal him. As she grasped onto her locket, a thought rose to her mind.

No, Salem's limited powers couldn't save him, but her full archangel magic could.

"War," the captain stated, piercing the veil of silence. His deep voice echoed against the metal helmet encasing his face. "Tell me, Paladin of Dawn, when you chose to become a mercenary, was it to avoid instances like this?"

"Yes," Salem announced honestly, unclasping the gold from around her neck and gazing into her reflection. The armored man hadn't stirred, as if unaware of her actions. "War is a consequence of the selfish choices of rulers, sacrificing their people in the process."

"War is a necessity of change," the captain retorted, not wavering from his position to stare out into the depths. It was as if he enjoyed it, reveled in it, gaining adrenaline from blood spewing across newly soiled dirt. "Without change, we cannot grow. If we cannot grow, we cannot destroy the chains that bind us."

Salem sat for a moment, pondering his words. They were something she agreed with. Change was a necessity of life and growth. She grabbed Veeris' non-mangled hand, unravelling his curled fingers to place her locket against his palm.

I'm sorry I can't return your feelings, Salem thought, taking a breath of guilt. As tears fell, she wrapped her fingers around his. *But I can give you something more valuable than my love.* She tightened his grip, cracking the locket underneath his touch. *I am so sorry, Veeris. Please, forgive me.*

"You and I have much in common," the captain said, his voice booming in the confines of his helmet. Finally, he turned to her, paying attention to her instead of the crying voices behind him. She hid the locket within Veeris' palm as she returned the soldier's gaze, though she could not see it beneath the shadow. "We believe in the same things. We believe in a better world. We believe in the fall of tainted kings and selfish ambitions. We believe in change."

Salem scoffed. "You serve a king."

"I serve no one." He raised his chin. "War serves no one."

"Then why are you here, if not to serve your selfish ruler?" Salem seethed, rising to meet the soldier with her sword and shield in hand.

"To bring you back to the Kingdom of Esperin," the captain answered, holding onto his hammer steadfast. "You are wanted in the north."

"And who calls upon me?"

"Alecain."

Salem practically dropped her weapon. "And he would take me from the battle? When I am trying to help save his people? Didn't he want my help in the war?" Salem questioned with a growl.

"Not when you'll likely die with the rest of them," the captain motioned to the falling townsfolk with a lean of his head.

"You and I both know there's more to it," Salem declared, peering away from the dying to avoid the overwhelming guilt. "So, what is it he truly wants from me?"

"He believes you to be able to forge the decidite into the weapons he wants."

Salem laughed, though only sadness lingered within her verbal response. "What makes him think that I could?"

"Angelic powers have been told to have seared so hot that they can pierce through anything." His voice presumed a callous tone. "That is what they call you, the merc whose holy magic can pierce even the Heavens."

"H-how did he know?" Salem stuttered.

"I told him," the soldier admitted, unconcerned about its truth.

"And how did you know?"

"The magic of archangels is too difficult to hide," he responded, glancing down to Veeris, as though noticing him for the first time. "At least a lesser angel resembles that of a mere mortal."

Salem stifled her anger. Before then, she had questions that the captain needed to answer.

"It is a lie," Salem told him. "Angels can't forge decidite. Even the power of archangels cannot burn so hot."

"I know," the soldier admitted again, initiating a saunter in her direction.

Salem strode backwards towards the town, hoping to put space between the captain and Veeris' unconscious form. She tried to portray a confidence that matched the captain's, but she had difficulty concealing the quivering in her knees.

"Who are you?" she whispered, suddenly finding it difficult to lift her sword that swayed loosely in her grasp.

Then, Salem realized that she could hear everything. It wasn't due to their ongoing conversation, or the cries of the people, or the sputtering of the undead that grappled her senses.

It was a bell.

A majestic resonance echoed across the plains. The bell, from the hill's tower, rang with a ballad of brilliance. It was beautiful and hollow, yet ghostly and terrifying, as if it was preaching untold stories of future events. Salem heard the undead in the distance quiet at its call, listening to a language the rest of them couldn't understand.

The captain of the guard seemed unbothered by the music. Instead, it projected more confidence in his strides. While he sauntered forward, his wide shoulders and massive form crushed the land beneath him.

"War," he declared.

FORTY-EIGHT.

The undead around Korbyn were rendered silent for the first and only time.

The tower's bell sang a deep and rich tintinnabulation, like a grave hum. An echo followed its ring when it parroted across the lands, only dimming into complete silence when the voices of the undead matched its ghoulish stillness. The monsters, no longer concerned for their party or the awaiting town, turned towards the bell's chimes. For a moment, he saw emotions in their eyes, as if they were able to feel something. Then, Korbyn realized they could—they were deeply afraid.

The monsters trembled, as if plagued by a mix of rage towards the disruption of their own ensembled groans and pained by the chime's resonances. The gong sang again, louder than the first. The cries of the undead amplified, like a chorus matching a director's tune. They clawed and tugged at their own ears as though to rid themselves of the epic ballad, but tearing away their frail cartilages wouldn't prevent them from listening. Even as brittle skin plummeted to the dirt in heaps and layers, still they whimpered and sang to the beat of the bell.

Despite Korbyn's inability to focus, he could see Gilben at the top of the bell tower. He jumped, pulling his full weight into the instrument. Every movement was like a choreographed dance, his shoulders and legs rallying against the bell's weight. Korbyn could tell, even from this distance, that the dwarf was smiling, enriched in his own bravado upon his grand stage. Korbyn huffed out a smile, enraptured just like the undead, but contrastingly enjoying his performance.

The creatures realized they wouldn't be able to prevent themselves from hearing the bell. Instead, the entirety of the thousand undead, including the ones that penetrated the town, all turned away from their previous objective. In a fit of rage, insolence, and fixation, they charged the western hill.

"He's not going to make it, is he?" Oakley whispered, falling to his knees upon the newfound miracle.

The undead surrounding them disregarded their presence, all focused on the bell tower in the distance. When they finally arrived at the foothill, they raced and clawed upwards, using each other as stepping stools to propel themselves up the incline. It would only be a couple of minutes before the bell's chime ceased, leaving them once again in a field overcome with monsters.

"He's going to die."

With a saddened upward tug of his mouth, Korbyn replied. "But he's a hero."

"This is our only chance," Haven urged, his hands balled so tightly into fists that his nails penetrated his skin. Though he paid no attention to it, blood dripped down his palms as his jaw quivered. "Let's not waste the opportunity he gave us," Haven demanded.

"There's no way we'll be able to defeat all of those soldiers without horses. There's at least three hundred of them," Oakley stated, swaying when he reached halfway to a standing position.

Korbyn reached out to aid his balance, both wobbling against each other. A concussion still pounded against his head, but he tried to hide its symptoms to give his friend a bit more courage.

"We don't have a choice," Korbyn replied. From behind the soldiers, he could see the Revelation King. He was yelling at the men and women around him as if their presence was egregious, stomping much like a child who didn't get his way. "The soldiers might retreat if we kill him."

"We've come this far," Haven added, clearly agreeable to Korbyn's suggestion. "Gilben's sacrifice cannot be a waste."

"You're right." Oakley huffed and stretched, motioning to hide the tears that formed at the corners of his eyes. "I should have had a night of bliss before this. Damn it all. Now I'm starting to curse more often. You're turning me into a savage, Korbyn. Damn you."

Korbyn laughed somberly, stepping forward to lead them into the approaching army. "Damn us all."

Groups of archers ran forward to presume multiple wedge-shaped formations, the point in their arrangement leading the front. The soldiers were covered in cloth and chainmail from head to toe, wearing hoods of similar fashion. They grabbed their bows made of yew and strings made of hemp. In tandem, each archer nocked and pulled on the feather fletching of an arrow, taking aim at the three mercenaries across the field.

Knight-Captain Hadawaye, the leader of the Middle Guard, sauntered forward. He wore a different cuirass than the one he wore days before, the new piercing and armor glistening in superiority. With a smirk, he motioned with a point of his index finger.

"Loose!" he yelled.

The sounds of the arrows mimicked wild chirping that alternated into whizzing, like a fleet of swallows that harmonized the night sky. They claimed freedom as they soared, most having no destination other than the broad area of the mercenaries' approach.

"Shields!" Korbyn shouted.

He lurched forward to a fallen undead. It didn't have any legs, but it still swirled its neck and flailed its arms at the bell's ongoing chime. Korbyn pulled its body upwards, using it like a shield. Oakley sank behind him, and the undead thrashed widely with an unclamped jaw. He ignored the desperate clawing of the monster as the arrows descended.

"One..." Korbyn whispered.

Hundreds of projectiles covered the night sky like a blanket of repetitive design. In their volley, multiple arrows penetrated their temporary barrier, teetering the moment they soaked into the undead's flesh. Rotten flesh spattered across Korbyn's face when a projectile pierced the monster's jaw. It halted directly in front of Korbyn's eye, and he continued to count as the barrage ensued.

"Two..."

"Nock!" Hadawaye yelled from across the field.

The momentum of the bolts slowed, granting them momentary reprieve from the onslaught. From the corner of his eye, Korbyn saw Haven toss aside two undead that acted as his own tower shield before motioning to stand.

"Wait!" Korbyn demanded, listening for the archers on the other side of the field. "Three..."

"Draw!"

"Four..."

"Loose!" Hadawaye barked.

"Five," Korbyn concluded, clutching onto another dismembered undead with Oakley at his back.

Another volley of arrows unleashed, their cries reverberating to the bell's tune, whizzing in the glory of an epic song.

The music of war, a symbol of retribution. May the lands sing in utmost freedom, Korbyn thought, despite not understanding the entirety of its meaning.

After the silence of the arrows' flight, Korbyn dropped the wailing undead and grabbed another, its body only a torso with hips and four severed limbs. "Forward!" Korbyn demanded.

More arrows perforated the blockade, but Korbyn wasn't as undamaged as the first time. One of the arrows whisked through the winds at a higher arch, falling straight down into his right shoulder. He cringed, disregarding its call. Another pierced his calf, with most of his legs remaining unprotected. He felt Oakley's hand clench tighter to the fabric of his cloak.

"I'm fine," Korbyn stated, relaxing a bit when the next wave of projectiles ended. He pulled out the arrow from his shoulder, leaving the one in his calf unattended. "Just focus on not getting hit."

The Revelation King, growing impatient by their lack of defeat, pointed forward towards Brinshire. "Charge them and then attack the town!" he demanded, his garnet curls waving with the defiant wind. "Now! Go!"

"This is my army!" Knight-Captain Hadawaye yelled in defiance, shifting his angry expression towards the mage. "I said, loose the arrows!" The troops halted, as if unsure of who to listen to.

"You will listen to me!" the Revelation King screeched, surprisingly hardy despite his earlier tantrum.

Hadawaye responded with something that Korbyn couldn't hear, but the mage yelled even louder over him.

"What is a general to a king?" the Revelation King questioned, pushing away the Knight-Captain and pointing forward. "Charge! There are only three—kill them!" Korbyn was unsure if it was to their benefit or not, but the soldiers behind the archers ran forward with raised spears and blades.

The Revelation King is marked by illusion, a facade of hopes and dreams, Korbyn thought again.

The soldiers approached in uneven waves, their formations faltering when meeting adversaries of three instead of an army. The first confident soldier lunged with a spear in Korbyn's direction. Still holding onto the undead body, Korbyn pushed it forward. The spear penetrated its torso, and the man was unable to pull it back to his aid. Korbyn threw it to the side, and the man's grip loosened. Korbyn threw a left hook, slamming into the soldier's exposed jaw underneath his bascinet.

After the man fell, two approached Korbyn diagonally. One thrust his spear and leaned forward with terrible footing. It was as if he was sure he would kill with this one strike, his wide stance preventing him from a counterattack.

Korbyn dodged the spear and hooked it under his right armpit, spinning in a circle and hauling the soldier with him. With unmeasurable strength, he whisked the soldier into the other approaching man while keeping the spear locked in place. The first man let go of the weapon as he crashed into the second, allowing Korbyn to withdraw the spear and wield it for himself.

All fear and oppose Death, but none succeed.

Three soldiers attacked, all stabbing with the tips of their spears. Their stances, more robust than the previous ones, struck in practiced unison. Korbyn swept the spearheads away with a spin of his weapon, and the three shafts clanged into each other. Because of his dominant hand, their arms and bodies spun towards their left, leaving their right sides wide open.

Korbyn spun in a circle, swiping the spear across the open flap in the man's armpit. The soldier cringed in response, stumbling left and falling against the other two men. Unable to hold his weight, they crashed in a heap of ringing armor and clamoring limbs.

"Oakley!" Korbyn yelled, running past the three fallen men. He could feel the bloodlust of the assassin's advance behind him.

Korbyn launched forward into the air with a raised spear. His next opponent carried a shield with a rounded edge and a shining longsword. The soldier parried Korbyn's first attack, but not the second. As Korbyn landed, he raised his spear and thrusted it over the man's curved shield, piercing him in the eye slit of his bascinet. The man fell to the ground, dying before he contacted it.

Every battle is preparing me for the future battle to come—for when my king needs me, beside the throne I'll be, Korbyn thought.

Another soldier whipped his sword in an arc. Korbyn fell into a roll and inserted his right arm into the leather strap of the dropped buckler. He rose to his feet with ample time to block the next two attacks. Korbyn projected the spear forward under the man's lifted arm, pushing it straight down into his torso. With the weapon so deeply imbedded, Korbyn failed to yank it free.

Soldier, warrior, mercenary...

Korbyn sensed a presence flanking him, and he didn't fully dodge out of the way of the combatant's brutal thrust. Blood sprayed from the new wound at Korbyn's ribs before an arm wrapped around his neck. Not permitting his assailant's actions, Korbyn threw his head backwards into the soldier's nose. The man toppled, following his dropped bascinet. Korbyn thrust the shield into his exposed throat to end his rallying cries.

Ally, friend, brother...

"Damn it!" Korbyn cursed as more soldiers approached.

As one of them lunged, Korbyn lowered himself into an evasive roll. Having no more weapons, he broke off the arrow sticking out of his calf and thrust it into an approaching soldier's eye. As the man reeled, Korbyn ran forward and pushed him, utilizing his body as a shield when other soldiers swung their weapons. The stumbling soldier toppled into two others.

Korbyn's heartbeat clamored so forcefully in his chest that he thought he might keel over. As he surveyed the battlefield, he realized Haven and Oakley were in similar predicaments as him.

Despite their strength and prowess on the battlefield, they were outnumbered. His fear was met by the only heartbeat Korbyn noticed. It pounded loudly, echoing through his ears.

Shepherd, Horseman, Reaper...

Korbyn picked up another spear and leaned his body to the right. A spear's head whizzed past his cheek, merely grazing his skin. He thrust his spear back in retaliation, and the soldier blocked his incoming attacks. They parried each other for several more strikes before they were interrupted.

Another soldier approached Korbyn from behind. He ducked under the attack, and it struck the man's ally through his throat. Disturbed by what he had done, the soldier gasped and lowered his guard.

Oakley, silent in the soldier's shadow, attacked from behind. Two blades punctured the man's throat, and he grasped and clawed in confusion. Eventually, he fell forward, and Korbyn stepped out of his way as he descended to the dirt.

Haven sprinted forward when multiple soldiers flanked them on their right side. He dashed in a fit of audible rage, swinging his axe with unpredictable strength. Even with the formidable armor encasing the soldiers, the half-orc carved through the toughest steel with determination and grit. The three mercenaries reunited with weapons raised defensively.

"There's...no way," Oakley whispered, heaving in tandem with Korbyn and Haven. "We're not making a dent."

More soldiers initiated their approach. They weren't as boundless as the undead, but they were more knowledgeable and skilled. Even they, the most capable mercenaries in Terrisae, wouldn't be able to defeat these soldiers and live to tell the tale.

"*No matter what they call me, all mortal souls falter in the presence of Death's wake,*" Korbyn whispered.

It was then that Korbyn felt it—the beat of his heart pounding avidly against his chest, like incessant drumming or the echo of a bell. It was a surge of magical energy that lay dormant within him, demanding its use. It was profound vigor after awakening from a restful slumber, it was the ecstasy of overwhelming pleasure after the proximity of an entrancing lover, it was the power that was promised.

The Blood Moon adhered to his call, and Korbyn basked in its red light.

"Korb?" Oakley prompted as Korbyn straightened his back and inhaled deeply.

When Korbyn gazed at the Blood Moon, the Blood Moon stared back.

"When I recall the memories I've lost," Korbyn said, his tone containing a sense of surety that it lacked before, "just know that you two will always be my brothers."

And when he blinked, Korbyn knew his irises became reflections of the bloodstained moon.

FORTY-NINE.

The world was so much more beautiful than Korbyn thought. It strummed in an unheard cadence, withholding many entrenched sounds that mortals couldn't hear. Whispers of uncollected souls, the hums of the autumn breeze, the growth of natural fauna, the echoes of the moon's rays—he heard them all, and they demanded a listener.

There were so many colors that he previously couldn't see, and no names to establish them. He couldn't accurately describe its sheer exquisiteness with preexisting colors. Before, Korbyn would have depicted its essence as a crimson, but there were so many different shades that existed cohesively upon its textured surface. Coral faded into ginger and ginger faded into whitened gold, with hues of a deep, red wine merging with shades of darkened violet that resembled splatters of discarded paint. A faded pearl surrounded its circumference, illuminating it from behind.

"Korb?" Oakley questioned again with a raised weapon towards the advancing soldiers. Without regarding him, Korbyn could hear the trembling in his form, a mix of fear and fatigue. "Are you okay?"

"Yes," Korbyn replied with full clarity. "Yes, I think I am."

He felt the strength of Haven's hand before it grasped his shoulder. Haven shook him with what Korbyn believed to be reassurance and a response to his declaration of family.

"Same to you, brother," Haven replied.

Korbyn wouldn't let them die today.

"Stand behind me," Korbyn stated, storming towards the Avernos army. "And strike after I bring these soldiers to their knees," he stated loud enough for the men and women to hear.

The soldiers readied their weapons and charged, accepting his challenge.

As Korbyn lunged, his cloak fluttered behind him from his abrupt movements, greeting the approaching soldiers with a wave in the breeze. The Blood Moon hung in the sky, projecting their shadows to the fore like elongated coffins and the very weapons he would use to decimate an army.

Demons—such a colloquial term. That is what the Heavens turned me into, Korbyn thought, raising his spear mid-leap as he plunged into the fray. *Darkness only exists because it is the light that casts a shadow.*

Korbyn landed in front of the first soldier, the man seemingly unready for his proximity as he swung his sword haphazardly. Korbyn pierced his spear straight through the man's helmet and carved straight through the steel, blood spraying as he collapsed. Korbyn picked up the discarded sword to replace the lodged spear.

The Avernos soldiers hesitated. Weaving the shadows underneath their steps, Korbyn projected his arms outward. The shadows underneath the soldiers followed his movements and shot up like stalagmites from a frozen cavern, and feeling just as cold. Three pierced through the chins and the crowns of their respective soldiers. Korbyn lowered his posture into a run as they fell, soaring through the battlefield quicker than they reacted.

"Stop him!" one of the soldiers yelled, cut off by a wide swing of Korbyn's blade through his throat.

Korbyn reached backwards, ushering more darkness to his demands. Five shadows encircled the men they were attached to like phantom vines, holding them in place and rendering them immobile.

"D-demon!" a soldier cried, stepping away in fear.

Korbyn raised his blade and pointed to the quivering man in the following motion. "Draw nigh," he urged, and the soldier adhered to Death's call with a rallying cry and an ungraceful charge.

When the soldier entered his reach, Korbyn swung in a full, horizontal arch. The man's head toppled before he could let out a gasp.

Korbyn peered back at his allies. Haven and Oakley cut through the soldiers that were distracted by him. With the soldiers' backs turned, they fell victim to every strike of the duo's quick advances. While Haven hacked at several men, Oakley skulked behind unknowing individuals, shifting to other victims before the previous ones hit the terrain.

"Retreat!" the soldiers echoed across the lands, most of them falling back, caring not of leaving their leaders behind.

To Korbyn's surprise, the Revelation King hadn't reacted to the withdrawal of the soldiers. Instead, his gaze was fully focused on Korbyn, his jaw slack.

I will make the faux king fear me, he thought.

Korbyn stalked forward with the gong of the bell, the echo of its ring dimming the cries of the retreating forces. Multiple opponents flanked him on all sides. Their progression forward ceased when the trails of their darkened silhouettes wrapped around their forms and squeezed. The shadows reflected images of themselves as they terminated their breathing, pulling them down into incessant darkness.

The Revelation King stood motionless in the middle of the chaos with an unreadable expression other than perplexity.

As Korbyn closed the distance, the bell chimed again. It rallied his fast-beating heart, the fray of the army and the probable end of the battle. A smirk rose to his face, the ends of its curvature lifting towards the moon.

This was the man that had the gall to prevent the dead from being laid to rest, the audacity to kill the guileless, and the insanity to slaughter an entire town with no remorse. When he made those decisions, his life became forfeit, and it would be by Korbyn's hand.

Korbyn lunged at the king's exposed neck. The mage, expecting the advancement, raised his scepter of black and gold, which didn't shine against the frowning moon.

The extended blade halted mere moments from the man's neck. Korbyn froze with wide eyes, wondering what appeared in the way of his fierce assault. However, when he tried to step backwards, he realized he couldn't. It wasn't an invisible wall, or the fact that the smirking king was out of his reach; it was that he couldn't move at all.

"I knew it, I knew it, I knew it!" The Revelation King cackled.

The king's eagerness caused a swell of panic, and Korbyn tried to thrash against the hidden restraints, but he could barely move his jaw with his own approval.

"What?" Korbyn managed to question.

When he peeked upwards, Korbyn saw a thread of golden, magical energy in the form of a thread, connecting him to the scepter of gilded decidite in his grasp.

Feeble fowls of a feather flock forever, he thought.

"You are the heir to the Horseman Death," the Revelation King squeaked out, unable to contain his screeches of joy.

The retreating soldiers halted their movements, turning back when they realized the king had stopped the monster prowling in the darkness. Slowly, they returned towards the fields.

"No," Korbyn whispered, the hold on his form not faltering.

"Yes! Yes!" the Revelation King replied, as if Korbyn was talking to him. "You—you are a sign from Samael! A sign from the prophecy! *When Death, the Reaper of Souls, takes new form, it will initiate the start of the Revelation War, to make way for the new Crown of Horns and Blades seated upon waves of scarlet,*" he repeated in the unknown language, lifting his crude scepter of bone and fake retribution to the sky, as if anyone above was listening. His red, tangled hair shifted from his upward gaze.

"But," he murmured, turning back to Korbyn, "you have not yet fully become one with Azrael, have you?"

The Revelation King lifted his chin, and it was then that Korbyn could fully see the man's face behind his hood. He appeared young, no older than the age of twenty-five, but his skin protested. His skin was frail, so thin and wrinkled that it looked as though it might snap.

"Fuck off," Korbyn spat, projecting a glob of spit in his face.

Instead of angry disgust, the Revelation King bit his lip in eerie satisfaction, clenching his face and spreading the saliva as if he had just experienced his own silent pleasure.

"The time of the Revelation King and the Brotherhood of the Trinity has come," he cried out to no one in particular. He waved over the encircling soldiers. "Bring the two heathens to me!"

Knight-Captain Hadawaye motioned his soldiers to halt with a raise of his hand. "Clearly, we have won. We will accept their surrender and grant them mercy."

The Revelation King shoved his face into Hadawaye's, his vile excitedness disappearing from his face. "Did the Trinity receive mercy when they were slaughtered? No, but they will get their retribution, and I will lead them. Now step aside, foul insect."

Hadawaye did not prevent the Revelation King from directing

his army. The crazed man threw forward his arms like a toddler, ushering the soldiers forward with a pointed finger and spouted saliva. "Seize them!"

"No!" Korbyn screamed, reaching for the Blood Moon's aid, but it didn't reply.

The Revelation King spun Korbyn's body like a puppeteer controlling his most prized marionette. The entirety of the soldiers ventured forward with another battle cry.

Oakley and Haven fought off the advancing army as long as they could. Multiple soldiers fell to their bruteness and vitality. Oakley stayed light on his feet, dodging multiple onslaughts projected his way. He couldn't sidestep them all, and soon he was covered in cuts and wounds like newly purchased jewelry, ones that gleamed too brightly to be ignored.

As Oakley stumbled, one of the soldiers claimed the opportunity. He slammed his bigger form into Oakley's, knocking him down with ease. When he tried to rise, multiple forms overpowered him, halting his struggles with clasped hands.

"Let me go!" Oakley yelled, squirming against their restraints. "Bastards! Let me go!"

Meanwhile, Haven was clad in more wounds that he previously was, blood dripping from his legs like waves of crashing sand. Endless combatants surrounded him, each readying their attacks. Haven swung first, throwing his hefty axe in a flurry of spins. He cut through multiple of the soldiers at once. However, it was all a distraction for the one approaching from behind him.

Before Haven could turn around, a spear penetrated his stomach. When he tried to fight off that soldier, another stabbed from his side, both spears puncturing through opposite sides of his body to meet the hilt of the other.

"*Haven!*" Korbyn yelled.

Haven didn't fall. Instead, he dug his feet deeper into the ground beneath him. The soldiers gawked and tried to pull their weapons from his body. Haven dropped his axe and grabbed onto both of their hilts, preventing them from stepping backwards with their spears.

The first soldier was unprepared when Haven slammed his forehead into the first soldier's nose. The man's helmet caved inwards, and his body fell limp, a noise and smell of excretion following his death. Blood streaked down the half-orc's face.

Haven swung for the next one, grappling her by wrapping his fingers around her face. He squeezed until the iron caved in on both sides of her temples. Eventually, she stopped squirming, and he threw her into another approaching soldier.

A group of soldiers lurched forward. Instead of striking Haven with weapons, they jumped on top of him. They grabbed onto his arms, legs, back, and neck to halt his movements. Some clutched the lodged spears, twisting and thrusting them deeper.

Haven's knees wavered, but only for a single moment. He pushed upwards and swung his arms, shoving several of the soldiers off him. He grabbed one by the back of the head and threw them face first into the ground, stomping on the back of the armored head until the man's movements stilled.

"You wear a crown as though it means something! I will prove your bones are as brittle as the ones you wear upon your head!" Haven bellowed, his guttural cry matching the tone of the bell's slowing chime.

A soldier attempted to pry Haven's axe from the ground, but when he tried, it was too large and cumbersome. Haven punched the man in his jaw, and the human tripped and collapsed on his backside. The half-orc raised the axe and swung. It didn't cease until the man lay in half, in heaps of his own intestines.

Haven's unbridled anger allowed the next few soldiers to attack. Another spear pierced through Haven's stomach and out of his front, pointing up towards the Blood Moon. Finally, the half-orc fell to his knees.

"No!" Korbyn shuddered, his voice cracking from his pleading.

Two soldiers approached Haven, thrusting two spears through his thighs and calves, sticking them all the way through his muscles and into the ground. He cried out, but it sounded more like enraged fury than pain, as if waking him from slumber.

Oakley was thrown forward on his knees beside Haven, his arms behind him wrapped tightly in hemp rope. He struggled against the hands holding him down by his shoulders, but there were too many. Blood poured from his brow as he stared up at his half-orc companion.

"Leave him alone!" Oakley screamed, causing one of the soldiers to punch him.

Oakley fell to the ground, and when he motioned to rise, the soldier pressed their steel-toed boot on his back. Even then, Oakley still wiggled against their grasp, tears forming into his eyes.

"What is it you want from me? I'll do anything you want. Just, *please*, let them go," Korbyn begged, his jaw clenching from the pain of use.

The king's remarkably strong hand wrapped around Korbyn's throat as they locked eyes. For a few seconds, he couldn't inhale. The laugh that erupted from the mage's mouth was venomous. It was like he had just heard the most hilarious gag he had ever heard, truly not believing the sentiment behind Korbyn's words.

"I am the Revelation King, prophesized centuries ago when the Garden fell," the Revelation King explained, waving his other arm in the air like a proclamation. "I am Samael's chosen heir and the hero who will conquer Elohim's chosen lands of Esperin, soon to be a kingdom no more." He grinned, a sadistic smile that his skin rebelled against. Instead of the skin lifting with his weakened muscles, it pulled down in wrinkles. A laugh emerged from his throat, though it sounded creaky and aged. "You will become the new Death, the Reaper of Souls, and I will finally ascend from mere heir to the seat of Abaddon, as new king and ruler of all three realms. And a king does not bargain with his minions."

The Revelation King let go of Korbyn's throat and pointed his scepter forward towards Haven and Oakley, the magical thread swaying in the silent breeze.

"Kill them."

Korbyn gasped from the lack of air and utter dread. "No."

"Yes," the Revelation King replied, another eerie smile spreading across his wrinkled face. "History is about to be made, and their blood will prove pivotal for the ritual."

The soldiers lingered in apprehension, clearly unsure of the mage's intentions and sanity. Knight-Captain Hadawaye, with a stoic mouth and unsure expression, said nothing. None did anything to stop him.

Korbyn lifted his blade upon the king's demand, carrying it at his side as he strode towards his allies with fearful eyes.

Haven's breaths had been slowing. The half-orc lowered his head, as if not wanting Korbyn to see the moment the glisten left his eyes.

I am not meant to save, Korbyn thought sadly as he thrust his blade into Haven's slow-beating heart.

The wave of the king's scepter caused it to be decisive and true, pushing the edge all the way through his torso until his chest met the hilt. He retracted his blade, and Korbyn couldn't stifle his cry when Haven's body fell to the ground.

"No," Korbyn cried as Oakley squirmed, fear filling his silver eyes. He writhed against the soldier's hold, but all held firm. "Please, please, not Oakley," Korbyn mumbled again, calling for someone's help.

No one came.

"Korb, brother—" Oakley yelled, moving his head the moment Korbyn lifted his shoulder and struck.

He missed Oakley's forehead. Instead, the pointed part of the blade pierced his eye. His brother screeched with so much agony that he flailed from his tied position. Blood sprayed from the wound, the eye popping and splattering. Oakley convulsed, his body panicking to try and fight off the pain. Korbyn could hear his friend's heart racing. Eventually, Oakley's heartbeat slowed, and then, Korbyn could no longer hear it over his own, panicked breathing.

Korbyn could only stare, the image of his slaughtered brethren forever soaked into his memory, even when the rest proved fragile.

"Very good! Gather their blood before it drains. Prepare the ritual as practiced!" the Revelation King announced, clapping his hands as if the soldiers were mere lackeys.

Though they weren't magically controlled by the Revelation King's commands, they still adhered to his call, daring not defy his wishes. However, it was Korbyn who did not listen.

"*I'll kill you!*" Korbyn screeched, dashing forward against the restraints of the magical vine.

As if at the end of his rope, Korbyn stopped just before the faux king's fearful expression. He hacked the blade through the air, fighting wildly against the invisible chains, barely missing him.

The king tripped and fell on his ass, his crown following his plummet. It tumbled, and pieces of the bone shattered when it crashed.

"*Do you hear me? Are you listening, pretend Revelation King?! I'll fucking kill you!*" Korbyn's voice mixed with hollow bellows, as if two voices were finally merging in a conjoined rally. Tears flowed freely from his eyes, anger and sorrow providing him with a strength even the gilded decidite couldn't stop. "*I'll tear out your heart and make you devour it. When the souls are set free from the Labyrinth, I'll leave you to waste and suffer for all eternity!*"

"Don't just stand there! Stop him!" the false king cried, reaching and clawing for his fallen scepter and crown.

Three men reached forward, failing to hold down his arms.

Korbyn proved too strong. He threw them off, trampling forward and slashing his blade. Six more joined their place, all endeavoring to encumber his crazed thrashes. It took nine to suppress him, trapping him under their weight. Even then, Korbyn didn't cease, never breaking eye contact with the king.

Some of the other soldiers collected the blood of Haven and Oakley in canisters, spilling their gore into a pentagram and carving the hellish sigil amongst its symbols.

The mage readjusted himself, holding his hands into a sign, with his fingertips touching one another. It looked like he was holding a ball between his palms from its careful placement. His ring fingers shook, power surging through them.

"Samael, I call upon your soldier of Death. Let them combine to form a product anew," he stated in the abnormal language. *"And make way for the Revelation King."*

When the ritual's preparations were complete, they tossed Korbyn into the middle of the sigil. They pressed his face into the tainted, red soil of his brethren, forced to taste their blood as they finished the ceremony. And before Korbyn could break free from their hold, his mind was thrown into the depths of a kingdom of blackened stone and a sky of permanent crimson.

The world wasn't as beautiful as he thought.

FIFTY.

Korbyn stood among a world of red ash and rubble. Valleys of deep-cut stone and rivers stretched across the lands for what seemed like hundreds of miles. Mists spread through the lands, tumbling like weeds with no destination of their own. The canyons encased halfway in ice sat beneath a dark red sky and what Korbyn believed to be an eternal Blood Moon. It was obscured by even darker clouds, threatening the world with an overcast of rain that had just begun to fall.

In the distance stood the same kingdom that Korbyn had seen before in all his visions. A gothic cathedral amongst a city made of black stone sat at the highest point on top of the farthest canyon he could see. It loomed with power and dominance over the lands beneath it. Fires sporadically spread through the entirety of the realm, seemingly counteracting the layers of ice that cascaded up the canyon walls.

Rain pelted the lands beneath, Korbyn's tears mixing with the rough pellets. At first, he thought that the rain was hot. Instead, it transitioned into a freezing touch, as if it was so torrid that it chilled. Under normal circumstances, he would have flinched from the pain it caused, but he welcomed it as the rain fell in heavier coats.

Korbyn either didn't hear the presence appear, or he didn't care. Through the thickness of the rain, a figure cloaked in the cloud's shadow had materialized from seemingly nothing. Instead of hovering over the land as he had seen before, the figure limped forward with the tall weapon in his hand acting as a cane. He leaned against it with every stride, the tall scythe glistening in the moon's rays. The feathers hanging from its bone snath fluttered in the breeze. For the first time, Korbyn could hear the ringing of the ball on the inside of the bell with each weak step the Reaper took.

"What's with the bell?" Korbyn asked somberly, caring not for the wet strands of hair that clung to his face.

When Korbyn spoke, the figure stopped, ending his strides with the rustling echoes of the iron ball within the pellet.

"It is a reminder," the Reaper replied. "Of when these lands will chant the Song of Revelation." His voice resembled a low growl, cracking like an old ship in a violent storm. It echoed around him amongst the foreign world's silence.

Korbyn ignored his response, for he didn't understand it, and instead continued with another question. "Are you Azrael?"

Despite the man—or the fallen—being unable to smile, he somehow felt a sense of amusement creep up him. "I am. And you are Dolion, though you do not remember this," Azrael responded. His words were slow and meaningful, thoughtful and careful. It was as if Azrael expected him to react, but Korbyn didn't so much as flinch. "Does your given name not surprise you?"

"It does. It just doesn't matter anymore," Korbyn whispered with tired eyes that failed to prevent his continual, silent tears. "My true family is dead."

"So you say."

Korbyn stood in silence, other than the occasional sounds of his trembling cries. He wasn't sure how long he stood there, relinquishing his confidence to his despair. He gripped his forehead, covering his eyes like a marquee from Death, who merely stood in perpetual quietude and gifted him a moment's grief while the rest of the world continued to turn.

Korbyn was unaware of how long he stood there, shaking with defiant knees. His mind spun with recollections of their deaths, listening to their cries as audible as the first occurrence and reimagining the one he did not witness. Although the voice was permanently silenced in his mind, he somehow could not prevent that wretched phrase from repeating in the depths of his mournful thoughts.

You are not meant to save.

At some point, Korbyn forwent Azrael's presence, failing to recognize the pain from the unceasing rain. His heaves simmered into quivering breaths, the tears finally slowing when the wells ran dry. Eventually, he wiped his face with his forearm, soaking the cloth and the hidden mark underneath it.

No, Korbyn could not save, but he could ensure retribution.

"You're dying, aren't you?" Korbyn probed, breaking the silence with his trembling voice.

The hooded figure raised his head beneath the hood, allowing him to see into the darkness underneath. Azrael was practically a skeleton wearing mortal clothing, with skin drooping across his bones. His permanent smile tilted to the side, sending chills up Korbyn's mark.

"As most do, at some point," Death responded, his voice a gasp, as if he hadn't had water in decades. "But without Death, there is no life."

Korbyn frowned, realizing his responses were just as futile as his internal, uncontrollable thoughts had been. "What is the point of all this? What's the point in anything? What's the point in me?"

"You are to become Death, the Reaper of Souls, in my place," Azrael explained, motioning towards his failing form. "You will accept the rest of the powers that have been promised from our contract." Korbyn gazed up at the Blood Moon, the only consistent ally he recognized that was still alive.

"And what of this Revelation King? And this fallen Trinity? The Revelation War?" Korbyn questioned, though emotion rose from his queries.

Azrael shook his head, the elongated hood's veil shaking in disapproval. "These are answers you are not ready for," he declared, leaning against the grand scythe in his hand. "But, in due time, you will be. I will ensure that you are fully ready before you accept my power."

Korbyn frowned. "I don't plan to wait," he replied, melancholy dripping from his words. "I need the scythe's power now." He took a step forward. "I need death. I need vengeance."

Azrael craned his head sideways. "Power comes with a price."

"And I've already paid that price," Korbyn snapped, referring to his form and a random direction that alluded to the outside world. "My friends are dead because whatever I am! There is no greater price than their meaningless deaths! You proclaim a price, but you're not the one to pay it!"

"*Do not tell me about price as if I do not understand. I have lost more souls than the entirety of the world's mortal flesh,*" Death spat, startling Korbyn from the usual raspiness. After a moment, his shoulders slackened. He turned his open arm towards the kingdom in the distance, the black stone standing almost as high as the Blood Moon. "This kingdom was built upon those who perished for a war that was lost. The castle itself will forever be a physical representation of their sacrifice." Azrael turned his full attention back to him. "There is no such thing as war without victims, boy. If you fail to recognize that, then you are not yet ready."

Korbyn glared. "I am ready."

Azrael's shoulders shook as if he was laughing, but no verbal confirmation of it erupted from him. "The responsibility and power that come with the existence of a Horseman is unfathomable. You are the right one, but it is not the right time," Azrael responded, tilting his head in the other direction, as if he was observing him from underneath his hood.

"Why did you choose me?" Korbyn asked.

Azrael shook his head, his hood fluttering in the breeze. "I didn't choose you; Samael did. One day, you will be needed. I am here to prepare you." Korbyn couldn't help but shudder. "This story, the current one you live, is but a prelude to what is to come."

"Needed by who? Samael?"

The Reaper paused, as if considering something. "No. Someone."

"Who?" Korbyn prodded further.

Azrael shook his head. "That is a story for another day."

Korbyn grimaced, turning his gaze away from him. The downpour still pained him with every single droplet that hit his skin. The water's descension pained his body, his cloak not protecting him from its ire. He eventually lost feeling between the rain and his curled, whitened fists.

"Am I just a piece of a grander puzzle?" Korbyn questioned sadly, trying to hide the secret defiance in his eyes. "Do I not matter? Are my efforts and wants meaningless? Are the deaths of my friends for nothing?"

The Reaper shrugged. "The weapons of powerful leaders and conquerors tend to be forgotten," Azrael croaked out before referring to the scythe. "Well, most."

Korbyn glanced at the scythe. If he was going to defeat this army, if he was going to avenge his fallen friends, save Salem—if she were somehow still alive—then he would need its strength, whether it was the intentions of the Revelation King or not.

"If I were to gain this power, what do I have to give up?" he asked, curling his fingers in his palm. "What price do I have to pay?"

"Eternal servitude under the sovereign rule of Abaddon."

A cold sweat, either from the pain or the fear, trickled over Korbyn's body. He shuddered, reactively grabbing his left forearm with his other hand, hoping he could diminish it completely.

He imagined himself next to Salem, with his fallen friends at his side. The image cracked and dispersed like glass into ash. It was then that he realized that there would be no happy ending for him.

"Fine," Korbyn retorted, his eyebrows furrowing. "I accept these conditions."

Korbyn stepped forward, upholding a strong composure despite the pain and the odds he faced. The Reaper's shoulders bounced as if he was laughing, though no audible noise followed.

"As I said, you are not yet ready," Azrael stated, cocking his head to the side. "If you were to gain this power too early, surely your heart, mind, and body would be lost."

"I don't have a choice," Korbyn stated confidently. He took a deep breath, inhaling the power the Blood Moon provided him. "If I'm going to avenge my friends and stop this putrid war, then I must have your power. I understand what I'm giving up, what I'm leaving behind. And I need it, now."

He imagined the Reaper was frowning. It appeared as though his shoulders slumped. "This is a prime example that you are not ready," Azrael responded, seemingly not threatened by Korbyn's approaching stride. "Death is not the end."

He ignored Death. "If you won't give it to me, then I will take it from you."

"You will," Azrael replied with a raised scythe. "Just not yet."

Amongst the cadence of rain and the silence of their voices, the bell chimed in the fluttering of the wind. It echoed within Korbyn's mind, reverberating in such strong successions that it grew in volume with every ding. The longer he stood here, the more irritable it made him. He slid his foot forward with impatience.

Korbyn rushed forward. Azrael didn't move, not until he was within reach.

Despite his limp, Azrael moved with grace, the brutality of the world around him not slowing him down. As Korbyn reached forward, the Reaper stepped backwards, his cape fluttering in the wind from his movements.

Whether this was a vision, an internal struggle, or if he really had teleported to this unknown realm, Korbyn still experienced the power under the red hue's touch. The moon glowed with an iridescent glow. He welcomed its power with an embrace, and he eventually felt the pain from the rain vanish. Whether he was so focused on endeavoring to grab the scythe from Death's grasp or if he was healing too quickly from his power, he wasn't sure. Either way, each pierce became forgotten or pushed away as a later problem.

When they had danced around the entire battlefield, Death's shoulders continued to bounce, as if he found the entire thing humorous. When Azrael dipped his head to the side in contemplation, his entire body followed and dodged in that direction. Korbyn's hand didn't even graze his hood. For some reason, the being older than even time was fast. Korbyn wasn't sure if using the scythe as a cane was a ploy or not.

Korbyn lowered his body and concentrated on pushing as hard as he could from the ground, hopefully giving him the strength and momentum to jet forward and grab the scythe before Azrael could react.

Instead of dodging this time, Death brought up the bottom of the handle, and the blunt of the bone met Korbyn's forehead as he jumped. He fell to his back, grabbing his face with both hands. He twisted and turned, the pulse of the strike sending waves of pain through his skull.

"We do not get to decide when we are ready for our destiny," Azrael stated, his voice heavy. It sounded like he was weeping, or struggling to breathe, as if any moment could be his last. "That is destiny's job, and we are foolish to take it from them."

When the pain finally subsided, Korbyn sat up with a growl under his breath. "Even if there was such a thing as destiny, it would wait for no one," he replied, rubbing his forehead and standing one more time. "Not even you."

Even though it wasn't possible without his skin or muscles, the Reaper smiled.

Korbyn reached for where Azrael's shadow would be but then realized nothing lingered there.

Death laughed. "Darkness does not work against a devil."

Korbyn scoffed. He raced forward again, following his next attack with a wide, horizontal swing. Azrael turned in the direction of his punch, not expecting the full arch of Korbyn's swipe, and faltered.

The archangel stumbled back with shuffling feet after the punch collided with his forehead. He used the scythe as a counterweight, utilizing its hefty form to remain upright. From underneath the darkness of Azrael's cloak, Korbyn watched pieces of bone crack and splinter before cascading like a waterfall.

Azrael's chest and shoulders twitched in delight. "Very well. If you think you are ready," he remarked, croaking each word with care, "then I will test you."

Death stood upright, twirling the scythe in circles as though it weighed equivalently to a feather. The gilded decidite's lines of gold gleamed in the dark sky.

"The metal." Korbyn's gaze became stuck in the trance of the makeshift pendulum. "What is it, truly?"

"Mortals call it decidite, but it is much more. It is raw. It is power. It is holy. It is the heart of all things sacred." Azrael halted his sad voice, as if he was saying too much. "The angels also called upon powers they weren't ready for and look what it caused. Chaos, corruption, and conflict. You should not make the same mistake."

Korbyn scoffed. "I didn't ask for this," he replied, ignoring the wound on his fist from his punch. It began mending the broken skin under a tint of scarlet. "I'm only attempting to survive in a war they instigated."

"Didn't you, though?" Azrael questioned. His words were much slower than his body. He flopped his head to the other side. The hood bounced with him, the fabric falling limp from the sudden jerk of his body. "If I recall, when I found you on the battlefield, you agreed to my contract. You said you would do anything, and anything you will do." Azrael motioned to the scythe. "Eternal service. That is the cost of a life."

The images of his dying friends plummeted in his mind—Andrid's wide eyes, Gilben's sacrifice, Haven's still form, Oakley's trembling mouth.

"So be it," Korbyn said, clenching his fists. Blood dripped from his right hand, matching the heavy pellets around him.

The Reaper adjusted his posture to stand straight once again. "Then it is a test you have already failed."

This time, Azrael struck first.

He shot forward at such an incredible speed that Korbyn didn't even see him. He barely dodged in time. Instead of controlling the weight of his body, Korbyn stumbled, raising his arms by his sides to alleviate his weight thrown backwards. The gilded decidite nearly grazed his face.

Azrael shot forward again, not missing the next attack.

The pointed edged of the scythe sliced through Korbyn's

right shoulder, and he groaned. He instinctively went to grab the wound to cease the pain, but Death didn't allow him a moment's amnesty.

Azrael swung with no sense of fatigue, with no breaths insinuating he was dying. Korbyn was only able to dodge every other strike. When one swing met air, the other sliced through his skin. Though not deep, each met cause. Every cut was more painful than a normal blade, as if the decidite exuded the same feeling as the rain around him. They burned so hot that they felt cold, sending such chills up his skin. His body slowed with each successful strike of Death's swings. Blood erupted from the fresh gashes.

Korbyn stumbled backwards, trying to regain his breath. When he finally did, the stinging of the bloody rain demanded remembrance. Rain streaked down his face, causing his cheeks to smart with every droplet. Finally, Korbyn ignored the pain in his legs and raced forward.

Death saw his approach and lifted his scythe to jab the blunt of his weapon backwards into his stomach. Korbyn dodged, grabbing the scythe and using all the strength in his arm to swing.

When Azrael dodged, Korbyn didn't let up. He kept his body close so that the fallen angel couldn't retaliate. Azrael jumped backwards, and Korbyn latched onto the man's cloak, which wasn't as controlled as the rest of his body. He held firmly onto the fabric with his right hand and grappled the scythe with his left. He pulled both forward, and Death stumbled. Korbyn smashed his forehead into the devil's nasal bones.

The crash of their skulls caused both to stagger. Korbyn tripped but barely caught himself. He breathed heavily, feeling a warm streak of blood trickle down his forehead and brush past his nose. Death also faltered, dropping to one knee as he clutched his face. Korbyn witnessed greater pieces of bone crack and shatter between his fingers.

Korbyn smirked, forcing himself to stand up a bit straighter, despite not being able to control his breaths. "Archangels are weaker than I thought."

The form of Azrael wavered, as if he was thrown in a pool of water. The illusion completely dispelled before his very eyes. Eventually, it mixed in with the mists around them, becoming nothing more than a broken memory.

"Confidence," Death whispered from behind him.

Korbyn flinched, spinning around and stepping a few paces away.

Azrael approached, his hunched form leaning in such an abnormal way that he resembled a creature. "Confidence is strong. Confidence is key, but confidence is a weakness, when in excess."

Korbyn sneered, despite trying to keep his expression hidden from his adversary.

"Tell me, Dolion, when you lose your way, your purpose, your destiny, what will happen to your confidence?"

"Don't say that like you know me," Korbyn responded, wiping away the blood that had trickled down to his mouth. It smudged, tainting his cheek in crimson. "And my name is Korbyn."

"But I do know you," Death responded. "I have known you for a long time. I know you better than you even know yourself. Even as you've collected your mind and power, you still know not who you are." He tilted his head again. "Hmm. Korbyn? Is that the name Cassiel gifted you? She has become quite rebellious. How interesting."

Korbyn peered into the gloom of the hood. "Cassiel? You mean Salem? You know her?"

"Yes, the archangel of the Heavens who chose mortality with a self-designated purpose." Azrael regarded the distance, as if searching for something. "Hm, permanently an archangel no more. A sacrifice indeed."

Korbyn stepped forward. "What? What's happening out there?"

Azrael turned back to face him. "War and Death."

FIFTY-ONE.

Every swing from the captain's hammer bellowed with such strength that Salem wavered, its pounds reverberating against her shield. He didn't slow after the first attack. Instead, he continued his strikes with a surprising amount of poise.

Salem had never seen someone with so much strength, so much vigor. Every attack was calculated, his form and strikes full of technique and skill. When she blocked his attacks, she couldn't keep her shield aloft. The force buckled her practiced technique. Rather than directly block his attacks, she diverted her shield at angles and followed the momentum of his swings.

Her muscles quivered from his next blow. Even as she bent her knees and dug her feet into the ground, she slid away from the force. She cringed at the discomfort, raising her sword and shield when he advanced again.

"Archangels are weaker than I thought," the soldier said from under the confines of his helmet. "Ignorant tyrants tend not to be prepared for war."

"We are not tyrants," Salem responded. She glared, fighting a dual battle within herself. "Not all of us."

"So, you serve a tyrant then?" he questioned. "You're all the same."

The captain rushed forward, slamming down his hammer in continuous strikes. Instead of blocking his next attack, Salem dodged, hoping to put some distance between the two.

Without her powers, her form slackened, and her speed decreased. The rejuvenation the locket provided previously allowed her to channel divinity. Without it, she was just a trained soldier. And that would have to be enough.

When the bull slammed his hammer straight to the ground, Salem dodged and stepped on it with one foot. Using it as a leverage for height, she swung the entirety of her body around and lifted a foot. Her heel soared, smacking right into the side of the man's helmet. She hopped back, analyzing her enemy with a victorious smirk.

The man's head barely turned from her strike. He rolled his neck, cracking it.

Her grin dropped into a gawk.

"Holy wings, hopeful dreams..." The captain lifted his hammer. "I will shatter both."

Salem ran forward, swiping her blade across his chest. He lifted his arm, parrying her attacks with his armor. It dinged, not even leaving a scratch behind. She repeated these actions, finding leverage. He blocked with his arms or not at all, letting the strength of his armor rebel against her attacks.

Salem tightened the grip on her blade and spun, adding rage and strength into her next attack. Even without her holy magic and his armor, she should at least be able to put a dent into it. However, the warrior didn't even bother to dodge it. He let his armor take the brunt of her full swing, and her blade shattered.

Stepping back, Salem gasped as the steel splintered into

pieces before observing his armor. Instead of a lightened gray, the armor the soldier wore was different. It was a darker shade, appearing more black than gray. Instead of shimmering against the light, the armor lacked luster completely.

"I thought Esperin hasn't been able to forge the ore?" Salem inquired, strands of hair clinging to her face.

"They haven't," the captain responded, stepping forward.

The next swing was more difficult to parry. Salem thrust her arms to the side to carry the strength of his momentum, but it caused her weak stance to follow his strike. Her body fell to the side, and she tripped over her own feet, rolling to the ground. The soldier followed her, raising his foot above her head. Salem spun out of his reach, pushing herself up to stand and raising her shield. He kicked forward, slamming into her shield and shoving her backwards and closer to the edge of the town.

Salem stumbled over to a brick well next to a wagon. The captain brought his hammer down, and she barely dodged out of his reach. The attack caused the well's edge to crash beneath his weight. Salem extended her arm and sliced through the hemp rope with her broken blade, and she heard the bucket splash into the water below. She grabbed onto the sliced edge of the rope, continuing her circle around the well.

The captain drove forward his hammer again, breaking the other side of the well to close the distance between them. Salem ran around his side and jumped on the wagon, pushing against it for height and added power. She leaped onto the soldier's back, wrapping the rope a couple of times around his throat, and then pulled their weights earthward.

The soldier toppled, landing on top of her. Salem wrapped her legs around his neck and clenched her defined muscles while tugging on the rope. The captain thrashed underneath her, but due to her strength and weight, he couldn't lift the top half of his body. When he started to pry her legs away from his neck, Salem clasped harder, wrapping her ankles around each other for added control.

She didn't see his next attack before she felt it. The captain smashed his elbow into her face, causing her hold to loosen. The soldier lifted his torso up and her along with it. Instead of standing up, he slammed them both back down to the ground.

Salem flinched, her cheek and back crying out in pain. The warrior was already out of her reach, and she twisted and pushed herself upright. Blood gushed from her nose and trailed down her mouth. She glanced around, realizing that she had lost her broken blade in the tussle, leaving her with only her shield as a countermeasure.

The captain ran forward and swung his hammer down. Salem couldn't dodge out of the way completely. Instead, she lifted her shield in the air, hoping it would halt his attack.

It sounded like a hammer slamming into anvil. Her shield shook beneath her grip, and it crashed into her face. The steel cracked and gave way, eventually splintering into countless fragments. Salem couldn't stop her wavering; she stumbled and fell to her back.

Salem was forced to stare up at the sky as world spun, blood spewing violently from her nose. Pain and nausea surged, but she somehow prevented herself from vomiting. As she lay there, attempting to figure out how to use her legs again, she could only hear a high-pitched ringing that reverberated against her skull.

The captain slammed his body on top of hers. He knelt on her sternum, disrupting her inhaled breath. Then, he wrapped one of his hands around Salem's throat and squeezed.

Adrenaline coursed through her once more, and she battered in desperate defiance. The entirety of his weight made it impossible for her to break free from his hold. She lifted her arms and rammed them into the inside of his elbow. His grip was steadfast, and her strikes slowed when her breath fled. Her head pounded against her skull, and her eyes drooped.

Darkness enveloped her in a tight embrace, unyielding in its horrid declaration.

"Sleep," the warrior mumbled. And so, she did.

FIFTY-TWO.

Phantom visions plagued Veeris' mind. Images of the Hells, fires so hot that they ran cold. They erupted into flames at the start of its internal war, with blades raised. He saw a warrior leading the fray. The monster, the one they called Korbyn, was at the figure's side with a tremendous scythe made of bone and black metal, decorated in numerous white feathers and a single, ringing bell. Rebels, lost souls, demons—all rallied at the warrior's side, instigating the battle before the war.

Veeris saw a sleeping woman with unnatural hues of purple hair. It glimmered with stars within her tresses, resembling a serene, night sky. She awoke from a long slumber, but there were two more of her. They emerged from the center of a familiar triangle, each copy of herself walking towards the knot's center point. Eventually, his vision cleared, and the silhouettes of the women formed into a singular one.

Veeris watched angels fight demons and souls that emerged from a forest clouded in mist. Blood stained the mortal realm them, each fighting for a cause they believed in. He heard their screams, their clanging weapons, and he wasn't sure if the world fell as prey or if it began anew.

Then, Veeris saw himself standing before closed gates, riddled with mortal scars, unable to gain entry.

His vision blurred.

The world was surrounded in mist and debris, filled with the clanks of iron and steel, screams and rumbling, much like his visions, but this time, they resembled reality more. He heard cries of fear, shrieks of the undead, and the slamming of a hammer on an anvil.

Veeris' heart didn't race. Instead, it was slowing. He could barely register which way the sky was facing, or if the ground beneath him was warm and cold. Maybe his body was the one that was cold. But he couldn't feel it at all.

There was a wound on his back. Veeris wasn't sure how bad it was, but he couldn't move it. He couldn't move anything; his arms, hands, or even the fingers he did have. They were still, just has his breaths were—just as his mind was.

There was something moving far in the distance, silhouettes of two people. One was large, covered in dark armor, with pointed edges and horns that resembled a bull on the top of his helmet. The second was a woman. She was unconscious, currently being thrown over the shoulder of the first one.

"Salem?" Veeris rasped out as his eyes found some clarity. He instinctually went to reach out to her, but his arms felt as though heavy weights were pulling him down. That was when he felt the healing.

When Veeris craned his head to the side, regarding his limp arms, pieces of gold cracked underneath his palm. Swirls of radiant energy seeped through his fingers and surrounded his body in hushed pulses. They were soothing, alleviating the overwhelming pain that would have addled him if not for the magic encasing him.

"What have you done...?" Veeris questioned, watching her holy, archangel magic seeping into his body.

Veeris wanted nothing more than to run to her, to help her, but his mind and body refused. He knew not if she was alive or dead. Despite his inward, desperate pleas, he could do nothing. Instead, he watched the captain of the guard and Salem disappear into the shadows of the forest, leaving Brinshire in utter demise.

Once Salem disappeared from view, Veeris fell into the world of unconsciousness.

FIFTY-THREE.

Korbyn's left arm was numb despite the gash's sting, his muscles not abiding his commands. Azrael's strike cut too deep, leaving it drifting unresponsive at his side. His fingers dangled just as stagnantly as the rest of his injured appendage, though sometimes it lurched from the spazzing muscles underneath.

He wasn't sure how long they fought for. It somehow felt like only a few minutes, but also like days. He was exhausted beyond control, hunched on quaking knees that urged to defy his wishes. With every inhale, his lungs demanded solace. Blood heavily soaked his body, mimicking dripping water. No matter what Korbyn did to escape the water's flow, rough hands held him under.

Unlike him, Azrael appeared unperturbed. He didn't grow tired, or wary, or impatient. He sought to teach him some sort of profound lesson, to Korbyn's indifference. Korbyn leaned down, wrapping his working arm around his pained stomach. Azrael had sliced there too and deeper than the rest, hindering his ability to stand upright.

"Have you learned? Contemplated the consequences?" the Reaper asked.

Korbyn replied with heavy breaths, avoiding his gaze.

"I wish for you not to make the same mistakes as I. You must understand, Dolion. This all is for a greater purpose. You must trust those before you with more knowledge and experience to guide your way. Adhere to my wishes."

Azrael continued his lecture, though Korbyn only heard every few sentences. Instead of listening to his commands, he focused on a sound that felt just as far as it did close, leaving him with the inability to decipher its words. He closed his eyes, focusing on its call.

It sounded like the crash of an ocean wave, though continuous and canorous, or walls of a kingdom's battlement crashing down, disruptive and vehement. Then, Korbyn decided it sounded like a drum, one with echoes that erupted with beautiful cadence. With each beat, it rose in volume, demanding Korbyn's attention just as desperately as he wanted to listen.

"They may all be dead," Azrael stated, unmoving underneath the red rain. "When you go back, you must leave. Allow the war of mortals to decide for themselves."

Korbyn heard him but said nothing.

The sound emerged again, a boom reverberating against the lands, shaking his body. No, that was wrong. It originated from his body, his mind, his heart. It was somehow more powerful than all three, each gazing upon the brash clamor with jealousy, but he could not unravel its identity.

No, it wasn't the ocean waves, or a kingdom's fall, or a reverberating drum. It was a gong, battling for remembrance, thrumming within him. It echoed against cavern walls, growing louder and louder like the rally of an army. It dimmed the Reaper's voice, though still he heard both in perfect clarity.

It was Korbyn's spirit.

"You must listen, Dolion," Azrael urged, taking several steps forward. "You are not like them. You have a greater purpose than most. These human wars mean nothing in the face of a greater plan." Death's poise wavered, a slip of desperation contrasting his usual, composed demeanor. "But you are not yet ready."

"No," Korbyn muttered.

The deep cadence chimed louder, and Korbyn raised his responsive hand to his head from the budding irritation.

"One day, the Song of Abaddon will ring, and you will be fighting in the War of Revelation in my place," Azrael explained. "You will aid the throne and start the world anew. That is your destiny! But you are not yet ready!"

"No," Korbyn moaned, the sonorous bell repeating with little pause in between, each strike of the metal also a physical blow to his head. His teeth ground, jaw clenching and locking from the agony.

"You will be the Shepherd, the Reaper of Souls. You will be Death." And then, like a stab to his soul, Korbyn heard the one phrase that had haunted him since his awakening: "For you are not meant to save."

The quote reverberated in his skull, and powers reawakened upon necessity. Surges of visions and memories crashed like conflicted waves, the remnants of his inner voice speaking in intangible jumbles, and he recognized none of it. However, each word, each phrase resembled a wailing inside his mind, his internal thoughts ready to claim its victory. The powers repressed in the depths of the forest merged fully with the husk of his body, and Korbyn couldn't control it.

Korbyn glowered in pain, stepping back a few paces. His scream echoed against the rock walls, penetrating even the continuous pitter of the rain of blood as it poured. He fell to his knees, clutching his head to rid the agony, disgorging an ear-piercing scream.

Then, the screaming stopped.

Korbyn took a deep breath. An unearthly cackle emitted from his lips, and he leaned his head backwards, staring into the sky and accepting the rain's pellets. For some reason, he started to enjoy the pain, reveling like a masochist under a knife's care.

"*Archangel turned fallen angel...fallen angel turned Horseman...Horseman turned Death...Death turned* nothing." Korbyn stared at Azrael with wide eyes and a smile. "*Tell me, Azrael, archangel of Death, are you afraid? Where do angels go when they die a second time? Where does one go when they have already been to the Hells?*"

Azrael ignored his questions. "Your mind is already turning against you. I hid away the gifts of your mind and powers because you weren't ready. Now you will end up losing what you tried so hard to gain."

"*Azrael, Azrael, Azrael...how amusing you are,*" Korbyn teased. "*You hide behind a knowledgeable persona, but what would happen if Samael found out you were afraid of your own failures?*"

Death frowned.

"*Yes—yes, yes, yes! There it is! A sign of weakness. Even Death has limits.*"

"I told you that you are not ready," Azrael said. "You cannot even control the little power I gave you."

"*Just as people can't make law and call it justice, you can't take my future and call it destiny.*" Korbyn sluggishly rose from his kneeling position, trudging forward. "*If I cannot save, then I will avenge, and you will not stop me.*"

Korbyn shifted his casual stride into a sprint. Azrael raised his scythe to mimic a shield, but it did not cease Korbyn's constant jabs. With every blow, he coerced Azrael into a backwards slide. They scrambled in perpetual collision, Azrael blocking Korbyn's punches with each lift of his weapon.

Eventually, Korbyn reached to seize the scythe. Instead of blocking, Azrael parried. With every reach of Korbyn's arm, Azrael spun and sliced its sharpened edge along his elongated arms. Blood sprayed with each strike, but Korbyn didn't care. He could sense growing trepidation in the devil's posture. Azrael was getting impatient.

Finally, Azrael swung his scythe hastily compared to his usual collectedness. Korbyn stepped forward into the blade's swing and extended his arms, revealing his chest with more clarity.

The scythe pierced his torso, the pointed edge angled towards the Blood Moon. Azrael stood in a panic amidst his own shock, staring into Korbyn's eyes. He released the handle, and both Korbyn and the weapon collapsed to the ground.

Blood sprayed from the wound that seared from his chest all the way down to the bottom of his torso, an eruption of color that intermingled with the sky. Korbyn coughed up blood all while trying to halt the world's spinning.

"Why?" Azrael croaked out. When Korbyn didn't respond immediately, the Reaper asked, "Why did you do this?"

Korbyn's voice quivered with every painful inhale, resembling painful croaks despite his confidence.

"Because...you...need me," Korbyn rasped. Blood spilled in a darkened pool beneath him. "If you believe...what you say...about destiny, then...you can't let me die," he murmured, a partial chuckle pervading the thunderous silence. "We had a deal; eternal servitude...for life." Despite the pain, he grinned wider, blood staining and trailing down his lips. "I guess you'll...have to make me immortal now...devil."

"You are not ready!" Death snarled. "There is no point if you lose yourself along the way! Not when she will need you!"

Korbyn's smirk with bloodied teeth. "Try me."

Azrael exhaled a breath; one he probably didn't need and would no longer have. "It seems you have outsmarted me today,

Dolion."

Blood spilled from the deep gash in Korbyn's abdomen, and his position prohibited him from seeing the stagnant, crimson moon.

Death was forced to answer his call today.

"What is it that you would give?" Azrael questioned, his magic, form, and existence dispersing under the moon's gaze.

And with the Blood Moon bearing witness, Korbyn whispered into the night with his last breath.

"Anything."

FIFTY-FOUR.

Daunting spins of the world cooed in defiance as Korbyn groggily peeled his lids open. He was being lugged by his arms, hoisted and dragged through the blood-ridden dirt beneath him. He could no longer hear the tower's bell atop the hill. Instead, the Revelation King seemed to have reobtained control over the undead.

Gurgling spits and moans encircled the town as the monsters devoured the living, in frantic search of something they couldn't find. No longer did the cries and the fear of the people permeate the air, for they were all gone. Korbyn could see their souls fluttering deep within the town's walls, overtaken by the hoard.

In front of the gates, Korbyn saw Veeris' collapsed form. He was lying on his side, drenched in layers of blood that erupted from a wound from his back. From the grogginess of his own temporary sleep, Korbyn couldn't tell if he was alive or not. He imagined not.

And Salem was nowhere to be seen.

The Revelation King trekked through the town, with the soldiers hauling Korbyn behind him. Bodies lay scattered across the lands, each under heaps of desperate moans of the undead. The soldiers ignored them, following the Revelation King further into the town and towards the mines carved into its grandest hill.

The pits were immeasurable in size. Primitive shovels, pickaxes, hammers, chisels, minecarts, and random barrels lay scattered and forgotten throughout the cavern, with no signs of life wandering through them. Korbyn imagined at one point, many voices filled this place, hopes and wishes to start the world anew.

How wrong they'd been.

"Gather the decidite!" the Revelation King demanded.

When the soldiers abided his command, Knight-Captain Hadawaye grabbed the sovereign's arm and pulled him away. The Revelation King's haughty expression was replaced by an angry one as he thrashed against his physical coercion.

"Do not forget, mage, that this is *my* army—"

"*Your army?*" the mage hissed, wrenching his arm away from the man. "You are nothing but a figurehead. No, you are less. You are a soldier, your promotion given only to ease your wavering heart. Do not forget, it was *my* undead army that led us to victory this day. One day, even the emperor will bow before me."

"Victory? This was not a victory; this was a *slaughter*. We were supposed to capture the town, not kill innocent civilians!" Hadawaye spat, turning away from him and stomping towards the outskirts of the mines. "You will be hung for your crazed arrogance."

Hadawaye saw not when the Revelation King pulled a spear from an unsuspecting soldier. The mage thrust the weapon directly into the back of his throat, piercing it through to the other side. Hadawaye lurched, hands fumbling behind and in front of his throat as blood and saliva poured.

"And I will tell him of your noble sacrifice," the Revelation

King whispered in his ear.

He threw Hadawaye forward and wrenched the spear from his neck. The soldier died before ever hitting the ground, blood and gore erupting from the betrayal.

The mage handed the spear back to the man he took it from, wiping the blood on his armor made of newly tarnished steel. When the other soldiers looked upon each other with horrified expressions, the Revelation King frowned.

"Are there any others who wish to proclaim their blasphemous ways?" he bellowed.

None spoke up for their dying leader. Instead, they obeyed the crazed man's commands and searched for the ore. The ones holding Korbyn dropped him to his knees, leaving him to hang his head. The vertigo finally began to recede, as the blurs of Korbyn's surroundings formed into single, cohesive images. He felt as though he was beginning to awaken from a deep sleep.

"Horseman," the crazed man called, gently slapping Korbyn's face to grab his attention. "Let me see you now."

Korbyn took a deep, even breath. When they met eyes, the Revelation King gasped in eagerness.

"Pale eyes permanently no more. I see more power behind them than before." He smiled, the edges of his mouth creaking upward. "The Blood Moon will forever taunt these lands, until the end and before the beginning. Stand, my warrior. You now serve the Revelation King."

"Um, Revelation King." A soldier approached, voice and stance gauche.

The mage frowned, pivoting to the interjecting voice. Before the man could continue, the Revelation King spat, "What?"

The soldier's posture straightened. "There's, um...well. A problem. There doesn't seem to be anymore decidite."

"What blasphemy is this?" he yelled with a glare, thrusting his scepter in a direction as if they would immediately obey. "It has only been a few minutes. Scavenge the entirety of the caverns." He pointed towards outside the cave. "Check all the mines!"

The soldier was right, Korbyn knew. The Kingdom of Esperin had taken all the decidite long before the Avernos army arrived. Even if he hadn't been told, he could sense it. Not a single piece of ore was left in the confines of this place. It was the cavern where the decidite was discovered, the cavern that propelled the initiation of war, the cavern where all of this began, and it would become the Revelation King's grave.

Korbyn rose from behind the unsuspecting king like his extended shadow.

His fingers tingled in avidity, though his stoic expression contrasted it. From the darkness of the cavern, no one saw when the hilt of old bones was summoned from the depths of nothingness, Korbyn readying himself to decapitate the man with gilded decidite in the form of a crescent moon.

And that was when Korbyn smelled it. It was familiar, somehow, yet foreign at the same time. It resembled sharp smoke mixed with eggs that had long rotted, the stench filling the air and spreading from the cavern's entrance.

Then, the Revelation King joined his confusion. He inhaled deeply. "What is that vile smell?"

"Everyone, run!" a soldier yelled, the men dashing towards the exit as fast as their legs could carry them. "It's going to explode! Everyone, get ou—"

Korbyn didn't get to enact his vengeance on his own behalf. Instead, he watched the soldiers and the so-called Revelation King combust in a wild blaze that would have made even the Hells frown in jealousy. When Korbyn's skin seared under the pleas of the fire, he couldn't help but smile, watching the false king burn.

The mines ignited and burst in hellish flames.

EPILOGUE.

The ground rumbled in cadence, like small, reoccurring tremors beneath her. Salem's head pounded, a groan passing her lips alongside unfastening eyes. Usually, she would have risen to assess the situation, but her arms were bound behind her. Tight metal chains encumbered her limbs alongside a pair that constricted her ankles.

She was in a caravan, which explained the shifting. As Salem assessed the contents of the wagon, she noticed it didn't contain anything other than her. The wood creaked in recognition of her waking but did little to inform her of her situation. Luckily, there was a window pointing towards the front of the wagon, next to her head.

When she peered through it, she recognized the captain of Esperin seated at the front seat, guiding the horse on the empty path and enveloping trees. The amber and honey leaves continued their descension from the branches, initiating the severity of winter's call.

The captain was slack compared to his previously daunting stature, idly holding the reins as if they could have torn in his grasp. Instead of his usual bull-like helmet, she saw thick black strands dragged into a messy bun at the base of his neck. A thick beard surrounded his jaw with matching strands of jet-black. His chin was set, focused on the quiet path ahead. He probably already knew she was awake, but she shifted to get his attention.

"Get comfortable. We have a bit before we get to the capital," the soldier said, his gruff voice sounding a bit more normal than it had been under the constraints of the gilded decidite helmet.

"You still haven't told me who you are," Salem rasped, leaning her aching head against the wooden frame. "Somehow you have forged the inimitable ore and know who I am."

She waited for his response, but he gave her none.

"So, what is your plan?" Salem questioned. "You claim to not serve a king, yet here you are as his esteemed hellhound."

The captain gripped the reins so tightly that she was afraid the rope would snap. The effort to alleviate his anger failed, as displayed by his clenched jaw.

"You will serve a purpose—to aid in my retribution," he murmured. "Kingdoms will fall and be set anew."

"Who are you?" Salem asked, analyzing his features with intensified scrutiny.

The captain turned his head in her direction, allowing Salem to analyze his features with intensified scrutiny. An abnormal pair of eyes stared back at her, with eyes like pools of black water and crimson pupils submerged in its depths, like reflections of the Blood Moon.

Salem gasped. "Kanen?"

Acknowledgements

When I turned 30 on July 2nd, 2024, I was scared. I saw myself as a failure and thought it was too late to achieve my dreams. Exactly one year later, I overcame my fear and published my first book. I have a lot of people to thank for that.

Thank you to my mom, who supported me in my dreams. You always believed in me. Thank you to my stepdad and grandma, who cherished and supported me always. Thank you to my grandfather and great grandfather for all your wisdom. I hope I've made you both proud.

Thank you to my father for believing in me enough to help me get this book off its feet. I could truly never thank you enough. Thank you to my sister and niece for your kindness and faith in me. You're in my heart always.

Thank you to my editor, Clara, for dealing with my countless questions. You really helped me make this story become the best version it could possibly be. Thank you to all my beta readers.

Thank you to my friends, the real ones who cared. You know who you are.

Thank you to Fresa, my alpha reader. I don't know how you read my story so many times. I can't thank you enough.

Thank you to Amir for my beautiful cover and having so much faith in me. Thank you to ALL my artists and contributors.

Thank you to my husband and best friend. I truly couldn't have become a writer without you. I know that no matter where life takes us, we will always be writing together until the end. I love you.

Lastly, thank you *you*, reader. I hope you enjoyed this story as much as I loved writing it. There's a lot more stories in this universe I have left to tell, and I'd love for you to join my journey.

About the Author

Ashen Huston grew up in central Florida, where she obtained a bachelor's degree in communications to pursue her love of writing and the arts. Now, you can find her in North Carolina with her husband, family and two cats, Lethe and Tobin. In her free time, Ashen likes to hangout at her favorite bookstore and coffeeshop and play online games with her friends.

Extras

Kendra Dawn
Esperin
Avernos

The Legend of New Beginnings

After the War against the Heavens, the rebelling angels fell
to Abaddon. With their lack of wings and depleted holy light,
the Fallen succumbed to age.
But when tales end, legends start anew.
When Death, the Reaper of Souls, takes new form, it will
initiate the start of the Revelation War and make way for the
new Crown of Horns and Blades seated upon waves of
scarlet.